Age of Quintessence

Synthetic Genesis

Vista Townsend

AGE OF QUINTESSENCE: SYNTHETIC GENESIS

Print Edition 2015 ISBN 978-0-9906168-3-2

Second Edition

Printed in the United States of America

Books By Vista Townsend

Science Fiction
Age of Quintessence series

Synthetic Genesis
Shadow Legacy
Vortex Crucible

Fantasy
Salt Legacy series

Masters of Souls

Historical Fiction

Jagged Road To Sainthood

Dedication

To my Creator who never ceases to amaze me with his wonders,

my parents who have been my moral guide,

my sister who has supported me during these many years of writing,

and Monica with whom I have enjoyed debating *Frankenstein* and other literary works.

Prologue

Eras begin in different fashions. Most start with a whisper as a new technology or idea slowly becomes widely used, changing an entire culture over many decades. Ages are usually progressive, but sometimes they usher in society's collapse. Many happen naturally while others are engineered.

The Age of Quintessence was all of these. Jealousy and arrogance became the parents that begot unnatural offspring—*Homo sapiens profectus*.

Humans had become powerful, spreading across many worlds. But we were not the first to reach the stars. That honor was claimed by the edietheans, an ancient race who formed an alliance with us. Together the two species expanded the Basanti Empire across the entire galaxy, befriending some sentient species, conquering others. While the linage of Emperors remained human, the edietheans wielded immense power in the Galactic Senate.

Through ten thousand years of arranged marriages and a strictly enforced caste system, the edietheans had produced a race of super geniuses that dwarfed all others. Jealousy filled the hearts of influential humans, leading to the creation of the Coalition of Human Advancement. For decades they pushed to change genetic laws, allowing the editing of sentient DNA. Emperor Anayasini finally agreed, but when he died five years later, his son's first act was to pass the Sentient Purity Law, forbidding such tampering.

Yet five years was all the Coalition needed. Within that time, five hundred of us were born to surrogate parents. We were mostly human, but a small strain of ediethean DNA was used to give us super intelligence and a longer life. For seven years we lived as ordinary children, raised by parents who loved us, but taking advance classes as soon as we began to talk. As our eighth birthday neared, our parents willing gave us over to the Coalition, sending us to a newly built university tailored just for us.

We came, one hundred new ones each year. They told us to be fruitful and change the universe. Who were we to question our elders? What they did not tell us was the heavy personal cost we each would pay.

Historians will debate for centuries to come which individual had the most influence, which groups caused the greatest upheavals, and if the era's title is misleading. One name always remains central in the debates—mine. Layla Rangan. In my naïve pursuit of science to create a sentient with perfect genes, I designed a new being both wonderful and terrifying that the galaxy was not prepared for.

The Age of Quintessence had begun.

Part I

Creator

"So much has been done, exclaimed the soul of Frankenstein—more, far more, will I achieve: treading in the steps already marked, I will pioneer a new way, explore unknown powers, and unfold to the world the deepest mysteries of creation."

—From *Frankenstein* by Mary Shelley

Chapter One

A blue hover car turned off a busy highway. The tall skyscrapers from the city it had just left faded out of view. The vehicle slowed its speed along the country road, passing in and out of shadows cast by bare tree limbs. The forest was carpeted with snow.

It's spring back home, thought the younger of the two occupants. Layla Rangan stared out the window, trying not to appear nervous. Her reflection in the window showed a dark-haired girl of Indian descent. She was nearly twelve but felt far older. Childhood for her race had been brief, replaced with intense, advanced-level classes which were spiced with lectures of destiny.

She had just arrived on the planet Bontinc yet already she was homesick. Bontinc was so different. Beyond the cities and towns lay real wilderness. Dense forests full of bushes and biers, hiding predatory animals hunting down prey.

She yearned for the tall, eco-friendly skyscrapers of her home planet Mansoor. Endless manicured parks surrounded the narrow bases of the towers which rose high up before mushrooming into bulky, yet elegant structures of apartments and businesses. Her adopted parents, both scientists, worked in a lab so high that when she was two she had believed it touched the clouds. But that fanciful notion was long forgotten—till now. What was her older brother Blaaze doing right now? Riding a hoverboard or watching a movie with friends?

He had been her parents' only biological child while she had been sent to them as a frozen embryo after they had been accepted as surrogate parents for the genetics program sponsored by the Coalition. They loved her, giving her a childhood of family picnics, games, and laughter. Even when she started school at the age of three, studying at first seemed like play. But the work had grown exceedingly harder, and the time for games ended. At the age of eight she was sent away to another planet to attend the newly constructed Luncaster University, just like every other profectus. After four years they received a Ph.D., if they did not break under the immense pressure.

Lifeless eyes, bleeding head, limbs sprawled in unnatural positions. Layla shook her head, pushing away the image of a boy who had jumped from the window of his dorm room. Most profectus had graduated.

"It's another hour before we reach BGF," said the driver, cutting into Layla's thoughts. Mera Walkins was a fortyish woman dressed in a business suit, hair pinned in a tight bun. As head of Genetic Enhancement Department, she kept a stern, no-nonsense manner.

"Why is Bontinc Genetics Foundation built so far from a major spaceport? Surely it slows down shipment processing and raises cost." Layla was cautious with her questions, wanting to appear sophisticated, the opposite of how she felt.

"BGF is nearly a hundred miles from Austin City. The founders wanted it isolated from populated areas in case of accidents. The closest town is Taylorville where many of our staff live. Since you are not old enough to drive yet, you have been given an apartment on campus."

"My own apartment?"

"It is not fancy, barely more than a hotel room we keep for guests. We have a cafeteria where you can buy meals."

"Where will I be working?"

"My department. We customize embryos by choosing the best DNA provided by paying parents."

Trying to impress her new boss, Layla recited, "The Genetic Enhancement Department creates the highest capital for BGF, serving rich clients from over one hundred planets. Customers choose the colors, sex, and predisposed talents of their offspring. Originally, it was the only section of BGF, but Experimental Genetics and Human Advancement were added later. I read your manual."

"Did the manual inform you that we workers just call them the Baby, Freak, and Advance Departments? Though now we call the last one the Abandoned Department."

"No."

"There is much you will not find written in manuals."

They rode in silence for a while. Suddenly Mera hit the brakes, stopping the hover car two yards from a large antlered beast standing in the middle of the road. It lowered its head, shaking its sharp spikes threatening. Behind it, several of its offspring sprinted across the road. Seeing its children safe, it snorted one last time at the vehicle then disappeared into the wilderness.

Layla stared wide-eyed at its retreating form as Mera began to drive again. "What was that?"

"Locals call them spike deer. Harmless as long as you leave them alone. You will see many things far more dangerous, not all of them animals. I should warn you that there was a heated debate over who you should be partnered with. You are a bit of a celebrity at BGF."

"Celebrity? I'm just the newest employee."

Mera gave an ironic laugh. "You are a symbol of genetic engineering, the results of over a century of planning and decades of tinkering from our scientists. Out of the five hundred we sent off, you are the only one who choose to return to us. The older members of my department feel...a strong connection with you. You are the crown achievement of their life's work."

Layla squirmed in the leather seat. "I am just here to learn to be the best employee I can be."

"I'm glad to hear that, because I have strongly warned them not to smother you, to treat you as normal as possible. I choose for your partner someone relatively new who will not be hindered by their possessiveness."

Eventually a sprawling campus came into view. It was nothing like Layla expected. Bontinc Genetics Foundation was located on an old military base closed down several centuries ago. The ancient base consisted of hundreds of acres dotted with various buildings, hangers, and training fields which had fallen into ruin long ago. Only the central area of the campus had been renovated after BGF purchased the land over a century ago. From the outside, the dull-painted complex looked cold and sterile.

Mera parked in a spot reserved for her near the entrance of a huge, three-story building. Layla followed her inside, leaving her luggage in the vehicle. The corridors were warm and well-lit, but peeling paint and smudges revealed the building's long use. Mera took several turns and climbed a flight of stairs before entering a large office where one wall was made of glass. Beyond lay a vast chamber that had once served as a hanger for aircraft. Now it was the busy center of Genetic Enhancement Department. Below, several hundred scientists bustled about among various workstations and laboratories which were partitioned off from each other.

Layla walked to the window and looked down at the labyrinth of workstations. Everywhere was movement. Some scientists studied computer screens intently. Others bent over microscopes or carried glass tubes to freezers. Near the far wall, cranes were picking up stacks of refrigerated containers. Despite the disarray, everyone seemed to know exactly what to do. Layla's tender age bore heavily down on her, and she felt intimated.

Behind her, Mera was speaking on a telecom. A few minutes later, a young woman entered. Like most of the other scientists, she was dressed in a white lab coat and slacks. Her long, red hair was pinned tightly up.

Mera said, "This is Rosetta Thomson. She will show you around. I will have your things sent to your apartment."

Rosetta smiled. "You must be the profectus. You look even younger than I thought you would be."

"I'm almost twelve."

"My sister is twelve, but she has not finished middle school yet. Ready for your first day of work? I have many exciting things to show you. I know how you must feel being new. I only started working here six months ago myself."

Rosetta chatted merrily as she gave Layla a tour. They passed through a breakroom which had several tables and vending machines. On one wall hung a huge board with various news clippings about profectus covering it. Layla noticed most were positive articles but two caused her to shudder. The title of one said "Profectus Takes Own Life: Was Pressure Too Much?" Beside it was an image of a somber boy staring towards the camera. At least the image of him dead on the sidewalk had not been published. Another headline read, "Profectus Hopes Die: Virus Claims Its First Victim." Under the title was a picture of a blond-hair child, happy and smiling. Layla stared, remembering the last time she had seen that same face. It had not been cheerful, but full of pain, a child facing death.

"Are you alright?" Rosetta came up beside Layla.

"Yes, fine." Layla averted her eyes and walked away from the bulletin board, hiding her shaking hands.

"Workers who transferred from Advance Department when it was closed down like to keep up with the lives of their creations. They are very proud to have you here. One of their children returning home."

Layla fidgeted uncomfortably. Rosetta led her through a locker-room and into the main hanger where hundreds of scientists worked. Rosetta introduced the people they passed, their names and positions blurring together to Layla. What did stand out to her were the overfriendly greetings and stares, leaving her feeling they viewed her like a cute pet instead of a fellow co-worker. Would anyone take an eleven-year-old scientist seriously?

It was a relief to Layla when Rosetta said it was lunch time. The cafeteria was located in a different building which meant they had to endure cold blasts of snowy wind which threatened to knock Layla off her feet. Before today, she had never even seen snow with her own eyes. The large cafeteria was full of delicious smells and chatter that reminded Layla of Luncaster University. There was a decent selection of foods to choose from. They sat at an empty table. As Rosetta talked, she kept glancing around. A few minutes later, a young man sat down beside her.

"This is Derrick Cashman," said Rosetta. "We both went to the same college together."

The tall, slim man held out a hand in greeting. "You must be Layla. There has been much debate over who would have the privilege of shepherding you about."

"I am just here to work."

"Good," said Rosetta, "because that is what Mera expects. You will be working with me to create blond, athletic boys for the planet Urke. They all must have green eyes. It's the current fad there."

Derrick sighed. "What ever happened to natural selection?"

"As if your Freak Department had anything natural in it."

"At least our creations never spread their spliced DNA into the public gene pool."

"You know that we only use pre-existing DNA of the parents. We just chose which traits are passed on to their offspring."

"Which is subjected to the whims of fashion. Darwin must be rolling over in his grave."

The two continued to bicker good-naturally through the rest of the meal about evolution versus intellect design. Afterwards, Rosetta showed Layla her workstation and introduced the various equipment. Layla was fascinated. Though she was familiar with the concepts of genetic engineering, it was her first hands-on experience. Luncaster University did not have the super computers and other expensive equipment which was needed. Near quitting time, Mera sent a message that Layla's apartment was ready.

Rosetta led her to a nearby locker room where the woman took off her lab coat and unbounded her red hair. "That's better. My only complaint about BFG is that the dress code is too strict. No earrings or jewelry is allowed because it might get caught in a machine." She untucked a cross on a silver chain which she had worn under her blouse. Then she pulled a thick, hooded parka out of her locker. "It's a bit of a walk to your apartment. Let me see if I can find a jacket you can borrow."

A few minutes later, they walked out into the freezing evening. Layla shivered inside the adult-sized parka which seemed to swallow her whole. *When I get my first paycheck, the first thing I will buy is my own*, she told herself.

The short walk across the grounds took twice as long as needed due to deep snow drifts. They finally reached a long row of adjacent apartments. The only decorations outside the brown building were untidy, snow-covered bushes. A couple of hover cars parked in front of apartments announced that Layla had neighbors.

The ID card that Layla had been issued unlocked her door. There was a large bed in the middle of the room. A desk and chair were against one wall. A tiny cooking area and mini-fridge were located near a video screen. Layla's luggage was stacked beside the bathroom door.

"I know it's not much," said Rosetta.

"It is the biggest bedroom I have ever had. My first apartment."

"I was excited to get my first apartment too, though I have to pay rent. It's in town. Whenever you need a ride to a store, let me know."

"Thanks, I am fine for now."

After Rosetta left, Layla let the excitement of the day wash over her. She was truly on her own for the first time in her life. No parents or teachers to tell her what to do. No more tests or assignments to pass. Only eight hours a day she would be on the clock doing others' bidding. The other sixteen hours was hers to do as she pleased. But what would she do with the time? Besides reading novels for fun when she was home on breaks, she had developed no hobbies. She began unpacking a suitcase and saw a book her brother had given her. A wave of homesickness hit, but she pushed it back.

"You are no longer a child," she said aloud. "Adults live on their own all the time. You can do this."

Packing finished, she sat on the bed and stared at the bare walls of the room. She pulled out her e-tablet and within a few minutes had it linked to BGF's wireless network. She sent several messages off to family and friends. It would take hours for the messages to jump light years across space through various relay stations. Several communications already awaited her. Her parents said they were proud of her. Her brother asked if he could have the board games she had left behind. Her college friend Roobaroo sent a video showing her happy reunion with her own parents.

It may be years before Layla saw her parents again. She turned off the e-tablet and stared at its blank screen. Loneliness came, this time too powerful to be shoved away. Memories of the past stirred, reminding Layla why she had given up family and friends to step into the adult world before she had even experienced adolescent.

Chapter Two

Twenty-five children scribbled intensely on their e-tablets. Occasionally one would stare blankly in the air for a few minutes until sudden insight led to renewed effort. A few furrowed their brows or puckered lips in concentration. Most worked steady, occasionally glancing at the timer at the corner of their screen counting down the seconds.

"Time is up. Please submit your exams now," said the middle-age professor at the front of the classroom.

Layla placed her thumb on the send button which briefly flashed green, accepting her fingerprint. Relieved the test was over, she put her e-tablet in sleep mode before placing it into her bag. Without seeing the score, Layla knew she had earned the top mark.

As students began to file out, an eleven-year-old boy strutted up to the professor. "You dared gave me a B on the physics project last week? We both know I understand these concepts better than you."

"I gave you the score you earned." The blue-skin neodite began packing up his computer.

"You gave an A to an underclassman of your species who was doing work half as complicated as what I did."

"He achieved his best and earned that grade. You could have done better but took shortcuts."

"My final answers were correct. What does it matter if I cut out the middle?"

The professor towered over the youth. "There are no shortcuts, not even for profectus."

As the boy continued to argue, Layla ducked her head as she hurried passed. She hated when fellow profectus scorned non-human professors. So what if the teachers were slower than their prodigy students? There was still much for profectus to learn.

The crowded hallways were filled with activity as students rushed to lunch. Occasionally conflicts broke out as older underclassman refused to be bullied by younger upperclassman—one of the paradoxes of Luncaster. After the last wave of profectus had been promoted a level, the college opened its door for prodigy youth across the empire. The new students were adolescents representing dozens of different species of sentients. Some of the young profectus resented the sudden invasion of older and—as they claimed—dumber aliens.

The tight crowds thinned as Layla walked outside into a courtyard decorated with flowerbeds, trimmed shrubs, and a sparkling water fountain. The designers of Luncaster University had spared no expense in creating a beautiful, contemporary campus whose glass-covered buildings of dorms, classrooms, student union, and cafeteria reflected the meticulous landscape. Birds chirped from trees overhead as Layla took a seat on a bench and waited for her friends to arrive. She brushed her long, black hair away from her face then pulled out her e-tablet. Sunlight hit its dark screen, briefly reflecting her Asian face and brown eyes. Her parents had told her the story of their ancestors emigrating from the country of India on Earth to the small colony of Mansoor which became, over the centuries, a thriving megalopolitan planet. She missed its mushroom-shaped skyscrapers and endless parks. Homesickness struck as she thought of her parents and older, protective brother Blaaze. At the end of each term, she stayed with them for a month, but the next break was still four months away.

"Starting your dissertation?" asked blond-hair Janti, glancing at the file Layla had open. Janti sat beside Layla on the stone bench.

They had originally met at the Mansoor spaceport, nervous eight year olds about to leave their families for the first time to fly to Luncaster. Layla's parents were giving her last minute instructions and hugs, but the sober child was already wishing to be free of them. Blaaze gave her the novel *Frankenstein* as a parting gift, his own unique way of showing his approval of having a genetically enhanced sister. As Layla waved her last goodbye, her eyes moved across the dozen other young profectus doing the same. Janti happened to be standing beside her. Layla smiled and Janti grinned back, as eager as her for their adventure to begin. Both needed a friend and a bond quickly formed between them on the flight. Once they reached the university, they were assigned as roommates and had been best friends ever since.

Layla turned off her e-tablet. "I have not chosen my topic yet. I was just pondering if my ancestries are Indian since I do not share my parents' DNA. Would be nice to know who contributed the genes for our creation."

"Do not start that again. You look like your mom and dad. They are your real parents, just like my mom and dad are mine. So what if we are adopted?"

"We are not adopted. Our moms birthed us, but we were designed at BGF. Do you ever wonder about who made us?"

Janti shrugged. "I prefer to wonder about the stars. They are more fascinating. Oh, we are going to be late for lunch. Where is Roobaroo?"

"No telling. Probably caught up in some debate again."

The girls headed towards the cafeteria. They had not gone far before spying several profectus surrounding a much taller grey-skinned youth whose fiery red hair was recognizable from a distance. Roobaroo had become close friends with Janti and Layla a years ago when they had defended her against racial slurs by their classmates—not that Roobaroo needed help. She was very agile with her tongue.

A profectus named Teno confronted the ediethean. "We profectus have the highest IQ scores in the universe."

"For your age," said Roobaroo calmly. "There are still many individuals, including some of my own race, who have scored higher."

"Just wait until we reach our prime. One day we will score so high that they will have to recalibrate the entire scale to make room for us."

"Perhaps, but intelligence does not equal wisdom."

"You cannot test wisdom."

"Ah, but it is tested all the time by time itself."

"And what is that supposed to mean?"

Roobaroo smiled. "Perhaps in time you will come to know."

Teno balled up his fists while glancing at his classmates, angry at being outwitted. "Edietheans don't belong here. You should go back where you came from, alien."

Janti moved to the side of Roobaroo. "As we share some of her noble race's DNA, does that mean we must all leave too?"

"You know what I mean."

"No, I do not. The edietheans are part of us. Why should we fight against them?"

"We are nothing like them." Teno turned to his buddies. "I have learned from time that it is useless to waste conversation on alien lovers."

Layla hung back, watching the conflict silently. Only after Teno and his peers left did she speak. "You should not keep angering them."

"They started it. I refuse to let them bully me." Roobaroo bent to pick up her bag which had been knocked to the ground earlier, but a fit of coughing stopped her.

Janti grabbed the bag for her friend. "That cold still bothering you? We should cancel tonight's study session."

"No, I am fine. History is the one subject I know more about than you two." As a daughter of ambassadors, Roobaroo had traveled to many planets, absorbing vast knowledge of cultures and civilizations. Before meeting her,

Layla and Janti had found history boring, but Roobaroo had a way of bringing it alive.

That evening they all met in Roobaroo's dorm room. After several hours of studying, they took a snack break, munching on sweets sent from home.

"Sorry that some of my classmates are so rude to you," said Janti, selecting a pastry. "You would think they would be grateful to edietheans for our super brains they keep misusing."

"It is good for me." Roobaroo lounged on her dorm bed while the other two sat on the floor. "My parents sent me here, hoping I would receive a top education free from the political propaganda back home. But they were wrong. The same elitism I see at Edieth is here too. I try not to mind too much because it allows me to feel what it is like to be on the bottom. When I return home, I will be able to identify better with the lower castes, and maybe find ways to help them."

Layla licked icing from her fingers. "How many castes do you have?"

"Twenty-two. I am an Alz, born to the highest caste on Edieth which comes with prestige opportunities like choosing my own career and home, but our marriages are arranged. The further down you go, the less freedom you have. Yaz are treated no better than livestock. They receive no education and are assigned tedious, hard-labor jobs. Not everyone agrees that this is right. Over the centuries, there have been rebellions which were quickly quenched."

"I do not remember having a test on that."

"You will not. Our High Council tries to portray to the galaxy our people live harmonious, pleased with the positions they are born into. My parents fight to change this." She paused to cough, covering her mouth politely. "Though highly privileged, my parents have chosen to speak out about the mistreatment of the lower castes. That was why my parents were appointed ambassadors. It is the polite way of being ordered into exile. Still, they try to raise politic awareness of the problem."

"Improving society is important, of course." Janti reached for a piece of rich, pink fudge sent by Roobaroo's parents. "Personally, I prefer improving lives through science, not laws. My goal is to find a limitless energy source so powerful that it will change everything we know."

"And where do you expect to find this endless power? Even stars eventually burn out." Roobaroo sat up, ready for a new debate.

"In that which eats stars for breakfast. Black holes." Janti's passion showed in her eyes. "They swallow entire solar systems and are so powerful that they even slow down time itself. Image if we could harvest just one millionth of a percent of that energy. Perhaps we could power the entire empire from just one factory. "

"Impossible. How could anyone get close enough?"

"I will design a ship which can fly beyond the event horizon and safely come back."

"Yet another impossibility."

"I will be the first," bragged the eleven year old. "Profectus were created to make the impossible possible."

Roobaroo signed. "You believe too much that propaganda they feed you profectus. Some things really are impossible like…" Another coughing fit stopped Roobaroo from continuing, and she took several swallows from her cup.

While waiting for her friend to recover, Layla said, "Manipulating laws and energy is one thing, but I prefer manipulating life itself. As a geneticist, I can correct the faults of evolution by improving the original design."

"Who is to say the original was not the best?"

"The current beings we see are only at the end of a long chain of random mutations. What if we could control those changes instead of the chaos of nature? My very existence is a perfect example. We profectus are the improved version of *Homo sapiens.*"

"Improved version? You two are my best friends, but I am going to be blunt. Profectus are arrogant."

"I am not arrogant," said Janti.

"You two are not near as bad as some of the others, but all of you have been indoctrinated to believe that higher intelligent means higher worth. You sound just like the ruling class on my home world, and I have seen firsthand where that philosophy leads. Horrible things have been justified in the name of improving our race. It will be the same for you, Layla, in pursuing the creation of the ultimate super being. It is not just my race which has made this mistake, but many other civilization including humans. I have studied your history, your wars…." Coughing prevented her from saying more.

Layla tried to smooth her friend's concerns. "Roobaroo, the most I will probably ever achieve is creating glow-in-the-dark pets which will never reproduce outside a lab. And I will never become involved in politics. I will leave that for you."

The ediethean's green eyes studied the child. "Are you so sure? You profectus believe it is your destiny to make the impossible possible."

The friends returned to their studying, not knowing it would be their last night together.

15

The next morning after class, Layla found Janti sitting on a bench, face pale, eyes feverish. "You look terrible."

"I think I caught Roobaroo's cold. Did I keep you up last night with all my coughing?"

"Not too much. You should go to the infirmary for some medicine."

"Hi," said Roobaroo, walking up. "That chemistry test was tough, but I believed I passed. Ready for lunch?"

"Yes," Layla glanced worriedly at her roommate.

"Go ahead without me," said Janti. "I am not hungry."

"Are you sure?"

"Yes, I just need some sleep." Janti turned and took two steps before slowly sinking to the floor.

For a moment Layla and Roobaroo stared in shock then rushed forward. Janti's eyes opened and she looked about, dazed. A small crowd of curious students gathered around.

"What happened?"

"You fainted," said Roobaroo.

"I suddenly felt dizzy."

"Come on. Let us get you to the infirmary."

Layla and Roobaroo helped their friend off the floor and walked closely beside her. When they entered the quiet clinic, the nurse on duty had Janti sit down and ran a few diagnostics tests.

"You have an infection that is affecting the vestibule in your ears which controls balance," said the stern middle-age human nurse.

"I could have told you that."

"No need for rudeness, youngster. I will keep you here tonight for observation."

"Just give me some medicine and let me sleep in my own bed."

"This is my ward, and you will do as told."

As the nurse marched off, Janti whispered to her friends, "My misfortune to ask for cold medicine from an overzealous nurse. Will you bring me a change of clothes later?"

"Sure. And some snacks," said Layla.

"At least I will be able to catch up on some reading."

Several hours later when the girls returned, the clinic's lights were dim. The nurse heard the door beep, announcing visitors, and she entered the ward from her connected living quarters.

"Your friend is sleeping and should not be awakened."

"We brought her some clothes and fudge."

"I will give her the clothes when she awakens, but she has no need for sweets right now. She needs healthy foods."

Reluctantly the girls handed over the clothing then headed back to the dorm with the uneaten snack.

The quietness of the dorm room bothered Layla that night. It was the first time in her life she was completely alone. She listened to recent video messages from home and sent one back wishing her brother a happy birthday. She tried reading a textbook, but grew bored with it and found herself picking up *Frankenstein*. During bouts of homesickness she read it, feeling connected to her brother, her fears melting away despite the novel's dark plot of a creator and his creation at war with each other.

Her throat felt scratchy. She grabbed a drink from the small refrigerator, but it offered no relief. Throughout the night, coughing fits kept awaking her. She had little appetite at breakfast which concerned Roobaroo. Layla let her believe it was due to worrying about Janti. They headed back to the infirmary. Entering, they saw the nurse talking in a low voice with a doctor from the city hospital.

"Is Janti awake?" asked Layla.

"Yes, she is eating breakfast." The girls headed for the side room where Janti was, but the nurse stopped them. "Keep your conversation short. She had a rough night and needs rest."

Layla watched as the nurse turned back to the doctor. The two continued speaking in low, grave voices. Layla entered the room where Janti lay on a bed. Her friend looked paler than before. Damp hair clung against a feverish face. The clothes they had brought for her lay unused on a nearby table. Her breakfast was barely touched.

"How are you feeling?" asked Roobaroo.

"Like I have been hit by a flying ship. Do you have any fudge?"

"The nurse would not let us bring any, but we will try to sneak some in later."

"I might be at the hospital later."

"Hospital?" said the other two in unison.

"That is what I gathered from eavesdropping. Doctor Philips thinks I have the flu or something similar." A fit of coughing left her breathless for a moment. "Now stop looking so grave. I have had the flu before."

"So have I," said Layla, "but I have never been sent to the hospital for it."

The nurse poked her head through the doorway. "You two should leave now."

17

As both girls left the room, they heard the doctor on the telecom asking for an ambulance. In the main lobby, Layla confronted the nurse, "What is wrong with Janti?"

"Just the flu. Now you kids don't worry. She will up and about soon."

"We are not kids, and we will worry," said Layla. "Why is she being sent to the hospital?"

"Just a precaution."

"Precaution for what? How are her symptoms worse than a normal flu?"

The nursed sighed. "You profectus are too smart for your own good. She has body aches, deep coughing, vertigo, high fever, and fluid in her lungs. It may be developing into pneumonia."

"Fluid in the lungs?" Layla suddenly felt lightheaded and reached out, grabbing a wall to steady herself.

"Are you alright? You look feverish also. Here, sit down."

Layla was escorted to a chair while the nurse ran a diagnostics sweep with a sensor.

"They are roommates," explained Roobaroo.

"When did they begin showing signs of sickness?"

"Just yesterday, right after I got over my own cold."

"You had a cold?" asked Doctor Philips who had walked into the room after sending his message.

"Yes, just a mild one that only lasted a couple of days. It is already completely gone."

A frown creased the doctor's face. "Both of you should come to the hospital for further tests." His somber tone perplexed both girls.

The ambulance soon arrived and carried Janti, Layla, Roobaroo, and Doctor Philips to the large hospital located in the heart of the city. Several nurses pushed Janti's hoverbed down the hallway and out of sight. Layla and Roobaroo were sent to an examination room where several tests, including blood work, were done. While Roobaroo protested that she was healthy and the tests unnecessary, Layla fought against lightheadedness and deep tiredness. She could hear Roobaroo and the doctor talking, but their words were incomprehensible.

"Layla! Layla, wake up."

The eleven year old opened her eyes, surprised to find herself on the floor while Roobaroo and Doctor Philips bent over her in concern.

Doctor Philips beckoned to some nurses who helped Layla to a hoverbed. "We are checking you in as a patient right now."

A telecom beeped and Doctor Philips read the message aloud. "Another student has passed out at Luncaster University."

The last thing Layla heard as she was floated out of the room was Doctor Philips sending a video message, "Xi'an Health Department, I am officially requesting immediate quarantine of Luncaster University. We have a possible species-jumping pathogen."

Layla was carried to a room and placed on its single bed. Almost immediately she fell asleep, but it was shallow, leaving her half-conscious of aches in her body and burning fevers which flip-flopped to icy chills. Hours later, it became difficult to breathe. She felt like she was gasping for air through a heavy, wet blanket. Healthcare workers came and went from her room. In one of her more wakeful moments, she noticed a nurse monitoring the equipment beside her.

"Where's Janti?"

"Next door." The nurse's greenish reptilian face was hidden behind a breathing mask.

"Is she better?"

"Sleep now." The nurse pressed a button on the machine, and Layla felt deep sleep steal over her.

Days later, her fever finally broke and a light meal consisting of a sandwich, a small salad, and fruit was brought to her. Weakly she sat up in bed and slowly ate. Weary of sleep, she flipped on the vid and surfed through channels. A newscast showing the campus of Luncaster University caught her attention, and she turned up the volume.

"...where three out of every four profectus showed medium to severe symptoms. A hundred and fifteen students were hospitalized."

The scene switched to a close up of Doctor Philips speaking in front of a group of reporters. "Luncaster Hospital has been working closely with the Xi'an Health Department to monitor the situation. We believe virus H4C34 has ran its course, and there have been no new cases in three days."

"What caused the outbreak?" asked a reporter.

"H4C34 is usually a mild cold virus who host is *ediethean*. The virus was able to jump species due to *ediethean* DNA used in the controversial genetic engineering of *Homo sapiens profectus*. Tests have confirmed that normal humans are in no danger from this virus."

The view switched again, this time to Dean Palakkad in his office at the university. "We are deeply saddened by the loss of one of our students, but we profoundly appreciated the health care workers who responded quickly and labored so tirelessly in preventing the loss of more lives. Friday we will have a memorial service and classes will resume on…"

Layla heard no more. Her heart rate quickened and the equipment monitoring her beeped, summoning the reptilian nurse wearing a mask.

"Where is Janti?" sputtered Layla.

"Janti?"

"She came in when I did. Where is she?"

"I will find out." The nurse left.

A few minutes later Doctor Philips entered. "It is good to see you awake."

"Janti. Where is she?"

The sadness in his eyes strangled Layla's hope before he even spoke. "Her symptoms were severe. We did not know at first what we were treating. I am sorry, but she did not make it."

Tears had already begun trickling down Layla's cheeks before he had finished his first sentence. The last words he spoke ripped a hole in her heart. She sobbed so uncontrollable that Doctor Philips ordered a tranquilizer to be given to her. For the next few days, Layla lay in bed, lifeless, refusing to eat. She went through bouts of crying and staring blankly at the wall or the video screen.

On the third day, she awoke to find Roobaroo sitting beside her. "Hi, they finally lifted the quarantine today. How are you feeling?"

"I feel nothing."

"Uh…classes resume Monday. They say you might be released tomorrow." When Layla did not respond, Roobaroo sat in awkward silence until the quietness became unbearable. "This is all my fault. Everyone hates me, including you." A tear slid down her smooth, grey cheek.

Layla reached out and took Roobaroo's hand. "I am not mad at you. It was just a mindless virus carrying out its programming."

"But I was the carrier. Everyone at school knows that. If I had not come to Luncaster University, then Janti would still be alive."

"And the doctors would not know how to treat us. Sooner or later some of us would have come in contact with other edietheans, and we may have died off one by one without understanding why. Here, the virus was identified quickly and treated. Do not blame yourself."

Roobaroo wiped tears away. "I…I will try not to, but others will."

"And if they do, I will tell them to their faces that they are numbskull throwbacks from the Cambrian Period."

The teenager smiled weakly. "That was always a dull era in history."

The next day Layla and several other profectus who had been hospitalized returned to school. The atmosphere was subdued and quiet. Clusters of students studied or talked in low voices. Some offered Layla their condolences, though all she wanted was to hide in her dorm room. But once there, she felt even worse. Janti's belongings had already been packed and sent home to her parents. Only a bare bed was left as a testimony for the girl whose bright dreams of being an astrophysicist would never be realized.

A knock at the door caused Layla to jump. "Come in."

Roobaroo entered, and both girls stared at the empty bed, unable to talk. No words could ease the ache in their hearts.

Two freshmen, one human and the other a neodite, shyly poked their heads into the room. "Some of us made some synthetic flowers yesterday for the memorial service. We're sorry you missed it. If you don't mind, can we bring them here?"

"Um, no. Go ahead."

The freshmen entered, each carrying an artificial flower and placed it on Janti's bed. They had barely left before another human came with a bright daisy, followed by a ten-year-old profectus with a sunflower. Yet still more students entered and each placed a flower on the mattress, creating a bright, mismatch blanket of petals and green leaves. Some students came and went silently while others lingered, chatting about pleasant memories of Janti.

The colorful heap of flowers offered comfort over the following weeks. There were many nights Layla cried herself to sleep, and some nights she took her blanket and pillow into Roobaroo's room and slept on the floor. When the term ended, she left the flowers on the mattress as she traveled to Mansoor.

Back home, she could no longer pretend to be a child easily amused by zoos and theme parks. Her parents and brother tried to connect with her, but the distance between them had grown too great. She rarely spoke about Janti, for to do so meant opening a wound that was still too raw and deep. There were good days when Blaaze made her laugh, she joined her mom in sing-alongs, or her dad's lame jokes caused her to smile. Still, her family sensed that her childhood had ended.

Layla returned to Luncaster University for her final term. In her dorm room, she found the flowers gone, leaving only an empty bed. Too many nights Layla stared at it while she struggled with writing her dissertation. Her original topic had changed after Janti's death. Now she researched immunity systems of various species and theorized how genetic engineering could improve on the original designs. Her adviser praised the research passages but offered caution about her theories, warning that the paper needed to stay in the realm of proven facts. Layla dismissed the professor's advice, seeing him as too short sighted.

Several months into the term, Layla was summoned by the dean. As she walked to his office, she went over arguments in her head why she should be permitted to continue writing the dissertation her way. Palakkad gave a friendly greeting then invited her to sit down. His office was airy and inviting with huge windows stretching to the ceiling and potted plants in the corners.

"Layla, with graduation drawing near, I am concerned about your future plans." Grey streaked Palakkad's dark hair, his aged face charismatic and friendly.

"I have been thinking about that too. I know the ideas in my dissertation are a tad extreme, but they are backed by careful research."

"I'm not concerned about your dissertation. I have read over the draft you submitted, and it shows creativity and imagination. What I am concerned about is your future. According to our records, no company has asked for your transcripts. Have you begun applying for jobs yet?"

"Ah, no. I have been too focused on my dissertation and classes."

"You should begin thinking about it. Graduation is only two months away. If I might make a suggestion, you should send an application to Bontinc Genetics Foundation."

"You mean BGF, the company which created profectus? I could not…I mean…how can I be qualified to work where I was…made?"

"You will soon have a Ph.D. in genetic engineering. You are as qualified as any other geneticist. It would be fitting to have a profectus at BGF. Dare I use the term poetic?"

"Sir, I…it would be an honor which I have never considered."

"Then consider it. You will find that you will have some pull with the new director at BGF."

"Mikam left? I had not read about that."

"Nor could you have. It has not been made public yet. Next week Mikam will announce his retirement and the replacement he personally chose—which will be me."

"You are leaving Luncaster University?"

"My heart has always been for the betterment of humankind through genetics. I worked for over twenties years at BGF, eventually heading the profectus project. I only became the dean of this academy because I felt no one else understood the needs of the profectus as I do. Who would shape your potential? Someone else would just see children, very smart children, but just children. I see the influential leaders of our future. With the last of the profectus graduating, my work here will be completed."

"The last group will not graduate until next year. Surely you will be here till then?"

The dean glanced away briefly before answering. "There has been some disagreements between myself and the board members. We have different opinions of who should be allowed at Luncaster University. It had been my understanding from the beginning that this would be an elite school for humans, but most of the members of the board believed it should be open to all species. The virus outbreak drove a final wedge between us. I blamed the board for your roommate's death. Janti had such potential. I keep imagining how she might have revolutionized what we know about astrophysics. She was a star which burned out before she even had the opportunity to blaze across the heavens."

Palakkad's genuine grief moved Layla, and she sought to comfort him. "Her death is no one's fault. It was just a mindless virus."

"Either way, I still would have left here after one more year. There is a job waiting for you at BGF if you choose to apply. I am very pleased already at the privileged positions my profectus have acquired across the Empire. Still, I would be delighted to have one working at BGF. Very poetic indeed."

For the next few weeks, Layla pondered the job opportunity while juggling her intense work load. Part of her was terrified to think about the future. Her entire eleven years had been spent either at Mansoor or Luncaster. Soon this predictable, comfortable life would end. All profectus were expected to begin careers, not move back home. Was she ready to take on the responsibilities of an adult before she was even a teenager?

Chapter Three

The first weeks at BGF blurred by in a blend of excitement and frustration. Though Layla knew the theories used in genetic engineering, it was her first opportunity to attempt it herself. The Baby Department was divided into many sections, each focused on a different sentient race. Would-be-parents sent in sperm and eggs along with a checklist of which traits were desired in the offspring. Scientists searched through the donated genetic material, editing the DNA then allowing sperm and eggs to interact. The resulting embryos were frozen and sent back to reproduction clinics on the parents' planets. There, the female would be implanted with her child. The entire process was very expensive, thus only the rich could afford purchasing the perfect baby.

Rosetta was a cheerful teacher who patiently answered Layla's many questions. She did not fuss when the preteen made mistakes, causing the destruction of products worth thousands of credits a piece. Rosetta missed her own sister who lived many light years away and embraced Layla as a surrogate sibling.

Most of the other scientists were friendly—some too much. Leana Sebok was the worst. The chubby, middle-age woman would corner Layla and quiz her with basic scientific questions like "What is a genome?" and "What is the RNA's role in DNA replication?" As Layla prattled off the answers which any freshman at Luncaster University knew, Leana would beam gleefully and call others over to hear the recital.

One day Rosetta spotted Layla hiding under a desk. The preteen whispered, "Is she gone?"

"Who?"

"Leana."

"She is going out the door with the others for lunch, where we should be heading." Rosetta watched Layla crawl out and dust herself off. "You should be more patient with Leana. She is not as bad as you think."

"You are not the one being treated like a performing monkey."

"Leana worked on the profectus project for thirty years. Near the time the project was cancelled, her husband and only child died in a car accident. I have been told she had a difficult time dealing with their lost."

"I am not her dead child."

"No, but she did help to create you. Be patient with her eccentricity."

Layla had only been working at BFG for three weeks when Rosetta decided to throw a surprise party for Layla's birthday. Rosetta claimed on the way to the grocery store that she needed to pick up a missing item at Mera's home. When they walked into the house, there was a big banner saying "Happy Twelfth" and Mera's family yelling "Surprise." Layla sputtered a shock reply. Several local teenagers who knew Mera's children had been invited. Layla struggled through the party, grateful for the thought but she felt awkward around the youths whose lives were far different than her own.

Spring brought sunshine and flowers. The hedges bordering Layla's apartment burst into fragrant pink blooms. It was a relief to walk to work without stumbling through snow and ice.

Over the winter, Layla had mastered the techniques of creating genetic engineered embryos and became bored. She knew there were still more challenging assignments in the department, but they were reserved for veterans. She would have to work for years at BGF before being allowed to tackle them. The Freak Department where Derrick worked became a lure which pulled her. Splicing DNA to add new traits to animals sounded more exciting than endlessly changing eye colors of babies-to-be. She wanted to ask for a transfer but was afraid that Rosette would take the request wrongly. Layla was dependent on Rosette to drive her to Taylorville when she needed groceries and other supplies. Rosetta and Derrick spent much of their time off work together, often inviting Layla along.

One day while they enjoyed a picnic lunch at a park, Layla said casually, "Derrick, I have been very curious about Freak Department. I would love to see the creatures there."

"I wish we were allowed to visit other departments. I would be spending all my free time with the babes." He grinned at Rosetta.

"And I with the freaks." She gave Derrick a playful push.

"Perhaps I will apply for a transfer," said Layla

Derrick shook his head. "Completion is too stiff. Banican Zine, my department head, would never let you in."

"Why not?"

He leaned forward and kept his voice low so passersby would not hear. "Well, rumor is that Banican and Palakkad have been lifetime rivals. Banican hated the Advance Department which Palakkad oversaw. After Emperor Kalyuga passed that Sentient Genetic Purity Law, cancelling the profectus project, Banican only allowed a few of the Advance scientists to transfer into his department."

"That was years ago."

"But if he hates Palakkad then he hates anything that Palakkad made."

That meant her. Layla studied the melting ice in her cup for a long moment. "Palakkad is now director. If he approves my transfer, then Banican cannot refuse me."

"No, but you may regret it. The two men are still enemies. Banican had expected to be named the next director then suddenly Palakkad swooped in and grabbed the title."

Rosetta asked, "Why do you want to leave the Baby Department? Are you not happy?"

"I feel I have reached a plateau. I need new challenges."

Once a week Palakkad invited Layla to his office to chat. He was always eager to hear about her latest achievements. She only had to mention her desire to learn about experimental genetics before the director quickly suggested her transfer. Two days later, she found herself standing in the office of Banican Zine. Behind him was a large glass wall through which could be seen the vast, only partly lit hanger housing the Freaks Department.

"Why have you asked to be in my department?" Banican looked at her with distaste. He was a middle-age, heavyset man who seemed to have a permanent scowl.

"I am interesting in designing new creatures." Layla tried to hide her nervousness.

"If you want to play with building blocks, I suggest that babies should stay in the Baby Department."

"With all due respect, sir, there is nothing new being created in the Genetic Enhancement Department. For decades, the same techniques have been used to produce the same results. It is here in your department where the action is. Your team pushes the boundaries of what is known. You are not afraid to try something innovative."

The frown did not leave Banican's face as he studied her. "You will start at the bottom like every other newbie. I do not care that you are a favorite pet of Palakkad."

"I ask for nothing more."

An aide escorted Layla to her new job. Freak Department looked very different from what she was used to. Baby Department had been well lit, clean, and tidy. Here, only certain sections were always kept lit while other areas were kept on timers to simulate day and night cycles for various animals.

She carefully treaded through the labyrinth of workstations, cages, incubators, and crates. The damp air was filled with odors of beasts, rotten fruit, and waste from cages waiting to be cleaned. Strange snarls and hisses rose from pens.

Finally the man guiding her stopped. "Lunk, she's all yours now. Banican asked for her to be shown the operation from the bottom up."

Lunk was a tall, scrawny man of few words. "Can you use a shovel?"

"I can learn."

"That is a start."

He led her pass several rows of cages to a large pen where two young men shoveled manure. She was delighted to see one was Derrick. In the adjacent pen were fluffy cow-shaped animals about three feet high. Lunk handed her a shovel and walked away. Layla took off her lab coat and hung it on a peg beside several others.

"Good to have you join us," smiled Derrick.

"Thanks." She attempted to scoop up a steaming pile of waste but it only slid away from the edge of her shovel.

"Have you ever used a shovel before?"

"No."

"It is nice to know I can teach a profectus something."

"What are those creatures?"

Derrick shoveled as he talked. "Cowoons from the planet Polat. They are known for both their milk and wool, but we are focusing on increasing the quality of their wool which fetches a high price in certain markets."

Layla copied his shoving technique and found that the task was not difficult, just dirty. Once the pen was cleaned, new wood chips were scattered on the concrete floor and hay forked into bins. Then the gate was opened to let in the hungry cowoons.

"Are you sure you really want to work here?" asked Derrick.

"Yes," said Layla, ignoring the ache in her arms. "What's next?"

They spent the rest of the day cleaning cages and pens. Layla had rarely been around animals and had to be instructed in how to handle them. She was glad that the insect, reptiles, and fish sections were not on their duty list. Still, she was almost bitten by an albino snake which had escaped from its cage and was hanging around lavender mice, hoping for a meal. She was pecked twice by a cranky blue-feathered raven which kept croaking one word, "Nevermore."

"That's Lunk's attempt at humor," explained Derrick. "He reads too much Gothic poetry and decided to test the bird's memory by having Blue Dust memorize the poem *The Raven*."

"Isn't that a very long poem? Can a bird actually remember that much?"

"His is genetically enhanced, hence the blue color and long memory. Right now, when Blue Dust is in a good mood, he can make it through half the poem."

When the workday ended, Layla headed to the women's locker room to shower off the dirt and grime. Every muscle in her body seemed to ache. When she reached her apartment, she crawled into bed and sleep for the next eleven hours. The beeping of her alarm pulled her out of deep slumber. The moment she moved her arms to hit the snooze button, she cried out in pain. The dull muscle ache from the day before had deepened into agonizing throbs every time she moved a limb. For a long time she lay in bed until she visualized Banican's stern face. He would love for her to quit after just one day. She clenched her teeth against the pain and crawled out of bed, reminding herself that within a couple of weeks, her body would adjust to the physical labor.

Despite aching muscles, Layla worked hard. There was so much to learn, to see. While she cleaned, she observed the veteran scientists and occasionally asked them questions, but most were too busy to give her much attention. After lunch as Layla scoured a rodent cage, she watched a tall scientist recording data. In his hand was a small scanner which he waved over a cage full of half-grown mice with deep lavender fur. After he finished, he touched a button on the earbud he wore. It beeped once then began recording his voice.

"Generation Fourteen has increased colorization by point two percent. Observation is complete." He walked over to another container. "Generation Fifteen was born yesterday and seems healthy."

He picked up a small container from a bin and walked back to the first cage of mice. With one hand, he gently brushed the dozen young mice out of the cage and into the plastic box. Then he handed the container and its squeaking occupants to Layla.

"Dispose of them." He walked away to another cage and began scanning a green gerbil.

Uncertain what to do but not wanting to show her inexperience, Layla walked away. After putting several rows of cages between her and the scientist, she paused to examine the mice. Several ran about, investigating their new environment. One stood up on its hind legs and looked her in the eyes.

"I am supposed to kill you? How? You're so cute." She had never killed anything in her life, at least not on purpose. Stepping on insects by accident did not count.

With no clue how to proceed, she searched for Derrick, ignoring her aching muscles. He was not with the cowoons or near the rodent area. She headed into the avian section. Still no sign of Derrick, but Blue Dust noticed her and cawed, "Deep into the darkness peering, long I stood there, wondering, fearing. Doubting, dreaming dreams no mortals ever dared to dream before."

Frustrated, Layla said to the bird, "Could you tell me where Derrick is?"

The bird tilted his head, studying her. "Nevermore."

"Thanks a lot."

Hearing the sound of metal hitting concrete behind her, Layla turned and spotted two feet poking out from under an incubator. She walked over just as a dirty Derrick, holding a wrench, rolled out from under the large machine.

"That should fix it. Just needed a new heating element," he said to a nearby scientist in a lab coat. "Give it a couple of hours to heat back up."

"Thanks," said the scientist. "Too bad you were not here last night. We lost the entire clutch of eggs."

Layla said to her friend, "I did not know you were a mechanic."

"It runs in the family." He stooped to pick up a fallen screwdriver. "My dad and grandfather run an engine shop. Perhaps I am the only kid ever encouraged to take things apart while growing up. They wanted me to follow in their footsteps, but I had my own plans." He placed the screwdriver into a toolbox that had his name printed on it.

"You look like a professorial handyman. Are you sure you are really a geneticist? Maybe you missed your destiny."

"Funny. This was a going away present from my dad when I went to college. It does come in handy sometimes." Squeaking from the container Layla carried drew Derrick's attention. "Why are you carrying around a box of mice?"

"I was told to dispose of them. How is that done here?"

"It's a simple enough procedure. Does take some getting used to, though. Come, I'll show you."

He led her through the maze of cages to a side room built into the wall of the ancient hanger. At the doorway, he typed in a password and the door unlocked. An odd smell drifted from the room, and Layla hesitated for a moment before following Derrick. On one side of the room was a series of clear canisters of different sizes attached to hoses that ran down through the floor. Derrick opened the smallest tube and placed the box of mice inside. He locked the door and showed Layla how to use the touchpad of the connected computer to input the weight and number of creatures to be euthanized.

"Why must they be destroyed? They look healthy. Cannot they be sold in a pet store?"

"They are part of a breeding experiment and have not been sterilized. We can't sell creatures that are fertile. If just one genetically altered animal breeds with their natural counterparts, the effects could be staggering and far-reaching. BGF would be slammed with so many lawsuits it might have to close for good. I'm sure you have studied about it happening to other genetic companies. It is essential we keep a high safety record here."

"I remember reading that half the cows on Alphos had to be put down when a gene introduced though one bull caused cancer in humans who ate the beef."

"Then I'm sure you studied the Linberm incident where fifteen hundred citizens died from a virus carried by a ruby butterfly which escape from a laboratory and breed with the local insects."

Derrick pressed the ready button. Machinery under the floor hummed, and a murky gas began filling the clear canister. Layla pitied the mice. They sensed something was wrong and began scampering about, squeaking loudly. Some tried to climb out of the box while others attempted to dig through the hard plastic. One by one, each died. Some curled up into a ball while others dropped dead in the midst of frantically trying to escape.

It is part of the job, she told herself. *I will get use to it eventually.*

After the lethal gas was sucked out of the canister, Derrick opened the tube and took out the box of dead mice. He walked over to a conveyor belt and placed the container on it. He hit a button on the wall which caused the belt to begin moving and the container of mice disappeared into a hole in the wall.

"The bodies are burnt, unless you fill out a request for an autopsy. We have a lab which handles that." He glanced at his watch. "Looks like our shift is over today. Rosetta wanted me to ask if you wanted to eat out with us tonight. She has something to show you."

"Sure, anything is better than cafeteria food. What does she want to show me?"

"Sorry, I'm sworn to secrecy." Derrick grinned mischievously.

After Layla had showered in the locker room, she met up with her friends near the cafeteria. Rosetta could barely contain her excitement as she held out her hand to reveal a ring with a light blue crystal which sparkled in the sunlight.

"Derrick proposed last night down by the lake."

"It's not a real jeremejevite," said Derrick. "I can't afford that on my salary."

"It looks like a jeremejevite, and I think it's beautiful."

"Not as beautiful as you." Derrick grinned, and Rosette blushed in delight.

"Congratulations," said Layla, trying to change the subject before it became more sentimental. "I learned today that Derrick is a mechanic."

"It's just a hobby," said Derrick,

Rosetta defended her fiancé. "He is just being modest. A month ago, he fixed in half an hour that NDB in Building B which the maintenance crew had been trying to do for two days."

"I was crawling under it and happened to be the one who spotted the cracked gear. Any one of them could have fixed it if they had seen which part was broken."

Layla cut in, "Building B? Is there a second building to Freak Department?"

"Actually there are three others, but you must have specific clearance for each one. I have been in a couple of them to help out with broken equipment."

"What experiments are done in them?"

"None. They produce our final products which go to market."

"Can I see them?"

"Not from the inside, but we can peek through windows."

Derrick led the way across the campus to several huge, plain-looking buildings. Though only one-story tall, each was vast with multiple wings added onto the structures over the years. At docking bays, cages were being loaded onto freight vehicles. Animals squawked, squeaked, neighed, mooed, or hissed in protest.

There were only a few small windows scattered about, but Layla found the glimpses they offered of the production lines fascinating. Derrick explained that the process started with the machines called Nanotech DNA Builders. Scientists told the supercomputers what to build, and nanites used proteins to synthesis the chromosomes of the desired animals. The DNA was inserted into a blank egg which had its own DNA already removed. A brief

31

spark of electricity fused the egg and new DNA together, and the egg began to divide. The embryo, if it was a mammal, was then placed into an automatic fetus developer and grown to birthing age. Shortly after birth, the infant was sterilized. Depending on the species, some newborns were shipped out immediately, but others were kept in growing pens until older.

Rosetta brushed dust from a window to see better. "Your procedures are so different from what we use at the Baby Department. We can't use NDB's because it produces, in essence, clones. And, of course, it is illegal to clone sentients."

"It would be much quicker and cheaper if you used NDB's to mass produce babies," said Derrick.

"And take the randomness from life? We don't need a thousand Derricks running about. One is quite enough."

"I would hate competing with a thousand other me's for your attention."

A man's deep voice boomed out, "What are you doing here?"

The three looked behind them to see a security guard walking towards them. His stern face and muscular build gave him a menacing look.

"Hi, Anthony," said Derrick. "I was giving my fiancé a peek at what I do. Don't worry, she works here too. Enjoying your new night shift?"

"The night part, no, but I am enjoying the promotion and raise. Congratulation on your engagement." The sternness, though, stayed in his voice.

Taking the hint, Derrick led Layla and Rosetta away from the building. After they had turned a corner, they paused to figure out where to eat. While the couple debated between fast food and a café, Layla's attention was drawn to a dingy building on the other side of a large parking lot. Beyond it grew a thick forest broken occasionally by husks of military barracks fallen into ruin long ago.

"What is in that building?"

"Which one?" said Derrick, still thinking about dinner.

"That large one there. Is it part of Freak Department?"

"No, it's just the Abandoned Department."

"You mean Human Advancement which oversaw the profectus project?"

He nodded then continued his defense about fast food.

"I want to see it."

Layla began walking across the huge parking lot, pausing to let several cars drive pass as workers headed home. Derrick and Rosetta followed, still debating about dinner. As they neared the building, Layla noticed the grass was kept mowed around the building yet vines had been allowed to climb up its walls. The few windows were covered with a thick layer of dust. Birds nested in crevices along the roof's edge. In a few more years, the building would disappear into the forest like the forgotten military ones of long ago.

"Can we get inside?" asked Layla.

Rosetta said, "I don't think that is a good idea. We will trigger an alarm."

"Not anymore," said Derrick. "The electricity has been off for years." He walked up to the nearest door and tried to open it. "Locked, of course."

"We should be heading to dinner now."

"Where is your spirit of adventure?" Derrick walked along the wall, peeking into cracked windows.

"I happen to like my job and don't wish to be unemployed."

"We are not going to get fired for exploring an abandoned building. There are tons of them scattered about, left over from when this was a military base."

"But this one was once a BGF department."

They rounded a corner and walked along the wall that bordered the forest. Layla tried another door and found it locked. "There must be a way in."

"Let me give it a try." Derrick bent down and examined the old lock. He then pulled a small pouch from a pocket and selected a long, thin rod from among an odd assortment of tiny tools.

"Don't tell me you carry a lock pick?" said Rosetta.

"My dad taught me to always be prepared. You never know what you might find yourself facing."

"Like breaking and entering?"

"Relax. No one cares about this building. If there was anything valuable left, the alarm would not have been turned off."

"How do you know the alarm is really off?"

Derrick held up a hand for silence and placed the rod against the lock. A spark of electricity jumped from the rod to the lock which hummed softly. Derrick began punching in passwords. On his sixth try, the lock clicked open.

"Ha, I guessed right that they never bothered changing it from one of the old passwords Lunk shared with me while I was helping him repair equipment."

He stood up and opened the rusty door. Only the hum of insects greeted them. Derrick gave his fiancé an I-told-you-so look then stood politely aside to allow the two ladies to enter first.

The large laboratory was the size of a small warehouse, dim light filtering in through dirty windows. Swirls of dust rose with each footstep they took. Insects scampered about among old equipment and forgotten crates. Here and there were marks on the floor where large machinery had once stood but had long ago been removed through a large freight door. Exoskeletons of dead insects decorated empty shelves and windowsills.

"Lovely place," said Rosetta.

"Does my eyes deceive me, or is that a NDB X1800?" said Derrick excitedly. "Those have been obsolete for over fifty years." He ran his hands gingerly over its bulky, tarnished frame. "I wonder if it still works?"

"Probably broken. That's why it was left here."

Despite arachnids' webs, Derrick lay on the floor and scooted under the large machine.

Rosetta stood with hands on hips, shaking her head in disapproval. "Show him an ancient contraption and he forgets all about food."

Layla explored deeper into the room. Despite its decay, the lab seemed sacred to her. This was where she had been created. In her childhood she had read the official story countless times. She tried to image what the lab had looked like when Palakkad and Leana Sebok had worked here so long ago. The chamber would have been filled with top quality equipment purchased with funds provided in part by the Coalition of Human Advancement. Some of the best geneticists from across the Empire had labored in this room for decades, not knowing if their work would ever become reality. Though they had successfully grown human embryos spliced with ediethean DNA, imperial law forbid the embryos to be allowed to develop beyond the early blastocyst stage. The embryos had been frozen, some for many years. The Coalition had continued to pressure the aging Emperor Anayasipi who finally signed the Human Advancement Law, allowing Layla and her fellow profectus to be born.

Layla paused in front of a cryogenic freezer whose door hung half off its hinges. *This may have been the same freezer where I was frozen. Perhaps for decades. Maybe Janti had been right beside me, both of us destined to be sent to the same planet.*

A feeling of deep sadness welled up, threatening to overwhelm her. She wiped away a tear and turned away from the freezer. Several dirty culture dishes on a desk caught her attention. She might have been formed in one of these, created from genetic material donated from both human and ediethean. The donors might still be alive or long dead. It did not matter. Her parents were Kalai and Sargam. Kalai had given birth to her. Sargam had held her hand when she took her first steps as a toddler. Her brother Blaaze sometimes teased her mercilessly, but he had always been quick to defend her against other children who made fun of her strange adult language.

"It just might work," said Derrick, dusting himself off. "They were considered the most advanced nano technology for over a century. The newer models break down so much easier. Just proves that newer does not always mean better."

"Where did you learn to pick locks?" asked Rosetta, arms crossed.

"During my adolescence. I wasn't always a respectable geneticist."

"You still aren't. You spend more time cleaning poop and fixing machines than editing DNA."

"Every scientist must start somewhere. Besides, you love seeing me dirty."

Rosetta changed the subject. "Layla, are you ready to eat yet?"

"Yes," said the twelve year old, walking back towards them.

While Derrick locked the door, Layla gave the dusty lab one last sentimental look. *My genesis, my beginning. But it is not my ending.*

Chapter Four

Chatter surrounded Layla as she munched on a sandwich in the crowded cafeteria. Across from her Rosetta and Derrick discussed wedding plans. To her left, Mera and Leana debated the rising cost of bioengineering. Layla paid little attention to the conversations as she pondered a bizarre reptile she had seen that morning. The vingoto lizard had been bright blue with neon purple stripes, a favorite at pet shops, but completely alien in appearance from its wild counterparts.

Mera chatted with Rosetta. "How are your parents taking the upcoming wedding?"

"Stressed but happy. Both our families will be flying in next month for it."

"Did you finally decide if it will be held at the church?"

Rosetta glanced at her fiancé before answering. "We are compromising. It will be outdoors in the park, but the reception will be at my church."

Layla whispered to Derrick, "How many different species were used in engineering that vingoto?"

"Six. That is actually a record. Before now there has never been a commercial successful product of more than four. There have been laboratory experiments of up to ten, but they always end in disaster. The more foreign DNA added, the more unstable the original source becomes. Even with the vingoto lizard, only half of one percent of its DNA is foreign."

"What if you started from scratch? Instead of using one primary source and editing its DNA, you started with nothing and added bits and pieces of different creatures, creating something brand new. Something that has never existed before."

Derrick laughed. "Start from nothing? You know it doesn't work that way. DNA is far too complicated. You cannot simply take an arm from this creature, a leg from that, throw in a brain from yet another one and suddenly have a brand new working animal."

"Why not?"

"Are you trying to be factious? I thought you had a Ph.D. in genetics."

"I am being serious. Why do we not design creatures from scratch? We could make something far better than what randomized evolution has."

"Well, for starters, it has never been done before. Creatures have different hormones and enzymes, even among related species. If you step beyond related kinds, say using both insect and mammal, then the very cells and skeletons are completely different. If you want to be really crazy then you could throw in animals from different planets that are completely foreign to each other."

"We should do it."

Derrick laughed again. "It is statistically impossible. We cannot make it beyond six species, let alone a dozen."

"Fifty or more creatures will be needed."

"Fifty? And what would be the purpose? A lot of wasted time and money to create a monstrosity no one would want to look at, let along buy."

"We should do it simply because no one has ever done it before. "

"It cannot be done. You're talking about writing the DNA for a brand new creature. A bacteria alone has six hundred thousand nucleotide pairs. In humans it's over three billion. Within the human genome are twenty-five thousand genes. Even if you tried to write the DNA from scratch for a simple worm, it could take many live times to achieve."

"It should be sentient, not animal."

Derrick stared at her. "A sentient Frankenstein? I will grant you that would turn heads in the scientific community, yet it would be opening a Pandora Box no one has dared peek into before."

"Actually Frankenstein was the name of the doctor. The monster never had a name, but it could think and talk."

"That is fiction and this is real life."

The conversation snagged Rosetta's attention. "Creating a brand new sentient is playing God."

"We could design the perfect being that neither evolution nor God ever achieved."

"Now you're crossing into metaphysics. There is only one perfect being and that is God. You could never create something even remotely like him."

"Should that stop us from trying?"

"Yes. You should try reading about the Tower of Babel. When mortals try to take on God, they always lose."

"Like Derrick just said, this is real life, not fiction. It ought to be at least attempted."

Derrick said, "Pushing aside all that morality ethics argument, I say it simply cannot be done. It will just end in a cancerous pile of mush, even if you spent a thousand years writing DNA."

Mera added, "The idea is intriguing, but I agree with Derrick. Even if it was feasible, it shouldn't be done. There are many religions across the galaxy which would find such an undertaken sacrilegious. That was why Emperor Kayuga passed the Sentient Purity Law."

"That was to protect existing sentients from genetic contamination," said Layla with a shudder. She was a living example of that feared generic pollution. "An artificially made sentient would be immune to the law."

"I never did like that law," said Leana, joining the conversation. "While working on the Profectus Project, I believed we had finally taken hold of the reigns of evolution. No longer need our race be bound by random mutations of nature or the whims of gods. We controlled human destiny." The woman's voice broke. "Then my husband and child died in that accident. A week later that horrid Purity Law was passed, and I was left with nothing to believe in. Nothing. We are still controlled by the cruel whims of nature. There is no freedom."

Mera reached out and touched her friend's hand. "Freedom still exists. You just have to know where to look for it."

Layla felt excitement. "We can write that freedom, at least for a new being. Just image. We can make up for evolution's faults. We only take the best DNA and toss the rest. No more wasted duplicate sequences. No junk DNA which has built up from millenniums of mutations. This being would inherit no genetic disorders and be immune to many diseases which our faulty DNA leaves us susceptible to. If nanites are used to build the DNA sequences then troublesome mutations will be banished. Every generation will be perfect."

"It still should not be done," said Rosetta. "You are not God to say what qualities as a perfect being."

"Do you not play God every time you choose which genes will fertilize which egg?"

"That is different. There is still much randomization for many of the genes, though we tweak certain traits."

Mera's watch beeped. "Well, time to fertilize those eggs again."

Everybody rose and headed in various directions. Rosetta and Mera discussed wedding colors as they went out the door.

Leana whispered to Layla, "Your idea is lovely. Youth need dreams. Hold onto it tightly. Relish it before reality snatches it from you."

Derrick gave Layla a pat on the back. "Thanks for the debate. It was far more interesting than talking about invitations and decorations."

The discussion was quickly forgotten by the others, but Layla thought about it the rest of the day. She played with various mental images of what an artificial sentient might look like. A greenish monster with bolts coming out its neck popped into her mind several times. She laughed at her foolishness, telling herself the idea was just a child's fantasy. All that math she had studied in earning her Ph.D. shouted that Derrick was right about the statistics.

I am sure there were critics who said it was impossible to create profectus, yet here I am, she told herself. *We were created to make the impossible possible.*

Back in her apartment that night, Layla sat on her bed and used her e-tablet to surf through a research database of known species from across the galaxy. The collection was vast and enormously diverse. She began making a list of creatures that caught her whim: the unique mouth of a mika, the beautiful wings of lunar moths, the razor-sharp dorsal fin of a diamond fish. Her dreams that night were filled with unnatural creations so bizarre that they seemed to have stepped out of a child's whimsical drawing.

The next day, Layla tried to keep her thoughts on work, but as she cleaned cages, she wondered what a perfect sentient would look like. It would need to be smart, adaptable, and able to blend in with main society without its appearance being too peculiar. Other useful enhancements included a strong body, long life span, and robust immune system. That night, Layla again examined the species database and wrote down creatures' names, but this time she searched more carefully, seeking for a realistic blend of parts.

The project slowly became an obsession. Whenever she had a spare moment at work, she was sketching weird creatures and pondering how their DNA would be coded. After work, she stayed in her apartment and made lists, categorizing creature parts, and labeling sketches. Eventually, her randomized ideas became focused on a single creation. She decided it would be made in her own image—human. The appearance, though, would be misleading. Less than half of one percent of its DNA would come specifically from *Homo sapiens*. Like a sculptor, she would mold her creation into a humanoid shape, but it would be an illusion formed by carefully crafting DNA from other creatures. Each part would be vigilantly selected to be compatible with each other yet somehow an improvement over the original human design.

Weeks flew past in a blur of excitement as Layla read through the endless database. The bones of the Isguard had the highest breaking point known in mammals, but as they were four-footed herd animals, their bone structure was undesirable. Fortunately, a research team long ago had isolated the genes related to the creature's bone strength. She only needed to find a way to splice it into DNA sequences of humanoid-shaped bone structures. The eyes of some predatory birds could see three times as far as humans. The coakyatte, a desert rodent, rarely shed its smooth, thick fur that closely resembled human hair. Her list grew longer and longer.

Altering growth rates and extending life had been researched for centuries by many scientists across the galaxy. Herd animals which grew up extraordinary quick cut production cost for farmers. Though there had been many successful experiments, catastrophes like the cows on Alphos causing cancer had led to a ban on using such DNA techniques on livestock grown for food, but it was used on some animals like the cowoons at BGF who were raised for their wool. Extending life was a touchy issue affected by environment, food, and disease—besides the aging process itself caused by the accumulated buildup of damaged DNA over time. While experiments had led to genetic companies producing pets who lived decades longer than their unaltered kin, never had it been done to a sentient—legally. There were several court cases of companies or lone scientists attempting it, usually with tragic results. After much searching, Layla managed to discover several published papers written by the culprits who spent the rest of their lives in jail for attempting to defy nature—and imperial law.

A major concern to Layla was the immune system. The virus H4C34 incident was still very fresh on her mind. This new sentient would need to fight off countless viruses which might jump species. The enormous amount of research Layla had done for her dissertation became very useful, yet she was unsatisfied with her various theories. What if there was a way to avoid sickness altogether or the host healed as quickly as a virus invaded? She typed the term regeneration and hit the search button. Names of numerous primitive invertebrates popped up, but there were few higher-level creatures. Salamanders regrew tails. Each arm of starfish could be cut off then grow into new animals. No mammals or birds were listed.

She typed *rapid regeneration* to narrow her search. The list was short. She clicked on the picture of a predatory slug with small, clawed tentacles. The data about *epulo infestus* turned out to be as fascinating as reading a novel.

A small research team landed on the primitive planet Z 5907 to categorize new life forms. While they were exploring a swampy region, a tentacle slug dropped from an overhead branch onto one of the scientists. The parasite immediately attached itself to the back of the human's head. The man made one attempt to pull it off before falling to the ground, paralyzed. His teammates tried repeatedly to cut the slug off him, but each time it was sliced, it rapidly healed. Within five minutes, the man was dead and the animal released him. A scientist cut the creature in half. After a bit of wiggling, the parasite died.

The research team carried the dead man and the tentacled slug back to their ship for autopsies. It was learned that the creature had a proboscis mouth similar to a mosquito which allowed it to feed on the electrical impulse of neutrons in the host's brain. As long as the creature was feeding, it could heal quickly. Like a mosquitoes which injects saliva into the host which acts like a local anesthetic, the slug inserted chemicals into its host which quickly subdued its prey. The team officially labeled the new species *epulo infestus* but its common name was *energy leech*.

Though saddened by the loss of one member, the team realized that rapid healing could be useful in medicine. They set out, determined to capture an energy leech alive. It turned out to be much harder than they planned. The group split up into pairs and searched the swamp for a week. On the seventh day, one pair of scientists never returned. When no trace of the missing scientists was discovered after a few more days, the nervous scientists left the planet, classifying it as extremely hostile. In the fifty-odd years since the expedition, no other scientists had visited the planet. The wife of the killed man did map the DNA of the energy leech but abandoned furthered research.

Layla added *epulo infestus* to her list of potential DNA sources.

Chapter Five

Laughter and music filled the fellowship hall of First Zion Church. Lights from flashing cameras distracted Layla from her food. She glanced at her watch, wondering how much longer the reception would last. She had DNA sequences to write. Layla sat at a table near a wall of glass which looked out onto the garden where the wedding had taken place. Summer flowers surrounded a gazebo covered in blooming vines. Layla turned her eyes from the window and sighed. She was tired of chatting with strangers and smiling at dull jokes. Several of the guests eating nearby worked at BGF. One or two looked like they were about to leave, and she wished she had arranged a ride with one of them. Too bad she was still too young to drive even though she could afford to make payments on a vehicle. A week ago Mera had volunteered to drive her to the wedding, but the woman failed to mention that she had also volunteered to be part of the clean-up crew after the reception. Now Layla was stuck waiting for everyone to leave.

Her impatience was not because she hated the wedding. No, she was truly happy for Derrick and Rosetta. What she disliked was all the social interaction which was attached to weddings. Most of the guests she would probably never see again. Why waste time listening to stories about their kids or how their flight from wherever had gone? The noise level suddenly increased and Layla looked up see a crowd forming near a door, blocking the bride and groom from view.

"Here," said Mera, placing a colorful lump of cloth into Layla's hand. "They are leaving. It's time to throw the birdseed."

Layla kept to the back of the crowd as it moved into the church's parking lot. Birdseed seemed to be flying everywhere. She caught a glimpse of Rosetta ducking into a hover car wrapped in layers of bright paper. The words "Just married" was written in foam on the back window. The car sped off among shouts and waves from the crowd. Several guests headed to their own vehicles. Layla went back inside and tossed her unopened birdseed into the trash. A few people began cleaning tables. Having nothing better to do, Layla gathered dirty silverware off plates. An hour later, Mera was finally satisfied that the cleaning was finished.

As they headed through the church towards the vehicle, Mera suddenly said, "Did I turn off all the lights? I'll be right back."

Layla was left standing in the lobby of the quiet church. Having never been in a religious building before, she glanced curiously at the pictures hanging on the walls, but they were meaningless to her. Seeing the door to the main sanctuary slightly jar, she pushed the door open and stepped inside. The peaceful quiet was welcoming after being surrounded by strangers most of the afternoon. Wooden pews filled most of the floor space. A podium and several chairs were on a dais at the far end of the room. Stain glass windows depicted ancient scenes from another era. For the briefest of moments, Layla considered if perhaps she was standing in the doorway to a netherworld where beings existed that could neither be seen nor touched. How did one prove or disprove the existence of a god? What tests could be conducted? Which measurements could be evaluated? A door slamming shut at the end of the hallway caused Layla to jump. She quickly backed out of the sanctuary and met Mera in the hallway.

Half an hour later, Layla was relieved when she entered her small apartment and could shut out distractions. Though she had lived here for nearly six months, she had added few decorations. On the desk was a digital photo frame which cycled through pictures of family and friends. On a wall she had hung a quote Blue Dust sometimes cawed when she passed his cage, "Dreaming dreams no mortals ever dared to dream before." Above her bed hung a large poster of a double helix.

Off went the blue maid of honor dress she had worn to the wedding. It was the only dress she owned, and Rosette had actually chosen it. She slipped into a comfortable tank top and shorts, flipped on her e-tablet, and settled on her bed. This was the moment she lived for each day—when the code of life flowed under her fingertips. It was hers to manipulate, to control. Four building blocks which were the foundation of all life. Beautiful in its simplicity yet so intricately complex. This she understood. DNA could be tested, measured, observed. From it she would build new life. She walked in the footprints of many great scientists who had pioneered the field of genetics. They had mapped the genes of countless species from across the galaxy, pushed against the limits of nature, and broken beyond. The heroes whose works she had poured over in her studies had twisted the very laws of nature, forcing it to do their bidding. Now she dived into the mysteries of life and creation, deeper than anyone had dared explored before.

An hour into her work, her elation had melted into frustration. The software she was using kept flashing warnings as she dropped DNA sequences into the virtual chromosomes. She finally hit the render button and the computer created a 3-D image of what a possible creature would look like. The result was a blob. Red lettering flashed across the screen, "Data incompatible."

"I know it is incompatible, but it will work anyway. I am sure of it."

Layla tossed the e-tablet on the bed and paced back and forth across the room in frustration. She was using the best, most expensive software on the market, yet it could not handle her demands. The problem was it based its data on centuries of real-life experiments. As long as she kept in the realm of what was known, the program worked just fine. Yet she was stepping far beyond. She was certain her ideas would work, but she could not prove that to the computer.

"I need better software. A program which lets me override any disagreement and set my own variables." Frustrated, she ran a hand through her long hair.

To continue, she needed a new program to be written which could handle her daunting demands. She had not studied computer programming and was too impatient to start now. Grabbing her e-tablet, she scanned through the list of graduates from Luncaster University. Finally, she found one who majored in computer engineering. Richard Cambridge had been among the first profectus to enter the school, and probably would not know her. It was his roommate that had committed suicide. He might help her just because she was another profectus. She carefully wrote a message stating she was working on a DNA project which could revolutionize everything which was known about genetic engineering, but she lacked software to complete the project. She added several sentences calling him the best computer programmer in the galaxy and her desperate need for his aid.

She sent the message and faced the dreaded wait. It would take hours for the message to travel the many light years to his planet. He might be busy or sleeping. When he finally read it, would he trash the message or answer her? She filled the hours wrestling with her software over where DNA sequences belonged. Sleep finally claimed her. A beeping alarm pulled her slowly back. Her blurry version stared at the blank screen of her e-tablet, and she touched its screen to awaken it.

The words, "You have one message" jolted her fully alert.

Her heart pounded as she read Richard's response. "Sounds interesting. I am bored into insanity at work. Send me the specs you need, and I will see what I can come up with. I need a new challenge."

Layla smiled and typed back. "We profectus are very similar. I came up with this project because I love challenges. My co-workers say it is impossible. I plan to prove them wrong."

That exchange began a friendship between Layla and Richard as they continued to send messages back and forth over the following weeks. Within a month, Richard had a rough prototype that Layla began testing. Richard continually improved the program, ironing out bugs and glitches.

Five months later Richard wrote, "Thanks to this project, I have decided to start my own software company. Imagine me a CEO at seventeen! My first commercial product, of course, will be Ultimate Designer. It will be limited to a niche market, but at least it is a start."

"Once I show your program to my co-works, I am sure you will have orders flying in," Layla texted back.

She was eager to show off both the new software and her virtual chromosomes, but her own work was far from complete. Writing coding for a creation using three billion nucleotides would take a very long time, to say the least. There were helpful shortcuts. All animals shared certain common DNA sequences. It was a simple task for Layla to copy the needed strains from other creatures. Still, she needed to double check the nucleotides, looking for fragmentation. Then she had to isolate the genes of traits she wanted from various creatures and copy those DNA sequences.

So far, what she had essentially done was window shop for clothing she liked and tried on a few outfits. Now she needed to rip the fibers of the clothing apart and rebind their molecules together to create a brand new, functional outfit. This was the hardest and most mysterious part. The relationship of genes to each other in popular species had been studied for millenniums, yet there were still many unknowns. Change a few nucleotides in one gene and nothing may happen or something seemly unrelated could be altered. It was like painting a car a new color and suddenly the engine stops working. The two should not relate, yet somehow they did. Into this minefield Layla boldly marched, too naïve to believe she would fail.

There were countless variables to consider. Her creation was to be a warm-blooded mammal, yet some of the DNA she had chosen came from cold-blooded creatures like *epulo infestus*. Ten major systems including circulatory, endocrine, nervous, and muscular needed to work together perfectly. Then there was the cellular level to deal with. Over two hundred cell types performed different tasks in *Homo sapiens* alone. Her creature would be even more varied. Every cell had to function as an individual machine yet work in harmony with the entire organism. On the molecule level hundreds of chemical processes had to perform correctly, or the cell would not function.

The process was intensely tedious. If Layla had been better-adjusted with close friends to drag her off to fun activities, she would have soon given up on the project. Instead, she was isolated and alone with little to distract her. There were still days she went shopping or walking with Rosetta, but the new bride's attention was focused on her husband. Layla did not mind. Her own obsession filled her waking hours and ruled her dreams. Even at work, Layla constantly searched for new insights.

Eventually Layla reached a plateau in her research. Computer models based on guesswork could only reveal so much. She had constructed a dozen virtual genomes, each built on a different theory of how the genes might function. The next stage was field-testing. She needed a Nanotech DNA Builder but knew her supervisor Banican Zine would never let her attempt the experiment in his department. Neither could she afford to buy her own NDB which cost nearly a million credits.

After work each day as she walked to her apartment, her eyes would drift to the vine-covered Abandoned Department. Perhaps her future was intertwined with her past.

Chapter Six

Three adults sat on benches under a shade tree across from the nervous thirteen year old. Though Layla would be presenting to just Rosetta, Derrick, and Mera, she felt as anxious as if she was speaking in front of a crowd of thousands.

"Well, I thank you for taking time after work to see my demonstration."

"We are dying to know what it is. You have been hinting about it for two days," said Rosetta, leaning against her husband. They had just celebrated their one-year anniversary by spending the weekend in Austin City.

"Everyone brought your e-tablets, I presume."

The adults pulled their computers out of bags. Layla hit the synch button on her own e-tablet and waited for each person to accept her link.

"Do you remember the conversation we once had about engineering a new sentient?"

Rosetta and Mera shook their heads, but Derrick said, "Vaguely. I thought you had a good argument about improving upon evolution's design."

"Well, I did it. At least I mapped the DNA for a possible new sentient." She opened up Richard's program and pulled up a 3-D image of a genome. She zoomed in, showing a close-up of DNA. "As you can see, I have written the complete genome for a new being."

"What program is this?" asked Mera, peering closely at her screen which showed everything that was on Layla's.

"I was wondering the same thing," said Derrick. "It looks far better than what we use in Freak Department."

"Nice zooming effect," said Rosetta. "Very fast."

"The program is called Ultimate Designer." Layla continued her rehearsed speech. "I have mapped out twenty-one pairs of chromosomes for a male specimen."

"That is a bit small," said Rosette. "Humans have twenty-three."

"I needed fewer chromosomes because I was able to cut out a lot of unneeded genetic trash."

"Where did you get this program?" asked Derrick.

"A profectus classmate named Richard created the program for me. Now taking a closer look at the Y chromosome…."

"He just sat down and wrote a computer program for you? It looks professionally made."

Mera said, "I would not mind having a copy of that program myself."

Layla closed her eyes in frustration and tried to calm herself. She was only trying to give the biggest speech of her life while her audience chatted about software.

"Go ahead, Layla," said Rosetta. "We are listening."

"The sentient will be a warm-blooded humanoid mammal." She touched her screen and pulled up a 3-D model which rotated slowly. "Though it looks human…"

"That is so cool," exclaimed Rosetta. "Very realistic skin tone. The hair is so lifelike. Far better than the cartoonish babies I have to stare at all day on my monitor."

Mera nodded. "I agree. We need this in Baby Department. Layla, is your friend selling this program?"

"Yes. The official release date is three weeks away." She zoomed in on the face. "The being is not human. It will have stronger bones, better eyesight, greater…."

"Banican will die of jealous if your department gets it and not his," said Derrick.

"….strength, hair which rarely sheds, high intelligence…."

"Little shedding? Now that would be a cool trait to add to cats."

Layla lost her patience. "We are not talking about cats, and the program is only a tool. I am talking about creating the first complex synthetic life form. No one has ever done it before, but I can. They will be the quintessence of genetics—sentients with pure, unfragmented, perfect DNA. No gene mutilations."

The adults glanced at each other before Mera said, "Your model looks very nice." It was the same tone a parent uses when praising a child's first drawing.

"What about moral and religious issues?" asked Rosetta. "Have you considered that some will be outraged if you are successful?"

"I don't care about philosophers debating over the meaning of life." Layla took a deep breath to calm herself. "I am ready for field testing and need a NDB."

"We do not have NDB's in my department."

"There is no way Banican is going to let you use one of his," said Derrick. "He has not even let me perform a trial run. The closest I can get is repairing the broken ones."

"There is one that is not in Banican's department. Remember that X1800?"

"Yes. Has a busted shaft rod."

"Think you can still get it to work?"

Derrick smiled. "I am certain I can."

Mera cut in. "Where is there another NDB?"

"In Abandon Department," said Layla. "We found it while exploring one day. I am seeking permission to field test using the X1800. Most of the supplies I need can be leftovers from your department. I can use low-grade oocyte eggs which are going to be tossed. There is even an incubator and cryogenic freezer at Abandon which Derrick might can fix. I know I can do this. I just need permission."

"You have spent a great deal of time thinking about this."

"Yes, over a year."

Mera sighed. "You have my backing, but it is not my permission you will need. You will have to write a proposal and present it at a management meeting."

"Alright. I can do that."

For the next week, Layla spent every night writing a proposal based on an example Mera had given her. She practiced her speech repeatedly in front of her bathroom mirror. The day before the meeting, Rosetta and Derrick volunteered as a test audience and were better behaved than before, though their occasional tickling of each other was a bit of a distraction for Layla.

The meeting took place in a conference room. Palakkad sat at the head of the huge oval table. Department supervisors sat along each side. A large flat screen on the wall displayed the BGF logo as Layla walked into the room. She had been waiting in the hallway for nearly an hour, tension building by the minute. It did not help that the first face she saw was Banican with his perpetual scowl.

Palakkad smiled encouragingly. "Mera said you have an interesting project to show us."

"Yes, I have been working on it for over a year." She attempted to synchronize her e-tablet with the wall screen but after two failed tries, Mera had to do it for her. Finally, the opening window for Richard's program came up. "I have mapped the DNA for a new, completely synthetic sentient." She pulled up the 3-D model of the completed specimen. "This is what I believe it will look like. Though it appears human, only one hundredth of a percent of its DNA comes from *Homo sapiens*."

"I don't believe I have seen this program before," said Palakkad leaning forward in his chair.

"It is called Ultimate Designer and was written specifically for my project by a fellow profectus named Richard."

"Ah, Richard Cambridge. He was one of our first graduates. Brilliant programmer. I am delighted to see that he is putting his talent to excellent use."

"You will see the capabilities of Ultimate Designer as I show you my project." For the next five minutes no one interrupted as she went through her speech. She wrapped up the presentation by listing the reasons why she should be allowed to use the Human Advancement Department for testing.

There was a moment of silence, then someone halfway down the table asked, "What is Richard's company address?"

Layla tried to hide her disappointment that the software was more impressive that her research. "Search for Cambridge Software and you will find it. Ultimate Designer will be on sale in two weeks, but he is already accepting pre-orders."

Palakkad said, "You ambition is to be praised."

"Profectus never do things halfway."

"If I may," said Banican. "There are a number of flaws which you have presented. First, the cell structure will be too unstable with so much foreign DNA. How many creatures did you say you used?"

"One hundred and seventeen."

"Never has any successful experiment made it pass six."

"That is because they were splicing foreign DNA into an existing creature. I started with nothing, added the basic DNA that all animals needed then built from there. There is no base model."

"That is not how proper genetic engineering is done."

"I rewrote the rules."

"You sound like a first year genetic student who forgot to study for the final. Real science is based on real facts. Do you have any proven statistics behind your theories? Any primary DNA software would have told you that your plan is impossible."

"It did. I decided the program was wrong, so I had it rewritten."

Banican glared at her. "Those who defy reality are fools."

She glanced at Palakkad. "A great man at Luncaster once told me that profectus were created to make the impossible possible. I believe those words."

The Freak supervisor retorted, "You are a child playacting as a scientist. There is much you have not thought out. For example, you did not list the sterilization procedure you will use to protect the experiment's DNA from polluting other sentients."

"I will only design one sex, as we often do with our products here. There is no need for sterilization for they will have no genetic equal to breed with. We both know that if two unrelated species copulate, then no offspring is produced. Besides, early castration of some species can stunt full development. I need to be able to study their entire natural life cycle."

"You have our permission." All eyes in the room turned to Palakkad. "I will have an electrician check out the wiring of the building tomorrow, and the water will be turned on."

"Thank you."

"Palakkad, the child is wasting valuable resources and money," said Banican. "If she was anyone else, you would not do this. If a janitor asked permission to create a talking broom, would you say yes?"

"You speak out of line."

"Do I? She is a child chasing a fantasy while wasting company time."

"As she has already pointed out, the cost will be kept low. As for wasting time, will she not learn more with hands-on experiments than cleaning cages? And who knows, she might actually succeed."

As the meeting ended, Mera pulled Layla to the side. "Excellent job. I am impressed how you stood up to Banican."

"I was terrified."

"You did not show it. That is what counts. "

The following days were filled with excitement and hard work. Human Advancement Department had to be cleaned and was renamed Advance Department. Mera rounded up a group of volunteers to help sweep floors, patch windows, and clear debris. Derrick spent hours crawling under dusty machines, taking off various parts to clean. The X1800 and the incubator were savable but the cryogenic freezer had to be tossed. Fortunately, Derrick found a replacement in the maintenance shed were a lot of rundown equipment was stored. At Baby Department, Rosetta and Layla hunted through closets and dusty bins, looking for aging supplies which would not be missed. Leana often joined them and quickly proved she had a talent for finding lost treasures among broken beakers and cultures growing long-forgotten experiments.

Finally the day came when Derrick announced that the X1800 was ready for a test run. Layla and Rosetta stared anxiously at the various readouts on the machine as it warmed up. Derrick prowled round the bulky machine, occasionally ducking under to investigate. When the dials had leveled out, Layla hooked her e-tablet up by a cable to the antique NDB and downloaded to its computer the genome she wanted produced. The machine hummed loudly and readouts fluttered.

"I don't think the nanites are working," said Rosetta.

Derrick opened a panel midway down the bulky body and pulled out a small canister half filled with what looked like silvery powder. He thumped the container. "They just need to loosen up." He shook the canister roughly then banged it on the concrete floor several times.

"Will you not break them?" asked Layla.

"Nanites? Nah. They are hardy buggers." He replaced the canister. "Give it another shot."

This time the dials stayed level and the computer screen showed a rough picture of a DNA being slowly built. All three stared in fascination at the blurry pixels on the screen.

"I never knew machines could be so interesting," said Rosetta.

"That's because you didn't have me around," replied her husband.

"The nanites are very slow," complained Layla.

"If you want speed, then you have to use a newer model, but the trade-off is lower accuracy. Despite its age, the X1800 is still the best ever made."

Rosetta laughed, "You look like an excited school boy. Are you sure you chose the right major in college?"

"Hey, if I didn't major in genetics, would I ever have had the opportunity to even touch a NDB?"

"So genetics was only a gateway to your true love."

"Yep. You." Derrick kissed his beaming wife.

Layla said, "How long will it take?"

"I estimate a day, give or take a few hours."

"A whole day?"

"Your cute little nanites are only building three billion nucleotide bases using amino acids and you cannot wait one day?"

"God made all land animals in a day," said Rosetta.

"Sorry to disappoint you, but I am not a miracle worker."

Rosetta tossed him a rag. "At least you can dust."

The rest of the day passed slowly with Layla constantly checking the NDB's slow progress. That night she dreamed she was surrounded by double helixes that suddenly crumbed into billions of atoms, and she spent the rest of the night trying to force molecules back into their proper locations. The next morning, she was at work an hour early. The X1800's timer said ninety percent had been completed. Layla roamed about the huge, mostly empty warehouse of Advance Department trying to find something to do. She was tired of cleaning, but could not keep her mind focused enough to work in Ultimate Designer.

Mid-morning the NDB finally beeped, and Layla lifted the end door to reveal a small culture dish. It was empty or at least seemed so. Layla gingerly carried the culture to a microscope that Leana had managed to find. Peering closely at the computer screen, Layla could see a tiny egg with its chromosomes intact. Layla moved the culture to the incubator. Now came more waiting. The egg hopefully would begin dividing within a few hours. Layla programmed the NDB to make a new genome based on a different design.

At lunch, Derrick was pleased to hear that the NDB had worked properly. "What did I tell you? The X1800 are always reliable."

His wife teased, "How about you be reliable to wash the dishes tonight?"

At the end of the workday, Rosetta and Derrick stopped by for a visit and found Layla studying images taken by the microscope. She was both disappointed and happy.

"It did work. The egg divided twice then died."

"It actually divided? That's a huge step right there," said Rosetta.

"Lunk owes me fifty credits now," grinned Derrick.

Layla frowned. "You are betting on my work?"

"Actually on mine. Lunk didn't think I could get the X1800 running. Dinner is on me."

"I have much to do. I need to analyze what went wrong and then retune my design."

"Freeze it for tomorrow," said Rosetta. "You will spend the rest of your life designing."

Rosetta was glad Layla had experienced a success, for she worried about how the young profectus would be effected by failure. The girl had kept too much to herself over the past year, and this was the only project she had shown real interest in. Yet what happened if Layla succeeded? The teenager was not God. Could she handle the responsibilities of creating a new race? Rosetta kept these concerns to herself, rarely mentioning them to her husband. Like Mera, she expected Layla would eventually give up and move on to a new project.

None of Layla's first dozen attempts made it pass four divisions. Each day while Layla waited for a new fertilized egg to be created by the NDB, she analyzed why the last one failed. Unfortunately, the microscope's zoom was limited to only showing complete chromosomes. She needed an electrical molecular microscope with sensors which could detect many variables, but they were nearly as expense as a brand-new NDB. There were only a few at Bontinc Genetics. The Autopsy and Freak departments each had one, but it was unlikely she would be given permission to use either.

"You want a what?" said Derrick, almost choking on his forkful of pie when she asked for one.

"Just an EMM," said Layla, calmly eating her salad.

"You think I can just find an EMM sitting around analyzing dust?"

"You are very skillful in finding things, and I cannot do serious analyzes without one."

"I will look, but finding one is as likely as me hitting oil in my backyard."

"We rent," said Rosetta. "If you found oil, we wouldn't get any money from it."

Two days later Derrick showed up at Advance Department with an EMM. Even he was shocked at how easy it had been. "It was inside one of those rusty walk-in freezers at the maintenance shed. It's in bad condition, and I cannot make any promises that it will work. It's probably been there at least eighty years."

"I'm starting to think that nothing is truly thrown away here," said Rosetta.

"Hey, they have got to do something to keep us recyclers busy."

It took Derrick three weeks of tinkering before the EMM was functional, though it was prone to daily malfunctions. Still, it did work. The data Layla now collected was helpful, but laborious to shift through. She needed a way to import the information directly into Ultimate Designer which was far more versatile. After months of sending messages back and forth to Richard while beta testing software, Layla had what she needed and Richard had a new product.

"Ultimate Designer Two is going to sell big, I believe," wrote an excited Richard. "Thanks to you, it is backwards compatible with older programs they have been using and genetics companies will feel more comfortable buying it."

"Your first version has been a hit at BGF. I know many scientists who bought it for their own personal e-tablets. Once Palakkad sees your new version, I think he will order it for our entire company."

"My first big business contract. If a renowned company like BGF converts, then soon orders will be rolling in from across the empire."

Chapter Seven

Layla carefully moved a stylus over the computer screen, counting the number of cells. One hundred and twenty-eight. The zygote made it through seven divisions—a record. The cells were now more stable due to the countless revisions she had made. She began entering notes in her e-tablet.

"Happy fifteenth birthday."

Layla looked up and saw Rosetta a few feet away. "Thanks. I just made it to division seven."

"You are more excited about mitosis than your own birthday."

"It is a record for me."

"I bet you didn't even remember it was your birthday."

"Uh....I remembered once last week."

"You are as bad as Derrick. When he forgot my birthday this year, I gave him the silent treatment for two full days." Rosetta sighed. "But he does know how to make up. Those roses and chocolate were thoughtful. Then he took me out to Austin City were we ate at...."

While Layla pretended to listen, her hand slowly moved over her e-tablet. She managed to type several sentences before Rosetta said, "You're not listening to me."

"You went to Austin City."

"I have changed subjects twice since then. The last thing I said was Derrick is bringing you a birthday present, but you need to open the freight door."

"Oh. That is very nice of him."

"You might not think so when you see it."

The two walked across the large, mainly empty chamber to the freight door. Layla hit a button on the wall and the heavy door slowly rose. It the distance they could see two maintenance trucks heading their direction. The freight door had barely clicked into place when the first hover truck began backing into the room. Derrick slipped out of the passenger side and waved directions to Lunk who was driving. Between the two of them, the hover truck managed to barely miss hitting two support pillars and a metal shelf. Finally, Lunk turned off the engine. The entire bed of the truck was filled with a huge machine with so many rods poking out from it that Layla was reminded of a centipede that had rolled over and died.

Grinning proudly, Derrick said, "So, what do you think?"

"Uh….what is it?"

"Maybe this will help." He opened the door to the hover truck and pulled out a huge glass jar. Then he held the glass canister between several rods twisting up from the machine.

"Is it an AFD?"

"Yep. An automatic fetus developer that was sitting behind the maintenance shed for years. A bit rusty and dirty, but she will clean up well."

"A bit dirty?" said Rosetta. "Looks like a giant insect which forgot how to decompose."

A dozen men, mainly maintenance workers, entered through the freight door. They had ridden in the other vehicle which had remained in the parking lot. Lunk waved them over and supervised the lifting of the heavy machine out of the hover truck. Much grunting and muscle straining came before the men finally positioned the AFD on the floor near the X1800.

Lunk patted the side of the machine affectionately. "Nothing like an AFD N50. Broke my heart when we had to replace her with the Z80. Glad she's going to a better home now."

"I will take good care of the AFD…her," said Layla, wondering why some guys refer to machines with feminine pronouns. "Thanks everybody."

After the maintenance workers left, Rosetta said, "You don't have to pretend to like it."

"I would need an AFD eventually, though it will be years before I will be ready to grow embryos."

"Good," said Derrick, "because it might take me years to get her running. She has been sitting out in the weather for seven years. The least they could have done was put a tarp over her." He reached over and pulled out a cluster of leaves caught in the twisted rods.

"Happy birthday," said Rosetta as she tossed Layla a rag for cleaning.

Derrick became as obsessed with the AFD as Layla was for her synthetic sentients. Over the following weeks, Derrick would show up with some odd parts he had savaged. The ugly, bulky frame of the AFD became even more cluttered with hoses, rods, and glass jars that Derrick added. The machine, when working properly, could grow fifty embryos to birthing age. Watching the machine morph slowly into a proper automatic fetus developer, Layla was encouraged that her own project would someday become reality.

That day came far quicker than Layla anticipated.

"Sweetie, pass the one-fourth wrench," said Derrick hidden under the AFD except for his feet.

Rosetta sighed and rose from her stool. She placed the tool in his hand which suddenly poked out from under the massive machine. "When I said let's get out of the house this weekend, I didn't mean spend all Saturday at work."

"This isn't work," said her husband. "This is fun."

"For you." Rosetta sat back down on the stool beside Layla who was placing an incubated egg inside the molecular microscope. "I am stuck between a maniacal mechanic and a solemn scientist. Do either one of you know what the expression *get a life* means?"

"I think I may have gotten a life," said Layla softly, studying the computer screen.

"What?"

"This one has become a blastocyst."

"Really? It's that big?" Rosetta moved closer to study the screen. "It's large enough to be shipped out to a clinic for implanting."

"It kept growing all this week. Every day I expected to find it dead."

"Congratulation, you have set a new record for yourself."

"It is not the only one." Layla placed the blastocyst in the incubator and removed another culture which she placed in the EMM. "This one is just one day younger, and it is alive too."

"Honey," called out Rosetta, "you need to come see this."

"See what?" Derrick pushed the wooden roller he was laying on out from under the fetus developer.

"She has two living embryos."

Derrick walked over and peered at the screen. "Did you use the same DNA map?"

"No, but they were almost identical. I only altered one gene."

"Then you should freeze them. Create a control sample. Make five or more of each then incubate them all at one time in the AFD."

"You lovely AFD still does not work," reminded his wife.

"Don't worry. I still have several weeks before Layla will need it. I'll have Anya working before then." He gave the machine a pat before laying back down on his roller.

"You nicknamed it Anya? Is that not the name of your first girlfriend in college?"

"Just a coincidence," Derrick disappeared under the AFD.

"I think I am jealous of a machine," muttered Rosetta.

"At least we are ready to move on to stage two," said Layla happily.

Derrick kept his word. Anya was operational by the time Layla had a collection of ten embryos, each frozen at the same level of growth. Ten glass canisters were filled with nutrient fluids and contained a strip of synthetic fibers which acted like the wall of a uterus. If all went well, each embryo would attach itself to the strip and begin growing.

Everyday Layla monitored the embryos' progress. Two never implanted. The others grew at a steady rate for a while. A blown fuse in the wiring killed two more. A leaking jar took another one. A week later, a spike in the temperature ended the reminding five. Layla considered the experiment a success. The chromosomes had remained stable as the cells divided. While Layla worked on creating another control group, Derrick kept hammering out the many glitches of Anya.

For the next test, Layla used fifteen embryos. While she waited for them to grow, she continued to edit DNA maps in Ultimate Designer. She focused on map L498. All the successful embryos came from either it or a slightly altered version. The teenager felt hopeful. No longer was she testing random patterns but had discovered a roadmap in the darkness. Where it led, though, was still unknown.

Chapter Eight

Layla rubbed her eyes and leaned back in her chair. The huge, empty laboratory was cast in shadows except for the one corner where she worked. Nearby the NDB hummed as industrious nanites built life's code. They never tired, unlike her. The only other sound in the room was Anya's deep purr as pumps moved fluids through hoses. Every glass jar now contained an embryo, though Layla noted that at least two were lifeless. For a long time, Layla sleepily watched small bubbles rise in one of the jars. She felt too tired to move. The clock on her e-tablet warned it was nearing midnight.

What is today? Friday? Saturday, she wondered. They blurred together too easily. It did not matter since she worked every day of the week. To take just one day off meant one less embryo to test. This week had been quiet with only a couple of brief visits from Lunk and Mera.

For their third anniversary, Rosetta and Derrick had taken the week off to visit a vacation resort near the coast. She did miss them. Her groceries were running low. It was frustrating to have a job, money, an apartment, yet be too young to drive. She could have asked another co-worker for a ride, but she hated the feeling of being an inconvenient burden. It was different with Rosetta and Derrick. They felt like family as she filled the role of little sister. And she needed that comradeship. She still regularly sent messages to her real family and friends from Luncaster University, but she felt distant from them after four years working at BGF. Blaaze was engaged. Roobaroo had become a political activist. Richard was a CEO of a small, but thriving company. Their lives had led along many adventurous paths while she remained working in the same lab year after year. The fruit of her labor was a long list of dead embryos and a mountain of statistics that no one but her cared to read.

Normally, Layla never let self-pity enter her thoughts. She had chosen this life which allowed her to pursue her passion for genetics. Still, as her tiredness sank in, the feeling of abandonment increased. It would have been nice to spend a week at a resort. She had vacation days built up. But what was the point? She could not drive herself, and it would have been rude to tag along on Rosetta and Derrick's anniversary trip.

Layla continued to stare at bubbles rising in a glass jar until she realized there were no bubbles in the other jars. She sighed. *Another malfunction. Another dead embryo. The story of my life.* Sometimes she felt like an elderly workhorse which trodden along the same worn path, separated from the day to day happenings of the world on the other side of the fence. *I became old before I was ever young. Did I even have a childhood?*

Yes, she remembered a time of innocence, playing with her older brother, laughing with her parents. Yet even then she had sensed she was different, separated from those around her by a barrier she could not understand. That boundary she now understood far too well. Her genes. She was created to be one of the smartest beings in the empire. She never asked for this gift. Others had designed her and placed heavy expectations upon her, claiming her subspecies would usher in a new Golden Age for humans.

But her creators did not have to pay the high price of being a genius— countless hours of isolation, separated from the very people who she was created to assist. While other teenagers enjoyed friendships, flirting, the simple pleasures of growing up, she worked in a drab lab. The seclusion was of her own making, but she knew no other way. How else would she have the time to fulfill the purpose for which she was created? No one at the company she worked for expected her to succeed. Give the teenager a lab. Let her play childish games with her whimsical idea of crafting a brand new sentient. Eventually she will tire of the dream, realize its impossibility, then join the adult world, keeping to what was known and leave fantasy behind.

Layla stood up and began gathering her things. Though it was late at night and the building isolated, Layla was comfortable working alone— usually. A door slammed and Layla jumped. For a moment, she felt very much alive as adrenaline pumped through her body. Then she heard familiar voices and relaxed.

"Did I not tell you, Derrick, she would be here?"

"It's midnight. Any reasonable person would be in bed."

"Does that mean, then, that you are unreasonable?"

Layla smiled. "It is good to see you."

Rosetta said, "Since we were passing by, I thought we should take a quick peek to see if your light was on."

"You look like you had a great time."

"The best. The hotel was marvelous. Had an indoor swimming pool with an island. Oh, and the beach was beautiful. I got a tan and Derrick a sunburn. I found a buried bullion."

"It wasn't real," interrupted Derrick.

"I was about to explain. The bullion looked like real gold and whoever found it won a free meal at a five star restaurant."

"But it was only a free meal for one. I had to pay."

"Well, you would have never taken me there if I had not won."

"For the price of my one meal, we could have eaten three meals at a normal restaurant."

"Normal to you always means fast food."

Layla hugged Rosetta, catching the woman off guard. "I have missed you."

"We missed you too," said Rosetta, returning the hug. "I kept thinking about you. So, anything exciting happened while we were gone?"

Derrick thumped the tank with bubbles. "You have a leakage."

"That is the most exciting thing that has happened all week."

"Tightening the clamp on the hose might fix the problem. I'll get my tools."

His wife frowned, "It's midnight. Reasonable people don't work now."

"It will only take a moment. If I don't do it now, the embryo will be dead by morning."

"Men," Rosetta sighed. "Quick to be heroes but still will not take out the trash."

As Derrick worked on the hose, Rosetta walked around the AFD, examining fetuses in different stages. The last three rows held her attention. "How old are these?"

"It's written on the chart."

"Hm. Are you sure these dates are correct?"

"Of course."

"It says they are only three months old, but I swear they look five months."

"Remember, they're not human. If it says three, then it is three." Layla walked over and looked at the chart. "These fifteen are from Test Two."

"They're still alive?" came Derrick's voice under the AFD.

"Most. Tank eight and eleven are dead, though I suspect a few more will be soon."

Rosetta lay down the chart and pressed a hand against a glass tank. Backlighting revealed the outline of the occupant through its thin placenta. "They seem so human. Look. You can make out hands and the eyes. I have fertilized thousands of eggs but never been this close to an unborn baby."

"Fetus," said Derrick.

"Baby," said his wife.

"You're a scientist. The proper term is fetus."

"If you ever call any unborn baby of mine a fetus, you will be sleeping on the couch for the next week."

"Actually I could just sleep here. It is quite pleasant down here, hearing the roar of motors instead of snoring."

Rosetta gave her husband's feet a playful kick. "I do not snore." There was a sound of a metal hitting metal. Large bubbles formed in the tank as its level dropped by an inch.

"A warning before applying any physical abuse would be nice," complained Derrick.

"Oops. Sorry about that."

He rolled out from under the AFD and used a rag to wipe fluid off his face. "I think I've fixed the leak."

"Thanks. You are a lifesaver," said Layla.

Over the following weeks, the subjects of Test Two received much attention. Daily Layla monitored their progress, noting which ones grew the fastest and which looked sickly. Derrick silently watched them in the brief moments he could spare between trying to keep Anya running, mending the molecular microscope's latest glitches, or running errands for Lunk. Rosetta babbled baby talk while touching the glass tanks. When ten fetuses passed the four-month mark, Mera began stopping by every day after her shift ended. Sometimes Leana came with her.

"They recognize me," said Rosetta. "Whenever I first walk into the room and speak, they become excited and kick."

"It's your imagination," said Derrick. "They don't move much when I am around."

"That is because you don't talk to them but bang on their homes."

"I'm fixing those homes, or they would have no place to do their kicking."

Mera peered at the glass tubes, "They look so human yet grow so fast."

"Are you sure your records are right?" asked Leana with her face pressed against a tank. "They look seven months to me."

"Yes," said Layla for the tenth time. Every visitor asked her the same question. "Their current age is five months and two days."

"Number thirteen is not looking well," said Mera.

"It's not a mechanical error," said Derrick, "I double checked their tanks today."

"The fault lies in their DNA," explained Layla. "Group C is down to two and Group B has three. The more I altered from the original DNA map, the less stable the cells. In fact, all subjects in Test 3 and Test 4 have already died."

"Have you lost any in Group A?" asked Mera.

"No, they are the healthiest."

"When is the birth?" asked Leana. "With them growing this fast, surely you won't wait till they are nine months?"

"I haven't thought that far ahead. I doubt any of them will make it much longer. They are, after all, just Test Two."

"I wonder. I wonder." Mera held her own face an inch from the glass tube holding T2-1. The fetus wiggled its fingers and gave a kick. "Could you have actually succeeded in creating a brand new species?"

Month six brought much debate. Rosetta and Leana claimed the fetuses were ready for birthing. Mera thought it would be best to wait another month. Derrick claimed neutrality as he was only a mechanic on this project. Even Lunk got involved by starting a betting pool in Freak Department over how long each baby would live. Almost every day one or two curious visitors stopped by. Layla kept warning that the fetuses would not live long outside of their protective glass homes, yet the money in the betting pool leaned towards a long life for the unborn. Palakkad congratulated Layla on her research and agreed with her that hopes should not be raised too high.

Halfway through month six, the birthing debate was decided for them. The fetuses were running out of room in their artificial wombs. The time was now. Layla only wanted Derrick and Rosetta present for the first birth. Some of the regular visitors had become too attached to the fetuses and Layla feared they would become upset watching a baby die in front of them.

After the dayshift had headed home, the three moved an old table near Anya. Beside the table, Rosetta placed a huge bag of baby supplies which she had purchased the night before.

Her husband complained, "I think you bought out the whole store. We won't need most of those things."

"Consider this a test run for when we finally have a child."

There were only eight fetuses still alive, including all of Group A. Derrick turned a dial on the AFD, and the fluid drained from T2-1's glass tube. Carefully he unscrewed the glass canister from its base and unhooked all tubing and rods. The infant tossed about in its placenta. Derrick carried the canister to the table and opened it. He used a sterilized knife to cut the placenta. Fluid drained away and the infant took its first breath. Rosetta helped him remove the wet baby from its slimy covering. Finally, Rosetta wrapped a blanket around the freed infant, and Derrick cut the umbilical cord. Layla limited her role to handing out supplies and tools.

"You have a boy," cooed Rosetta. "A strong, healthy boy."

"All of them are boys." Layla experienced uncertainty. What was she supposed to do now? It was one thing to spend years writing DNA coding for an abstract sentient only visible on a computer screen. It was an entirely different matter to be looking at a living, breathing infant bearing the DNA she had written. "What now?"

"We could birth the other seven tonight."

"No, one is enough for now. We need to observe it, see if it makes it to the morning."

"He will." Rosetta rocked the baby gently in her arms. "What will be your name, little one?"

"Isn't it too soon for naming it?"

"Do you think it is too soon, little one? Which name belongs to you?"

"He is T2-A1. Test two, group A, subject one."

"You have no imagination."

Derrick approached with a small marking gun. His wife frowned. "Do you really need to do that?"

"We mark every subject that is born or hatched in Freak Department."

"But they are animals. He is not."

"He still belongs to the company, and we must follow procedure." He placed the muzzle on the infant's right arm and pulled the trigger. There was a brief snap, and Derrick pulled away the gun, revealing a small red mark. The baby let out a wail, but quickly quieted as Rosetta rocked him.

"See, it wasn't so bad," said Derrick. He picked up a small scanner and waved it over the baby's arm. The scanner beeped. "Good, the implanted microchip is working."

"How would you like it if I shot a microchip in you?"

"It's very tiny. He won't remember getting it or ever feel its presence."

"How do you know? Did you ever ask one of your genetic altered mice how it felt?"

Layla cleaned up the birthing table while Derrick wiped the knife. Rosetta reluctantly laid the infant in a warming pen Lunk had let Derrick borrow. Its large, flat bed was designed to keep young chicks warm.

"A chicken hatchery is not a proper crib," complained Rosette.

"It's the best I could do. It will hold them all and keep them warm."

"He will need feeding several times tonight."

"How often?" asked Layla, picking up her e-table to take notes.

"Every four hours. With it just being one, we could care for him at our house tonight."

"You know we cannot take him home," said Derrick. "That was in our contracts. No employee may take any specimen off campus without prior authorization. That is the quickest way to get fired here."

"I am sure they were not referring to a baby."

"All babies, may they be rodents or birds or mammals. All."

"We could take better care of him at home."

"And what will you do when there are eight of them?"

"I can feed it tonight," said Layla. "I will get some bedding from my apartment and sleep on the floor here."

Rosetta frowned. "Have you ever babysat?"

"No," answered the fifteen year old.

"Have you ever feed a baby or changed a diaper?"

"No, but once you show me how, then I can do it. How hard can it be?" Layla held her stylus over her e-tablet, ready to write notes.

"Can't be too hard," said Derrick, reading the back of the diaper box his wife had brought. "The directions are right here. Even includes diagrams."

Rosetta rolled her eyes. "Sleepover. We will all just camp out here tonight while I give you both lessons in Parenting 101."

The next morning Mera dropped by before her shift began to see how the first birth went. Derrick and Layla were still sleeping, but Rosetta was feeding the baby.

"He has a big appetite. Have you been up all night?"

"Most of it. You should have seen my husband try to change his first diaper. He used rubber gloves and complained the baby smelt worse than a hog pen needing two weeks cleaning. It took three attempts before he got the diaper on right. It was so hard for me not to laugh at him. He did better with the feeding."

"Good that you are breaking him in proper now before you have your own kids. How did Layla do?"

"Well, she tried. She was fine with changing diapers, but she lacks that mother instinct. You know what I mean? It's more like the baby is just an object to her, and all that is needed to care for it is memorizing a series of steps."

"She is only fifteen."

"At fifteen, I was babysitting my two younger siblings and several of the neighbors' kids. Thought I was making good money back then. I worry about Layla sometimes. She is too closed off from others, too detached."

Mera nodded. "Yes, I see it too. Palakkad and his team were too busy trying to make the smartest sentients in the galaxy that they never considered the emotional cost to their subjects."

Near the wall, Layla lay under a blanket with her back to them, listening.

Mera had barely left before Lunk swung by for a visit. Derrick sleepily greeting him, then both men headed off to find old chairs for visitors to sit in. Layla rolled up her bedding and reached for her e-tablet. As her hands touched its sleek surface to wake it up, she thought about what Mera and Rosetta had said about her.

Closed off, detached, emotional cost. This is how they perceived me. She picked up her stylus. *They are right. It is who I am.* She walked over to the AFD to begin recording observations of the fetuses.

Chapter Nine

Word spread quickly across BGF that the first completely synthetic sentient in history had been born. Visitors drifted in throughout the day. During the lunch break, there was a large surge as dozens came to see him. The infant barely spent any time in the warming pen for he was constantly passed around among much cooing, aahing, and baby talk. The unborn received just as much attention as visitors pressed their faces against the glass tubes to peer at them. Derrick and Lunk stayed busy hunting for more chairs and benches. Rosetta kept a constant eye on the infant, supervising who held him next.

Layla was completely at a loss. This had been her lab for over two years—a quiet, solitude environment where she controlled everything. Suddenly overnight, her lab had turned into a miniature amusement park full of people, chaos, and mirth. It was far, far worse than being trapped at a wedding reception. She could get little work done. Barely had she answered one person's questions about how the babies had been created before she had to retell the same story to yet another curious visitor. In between all the questioning, she vainly attempted to check cell division of eggs in the incubator, analyze dead embryos from test six, and edit a new DNA map. For the first time in two years, the nanites in the NDB rested silently, for Layla had no time to upload a new genome map for them to build.

Word got out that the other seven infants were going to be born after the day shift was over. Layla believed most people would have gone home by then. She was wrong. Over a hundred scientists showed up, and they did not want to just observe but take part in the birth. Frustrated, she became just another person in the crowd which sat or stood along the walls. Lunk, who had helped birth many animals over the last decade, volunteered with another co-worker from Freak Department to deliver T2-A2. The process went smoothly. Mera and Leana teamed up for T2-A3.

A few hours later, seven newborns lay asleep in the warming pen beside T2-A1. Though the crowd had thinned, many stood around chatting, congratulating Layla, or watching the infants. Half a dozen women from Baby Department volunteered to stay and babysit through the night. Derrick and Rosetta, exhausted, headed home for a decent night's sleep. Layla slipped away to take a shower at her apartment and sleep for a few hours.

It was nearly three in the morning when she made it back to her lab. She had only meant to take a nap, but she had been so exhausted that she had slept through her alarm. With e-tablet in hand, she carefully treaded around the volunteers sleeping on the floor to reach the warming pen. Several of the infants slept while others waved little fists or stared about. She had managed to weigh each of the infants right after birth, and C12 and C15 where underweight compared to the others. Besides weight, all eight infants looked identical. She picked up the scanner and waved it over the arm of the nearest infant to find out who he was. The scanner's screen read T2-A1.

I need to put armbands on them to tell them apart, thought Layla.

The infant reached out a hand and tried to grab the edge of the scanner. The gesture was unexpected, and Layla dropped the scanner. As she reached down for it, one of her fingers brushed the baby's tiny hand and the infant grabbed hold. Layla froze. The newborn's hand tightened about her finger. It was warm and soft. For a moment, the teenager's clinical attitude vanished, and she stared in wonder at this new life. *He is aware. He sees me, knows I exist.*

A baby further down the line began crying. A sleepy scientist on the floor mumbled, "Feeding time."

As the volunteers awoke, Layla pulled her hand free and grabbed the scanner. Back was her somber face as she heated formula for the infants. The women bottle-fed the babies while swapped stories about their own children. Layla listened politely, but her mind was running through a checklist of things which needed to be done. After the meal, her charge would not burp as she walked back and forth with the infant over her shoulder.

"You are not holding him right," advised Leana. "Watch how I am doing it."

Layla readjusted B9's position, but the results were the same. Impatiently, Layla handed the infant to another woman then helped wash bottles. The volunteers went back to sleep, but she worked the rest of the night, catching up on chores she had been too busy to do during the day. Rosetta and Derrick arrived shortly after daylight, just in time for another feeding. The six volunteers headed home, but new ones soon arrived to take their place.

Noon brought another swell of visitors, and the infants were showered with attention. Rosetta posted a signup list for volunteers to help for the rest of the week, and a crowd quickly gathered to write their names. Exhausted and cranky, Layla sat on a wobbly stool in a corner, wishing for a comfortable chair in her own lab but they all had been claimed.

"You look terrible," said Mera, handing her a bagged lunch. "You should go get some sleep."

"I need to weigh them after the next feeding."

"Someone else can do that." Mera sat down on another stool and pulled out a sandwich and juice from her own bag.

"They may not do it properly, and my e-tablet is programmed to only respond to my fingerprints. Plus, I need to prepare Anya for Test Eight's embryos."

"You are going to need more help."

Layla laughed wearily. "Look around you. I have more help than I could ever wish for in a lifetime."

"Right now, the infants are popular, but the newness will wear off. You cannot run a laboratory and raise eight kids on your own. You need permanent staff. Let's see." Mera pulled out a pen and began scribbling on the side of her lunch bag. "You will need three shifts a day with three or four workers for each shift. Weekends could be rotated, though you might want to consider twelve hours shifts for it. I estimate you need a minimal of twelve employees though fifteen is optimum."

"Twelve people here all the time? I am a scientist, not a manager."

"I am both. You have already been doing the role of supervisor, though you do not realize it. You have been managing Rosetta and Derrick quite well."

"They have just been helping me out."

"That is what employees do, help out. Officially, you are the Head of Advance Department. You need to choose several supervisors who will help you oversee the rest of your staff."

This was too much for Layla to take in. She just wanted things back as it used to be—quiet lab, humming machines, and occasional visits from co-workers. "I...uh... choose Rosette and Derrick."

"Someone called my name?" said Rosetta walking over with an infant in her arm. She settled on a stool while Derrick unpacked their lunches. "You will not believe how hard it is to just hold a baby around here."

"I was talking with Layla about the need of permanent staff. She just named you two as her top supervisors."

"My thanks, Layla," said Derrick, between bites of his apple. "That will rank me higher than Lunk. Hope he won't be too jealous."

"You already spend half your time over here anyway, before the births. I am surprised Banican has not reprimanded you."

"I've been too low down on the hierarchy for Banican to notice a lowly poop scooper like me. Besides, my direct supervisor Lunk has been my partner-in-crime *borrowing* stuff for Advance."

Rosetta expertly juggled a sandwich and baby at the same time. "I love the idea of being paid top credits to babysit. Makes me feel like a teenager again. Layla, have you considered who else you want?"

"Uh, no. Maybe send out a memo seeking volunteers."

"Good, I will help you go over the signup list. I'm sure there will be many. You should choose Leana, if she signs up. She will love watching them grow up. Maybe it will help make up a bit for losing her own daughter."

"I do not know if that is a good idea. It might crush her when they die."

"Die? They are as healthy as any children I have seen."

"A simple cold virus could wipe out all of them at once. I mean, there is so much we do not know. Anything could happen."

"Must you always plan for the worst? Have you even considered that they might actually make it to adulthood?"

"It is best not to get too attached to something that can die so easily. That is what scares me. All these people who keep visiting. They are going to be upset with me if something happens."

Mera said, "They might be disappointed but they will not blame you."

"I do not understand why they are even here. I have worked over three years on this project, and besides you three and a few others, no one has even cared or believed it was possible. I produce infants and suddenly everyone wants to know about my project. Why do they care?"

Mera sighed. "There is a lot you do not understand. Look around you. Over half of these scientists worked on the profectus project. They are your creators. Some of them worked for decades in thankless roles on a project that was unpopular and highly controversial. Even before you were born, they placed high hopes in you. While you grew up light-years away on another planet, they worried about you. When they heard the news about that virus outbreak at Luncaster University, they were devastated. They blamed themselves for the flaw in your genes which killed one of your classmates. They mourned her death like she was one of their own children. Then when one of their creations came here, they were delighted. They have cared about you all these years but did not know how to show you that. Until now. They love these newborns because they are yours. Their creation has created life. The cycle has been completed. They feel like grandparents, though you are too young to understand how that feels, what that means."

"I…I did not know they felt that way." Layla felt uneasy. The last three years she had lived in solitude of her own making. She could have formed many friendships if she had simply extended a hand.

"You have a huge family that has always supported you, even if you never succeeded in getting a zygote to divide."

"I guess that list for transfers might be very long."

"Very long indeed. Having staff means many new duties for you. You must plan for the future. Monthly budgets need to be submitted. You should start attending the weekly administrative meetings. There is a lot of empty space here. Do something with it."

"How about cots for the nightshift," suggested Derrick. "Sleeping on the floor is not a pleasant job perk."

His wife added, "This place is very drafty. The babies should have their own room which is heated in winter. Oh, and a playroom for them when they become toddlers."

"Alright," said Layla. "I would like to have my lab separated from the main room. Derrick, can partitions be built in here like in the Baby Department?"

"Sure, but I won't be able to scrape up enough supplies. It's going to cost money, a lot if properly done."

Layla looked at Mera. "Would Palakkad approve a building project?"

"The only way to find out is to ask. I will help you write the proposal."

For the next few days, Mera worked closely with Layla to create several proposals. Mera suggested sending in the request for new workers the first week then the building project the next. The first administrative meeting went smoothly despite Banican's complaints that Layla would be taking valuable workers away from more important projects. Mera countered that most of the transfers would be from her department. Once the proposal was approved, Layla sent out a memo inviting employees who were interested in working at Advance Department to fill out a transfer request. Within two days, fifty-six applied. Rosetta and Mera helped Layla narrow the list down to a final twelve which included Leana. Keeping with policy, Layla sent her building proposal to all the administrative staff three days before the next meeting. Once Banican read it, he finally made his first visit to Advance Department.

Busy analyzing C15's blood to figure out why he was barely gaining weight, Layla did not notice Banican storming into her building. Several volunteers were changing diapers. They froze as they followed Banican with their eyes.

"What audacity you have asking for a hundred thousand credits to build a fancy daycare!" Banican waved his e-tablet in the air.

Caught off guard, Layla said, "We are building sleeping rooms for staff too."

"Sleeping rooms? If someone is sleeping on company time then they should be fired. Who do you think you are? Just because you produce several babies does not give you the justification to go on a spending spree. You are not the first teenager to have kids."

Layla sat for a moment, unsure how to respond. "It is not wasteful. I explained how every credit will be used."

Banican read from his e-tablet. "Twenty-five thousand for walls, twenty thousand for a new heating and cooling system, fifteen thousand for surveillance equipment, five thousand for carpet. Carpet. My department is not carpeted."

"You do not have toddlers crawling on the floor."

"We are not running a daycare here. This is a serious company who does real science, unlike you."

Layla stood up. "My work is just as important as yours."

"My department produces a quarter of a million animals every year which ships out across the galaxy. We make money. Lots of it. What will your daycare sell? Who wants to buy a baby costing a hundred thousand credits when they can customize one for twenty thousand in Mera's department? Or better yet, make one the old fashion way. The last time I checked, you can still do that for free."

"My department is still new. It takes time to become profitable."

"I will tell you want will happen. Palakkad will, of course, give you your money. He enjoys patronizing his pets. But how long will the board keep a department that bleeds money? Ten or twenty years down the road, the board will choose a new director. By then your babies will no longer have cuteness to save them. When manufacturing lines are discontinued at BGF, we terminate any remaining inventory. I will be quite happy to be the one who gases yours."

Layla's heartbeat quickened. "How can you be so cruel?"

"Cruel? I am not the one producing sentient merchandise. What did you expect was going to happen to them? A product must make profit or it will be discontinued. That is the bottom line of every business."

"We will make money."

"How?"

"I do not know."

"That was what I thought." Banican turned and began walking away, but he paused by the warming pen where six of the infants slept. "Isn't that from *my* department?"

"We borrowed it."

"Well, return it. Today." He marched out of the building.

Layla stood with hands clenched, her chin quivering. *I will not cry. He will not get that satisfaction.*

"Vindictive barbarian," said Leana, picking up A3 from the changing table. "He always hated the profectus project. It never made a profit, but our work was featured in every major magazine and newspaper. The *Galactic Times* did a six-page spread about Palakkad. Imagine that—*Galactic Times*. Banican is just a jealous fool."

Layla tried to regain her composure but only half succeeded. "What are we going to do? Without the chick pen how are we going to keep them warm at night? Winter is coming."

"Then we make our own. Come to think of it, I still have my daughter's crib in my garage. I held onto it, thinking I was going to have another child, but then after the accident, I just couldn't throw any of her stuff away."

"I have a crib too," said a man nearby, checking the sleeping infants for wet diapers. "Our second child has outgrown it, and it is only taking up space. I will bring it by after work."

Leana gave A3 a motherly pat. "Now you will sleep in a far better bed than Banican's cage. I will ask Mera to announce you need more cribs. I'm sure you will have more than enough."

By late evening the warming pen was back in Freak Department, and each of the eight infants sleep in his own crib. Derrick moved several heaters near the cribs. Donations continued to pour in over the next few days including blankets, clothing, high chairs, stuffed animals, and toys. Layla was touched by the gifts, yet Banican's words still haunted her. How was her department going to make a profit? When the profectus project had been shut down, all remaining frozen embryos had been destroyed. If her project was closed, the same thing would happen to any specimens in her care.

Life was too hectic and busy for her to worry too much. Derrick ordered the building supplies and correlated with the maintenance department who agreed to do the construction work. Rosetta organized the new staff members into shifts, though there were still many volunteers eager to help, especially on the weekends. No one but Layla liked her system of calling the infants by a number. Soon choosing proper names became a hot debate between staff at BGF. Someone in the Baby Department started a naming poll. Staff at Freak Department, determined not to be outdone, began a pay-for-your-favorite-name contest. All profit would go towards buying baby supplies. Layla suspected Lunk was behind the contest, but she did agree to use the winning names.

Her immediate concern was for the health of C12 and C15, dubbed Miguel and Dylan. While the other six had hearty appetites and rapid weight gain, these two grew slower and slept more. Layla took daily fluid samples to examine under the molecular microscope, but she was not a medical doctor and lacked the expertise to know what she was looking for. The best she could do was isolate how the cells of Group C reacted differently from the others group's cells. The results of the analyze she kept to herself, hoping she was wrong.

When the infants were nearly two weeks old, Layla received a call in the middle of the night by one of the nightshift workers named Opal.

"It's Dylan. He still won't eat and that fever he had earlier is much higher."

"Just let him sleep, and I will check on him in the morning," mumbled Layla.

"His breathing is shallow. I think you should call a doctor."

"I will be right over."

Layla arrived to find the three nightshift workers and one volunteer gathered around Dylan's crib, all whispering anxiously.

Opal said, "His temperature is high, and he is not breathing well."

"Any sneezing or coughing?"

"No. Didn't you check his blood earlier today and said he was clean?"

"Yes, viruses are not the problem." Layla averted her eyes, pretending to read over a chart that had been handed to her. Viruses were the least of Dylan's problems. His cells were not breaking down sugars properly, leaving him weak and vulnerable. Colds could be treated. Rewriting the DNA for every living cell inside him was beyond even the miraculous skills of nanites.

"Perhaps he should be sent to the hospital."

"They will not know how to treat him. Remember, he is not human."

Layla took another blood sample and examined it under the EMM. Opal and the other workers debated about if he should be given medicine, and if so, what kind. They finally decided on a common cold medicine for children. Layla let them do as they pleased, already certain what the outcome would be. As the night wore on, Dylan's heartbeat slowed and his breathing became ragged. Dawn arrived but the sunshine could not warm the chilly fall morning. The dayshift arrived and joined the night workers who refused to go home, all worrying about the infant.

Mid-morning Dylan died in Leana's arms as she rocked him gently. Even after she knew he was gone, she continued humming a lullaby to him. Rosetta was the one who finally, tenderly, took the dead infant from her. Layla planned to have the baby sent to Autopsy Department for disposal, but the workers insisted on having a funeral first.

Word quickly spread across the campus and over two hundred people showed up that afternoon for the short ceremony. Several scientists, including Leana, shared fond memories of caring for Dylan. Layla stood against a far wall, aloof, watching tears running down the cheeks of many volunteers. She kept the knowledge to herself that Miguel shared the same cell malfunction that Dylan had. The other six seemed healthy, but there were so many unknowns. Would she have to endure seven more funerals like this one? Her project might close down far quicker than Banican had predicted.

Chapter Ten

Numbers blurred together as Layla looked over the monthly budget yet again. Banican had been wrong when he estimated her creations costing one hundred thousand a piece. Their value was steadily climbing to the millionth mark. Just to pay the salaries of the fifteen scientists in her department added up to over six hundred thousand per year. Then there were utilities, repairs, and baby supplies to be concerned about, plus meeting the many wishes of her staff. Opal wanted a kitchenette installed in the breakroom. Leana claimed the thermostat in the babies' room was broken though Derrick had checked it out three times.

Ah, Derrick. He was giving her the biggest headache at the moment. He wanted her to transfer over a friend from the Maintenance Department. She had politely refused, claiming that since she was no longer growing embryos, one person could handle any machinery malfunctions, which was usually limited to her molecular microscope. Derrick countered with a joke accusing her of being sexist since she had thirteen women working in her department but only one guy. Layla had explained she had simply written down the names Mera and Rosetta advised. Derrick went off in a humph, mumbling about being surrounded by feminists. Since then, he had been difficult to work with. If she wanted peace, she would need to transfer his friend, but that meant another salary coming out of her budget. Life had been far easier when she was a secluded scientist working in a run-down lab.

At least the construction work had finally been completed. The weeks of hammering and banging had gotten on everyone's nerves. Simple conversations were difficult since you had to shout to be heard over the racquet. The infants had difficulty sleeping in the day hours. The whole building had turned into a maze of half-finished walls, ceiling tiles falling unexpectedly, and corridors which were opened one day but blocked the next.

Layla's scrutiny of the budget was interrupted by Mera entering the new lab. A large chunk of floor space was taken up by the NDB and Anya. The rest of the space was filled by a desk, shelves, cryogenic freezer, and several tables cluttered with equipment and supplies.

"It's in," said Mera, dressed in a spotless lab coat and her hair pulled into a tight bun.

"What is?"

"Just that short, six page article about you in *Galactic Times*. I was going to show it to you first, but I got mobbed in your breakroom. Your staff can be a bit dangerous."

Layla sighed and put down her e-tablet. "I am not sure I want to see it."

"Of course you do. It is a great honor."

With dread, Layla followed Mera down the hallway to the breakroom. Rosetta, Leana, and two other women were attempting to read from the same magazine simultaneously. Derrick, sitting at a table, had settled for paying for a digital copy downloaded to his e-tablet.

"You made the cover," said Rosetta, holding up the magazine. It was a close-up of a smiling Layla holding one of the infants. The photographer had a difficult time taking that image. It took Derrick and Rosetta both teasing each other for several minutes before Layla had relaxed enough for the photo to be snapped.

"We are all in here," beamed Leana. "Remember that shot they took when we were holding the babies?"

Derrick scanned through his electronic copy. "There are no pictures of me."

"You were not feeding one."

"I was still there. I helped them set up the lighting, remember."

"They even have a paragraph about me and a quote." Leana read, "I am truly proud of everything Layla has achieved. We who worked on the profectus project had high hopes for our offspring, but her success is far greater than we could have imaged."

"I didn't get a quote," complained Derrick.

His wife pointed excitedly at a spot on a page. "Oh, they quoted me when I was explaining how our babies are growing roughly twice as fast as a normal human child."

"Why did they not quote me? I explained how the X1800 and Anya work."

"Maybe because of information overload. You drowned them in technical jargon."

"Interesting title," pointed out Mera. "The Quintessence of Genetics."

Layla studied the article's first page. "They must have picked that line up when I was explaining how pure their genes are."

"They refer to the babies several times as *quintessence*. Readers are going to think that is the name of their species."

Leana said, "I prefer the term *quintessence* much better than *sentiens purus artificialis,* that boring Latin title you gave them. No offence, Layla."

"I have been told I lack creativity when it comes to names. Was that a picture of Richard?"

"I think so," said Rosetta, flipping back a page. "He is explaining how you worked with him on creating Ultimate Designer. I bet his sales will jump high because of this article."

Derrick complained, "Even the computer programmer gets a picture and a quote, yet I get nothing."

"They may have thought you were just the maintenance guy."

"I am not maintenance but a genetic technician supervisor."

"Same thing."

"It's not the same thing. How many maintenance workers know the name of every single part of a Nanotech DNA Builder?"

"Just you and that crazy buddy of yours."

"Zylar is not crazy, and it would be nice that since I have a title of supervisor that I am actually supervising someone."

Tired of the bickering, Layla cut in. "Alright. I will transfer Zylar over after lunch."

Derrick's crankiness immediately vanished. "You won't regret it. He might be a bit...different, but he knows almost as much as I do about nanites."

"Takes one to know one," mumbled his wife.

"Layla, what are you going to do, now that you are famous?" asked Leana.

"Uh...buy my first hover car. I am sixteen now."

Derrick eagerly offered, "I'll help you chose the perfect one. Perhaps a Blazer Z50. The engine purrs like a kitten even when the RPM goes over ten thousand."

"She is not buying a racing car. She needs something more moderate like my Laken Sedan."

"Sorry to inform you, dear, but your hover car is boring. Layla has been saving for years and deserves the best."

"Layla is modest; therefore, she needs a modest car."

"I think everyone for their opinions," said the teenager, "but first I need driving lessons. I have never actually been behind the wheel before."

Rosetta turned to her husband. "That is your job, supervisor."

After several weeks of lessons from Derrick, Layla passed her driving test. Then she rode with her friends to Austin City to car shop. Derrick had a blast, test-driving every sports vehicle on the lot. If Rosetta had not intervened, he would have brought one home himself. Layla eventually chose a silver Zoomlander. Derrick raved about its sleek design, and Rosetta liked its safety record. Layla loved the freedom it offered her.

For the first time in her young life, she had the one power that had been denied her—freedom to go where she wanted whenever she wanted. When the whim hit, she could hop into her hover car and zoom along country roads, taking random turns. She shopped more, visiting stores Rosetta had never taken her into. Her one-room apartment became so cluttered that Rosetta began hinting it was time for Layla to get her first real apartment. Layla considered it, but she was concerned about being too far from her charges in case of an emergency.

She had cause to be concerned. Miguel was still underweight and sickly. The babies were now nearly six months old but looked like one-year-old humans. Miguel was easy to pick out because he was smaller, but the other six looked like exact copies of each other. Each wore an armband printed with the child's name, but it was too small to read from a distance. The caregivers soon began sewing names in large letters on the fronts of all the boys' shirts. Because of Miguel's ongoing sickness, he was showered with more attention than the others.

In many ways, the quintessences seemed human. They crawled on the floor, chewed on toys, attempted to stand, and responded to "no." They had even begun babbling baby talk and occasionally spoke real words. Many visitors still came to see them. During lunch breaks, it was common to see a dozen scientists sitting on the floor in the playroom, rolling a ball to a child or trying to get a child to mimic words. Some visitors commented that though the kids looked human, there was something different about their appearance, especially in the eyes. They belonged to no particular ethic group, though their darker skin tone and face shape hinted of Middle Eastern heredity.

Layla kept careful records of the children's progress. She took weekly blood and urine samples to examine under the molecular microscope. Their growth rate did not directly parallel humans. Though the quintessences were growing roughly twice as fast as human children, the rate varied as growth spurts happen at different times between the species. While still only one, the quintessences flew through their toddler and three-year-old stage. Layla asked the caregivers to fill out daily evaluations about their charges. Parents themselves, the caregivers often compared their own children to the quintessence.

"Another easy day. They are so quiet and obedient. You only have to say "no" once and they stop whatever they are doing. Wish my own kids were so well-behaved. Can we use gene therapy on my son?"

"I noticed they rarely cry. They used to cry whenever they were hungry or wet, but now they don't, even when in pain. Neither do they laugh or joke very much. So sober to be so young. It seems a bit unnatural."

"They eat more than my daughter, but they have better table manners. Not once have I seen any food thrown. Can I borrow one to take home to give my daughter lessons in proper dinner etiquette?"

"Alexander shared his cookie with me. Of course, all the others immediately offered theirs to me too—except Xavier. Somehow that one is different than the others."

"Miguel is sick again today. The others seem to sense it and are protective of him. When they thought I was speaking too loudly, as a group they shushed me. Except for Xavier. He twice walked near Miguel and yelled loudly. Both times he stopped as soon as I asked him to."

"Xavier hit Miguel in the head with a ball yet again. My own three sons fight all the time, and this is normal behavior for them. But as Xavier is not human (you keep reminding us this over and over), his behavior seems peculiar. Why is Xavier the only aggressive one in the group?"

"Caleb and Xavier were playing with a toy car during nap time. I took the car from them and placed it on a table. A few minutes later, Caleb had fallen asleep, but I spotted Xavier playing with the car again, knowing he was not supposed to. Note to self: Don't take your eyes off that one."

At the age of three and a half, they were as tall as an eight year old human. Leana took on the role of teacher and began instructing the quintessences in basic reading and math. They learned about as quickly as a typical seven-year-old human did. Layla, far too often, kept saying it was unfair to compare quintessences to humans. She preferred comparing quintessences to each other. Alexander, Mason, Caleb, Jacob, and Gabriel all came from the same DNA map used for Group One and behaved so similar to each other that unless their nametags were read, it was impossible to tell them apart. They were quiet, obedient, and helpful. They behaved more as a group than as separate individuals. If one ate, they all ate. If there was only one cookie, then they broke it so all had food.

Miguel was as quiet and cooperative as the others from Group One, perhaps even more so. As his twin was the one who died, the caretakers worried about his various colds and illnesses. He was given special snacks. At first, he tried to share his treats with his brothers, but when told it was just for him, he ate dutifully. Regular visitors preferred playing with him over the others, perhaps because he was the only one that could be recognized simply by sight. The caregivers picked him up more often and lavished attention upon him.

If there was any mischief about, Xavier was always at the bottom of it. He never directly challenged his caregivers, but he would disobey when he thought they were no longer looking. He was more aggressive, prone to throwing toys. Several times mysterious bruises showed up on Miguel who remained silent when asked where they came from. Caregivers suspected Xavier was the culprit.

Chapter Eleven

Ringing aroused Layla from deep slumber. Groggily she moved across her room, stumbling over a pair of hover skates, a recent purchase encouraged by Rosetta who thought it would be fun to skate in the parking lot after work. As Layla grabbed a chair to keep her balance, the closet mirror revealed her eighteen-year-old silhouette cast by dim street light. Her slim, Indian body had finally developed feminine curves, though she was still plain looking, the least noticed if placed in a crowd of strangers.

The teenager hit the talk button and heard Leana's upset voice. "Layla, you need to come. Miguel is dead."

"Dead? He was fine earlier. The fever was not that high."

"He is dead. I...I...think he was murdered. You need to come now."

"I will be right over."

She grabbed her keys and headed out the door, still in her pajamas. As she drove across the large campus to Advance Department, Layla pondered what Leana had said. Surely she was wrong. Who would murder Miguel? He was sick enough like it was. Maybe the twelve-hour weekend shift was getting to Leana. Layla had barely pulled up in the parking lot, when Opal met her.

The sixty-year-old grandmother looked pale and fearful. "It's Miguel."

"Leana said he had been murdered."

"Maybe...you need to see."

Layla followed Opal into the building to the quintessences' sleeping quarters. Leana stood in the doorway, trembling, staring wide-eyed at the six children standing quietly beside their cots. Miguel's lifeless body lay in the middle of the room, face down.

"How did this happen?" asked Layla.

Leana began crying, and Opal tried to comfort her but was shaken herself. Layla beckoned the two women down the hallway, out of the children's hearing.

"What did you see exactly? I need to know."

Opal answered, "A thump woke us, and we came to see the children. There was Miguel, dead, and Xavier standing over his body. Just standing."

"Did you actually see Xavier hurt Miguel?"

The women shook their heads, and Opal said. "No, but it was so unnatural. Xavier was so composed standing right there beside his dead brother. Normal children would be upset."

Layla was uncertain what to do. There was no protocol at BGF which covered this. "Miguel probably died from his illness, and Xavier just got up to see what was wrong with him. We all knew Miguel was sick."

"But not sick enough to drop dead," said Leana between sobs. "You said that on the phone."

"Leana, I need you to call Rosetta and Mera. Can you do that for me?" The woman nodded. "Good. Opal, contact security and tell them to send over a few men to take a dead specimen to the Autopsy Department."

The women left, and Layla went back into the sleeping quarters. It looked exactly as before. Each child stood by his bed, silent, showing neither fear nor grief. As Layla entered the room, the boys watched her closely. She knelt beside Miguel's body to examine it. There were no bloodstains or markings indicating violence.

"Can anyone tell me what happened?"

Five identical children's faces turned to look at Xavier.

"Xavier, what happened?"

"I could not sleep because of his coughing, so I silenced him."

"What do you mean by *you silenced him*?" Goosebumps ran down Layla's arms. Could Leana have been right?

"He was weak. Why have you kept him this long?"

"That was not your decision to make."

"Derrick told us about the experiments in Freak Department. Weak subjects are culled; healthy are kept. Why was Miguel not terminated?"

"That was my decision to make, not yours." Layla suddenly felt cold, clammy.

The boy cocked his head slightly to one side, studying her with predatorily eyes. "You are afraid of me."

"No," said Layla, slowly standing up. Over the years, she had felt fear of failing tests and the anxiety of moving to a new home, but never had she known terror—to this moment.

"You do not lie well, creator. Are you weak like Miguel?"

Layla felt she had just been measured and found wanting. That bond of respect for superiors that had always kept Xavier in line vanished. He took a step towards her, eyes intense. The other children responded immediately by forming a silent semicircle in front of Layla, blocking Xavier. Neither side spoke for a long moment.

"You have done wrong," said Gabriel.

"You will do no more harm," said Jacob.

"I have discovered a secret, brothers. A great secret which she never intended." Xavier gave a weird, unnatural grin. "We are designed superior to them."

"They are our caretakers," said Alexander.

"They created us," said Mason

"They provide us life," said Caleb.

"And we can take life," replied Xavier. "And their knowledge. With it we will become greater than our creators."

A door slammed at the end of the hallway, and there were voices. Relief flooded through Layla when she saw Opal and Leana accompanied by several security officers. She backed out of the room, never taking her eyes off Xavier.

The night security chief crossed his arms and said, "Where is your failed experiment that can't wait till morning for proper disposal?" Anthony Franklin was a board-shoulder, imposing man who had retired several years ago as a captain in the Imperial Army. He had no time for nonsense and had never been tempted to visit Advance Department to see the celebrated test subjects.

"Sir, arrest him for murder." Layla pointed through the door at Xavier.

Anthony frowned. "A child? We don't arrest children. If he killed one of your experiments, then talk to his parents."

"He is the experiment, and he killed another child."

The man stepped into the bedroom and saw Miguel's body for the first time. He also noted the semicircle of five identical children and Xavier standing alone, aloof. "What are these? I thought quintessences were some new, bizarre animal you scientists cooked up."

"This child killed the one on the floor. Please arrest him, now." Layla tried to keep her voice even, but her heart still pounded with fear. She was not about to be left alone with Xavier again.

Anthony signaled to his two guards, and they walked over and grabbed the arms of the boy. Xavier walked calmly out the door with his escorts, not showing fear or remorse. Leana broke into new, uncontrollable sobs.

"Opal, please take Leana home," said Layla.

"Are you sure?" asked the grandmother.

"There is nothing else you can do tonight. Mera and the others will be here soon."

As the women left, Anthony said, "We can't hold the child. If he really did commit homicide then he must be turned over to the local police."

"He is an experiment and out of their jurisdiction. He is property of BGF."

"A child that is property? I knew you scientists were strange, but this is pushing the limit. Are you really sure he killed on purpose? Accidents happen." He securitized the room with his eyes. "Is that security camera working?"

"Yes, my technician supervisor oversees that."

"Show me where you keep the logs."

Layla led him down the hallway to a small room that housed the building's mainframe computer. "My technician will be here soon."

"No need to wait."

Anthony sat down in front of the computer screen and easily navigated through the menus. He pulled up video feed of the boys' bedroom from two hours earlier. All the quintessences slept on their cots. Anthony hit the fast forward button. It revealed Miguel coughing occasionally, and in the next cot, Xavier twisting and turning restlessly. When Xavier climbed out of bed, Anthony slowed the video speed to normal.

For a long time, Xavier stood completely still, watching Miguel's body, whose back was to Xavier, shake in a spasm of deep coughing. Xavier turned and picked up his own pillow. Slowly he lowered the pillow over Miguel's head. The other boy began to turn in bed and spotted Xavier. Instinctively, Miguel rolled out of the way and clambered out of the cot on the other side. The two children looked at each other in the semidarkness. One sickly, the other still holding the pillow. Neither spoke. Finally, Miguel turned and walked toward the door.

"He was probably going to see Leana and Opal," whispered Layla.

Xavier dashed forward and grabbed Miguel from the back. There was a brief struggle which ended when Xavier bit the back of Miguel's upper neck. Several sleeping boys in nearby cots stirred, but remained asleep. Miguel went stiff, eyes wide. After a couple of minutes, Xavier straightened up, ending the bite. Miguel's body dropped to the floor. The thump awakened the other children. They climbed out of bed and stared at Xavier standing over Miguel's body. Xavier looked at the dead child and a twisted smile crept across his lips. Opal and Leana entered the room, and Xavier erased the grin from his face, looking identical to the other silent children.

"How is this possible?" asked Anthony. "Kids don't kill kids by biting. What type of perverse experiment is this?"

"They have never attacked each other before." But even as she said the words, she remembered reports of strange bruises on Miguel. How long had Xavier's abuse being going on? Why had she not searched security videos months ago to see the cause of the marks? Even as she questioned herself, the answer stared starkly back. Because a few bruises had not seemed serious to her, until now.

"These things you created are not kids. Not human."

"I know."

"You are lucky one of them has not killed before. You keep their bedroom door unlocked. It would be easy for one of them to slip out and kill a sleeping adult. I don't know how you scientists justify creating monsters like this."

"I did not design monsters…something just went wrong with Xavier. I never intended for this to happen."

Anthony, who was still watching the computer monitor, suddenly pointed at the semicircle that the children had formed in front of Layla. "That is a defense formation. Quick, unified response. They are very protective of you."

"Like I said, they are not monsters."

"What are they then?"

Voices in the hallway announced that Mera, Rosetta, and Derrick had arrived. Layla called them into the room and briefed them on what happened. All three stared at her in shock and disbelief. They were not convinced until they watched the video themselves.

Rosetta said, "I don't understand. Why would Xavier do this?"

"Jealousy perhaps," said Derrick. "You have always given Miguel more attention."

"But to kill? They are children."

"Not human children," said Layla.

"The board is going to be upset," said Mera. "They may close this project."

"No, they can't," said Rosetta. "They are still children. The others are not dangerous. We all knew that Xavier was aggressive. They can't terminate the project."

Anthony spoke, "If one can kill, so can the others."

"But if they terminate the project, it means they will cull the quintessences. We can't let that happen."

"Look, I don't know what your plans for this project are, but in my holding cell right now, I am detaining a creature for murdering its own kind. If it can kill its own so easily, imagine what will happen when it turns on you."

"They would never do that," said Layla.

"Really?" Anthony rewound the video and stopped it where Xavier began walking towards Layla still partially bent over Miguel's body. "If those others had not blocked him, you wouldn't be here talking with me right now."

"But they stopped him."

"And who will stop them?"

Derrick defended, "The rest are not killers. You cannot judge all based on the actions of one."

"All I know is you created creatures which kill. They are more like soldiers than children."

"We would never do what Xavier did." The adults turned to see five young quintessences standing in the doorway, faces somber. "What he did was wrong."

The adults glanced at each other, uneasy. Rosetta finally broke the silence. "You should be in bed."

"We cannot sleep. Miguel is still there," said Mason.

"Oh, um…we will remove him soon. You may go to the playroom."

The children turned obediently, but Layla called out. "Wait. Tell me, what do you think should be done to Xavier? He has broken the highest of all rules."

The children glanced at each other, then Alexander said, "Xavier followed the rule that the weak should be culled. But he is not judge, you are. He has tried to make himself higher than you, his creator."

"What punishment does he deserve?"

"Death," said Jacob, face emotionless.

Several of the adults shifted uncomfortable, but Mera asked, "Do you all think Xavier should be terminated?"

Five identical faces nodded in unison.

"You may go play now," said Layla, body trembling.

"Sin has entered paradise," muttered Rosetta softly, equally upset.

Layla took a deep breath to calm herself. "Is there anyone who disagrees with what they said?" She glanced from face to face. Pale, Rosetta clutched Derrick who looked ill himself. Mera wore her stern, no nonsense look, but a shaking hand betrayed her inter conflict.

Anthony was the only calm one. "I have been in war and seen how it changes people. These creatures of yours have the faces of children but speak like harden soldiers. I'm with those kids voting for capital punishment. Your only other option is keeping him caged the rest of his life, but if he breaks free, he will be more dangerous than ever."

"Are you okay with being the one to…terminate him?" asked Layla.

The man nodded. "Won't be the first time I've killed, but he will be the youngest."

Rosetta said, "How…how can you sleep at night?"

"Young lady, what I did in war, I did to protect others. You scientists live such sheltered, shallow lives, but you only do so because soldiers like me fight and die to protect your way of life." He stood up. "Now I'm off to see about the reason I came here in the first place—disposing of that body for you."

Derrick said, "I will help you…with everything."

As the men left, Mera looked at the computer screen still paused on the image of Xavier's predatory face. "Layla, what did you create?"

"I no longer know."

Chapter Twelve

Fifteen high-level staff members sat round the huge oval table. Some read from their e-tablets. Others tapped fingers impatiently. A few actually listened to the maintenance chief wrapping up his speech about why the parking lots needed to be repaved. After the issue finally passed by one vote, Palakkad introduced the speaker Dubuis Gollnick, chief pathologist of the Autopsy Department. Immediately the room became charged with tension as staff members turned attentive eyes towards the man.

Dubois stepped to the front of the room. "Our examinations of subjects T2-C12 and T2-B9 are still ongoing. They are, to say the least, the most interesting specimens we have studied at BGF since I started working here over twenty-five years ago." He tapped his e-tablet and a 3-D image of a young quintessence appeared on the wall screen. "Specimen B9 died, in simple terms, from a rapid energy drain from a source point in the lower brain. In humans, that is where our cerebellum and brain stem are located. Not so for quintessences."

The image on the wall changed to a close-up of an abnormal brain, distorted, with alien lobes in odd regions. There were gasps of surprise as scientists strained forwards in their seats for a better view. "As you can see, its brain structure is completely foreign from anything we have seen before. My staff has been analyzing this for three days now, but there is a great deal we do not understand yet about *entiens purus artificialis*. For example, there is a lower section which is…webbed into upper areas."

Dubois touched his e-tablet and different parts of the digital brain became colorized. The lowest section, painted a deep blue, was thin and stretched out with small tentacles which weaved upward, embedding into the higher regions. "That though, is not the strangest phenomenal we found." A cartoonish cross section of a quintessence head was revealed. From the lower brain stretched thin, blue tentacles which followed the jaw line and bunched into an oval under the tongue. "We are uncertain if this is a separate organ or still part of the lower brain. All of it is made from the same cell type for which we have no name for yet."

"This is all fascinating," said Banican, "but how do these things kill?"

"You are looking at the weapon. That part under the tongue can extend itself and pierce a host's brain stem. Once that happens, it seems to feed off the electrical impulses of the neurons belonging to the host. There is also a chemical process which takes place, though we are still analyzing that."

"What does that mean?" asked the maintenance chief. "Are they, what, energy sucking vampires?"

"No, I would not use that term. Actually, there are no terms for much of what you see—yet. Some of it does look familiar, but some is completely unique. I am hoping that Layla can share some insight on what we are seeing as she was the one who chose the DNA."

All eyes turned to Layla who had been staring at the screen with a sickening horror. She knew and it scared her. Never had she thought it would be used to kill another.

"Well," prompted Mera. "What are we looking at?"

"A...an...*epulo infestus*."

"A what?" came several voices simultaneously. Several people typed the name into their e-tablets and began a word search.

"They are a rare species from the planet Z 5907. So rare that only one has ever been...studied. It has high regeneration speeds so I thought that...it might...be useful in case of virus infections."

"An energy leech," read Banican from his e-tablet. "Only one specimen collected at the expense of three researchers' lives. What were you thinking?"

"I thought it would be useful. I never thought about it actually being used as a weapon."

"It killed three people and you thought it was not dangerous!"

"Only one. The other two simply disappeared. It was a hostile planet."

Murmuring filled the room as more staff read about the creature. Several people glared at Layla in angry or disbelief.

Palakkad held up a hand for silence. "Layla, I am sure you had good intentions. How much *epulo infestus* DNA did you use?"

"Thirty-one percent of its total, but it was a low-level animal. In quintessences it came to less than one percent of their total DNA."

Banican said, "You put a third of a parasite into a sentient and thought it was not perilous? How naïve can you be? Have I not said over and over that this project should never have been funded? BGF spent millions of dollars in order for you to create an intelligent leech. You should have named them *foeditas horribilis*, horrifying foulness."

Layla looked around in desperation at the many angry, betrayed faces. "They are intellect sentients. The others will not kill."

"Maybe they should." Staff members turned to see Anthony, arms crossed, leaning against a back wall.

Palakkad thought an introduction was needed. "This is retired Captain Anthony Franklin, our chief night security officer. He was present at the scene and has reviewed the video of the attack. I have asked him to share his unique insight."

The room quieted as Anthony spoke. "I am just a simple, retired soldier who knows little about your fancy diagrams and charts. What I do know is you are upset because these man-made beings have the ability to kill quickly. Have you not understood what this girl actually created? A weapon. An intelligent, trainable weapon, which, in the right hands, could do much good. Set one of these loose in an enemy camp and a lot of damage could be done."

"They are not weapons," said Layla. "They are children."

"Who kill. And they will not stay children for long. Look, it makes no difference to me if you gas them all today, but I will tell you what I saw. They work well together as a unit, are fearless, and will protect friendly targets. These are highly sought after qualities in soldiers."

The chatter began again, but the anger had vanished from most. Layla sat, stunned into silence. She could keep arguing against the soldier idea, but then she had nothing to fall back on. Her project had to make money or it would be closed sooner or later.

Banican said, "Million dollar soldiers? Quite expense weapons to send on suicide missions. I am not certain you will find many buyers for that."

"They could be mass produced like in your department," said Palakkad. "That will cut down dramatically on the cost. Of course, they would need to be trained and field tested first."

"You cannot seriously be considering making them a saleable product." Banican thumped the table in frustration. "The lawsuits alone would bleed our budget dry."

Palakkad looked at Layla who sat pale and anxious. "We should at least explore that option. Captain Franklin, are you interested in training them?"

Anthony studied Layla for a long moment. "Yes, I would like to see what these creatures can do, but if they turn just once against their handlers, they should be put down."

"Agreed," said Palakkad. "I believe the board will approve a one year training program. At the end, we will evaluate to see if quintessences might make a feasible product."

As people filed out of the room, Layla remained seated, staring at the rotating BGF logo on the wall screen. Soldiers. All those long years of designing them, of agonizing over how to find the perfect recipe for cell structure and they were to be turned into trained killers.

Mera patted her on the shoulder. "It went a lot better than I hoped."

"This is not what I intended. I wanted peaceful, intellect sentients, not predators that kill on command."

"They are alive. Be happy. I had feared that before the sun set today they would all be gassed. Soldiers are more than killers. They can save lives too. Have you thought about that?"

It was all Layla thought about the rest of the day—along with her upset staff. Three caretakers turned in requests to transfer back to Baby Department. Leana wavered but finally decided to stay at Advance Department a while longer. Many supporters of the quintessence project felt betrayed, and visitations dropped off sharply. For years, they had watched the cute newborns grow into well-behaved children, never guessing the parasite genes written into their genetic code.

Anthony Franklin came the next morning to discuss his training program. Officially he was assigned the position of military supervisor under Layla, but the moment he walked into her lab, he projected himself as dominate. Layla felt intimated as she gave him a tour of the facility, feeling tiny next to his large, muscular frame.

"A playroom?" He frowned, arms crossed, watching through the glass wall as the five quintessences played board games, quietly moving pieces on the digital boards.

"They prefer strategy games like chess."

"An excellent war game for building strategic skills."

"I did not know it was a war game."

"Why do you think there are knights and pawns?" he said in a deep voice. "Winning requires effectively using the unique qualities of each of your troops while manipulating your opponent into a trap. You must balance offense and defense effectively, attack your enemy while simultaneously defending your leader. A master player understands when to sacrificed pieces in order to gain the advantage."

The clock on the wall showed nine. As one, the quintessences turned off their board games and filed out of the room. Anthony and Layla followed them several doors down the hallway. The children entered their classroom and sat silently at computerized desks. Leana tapped on her e-tablet and a math program opened on their desktops.

"Yesterday we began division. You did well on your first assignment. Today we will divide by two digits. On your monitors, notice the example. Ten goes into one hundred how many times?"

"Ten," said five voices as one.

"Good. Now look at the next example. Ten goes into two hundred how many times?"

"Twenty."

The students paid strict attention to their teacher. There was no whispering, sly glances, or attempts to pass hidden notes.

As Anthony and Layla continued down the hallway, Anthony asked, "How intelligent are they?"

"We are still debating that one. They are almost four but just began second grade material."

"Then are they geniuses?"

"Not really. Their learning rate seems to about equal to an average human, maybe a little higher. It is just that because they grow so quickly, they begin studying younger."

"When does their schooling end for the day?"

"About midafternoon. Then we take them on nature walks if the weather is good or they play games with staff and visitors."

"That will be the time I will begin training them. Two hours every evening."

"How exactly are you going to train them?"

"I will start with the basics: exercises and drills. I will evaluate their progress and decide from there what they are capable of doing."

"What does that mean? Will you give them weapons and teach them to kill?"

"When the time comes."

For a week, Layla watched her quintessences silently follow Anthony outside every afternoon. They returned sweaty and dirty, speaking no complaints, even when several bore scrapes on arms and knees. The day one returned with a bleeding hand, Layla became very upset. She walked into the breakroom and saw Rosetta holding bloody gauze against Gabriel's palm.

"What happened?"

"One of Captain Coldheart's training exercises." Rosetta began wrapping tape around the gauze.

"It was my fault." The boy flinched when Rosetta accidently pressed against the wound. "I was climbing a fence and did not properly cover the barbs with my shirt."

"You are not referring to those fences by the old training field?" said Layla.

"Yes."

Rosetta looked at Layla. "Those are twelve feet high with barbwire at the top. No kid should be climbing them."

"This is getting ridiculous. I am going to talk with Palakkad."

Layla was still angry when she walked into the director's office twenty minutes later. Palakkad smiled and offered her a seat. His office was plainer than the one he had at Luncaster University, with only a few pictures on the walls.

"How is the training program going?"

"Terrible. Anthony is putting their lives in needless danger. One came back bleeding today from a barbwire cut he got twelve feet in the air. Twelve feet. He could have fallen and broken his neck."

Palakkad leaned back in his chair and studied Layla for a moment before answering. "No one wants to see your project succeed more than I do. To create coding for a brand new species is exciting. Watching your creations grow up to follow their own destiny, now that is tough. I probably understand this more than anyone else at Bontinc. It is hard to let go."

"They are still children."

"So were you when you left home at the age of eight. Did you think your parents wanted you to leave? But if you had not left, then you would have never grown into who you are now. Sometimes true growth can only happen when there is difficulty. For example, you had to study for tests. You did not enjoy those tests and lived with the fear of failure, but because you studied hard for those tests, you were able to retain knowledge which helps you now."

"This is not about memorizing math formulas. Quintessences could get hurt or die."

"Layla, I have stood in the gap for you, supporting this project while the hounds of war circled, calling for blood. The Xavier incident was the last straw. I knew the board was going to pull the funding, and I dreaded that it would crush you. Classifying your quintessences as a military project was the only way to save it. Military contracts can be substantial, and the board is patient enough to keep sinking millions of dollars into the quintessences as long as they believe the compensation will be generous."

"Can we find someone else besides Anthony? He is too harsh with them."

"Captain Franklin served in the military for thirty years, with over a dozen years of experience coming directly from the battlefront where he earned three Purple Comets. He was forced into retirement due to injuries he received while earning that last medal. He was in rehab for over a year. I consider it an honor having a war hero working at Bontinc. If anyone can turn quintessences into successful soldiers, it will be him."

Layla left the meeting feeling frustrated. *This is not what I want for my creations. A perfect being should be peaceful, not a weapon for war.* But she was helpless to stop the process of forging the children into warriors.

Chapter Thirteen

Skates hovered an inch off the pavement made hot from the summer sun. Rosetta seemed born for skating, gracefully glided across the parking lot. Layla, on the other hand, struggled to keep her balance, sometimes grabbing nearby objects to prevent a fall.

"You are so gloomy today," complained Rosetta.

"I have a lot on my mind."

"That is why we are out here. Forget about work and enjoy yourself. The sun is shining. The birds singing. What more could you ask for?"

"A new job."

"Don't be silly. Oh, look out for that…"

Too late Layla spotted the pothole. She tried to correct her balance but landed flat on her back. Rosetta glided over and helped her stand, which Layla had learned from many painful experiences was the hardest part of hover skating.

When Layla was finally on her feet again, Rosetta said, "One of your problems is that you take life too seriously. You should have more hobbies."

"I find this one dangerous enough."

"You should date."

Layla stumbled and grabbed a parked vehicle for balance. "No, thank you."

"You are almost nineteen and still have never been on your first date. You are an attractive girl, and I know several guys who would go out with you."

"I have far too many things to deal with to add a boyfriend in the mix."

"I'm not saying you should jump into a serious relationship. Just go out and have fun."

"I am not interested in fun. I am interested in protecting my quintessences from Captain Coldheart."

"Look, I don't like him anymore than you, but you can't let your hatred of him ruin your life. I am serious that you ought to start dating. There are several teenagers who have already asked if I could arrange a date for them with you."

"You know I cannot carry a conversation with another teenager. They talk about such shallow, meaningless fluff. And there is no way I will go on a blind date."

"Then how about going out with someone you already know. Zylar is only two years older than you and very smart."

Layla stumbled at the name but regained her balance. Zylar was Derrick's tagalong sidekick who had transferred from the Maintenance Department. "He dropped out of high school."

"Because he was bored. He really should have been placed in the gifted program."

"He is only gifted in one area—and that is not social skills."

"I know he gets longwinded when anyone mentions technology, but he is a nice guy."

"A little longwinded? He makes your husband look like a saint. If it was not for the fact that I can order him to go work on something else, he would keep the same conversation going all day. And besides, supervisors are not allowed to date subordinates."

"You could always have him transferred back to maintenance then date him."

"And deal with the wrath of Derrick? I think not."

"Actually Derrick was the one who suggested Zylar, and I promised I would mention him to you." They skated around several corners in silence before Rosetta spoke again. "Derrick and I have finally decided it is time for us to start a family."

Layla wobbled dangerously but remained upright. "You have wanted kids for years. What caused Derrick to change his mind?"

"He did not want to change diapers for seven kids all day then come home and do it again. Now that the quintessences are growing up, he felt it was time to become a dad."

"Be warned. Derrick never really changed diapers much. He and Zylar were always coming up with excuses to play with their machines."

"Derrick will make a good father. And some day you will make a good mother."

Layla did lose her balance this time and crashed to the payment, the safety pads she wore taking the blunt of the fall. After she regained her balance, they headed back to Advance Department where they spotted Derrick and Zylar taking boxes out of Anthony's hover truck. Both men looked excited.

"Uh, oh," whispered Rosetta. "It's some new machine. They have that gleam in their eyes."

As the women skated up, Derrick grinned, "You won't believe what Anthony is donating."

"I wish my grandfather was near as cool as him," said an ecstatic Zylar, wearing a T-shirt of two green aliens having a shootout. The Maintenance Department had not enforced the strict dress code that the other BGF departments did, and Zylar had brought the habit over with him. "Who knew the old man was so down with video games? I mean, this collection has some real classics like *Call of Death V* and *Bloodbath IV*."

"What are you talking about?" said Layla, gliding down the hallway after them and entering the breakroom.

As the men placed the boxes on the floor, Derrick said, "Anthony bought his grandkids a new Game Station 5000, and he is donating their old one to us."

"It is just a 4000," said Zylar, "but the games are still excellent. *Call of Dearth V* won many awards including Game of the Year and…"

Layla tuned Zylar out as she sat down in a chair to take off her skates. As she bent over to grab her shoes, she noticed the covers of several of the games in the box. All showed scenes of guns and violence. She picked up several of the cases to examine closer while Zylar spewed the detailed history of each game she held.

"Put these back in Anthony's vehicle. We cannot accept these."

"What?" said both men together.

"Send them back. They are too violent for children."

"They are classics," said Zylar. "Lots of kids play them."

"They teach kids to kill."

"Isn't that the point?" said Anthony, standing in the doorway.

Layla put on her other shoe. "I do not want them to play these games."

"You allow them to play chess."

"It is not bloody. These are graphic."

"They teach strategy, just like chess. The video games just increase the level of difficulty and prepares them for real life situations."

Layla held up *Call of Death V* which depicted solders fighting in a street with dead bodies lying about. "I do not want my quintessences fighting in a war. I did not create them so they could become pawns to be sacrificed so politicians can have more power. I want these games out of here now!"

Having never heard her yell before, everyone stared at Layla in surprise. Zylar was the first one who dared speak. "They are just games. I grew up playing them, and I turned out just fine."

Layla gave him a dark look before throwing the game at him and running out of the room, brushing pass Anthony.

"What did I say?" asked Zylar. "I mean, we don't really have to give them back, do we?"

Derrick sighed. "There are times when it's best for a man to remain silent. That was one of those times."

"I will go after her," said Rosetta. "She is just having a bad day."

"Does that mean we can keep the games?" asked Zylar hopefully as she left the room.

Rosetta found Layla in her lab, sitting at her desk, crying. Rosetta pulled up a chair and sat quietly by her friend.

After several minutes, Layla said, "I cannot take it anymore. I will not set back and watch him turn them into monsters. I am turning my resignation in to Palakkad tomorrow."

"Honey, you are just acting on emotions. That is not like you at all. You just need a good night's sleep."

"No, it has been like this for weeks. I cannot work with Captain Coldheart. He is taking my creations and twisting them into something I never intended."

"He is doing it to save them and this project."

"Well, he can have the project. He has wanted to be boss since he came here. I do not care anymore. I am through. I wash my hands of it all."

"Have you ever heard the story of Joash?"

"If that is one of your mythical stories, I am not in the mood."

"It does not matter if you believe the story is true or not. All good stories have a lesson to teach us. Joash was a seven-year-old boy who became a king due to the help of a kind priest. He was a great ruler, beloved by his people. Forty years later the priest died, and Josiah began making bad decisions. He fell into disgrace and eventually was killed by his own servants."

"This story is not making me feel better."

"There is a point. Joash represents your quintessences. As long as he had a moral mentor looking out for him, he made good decisions. Remove the mentor and there is no moral center. You and I are like the priest. Anthony teaches quintessences how to be soldiers but we teach them ethics. What do you think will happen if you walk away?"

"Anthony will take over and make them into mindless killers."

"Do you really want to abandon them? They need you. If you leave, then I will transfer back to Baby Department. Derrick and Zylar will then transfer. Leana, Opal, and the other caregivers will go next. No one will be left but Captain Coldheart and his goons. Is that what you wish for your creations?"

"No. I just want to protect them."

"Then protect them by staying. If the creator abandons the creation, hope itself is abandoned."

Layla closed her eyes, thinking. Softly she whispered, "Yet you, my creator, detest and spurn me, thy creature, to whom thou art bound by ties only dissoluble by the annihilation of one of us."

"Huh? I don't recognize that quote."

"It is from an ancient novel *Frankenstein*, which my brother gave me when we were kids." As Layla talked, she relaxed. "This doctor created a sentient by using dead body parts. Once he saw the ugliness of his creation, he abandoned it. The monster, who was gentle in nature, lived a solitary, lonely life. He tried to befriend humans, but they were afraid of him. Frustrated and misunderstood, the creation eventually turned to violence and killed his creator's bride. The creator and creation were at war with each other the rest of the novel."

"Now that is a tragic tale. I would hate to see it repeated in real life."

"So do I." Layla sighed. "Alright, you win. I will not abandon my quintessences, but I do not see how I can help them. Captain Coldheart has too much control over them."

"You are their creator. You have more influence than you realize."

Chapter Fourteen

A deep forest surrounded a vast, overgrown field broken by skeletons of half-fallen buildings. Creeping slowly through the tall grass and thickets moved a preteen, crouching, eyes alert. Two hundred yards away, a slight movement behind a broken windowpane attracted the boy's attention. He studied the landscape around the abandoned house, considering possible ambushes. Still keeping low, he moved to the right, keeping bushes between him and the house.

Out of the corner of his eye, he caught a quick movement. Instinctively he dropped to the ground and rolled. A flash of light ripped through the air above him and hit a tree. Before the boy touched the ground, he already had his own blaster aimed at the culprit. His beam caught the man between the eyes. A direct kill. Without slowing, Alexander rolled out of the way as another beam flew at him. Before he could lock his blaster on his next opponent, the man fell from a blast from behind. Through the bushes, Alexander spied a face identical to his. The other boy wore a camouflage outfit, the same as his own.

Alexander gestured with his hand, indicated the ruined house. Mason gave a brief nod and disappeared into the thick grass. Alexander continued his round about approach to the house. As he came within a hundred yards, he heard a distant blaster and saw flashing light somewhere to his far left. A thump indicated a body hitting the ground. Then silence. As Alexander moved closer to the house, his excitement mounted, for he was certain he had discovered target alpha's hideout. His slow movements and grim face hid his inter glee.

Fifty yards, forty, thirty. He was so close now. *Careful*, he reminded himself, *never let emotions control you.* There was movement near an old shed. He froze, waiting. Only Jacob. The other preteen gestured to him, and Alexander nodded, agreeing with the idea. He moved to his left towards the front of the building. There was little cover here. He crept around a bush then a rusty metal crate. A sudden blast of light caused him to duck. Right were his head had been, the crate gleamed silver. There was another flash of light and he rolled across the ground. Then he half-stood and dashed across the opening towards the nearest tree. More blast hit the ground on either side of him.

Logic told him the tree was too far away, and he expected to feel the heat of a laser any second.

Suddenly blasts came from the bushes off to his right, but the bolts were not aimed at him. Caleb and Gabriel were trying to draw fire away from him. Their blasts hit the broken window and the wall which protected their enemy. Their opponent ducked out of sight, allowing Alexander to reach the tree. Heart pounding, he flattened himself against the bark. More blasts came, this time from inside the house.

"All clear," came a loud voice over a megaphone.

Alexander stepped away from the tree. Caleb and Gabriel walked out of the bushes and headed towards the house. From a side door of the decayed building stepped Jacob and Mason. For a brief moment, Mason let a smile of victory flirt cross his lips, revealing to the others that he had fired the winning shot. Across the field, the dead men stood up and brushed themselves off. Laud applause burst from bystander setting on bleachers near the edge of the woods.

"Did you have to take me out so early?" complained Zylar. "I missed most of the fun."

"Then you should have chosen better cover than walking about under a barrel," said Calab.

"Hey, it worked in *Bloodbath IV*."

Derrick shook his head at his friend. "At least I almost made it to the end, but I have no clue which one of you shot me."

"That was me," said Jacob, face stoic, hiding the glee he felt. "Guard your flank next time."

Lunk stepped out of the ruined house. "Best fun I've had in years, though that was a dirty trick having one running about in front while two shot from the bushes. Then you two sneaking in behind me. I can't deal with five targets at the same time."

"Practice will improve your ability," said Gabriel, a slight curl of his lips indicating his amusement.

Many of the bystanders who had watched the training exercise walked into the field to congratulate the winners and joke with the losers. Several imperial officers dressed in full military uniforms were talking with Anthony and Palakkad.

"What do you think they're saying?" asked Zylar.

"That the fool in the barrel should really have been shot," said Rosetta, walking over and embracing her husband. "You look handsome when you're dead." She laid a hand on her swollen stomach. "Do you think your daddy makes a good soldier?"

Derrick put an ear to his wife's round tummy. "He says I am the best dad in the world, no matter if I am a soldier or a geek."

"Hey, they're coming over!" said Zylar. "Which one was the general again?"

"The tall one with the stars pinned on," said Rosetta. "I was sitting behind him the whole time. I think he was impressed with the show."

In front of the watching crowd, five quintessences lined up in a straight row, faces sober. The walking dead formed a loose circle and tried to look serious. General Colson and several of his aides walked up, followed by Anthony, Palakkad, and Layla. The quintessences saluted. The recently dead men tried to copy the gesture, but they failed to look impressive.

"At ease, soldiers," said General Colson, studying the preteens. "Five boys winning against twenty men. Well done. Captain Franklin, you have done an excellent job training them."

"The board members and I were pleased with the demonstration," said Palakkad, addressing the crowd. "I would like to thank everyone who was involved. Soldiers dismissed." He gave a clumsy salute which raised good-nature laughs from the crowd. The volunteer soldiers and onlookers began to head back to work. The quintessences remained in place, showing neither pride nor glee, waiting until Anthony personally dismissed them.

"I have read articles about them, but it is hard for me to believe these children are only four years old," said the general. "They look at least eleven, perhaps twelve."

"I added a rapid growth gene in their DNA," said Layla. "They are indeed four and a half years old."

"What is their expected lifespan?"

"It is unknown. If they keep growing at the same current speed, perhaps thirty years. But I included in their DNA triggers which are supposed to slow down the aging process as they mature. If it kicks in, they may live well over a hundred. We just do not know yet."

"I will admit this project has fascinated me since I read that article in *Galactic Times*. To create synthetic sentients is impressive. When my old war buddy Captain Franklin invited me to come, I could not pass up this opportunity to see them with my own eyes. Their military potential is intriguing. Still, I have many concerns. Are they mentally stable? Can they hold up under the pressure of a real battle? How well do they work with other sentients? In the heat of battle, a soldier must be able to trust his comrades.

We cannot put your experiments into a situation which might cost lives of real soldiers."

"We are concerned about this too," said Anthony. "They still need years of training. Eventually I would like to have them working with the police, perhaps on a SWAT team. Then we can observe how they respond in real-life situations."

"What is the estimated price tag for them?"

"A million credits apiece," said Layla.

"A million for one soldier? We can recruit and train several hundred soldiers for that price."

"We believe," said Palakkad, "that the final price will be far cheaper. Once we move out of beta testing, we can mass produce them."

"And how long will that be?"

"It will be some years yet. There is still much to learn about these five."

"Are you certain that you can make more that are exactly like this group?"

"BGF is renown throughout the galaxy for our cloned products. Our nano technology allows us to reproduce the exact genome as many times as we desire. In fact, I was talking with a few board members before the demonstration, and they believe we are ready to grow a new batch."

The general nodded in approval. "I would like to observe them in a younger stage. This project has caught the attention of Emperor Kalyuga, and he asked me to report my finding to him. Currently my advice will be to keep a watch-and-see attitude about your project. The benefit of a quickly grown army is tempting, but I don't see how your quintessences give us an advantage over using normal soldiers. Plus the price tag would have to come down sharply."

Anthony said, "Give the quintessences a few more years to mature. I believe you will be pleased with the final results. They still have talents yet to be discovered."

Palakkad asked, "How about a tour of Advance Department? Layla Rangan, their creator, can explain the entire process to you."

Layla, who never liked speaking in front of groups, felt uncomfortable guiding the general and his aides through her building which was more a home to her than her own apartment. They asked many questions, and she feared boring them with too many technical details. It did not help matters when Derrick went into a long speech about how the Nanotech DNA Builder worked. Still, they listened politely. After the tour, Palakkad invited Anthony and the general out for dinner. Layla was relieved to see them drive away.

"Whew, I can finally sit down," said Rosetta as they headed back into the building. "The general was really impressed."

"I do not know if I should be happy or upset," said Layla.

"Happy. Not only did the board not pull the funding, but they want you to grow another generation." She touched her large stomach. "It's a good thing I am already pregnant or Derrick would have used this as an excuse to again delay having our own."

"No, he really wants to be a father. Even I can see his pride in becoming a dad."

Loud talking down the hallway drew the women's attention. Through the large glass window of the game room, the women could see Derrick and Zylar sitting on a couch playing video games against several quintessences. When Layla had said that the Game Station 4000 could stay, the men had gone out of their way to turn the playroom into a geek's fantasy haven. They collected a dozen old flat screens, hung them on a wall, and synced them to work together, in effect, creating a gigantic room-size screen. Then they wired numerous speakers throughout the room, bragging that their sound system was better than the one used by the local cinema in town. When Rosetta had complained that she could hear their games all the way out in the parking lot, the men took that as a compliment.

"This is the best job in the world," bragged Zylar, not realizing his boss was watching through the observation window. "Where else can you get paid to play video games and they call it military training? Ouch, who just shot me? Now I have to find new body armor."

Derrick replied, "Sorry about that, but you did have your gun pointed at me."

"We are on the same team. I don't shoot you unless you shoot me first—which you just did." He fired a shot which barely missed Derrick's character.

Alexander said, "Will your team be obliterating itself or will this be an actual competition?"

"Hey, we are just getting our bearings. Give us a moment."

The characters of Mason and Alexander sprinted about the virtual city landscape, grabbing weapons and planting bombs while avoiding the human team.

"Are you hiding on purpose?" said a frustrated Zylar. "I haven't had the chance to fire one shot."

"We were waiting till you gain your bearings," replied Mason.

"Well, we're ready for some action now." Zylar regretted those words five seconds later when a red screen indicted the game was over. "What happened? I was just standing in the courtyard and suddenly I'm dead. There wasn't a shot fired!"

"I detonated a remote mine," said Alexander.

"I was checking the ground and didn't see a mine," said Derrick

"I planted it inside the fountain."

"You can do that? That's a dirty trick," complained Zylar.

"You knew that mines were a possible weapon," said Mason. "You should have spread out your forces instead of standing out in the open together. If the game had not ended, then you would have been hit by my grenade rocket."

"Now that the game is over," said Rosetta, "it's time for the real soldiers to train and the boys to work."

"We'll just getting started. One more round," begged Zylar.

Layla marched into the room. "You were not hired to play games. The board just approved the growing of ten new quintessences. We have a lot of work to do."

"About time," said Derrick, passing his controller to Gabriel. "I will warm up Anya, and you will finally get to see the X1800 in action."

Zylar jumped up eagerly. "Alright. This is the best day ever. I've died twice and now I get to see nanos making life. What better job is there?"

Rosetta whispered to Layla, "I can understand why you passed on dating Zylar. Good choice."

It took nearly two weeks to create the new genomes in the NDB, then the eggs had to be incubator for a week before being placed in the AFD. Derrick and Zylar found their skills pushed to the limit in attempting to keep Anya running in top condition. Mera announced a donation drive for baby supplies, which drew assistance from many BGF workers. Layla carefully recorded the progress of each fetus. Like the previous generation, they grew rapidly and at two months old, they looked like four-month-old humans fetuses.

"Are you ready?" Leana stood in the doorway of Layla's lab.

"Yes, send them in."

Leana walked into the room followed by the preteen quintessences. The youth stood in a straight line, silently taking in the details of the lab where they had been created but rarely visited. Leana pointed to the various equipment and asked the preteens to identify it. Layla then explained each machine's function. Finally, Leana pointed to Anya.

"It is a quintessence grower," said Jacob.

"That is the purpose of the Automatic Fetus Developer which we call AFD, though you may hear Derrick call it Anya. Come closer. What do you see?"

Obediently, the preteens stepped near the machine and studied the glass tubes housing the fetuses. Several of the boys reached out and touched the glass.

"They are your brothers, the same as you except for size. As they grow up, they will need you to look out for them and teach them what you have already learned."

"We will protect our brothers," said Caleb, watching a fetus wiggle its tiny fingers.

Derrick's voice boomed down the hallway, "She's here!"

Layla asked, "Do you know who we are expecting today?"

Three preteens responded at the same time, "Rosetta is bringing her son."

Rosetta had been absent several weeks on maternity leave. After the baby was born, Derrick had posted pictures in the breakroom and bragged constantly about his son's latest antics. Today Rosetta was stopping by to show co-workers the baby for the first time. Leana led the quintessences down the hallway to the breakroom which served as both kitchen and cafeteria. Several workers had already gathered around the proud couple and the baby.

Rosetta beckoned the preteens close to her child and said, "This is my son Allan Cashman." The quintessences studied the child closely, and several touched the baby's hands.

"Where are his brothers?" asked Gabriel.

"He does not have brothers yet."

"He will be lonely," said Caleb.

"Are we to be his brothers?" asked Alexander.

"He will like playing with you when he gets older, but he is not your brother. He will be different from you because he is human. He will grow slower and be more fragile."

"Like Miguel. We will protect him too, like our own brothers," said Mason.

Derrick glanced at the wall clock. "Layla, didn't that administration meeting start five minutes ago?"

Layla dashed out of the room and sped to the main building in her hover car. She had to circle through the parking lot twice before finding a place to park. She hurried upstairs to the meeting. It had already started, and she slipped into her seat inconspicuously as possible, wondering why Anthony was speaking.

"Those are my plans for Stage Two. I have already spoken with the county prison, and they are in agreement. The prisoners who volunteer will receive a deduction of up to half off their original jail sentence, depending on how well they cooperate. There will be prison guards on duty so our own security staff does not have to be involved."

"Why do you need prisoners for Stage Two?" asked Layla.

"If you had been here on time, then you would have known that Stage Two involves testing the quintessence's epulo attack."

Layla paled. "My quintessences are not about to be used as a tool for capital punishment against helpless prisoners that are being lured here by telling them they will receive a sentence deduction!"

Anthony sighed. "You are forming assumptions without being fully informed. As I explained earlier, the quintessences believe that the epulo attack doesn't have to be fatal. The prisoners know exactly what is going on and have volunteered for the training exercises."

Banican said, "Why would anyone volunteer to have their life energy sucked from them?"

Layla looked at Banican in shock, life suddenly taking a bizarre twist as she found herself on the same side as her archenemy.

Anthony explained, "Believe it or not, there are prisoners who prefer running around outdoors playing laser tag with kids than sitting for years in a barren jail cell. Some will actually find it fun. Stage Two does involve a lot more than just practicing the epulo attack."

Palakkad said, "I have already spoken with the warden, and he finds the experiment appealing. He believes we will have no trouble finding volunteers, though the prisoners will have to be screened to exclude the more volatile ones."

You had already spoken to the warden! Layla clenched her fists but kept her frustration to herself. Anthony had gone over her head and planned all of this in secret with Palakkad. This staff meeting was just a formal announcement of what had already been decided, and nothing she said was going to change anything.

Banican tried several arguments against it, including claiming he did not want to work anywhere near convicts, but Anthony countered every argument. Layla left the meeting in a fury, refusing to slow down and talk to Mera who tried to calm her. Once in her hover car, Layla speeded off BGF grounds and randomly zoomed down country roads. Only when her low fuel light came on did she head back. She stormed through Advance Department looking for Anthony.

"He has taken the quintessences out to train," said Zylar playing a video game against Derrick.

"Of course he would be training them! Why are you playing games at work? Turn that off and go do…some real work." Layla slammed the door on her way out.

"What did I do this time?"

"Nothing. Women get that way sometimes. Come on, let's clean out the leftovers in the breakroom. I think there was some pie left."

Layla marched into the woods. It took her half an hour to find Anthony high up in a tree stand, holding a stopwatch while barking orders at quintessences climbing up twenty-foot ropes. "How dare you go over me! I am department head, not you. You had no right to decide to use live prisoners without asking me first!"

The captain looked down at her. "Lass, I knew you were too close-minded to consider it, so I went directly to Palakkad. Jacob, you're slowing down. Come on, keep going."

"These are my quintessences, and I know what is best for them. If you ever go over my head again, I will have you fired."

"You don't have the authority to fire me, only Palakkad." The elderly man studied her with stern eyes. "I'm the one who is saving your precious project, youngling. If I had not agreed to train them as soldiers, it would have been terminated long ago. As for who knows what is best for quintessences, you don't know your creations nearly as much as you think you do. They enjoy this training. Do you really think they want to sit around all day playing board games? This is what they were made to do. The hunt. The battle."

Layla's hands clenched into fists. The five quintessences had all dropped back to the ground and stood by their ropes, silently looking at her. Did they actually like these harsh physical exercises that Anthony pushed upon them? Surely not. How could anyone like it? Unable to think of a response, Layla turned and marched back to Advance Department.

She retreated to her lab, the one place she still had control. She wished Rosetta was here to talk with, but the new mother had already headed home. Layla sulked and muttered to herself for a while then tried to organize embryo data into a chart. Nothing made her feel better. A knock at the door caused her to look up. One of the quintessences stood there, watching her with solemn eyes.

"I thought you were training."

"We are finished. Would you like to play a game of chess?"

Layla was caught off guard. Usually she just observed caregivers interacting with quintessences while she stood on the other side of the glass and took notes. Never had one asked her directly to play before. "Uh, sure."

She followed Alexander down the hallway to the game room where several of the preteens were playing *Call of Blood V*. Layla tried to ignore the game as she sat down. Alexander turned on the digital board and setup the game. They played several minutes in silence.

When Layla lost on her sixth turn, Alexander said, "Your mind is not on the game."

"I am upset. That is all."

Alexander setup a new game. "When you and Captain Franklin argue, everyone is miserable. You should make peace."

"He is wrong in what he does."

"How?"

"You are too young to understand."

The preteen looked at her with serious, keen eyes. "You underestimate us. It is your turn."

Layla moved a pawn forward. "Are you saying that Anthony is right? That I do not understand you?"

"You only understand what you see, but much goes on which is unseen." He slid a bishop into a direct line with her queen.

Layla moved a knight. "What is going on that I do not see?"

"One, you exposed your most powerful piece." His bishop captured her queen. "Second, it was we who approached Captain Franklin and asked to begin Stage Two. We told him we wanted to test the epulo ability."

"It was your idea? Why are you wanting to kill innocent prisoners who never did you wrong?"

"If they were innocent, why are they in prison? Do not worry. There will be no killing. We are certain we can control the attack. We will not harm them."

"What if they harm you? They are hardened criminals."

"A moment ago you worried we would kill them, now you worry that they will kill us."

"Look, it is just a bad idea using prisoners. Why do you want to try out that epulo thing?"

"To learn what we can do. You designed us. Do you not want us to understand ourselves?"

"Not at the cost of your lives."

"We will be careful. No one will be harmed." He slid his queen near her king.

"How can you be certain?"

"We just are. Checkmate."

Layla looked at her trapped king. She had not seen the attack coming.

Alexander turned off the game. "Dinner time."

He and the other quintessences stood and walked out of the room, leaving Layla wondering what other unseen things were happening right in front of her.

Part II

Creation

"He had come forth from the hands of God a perfect creature, happy and prosperous, guarded by the especial care of this Creator; he was allowed to converse with, and acquire knowledge from, beings of a superior nature; but I was wretched, helpless, and alone."

—From *Frankenstein* by Mary Shelley

Chapter Fifteen

Elegant skyscrapers filled the city skyline of the capitol city of Edieth. Each building had its own park with hundreds of trees and flowers growing on terraces built into the sides of the massive buildings. Small mammals leaped among the branches, heedless of the chasmal drop to the streets far below. Birds nabbed berries and insects to take to their growing nestlings. One vast structure rose higher than the others, its oval gold dome gleaming in the sunshine.

Roobaroo stood by an office window, looking out over the city where her parents had been born then exiled from.

"You stare too much at the High Council Forum," said a youthful male ediethean, moving to stand beside Roobaroo. Like all Alz, he was tall with an angular face and slim body.

She casually took a step back. "I never tire of the sight. It is the most beautiful building of them all."

"It is a shame that you will never be invited to become a member, with your family background." Ceroon pretended to feel pity. "Perhaps with the right union, you might find yourself married to a council member someday."

"I doubt that, as my parents are not here to make such an arrangement." Roobaroo turned away to stack files on her desk, keeping distance between herself and the flirting male. Roobaroo had treated him coldly since she first began working as an aide to a minor city official, but Cerron was determined to gain her attention, perhaps because of her high IQ, extreme even for an Alz. When it came to ediethean marriages, genes were everything. The higher the IQ, the greater the prestige.

"Pity. My parents are comfortable communicating by video conference with business partners on other worlds. Your parents could chat with mine anytime. Did I mention that our boss is considering promoting me to assistant?"

Roobaroo tried to hide her irritation. "Where you sent here to chat or pass along an assignment?"

Cerron looked disappointed. "The boss wants you to find a way to catch latrats humanly. They're overrunning Orion Park. Personally, I say we should kill them all, but he is worried about public opinion."

"You want me to catch rodents?"

"Not you personally, of course. Go talk to an exterminator. See how much it cost to relocate them." Cerron headed for the door then paused. "How about going to a restaurant with me tonight?"

"We are unmarried. How dare you even ask. Just because I grew up off world does not mean I act like a heathen."

He grinned at her offended expression. "My parents could change your single status."

"I will begin calling exterminators immediately." Roobaroo turned her back to him and pulled out her telecom. She was relieved to hear him leave.

After several calls, she got a text message. At first she thought it was one of the exterminators, until she read the last line. "Meet at Orion Park in one hour by fountain. Your hunt has met its scorpion." Roobaroo's heart quickened. The last line was an allusion to an ancient Earth myth which middle caste workers would be ignorant of. Could it be contact with the insurgents, after all these years of searching? If so, then the reference to *scorpion* was a warning that her quest would end tragically. She had always believed it would, yet she still needed to see the truth.

Roobaroo headed towards the elevator, pausing by Cerron's office to tell him she was meeting an exterminator. She took a subway across the city and exited near a popular park. Ancient trees cast deep shadows over the sidewalks. Several latrats leaped among the branches, while others closely watched picnickers, looking for an opportunity to steal food. Groups of Hym children too young for school dashed about in play, watched by caregivers. Their mid-caste moms should be laboring in factories at this time of the day, the only job allowed for Hym. Roobaroo moved deeper into the park and sat on a bench near the large fountain displaying a stone stature of the leader of the first colony to settle another planet. She studied the stone figure spewing water endlessly. He would have lived nearly eight thousand years ago. Many had followed his example, colonizing dozens of worlds, turning them into thriving copies of Edieth.

Several minutes later a Cuy sat on her bench and bent over to tie his shoe. Without looking at her, he said, "Follow me, huntress, but keep your distance."

He stood and walked causally along a path. Roobaroo waited till he was nearly thirty feet away then followed. He turned a corner. When she made it to the spot he had vanished, she spotted him disappearing behind some bushes. Once she reached the shrubs, he was no longer in sight, and there was no more paved path. She looked about, afraid she had lost him. Then she noticed a narrow dirt path through the shrubs. She moved along it, thorns snagging her stylish cloak. Fifteen steps into the bramble, she saw a small, earth-covered shed, the last remnant of an ancient, abandoned subway system. Its door was slightly ajar. Roobaroo pushed it open and stepped into a dimly lit entrance, cracked stone stairs beckoning her downward. Carefully she closed the door behind her and descended into darkness, her telecom the only source of light. When she reached the bottom, a large chamber opened up. An orange lantern dimly lit the central area, casting the rest of the huge room into deep shadows.

The Cuy sat on a crate in the middle of the chamber, his face a bit wider than hers, his height slightly shorter. She moved across the chamber, her feet kicking up dust. When she neared, he gestured for her to sit across from him.

The Cuy studied her with keen eyes. "Call me Hunter. Your quest is treacherous. Are you sure, Alz, that you wish to continue?"

"My parents' quest became mine. We seek truth, no matter where it leads us."

"It has already led you to strange places including the Coalition's university for their abominations."

"You have been studying me."

"Do you think we take it lightly, meeting with an Alz? We have monitored your communication for months, seeking if your request was genuine."

At the mention of the word *we*, his eyes glanced briefly into the darkness, and Roobaroo's tension increased. Anyone could be watching them with weapons aimed at her.

She forced herself to relax. "You are right to mistrust my caste, but I am not like them. Alz believe our super intelligent gives us the right to control all aspects of the other castes' lives. Yet I have visited worlds where things are different, planets where small groups of our species live alongside other sentients. There some of the Council's rules are lax. I learned that society does not collapse when a Hym decides to work as a florist instead of a laborer."

"What did you learn at the university of abomination?"

"That the profectus are very much like Alz, indoctrinated from youth to believe they are destined to lead their species. Some are as arrogant as my kind, while others are decent, willing to befriend those that are different."

Fire reflected in Hunter's dark eyes. "You were only allowed to come to Edieth because some Councilors of religious zeal believed you were an instrument of divine wrath causing the plague which affected the abominations. They complained that more should have died."

Roobaroo flinched and looked away. "Those are cruel words. The one who died was my friend."

"Your grief looks genuine, Alz. Perhaps a few of you have hearts after all."

"You would like my parents if you met them. They have sacrificed much in seeking truth. Have you found what they sought which led to their exile?"

"Your parents should have been more careful whom they trusted. Betrayed by a close friend. They were only spared execution because of their high IQ's and powerful family linage. Having ancestors on the Council will not save you. If you do not tread carefully, the Council will see your line as contaminated and vote to eradicate it."

Roobaroo leaned forward. "I am not afraid. Show me."

"Give me your telecom." Hunter pulled out an encrypted data stick and plugged it into her device. He navigated through several menus, entered a code, and then gave the device back.

She took a deep breath before looking at the screen. It was an official document containing the Council's seal at the top. Below was a long list naming all who were executed within the same month. Information including age, gender, and crime. Heart pounding, Roobaroo scrolled down till she came to the D's. The data read, "Perelaandra Dayal, age five, female, a Byk throwback."

"You expected this," said Hunter, his voice gentle.

Roobaroo's hand shook. "Yes. My parents were officially told she was being relocated to suit her IQ. Other parents want to believe their children are placed in adopted families of the proper caste. But we both know edietheans do not adopt children unless they are relatives."

"Were you close to your sister?"

"Yes…and no. They took her away years before I was born, but she has lived with me all my life. From the way my parents raised me, to my decision to come to Edieth was because of Perelaandra. She only scored two points below the line for Alz when they tested her the second time. My parents begged for more time, claiming as she grew older, her IQ would climb. But the police came anyway and drag her away, screaming my mom's name. My parents still grieve for her. It became their fire, making them question all they had been taught." Roobaroo's voice trembled as she became emotional. "Perelaandra was smarter than nine-tenths of all sentients in the galaxy. On many worlds she would have been seen as a brilliant, capable child. But because she underperformed what her birthright called for, she was killed. How is this right?"

Hunter leaned forward, eyes intense. "There are many atrocities which our esteem High Council is guilty of, but the Galactic Senate turns a blind eye because Alz weld much of its power. The Council is untouchable, or so they believe. My comrades and I seek to change that. You can join us. You would be the first Alz to turn against their own."

Roobaroo looked down at her sister's name. "Your methods only annoy the Council while changing nothing. Spray painting insults or hacking newsfeed makes you only look like pranksters, easily ignored."

"That is what the Council wants you to believe. They cover up many things we do, but they cannot do so forever. Insurgents have been around as long as the Council has existed. They try to silence our voices the moment we disagree, but if enough of us yell, we can wake up our sleeping society."

"I will help you if it does not involve breaking the law. My parents believe the best way to make permanent changes is from the inside. If I can climb high enough in political circles, I can use my influence to change attitudes, which in turn, will change laws."

"Fine dreams, but Alz and the other high castes do not want change. They like power and comfort. I should know, being a Cuy. I have seen the poison within my family. My father manages a Yaz sweatshop. There I have witnessed barbarous acts which would be called crimes in any other society. Our kind will not change unless forced to."

Roobaroo stood. "Thank you for this information. I will send it on to my parents."

"Beware. If caught with it, you will be charged with espionage."

"I will be careful." She turned, telecom in hand, treading through the darkness, alone, seeking the exit. Her soul lit with righteous vengeance. She would never forget or forgive what the Council had done to her sister.

Chapter Sixteen

Across the huge, overgrown field of ruined buildings Alexander spied the crowd of bystanders sitting on bleachers. The director of BGF sat beside General Colson and Captain Anthony Franklin. Nearby the warden of the county prison chatted with the police commissioner of Austin City. Each official was here to scrutinize the performance of the quintessences. Alexander kept his face stoic, hiding the tension he felt. The future of his entire species depended on winning this competition. Across the labyrinth field hid thirty-five highly trained officers from the Austin Police Department.

Alexander swept his keen eyes further down the crowded bleachers. Many of the caregivers had come to watch including Opal and Leana. Beside Rosetta and Derrick sat their three year old son, wiggling with impatience. Zylar made silly faces to entertain little Allen. Contrasting the cheerful crowd sat ten silent, solemn kids, each with a face mirroring his companions. The second generation of quintessences had followed in their older brothers' footsteps in both behavior and appearance. Alexander focused on the woman sitting beside the last child. It was her, his creator, sitting aloof from the crowd, that he and his brothers wanted to impress the most.

A buzzer sounded, announcing the beginning of the event. Alexander glanced at Jacob on his right and Mason to his left. Like him, they were dressed in camouflage and wore an electronic belt which monitored when they were hit by laser shots. To onlookers, they looked like eighteen-year-old humans, but they had only been alive for seven years.

The five brothers fanned out, keeping low to the ground. Though they were often out of sight of the others, each was constantly aware of his nearest neighbors' locations. Communicating through silent gestures, they warned each other about sentry posts. The first dozen guards were ambushed easily from shots taken through thick brush, but as quintessences worked deeper into the field, their opponents concealed themselves in ruined buildings. Great care had to be taken to avoid being seen while approaching near enough to take out the targets. Halfway across the field, they reached their first snag. Three opponents were inside a small house, each stationed by a window facing a different direction. The quintessences could not approach without being seen in the low grass near the building. One of their own would need to be sacrificed to break the stronghold. Gabriel made a wild dash across the clearing, shooting as he ran. By the time he was taken out, Alexander and Mason had slipped past the western guard and entered the house through a back door. Moments later, their three opponents lay on the dirt floor.

Ignoring Gabriel lying on the ground, the four remaining quintessences continued to tread cautiously across the field. The final stronghold was a small, roofless warehouse where two sentinels on the second floor had a clear view of a large area. Three others guarded the bottom floor. With difficulty, Alexander gained the front wall without being shot. He flattened himself against the concrete wall and crept along it to a window. Several inches above his head, a tip of a blaster protruded through the broken window pane. Alexander waited until the owner of the gun started firing at Jacob who had made a dash for the wall. Then Alexander partly stood and shot through the window, hitting the surprised man in the chest. Another guard inside shot at Alexander, but the youth ducked out of the way. Jacob reached the wall and crouched down beside him. The two brothers gestured out a new plan to Caleb and Mason, watching carefully from the bushes.

Alexander crept along the wall to a rusty door. He kicked it in then rolled inside. At the same time, Jacob stood and fired several shots through the broken window into the building. Caleb and Mason dashed across the clearing to the warehouse. With so many things happening at once, the guards had a difficult time choosing who to shoot at. Alexander managed to hit one officer by another window before he heard his belt buzz, announcing he had been shot and officially out of the competition. Jacob had managed to take out the third guard on the first floor while Caleb and Mason gained the safety of the outside wall. Alexander was forced to remain motionless on the dirty, cracked floor while Caleb and Mason walked over his body and headed up the rickety metal stairs to the second floor. Alexander's hands twitched in impatience. He wanted to rush up the stairs behind his brothers, but the rules of the contest stated that just one wound counted as a kill though Alexander believed the injury would have barely slowed him in a real battle.

From the corner of his eye, Alexander saw Jacob climbing up the half collapsed fire escape on the outside of the building. Caleb and Mason drew fire when they reached the top of the stairs, while Jacob easily took out the final two guards from behind. A bullhorn sounded, announcing the end of the contest. Alexander and the guards picked themselves off the dirty floor.

One brawny man gave Alexander a pat on the shoulder. "Good job, son. I didn't believe you would have made it halfway here."

"Think he is SWAT material, Sergeant Khan?" asked another officer.

"Just might be. I will suggest to the police commissioner to invite you to the boot camp we have for our trainees. Your buddies work extremely well together."

"We look forward to the opportunity," said Alexander, pleased.

He walked outdoors and joined his brothers standing in front of the cheering crowd on the bleachers. Gabriel, who had to walk across half the field, was the last to arrive. As Alexander lined up with his brothers, he scanned the crowd and spotted twelve people who did not join in the cheering: his ten younger brothers, Banican, and her—Layla. Sometimes Alexander thought his creator could have made a decent quintessence herself with her emotionless aloofness.

Anthony quieted the crowd. "The quintessences have one more demonstration they wish to show you. Please, no moving until it is finished."

Alexander and Gabriel stepped forward. Anthony handed Alexander a sharp knife then walked over to stand beside a prisoner from the local jail. The crowd watch in bewildered silence as Gabriel held an arm out and Alexander made a quick, deep slice across it with the knife. Blood immediately poured out of the cut and pooled on the ground. The crowd gasped. The ten younger quintessences leaned forward, eyes intense. The calm prisoner walked over, and Gabriel swiftly bit him on the upper back of the neck. Before the crowd even realized what was happening, Gabriel straightened up and the prisoner walked away. Gabriel held out his arm again. No more blood spilled from it. Anthony tossed him a rag, and Gabriel wiped off the wet blood from his arm. Then he held his arm up high over his head. There was not a mark on it. The crowd went wild in delight.

The five older quintessences scanned the crowd. General Colson, Sergeant Khan, and various officers began animated conversations. Quick healing was a useful skill in the midst of a battle. Several BGF board members swooped towards Palakkad. The crowd broke apart, and many approached the quintessences to congratulate them or ask questions. Banican silently made his way out of the thinning throng and headed back to his department, disturbed by what he had witnessed. The ten young quintessences sat silently, waiting for a command from a caretaker. Derrick and Zylar collected money from another co-worker who had lost a bet against them. Rosetta carefully guided her son down the bleachers, her swollen stomach revealing a second child on the way.

It was not for these that the quintessences scrutinized the crowd. It was her, their creator, who they sought. They looked for just one smile or nod of acceptance from her. There was none. She sat stiff, pale, with hands clenched.

Their creator had not been impressed with their victory or the skill of healing which she had designed them with.

A few hours later, the breakroom at Advance Department was crowded with celebrating staff. The ten younger quintessences sat in mismatched chairs and quietly ate white-frosted cake while their older brothers scattered around the room talking with the humans. Both quintessences and their caregivers sensed that today's test had been a passage from youth into adulthood for the quintessences.

"That thing with the healing was way cool. Wish I could learn that trick," said Zylar stuffing his mouth with a piece of Leana's cake. "A woman beside me almost fainted."

"Could it have been done with less bloodshed? Far too graphic," complained Leana.

"It would not have been as effective," said Gabriel without a hint of boasting.

The ten young quintessences finished their dessert, rose as one, and headed toward the game room. Little Allan tried to follow, but his mom grabbed him.

Rosetta wiped icing off her son's sticky mouth. "It will soon be time to go home. Do you want to play a few more minutes?"

"I stay. You go home."

"No, you will come home with us. You have fifteen minutes."

The boy crossed his arms and pouted. "I quintish. I stay with brothers."

Derrick called out. "Let him stay. We'll get a decent night's sleep, and the night shift can enjoy bringing him water every two hours. "

Rosetta placed hands on hips. "Derrick Cashman, I am ashamed of you. He is our son and you don't help matters when you keep treating him like a quintessence."

"Well, he practically grew up with them. He still doesn't understand what a human is."

"I quintish. I quintish," chanted the three-year as he ran down the hallway to the game room.

Zylar elbowed Derrick. "Your son will go down in some physiology textbook as the first human diagnosed with quintessence disillusionment. He will be famous."

Rosetta shot Zylar a dirty look.

"Fifty new ones ordered," said Mera in a corner chatting with several caregivers. "I am not sure you will have enough room for them all."

Leana shook her head. "It is hard enough having fifteen. The older group study in the morning and the younger ones in the afternoon. But there is not enough space for fifty desks or beds."

As the chatter continued, Layla slipped out of the crowded room and headed down the hallway. Only the quintessences noticed her leaving and guessed she would be going to her lab, the refuge where she spent most of her day, only coming out for meals or to collect data. Since Stage Two had begun three years ago, Layla had remained detached from the day-to-day activities of Advance Department. Rosetta supervised the caregivers while Derrick and Zylar dealt with maintenance and technical problems. Layla rarely interacted with the older quintessences and avoided Anthony altogether.

Alexander caught the eyes of his brothers. They knew each other so well that simply a look was enough to pass on a volume of information between them. Something had to be done to bridge the gap between themselves and their creator. Alexander sat down his empty plate and went to the game room where younger quintessences quietly played video and board games. Zylar was attempting to talk Allan into giving up his controller, but the three year old squealed loudly each time Zylar reached for it. Alexander walked through the cluttered room to a shelf and took down an old-fashioned chessboard made from wood. He left the room, headed down the hallway to the laboratory, and knocked on the door.

From inside came Layla's voice. "I'm busy. Unless someone is dying, go away."

Alexander opened the door and studied his creator sitting at a desk, head bent over her e-tablet. "I thought perhaps you would like to play chess. Technically, whoever loses the game dies."

For a moment, it looked like she was going to say no, but instead Layla put her computer in sleep mode and followed him into the hallway. Alexander headed outdoors instead of the game room. He wanted no witnesses to the conversation. He set up the chessboard on a picnic table. At the request of caregivers, a picnic area along with a playground had been built by Derrick and Zylar at the edge of the forest. Layla sat across from him, providing opportunity for Alexander to study her closely. Now twenty-two, Layla's youthful Asiatic face could easily pass for eighteen. Any stranger passing by could have thought them both the same age.

They played several minutes in silence. Alexander avoided a quick win. "You are displeased with the demonstration."

"I never said that."

"You do not have to say the words. We can see it."

"Alexander, I am glad you won and now get to join a SWAT team. And we have an order for fifty babies. It gives me plenty of work to do."

"Why does the epulo bite disturb you?"

"Why?" Anger flashed in Layla's eyes. "Did you enjoy slicing your brother? I thought you cared about each other."

"We would die to protect each other. The cut was not life threatening. We decided that a bleeding injury would be the most effective way to demonstrate our healing ability."

"Was it Anthony who ordered you to do it?"

"No, I volunteered just like Gabriel did. It made no difference who did the cutting or was cut. We were all in agreement. Why are you really angry? You knew we practiced the epulo."

"I was not informed you would be cutting each other in front of a large crowd. If this is what you do in public, what horrid experiments happen in private?"

"It was not a secret. If you had asked about our training, we would have told you."

"Well, I am asking now."

"We do a lot of physical training, pushing ourselves. There is still much we do not know about ourselves. Like what are our limits? How effective is the epulo for healing more serious wounds? We have learned a great deal, though."

Layla swallowed. "How serious have your wounds been?"

"Caleb broke a leg. It took less than two minutes to heal."

"When did Caleb break a leg?"

"Over a year ago when he jumped off a small cliff."

"He jumped off a cliff! Why would Anthony order him to do that?"

"No one ordered him to jump. We all did it. He just landed wrong. You designed us with superior bone structure. We wanted to test what that meant."

"Are you crazy? Only a fool puts themselves in danger on purpose."

"Are firefighters and police officers fools?"

"I did not mean it that way. Commonsense says you should not put yourself in danger needlessly. You did not jump off the cliff to save anyone."

"No, but someday we might need to jump out of a building to save somebody. We now know it can be done, along with the risks that come with it. Is it not better to know what you can do before a dangerous situation arises, than try to figure it out in the midst of a crisis?"

Layla sighed, "I do not understand you at all. You are both cautious and reckless at the same time. Do you enjoy risking your life?"

Alexander studied her for a long moment. "You are not ready for the answer yet."

"What do you mean? That you enjoy the hunt? You want to kill people?"

"You might as well ask a wolf why he leaps upon the charging moose or the falcon why he dives a hundred and eighty miles per hour to grab a tiny mouse. You will get the same answer. That is what we are created to do. How many predatory DNA did you use in our design?"

"Sixty-six, but my goal was not for you to be predators. I gave you the intellect to choose who you want to be. You do not have to be soldiers."

"We are what our DNA makes us. Our predatory instinct is strong and our minds allow us to fine-tune it. We can distinguish between friends and foes, between friendly and hostile targets. A lion may rip apart its prey but be gentle with its cubs. We understand the difference."

"When I designed you, I was trying to create a superior being who would be peaceful and smart. Then Anthony takes that all away, forcing you to be soldiers."

"Anthony never forced us. We wanted to be soldiers. It fits our personality. You made us superior warriors who can handle extreme environments. We can survive what others cannot."

Layla looked at the chessboard. Neither had made a move in a long time. "I did not want others to hurt you, and now you are the ones hurting yourself. There are so many who want to take advantage of you. I have been trying to protect you, but you are running headlong into danger."

"We do not want to be kept safe. We were created for challenges. There are two great desires we have: to be what we were designed to be and to please our creator. So far, these desires have been in conflict with each other."

"I…I will try to be more supportive of you. That is difficult for me because…you will be killed sooner or later in battle. It is easier for me to…to…"

"Stay in your lab and shut the world out. We are not as fragile as you think. Trust us. Our foes will find us a force to be reckon with."

Chapter Seventeen

Thick forests concealed five quintessences practicing bōjutsu. Their movements were clumsy as they swung long sticks at each other while attempting to avoid return strikes. They had only recently begun learning the ancient martial art by picking up tips from one of their SWAT team members. During downtimes between raids, Seit Tigon had shown them several basic techniques.

Jacob dodged a blow by Gabriel, only to be accidently hit by the tip of Alexander's staff. Jacob complained, "We need proper lessons."

"That is difficult to do," said Gabriel, ducking a blow, "since no one at BGF knows bōjutsu, not even Captain Franklin."

"There is a martial arts school in Austin City which Seit attends. If we could be stationed in the city, we could attend the school." Mason stood on the sideline, waiting for his rotation to have a partner.

"She will never allow it." Jacob dropped to the ground then rolled to avoid Gabriel's attack.

"She might if we explained what we wanted to learn." Gabriel managed to land a blow against Jacob's side.

Still on the ground, Jacob grunted as the stick hit, then swiped his staff against Gabriel's legs, causing his brother to fall. "She wants nothing to do with us bettering ourselves."

"She is trying to be more open-minded." Alexander deflected a thrust.

"Will she be open-minded enough to allow us to move to the city?" asked Caleb, pushing his staff against Alexander's weapon.

"I think not. She is concerned enough with the time we spend with the SWAT team now." Alexander pushed back against his brother, and his tree limb broke. They both lost their balance and fell.

Mason looked at his four brothers on the ground. "We need proper lessons and proper weapons. If we explained to her what we are really capable of, she may trust us more, allow us to live away from here."

Alexander sat up. "She is not ready for such knowledge."

"She holds on too tightly. Is this from fear or pride?" asked Caleb.

"Guessing human emotions is useless. We should find out for certain what she thinks," said Mason.

"She will think we are attacking her." Jacob rose and dusted himself off. "We will have to explain it to her first."

"We can wipe her memory afterwards," suggested Mason.

Alexander stood. "She is our creator. It would be wrong."

"If we do this, then she must be made to understand. There will be no going back." Caleb looked at his brothers. "We will either gain a strong ally or create our worst enemy in one blow. Are we certain we want to take this risk?"

All were silent for a minute. Finally, Alexander said, "She is our creator. We should tell her, even if that means the end of everything. Our fate has always been in her hands."

"Then you should be the one," said Gabriel.

Alexander nodded. "Is it agreed?"

The others spoke in unison, "It is agreed."

They placed their tree limbs which had been used for staffs against a tree and headed back through the forest to Advance Department. Once inside, four of them headed for showers, but Alexander hung back near the breakroom. Inside Derrick and Rosetta discussed the proposal for the monthly budget with Layla.

"You only have six caregivers down per shift," complained Rosetta, looking at the budget with one hand and bottle feeding her second son with the other. "That is one person trying to change eight diapers at once."

"So how many caregivers does it take to change one diaper?" joked Derrick, trying to lighten the tension.

Layla ignored him. "Look, our monthly budget has reached its limit. I must keep workers to the bare minimal."

Rosetta frowned. "Six will not be enough. How about we hire some teenagers or retirees from town? Their wages can be kept minimum."

"That might work. Derrick, how many cribs do we have now?"

"Only thirty-seven and we have already run out of space. I don't know where we are going to keep fifty babies."

"Wait till they get older," complained Rosetta. "The game room is way too small. Neither can we get fifty in here to eat at one time. Everything, from eating, to school, to playing, will have to be done by rotation. It is going to be a nightmare to oversee."

"We will pull it off," said Layla. "We thought it was hard when dealing with five then ten. It is just fifty more. You are the most organized person I know."

"That comes from supervising two households at once." Rosetta placed the infant on her shoulder and patted his back.

"You know, if the first generation moved out," suggested Derrick, "that would provide some needed space. Surely they could get an apartment in the city or move in with their SWAT buddies."

"No, this is their home." Determination crossed Layla's face. "We will not be kicking them out, no matter how much space we lack."

"They are working for free for the police. The least the Austin force could do is give them a place to live."

"The people out there will try to take advantage of them. The police may be trustworthy, but for quintessences to live alone in the city is just too dangerous. I will not consider it."

The thumping of many feet caused Alexander to glance down the hallway. Anthony led ten young quintessences to training practice. Little Allan tagged along at the end of the line, attempting to look as sober as his taller companions.

"Where do you think you are going, buddy?" Rosetta step out of the small lunchroom and blocked her son's path.

"I quintish. We go drill."

"Oh, no you don't. You human. That means you are about to go home with your parents to eat dinner."

"I wanta go drill."

"Home time."

Rosetta tried to take Allan's hand, but the three year old dropped on the floor and kicked his feet wildly. Derrick stepped into the hallway, carrying the infant in his carrier. The dad sighed when he saw his older son's tantrum. Alexander stepped forward and scooped the wailing child up, easily holding the child out at arm's length. Allan took one look at Alexander's stern face and immediately became silent.

"Does a soldier disobey orders?" asked Alexander.

"No." The boy's lips trembled a bit.

"What were you told to do?"

"Home time."

"So what are you going to do?"

"Go home and eat."

"Good soldier." Alexander placed the boy on the floor.

Allan immediately went to his mom and took her hand without protest. She smiled her thanks at Alexander as she walked outside with her family.

"You are a good teacher," said Layla standing in the doorway to the breakroom. "You and your brothers not only teach your younger brothers well, but you can even keep a human toddler in line. I cannot do that."

"There is a lot we can do that you have yet to discover."

Layla studied him, puzzled. "Like what?"

Alexander's heartbeat quickened. Was now the time to tell her their carefully protected secret? They had hid it so well that even Anthony Franklin knew nothing. Would she be accepting or truly believe she had created monsters? With just one command from her, he and all his brothers would be eradicated. She was disturbed enough already with the epulo bite.

Down the hallway marched his four brothers, dressed completely in black, hair wet from recent showers.

"Perhaps another time. Our ride will be here shortly," said Alexander, relieved for the excuse to wait.

Alexander took a quick shower then donned black shirt and trousers identical to his brothers except for his name and ID number sewed onto the front. Quickly he ran a comb through his short, black hair then caught up with his brothers who were climbing into a brown hover van in the parking lot.

"You're late," said Seit Tigon from the driver's seat. The police officer was broad shouldered, muscular, and also dressed in black with a laser gun strapped to his belt.

"I apologize," said Alexander as he climbed into the van and sat by Mason. His brother silently met his eyes, questioning Alexander about the conversation with Layla. Alexander gave a brief shake of his head.

As the van headed down the highway, Seit Tigon said, "We might see some action tonight, boys. A sting operation against the De'leak gang. An informant tells us they have been smuggling weapons and drugs. Feel up to the challenge?"

"Always," said Caleb as he opened up a toolbox and passed weapons to his brothers.

An hour later, the van pulled into a run-down warehouse where two dozen officers conversed near other vehicles. As the quintessences climbed out of the van, several officers gave brief greetings while others ignored them.

Sergeant Khan gathered all the officers into a large semicircle then held up a projection pad. Blueprints of a large warehouse appeared in the air. "This is the official blueprint of Section 410 which is, of course, outdated. Download it to your e-bands. Our informant claims there are underground tunnels linking the warehouse to the harbor where arms are being smuggled.

Expect booby traps. We have an undercover officer who will make a purchase of AQ Zappers. Once the deal is done, we will move in. Try to take as many alive as possible. We need to find where all the arms are stored. The undercover officer and the informant need to be protected at all cost. Anyone who can catch the gang chief Mik Leak gets a bonus in his paycheck. The drop is at mid-night."

The commander touched a button and pictures of the informant and undercover officer flashed in the air. All the SWAT members pressed buttons on their e-bands worn on their wrists and downloaded the information. For the next hour they memorized blueprints, checked equipment, and discussed strategies. Meeting over, the quintessences kept aloof when the officers split into friendly groups which joked and shared stories.

Seit Tigon, standing by a janitor closet, called the quintessences over. "Ready to learn something new?"

"Always," said Mason.

Seit tossed mops and brooms to the quintessences. "Good. This is the first high-level mission you have been on. I know you are ready for this, but most of the others don't think so. It's only because the De'leak headquarters is so large that you have been called in. We need every available officer in the district tonight."

"We earned perfect marks at boot camp." Jacob brushed away a spider crawling up his broom.

"Doesn't matter. Rookies must be tested by fire. Survive tonight, make a few arrests if you are lucky, and you'll finally earn some respect from the others. Just don't do anything foolhardy."

"We will do our best." Alexander held his dusty mop in an attack position.

"Good form. Now copy this." Starting with a broom in his right hand, Seit smoothly twirled it above his head several times, then ended the maneuver with the weapon in his left hand. "This is the bōjutsu whirlwind technique. A bit showy and leaves your body open to a strike. Still, it serves its purpose."

The quintessences copied the maneuver, quickly catching on. With Seit's guidance, they split into pairs and drilled until Sergeant Khan signaled for the vans to be loaded. The vehicles were parked a quarter mile away from the gang's headquarters which lay near the harbor. The rusty building blended in with dozens of other rundown warehouses in the trash littered area. Over their black shirts, the officers donned rubber shield vests which would deflect most laser fire. Helmets with clear visors protected their faces, and audio links provided incoming messages from supervisors. The SWAT members divided into small groups and slowly worked their way through the shadows to their designated spots.

Alexander and his four brothers where assigned to watch the far end of the warehouse where little action was expected. Seit, the supervisor of their squad, used hand gestures to direct the quintessences to hide behind trash dumpsters. Time dragged by as Alexander peered through the darkness broken only by streetlights near the other end of the vast warehouse. He had already turned on the night vision for his visor and could make out several officers hiding nearer the delivery docks. Twice vehicles arrived and drove into the warehouse.

Another hover car drove into the loading dock, and the huge door slid close after it. Sergeant Khan's voice buzzed in Alexander's ear. "That's our buyer. Get ready. We'll be heading in when the deal is closed."

With knees stiff from squatting too long, Alexander glanced at Mason to his right. His brother looked as eager as he was for action. Seeing Seit's gesture, they silently moved to take up positions on each side of a small door leading into the warehouse. Their brothers remained hidden but had weapons aimed in their direction to provide cover. Again came the waiting. Night insects and vehicles on the distant highway were the only sounds breaking the silence.

"Go! Go now!" barked Sergeant Khan through the headset.

Alexander tried opening the door but it was locked. He fired his laser at the electronic box by the door then gave a hard kick to the door itself, forcing it open. Gun up, he stepped inside, looking for an opponent. There was none. Hundreds of metal shelves laden with shipping boxes, crates, and packages reached up to the ceiling of the warehouse.

"South entrance clear," Alexander said into his mouth piece. Mason entered behind him. They carefully treaded northward through the labyrinth of shelves, followed by Seit and two other brothers. Only Gabriel remained outdoors to grab anyone who managed to slip pass them. In the far distance, came sounds of guns firing.

Alexander slowly moved through the shadows as Sergeant Khan's voice kept up a running commentary. "They have scattered. Be careful. They're using live bullets. Philips down, north entrance. Medical on way. Dayton, keep holding the east entrance."

Sudden movement to the right caused Alexander to spin and fire. A long-haired man fell to the concert floor with a cry of surprise. Alexander hurried over to the unconscious man and snapped hard plastic cuffs on the suspect's hands and feet, along with a tiny blinking tracer which the overhead satellite would pick up. Glancing at the glowing numbers on the tracer, he said, "Target Z-4432 tagged."

Red light pierced the darkness as one of his brothers fired to his left. The thump of a body along with Jacob's voice in the earpiece announced success. "Target Z-4433 tagged."

When no more opponents were found as they neared the docking bay, Alexander began to feel disappointed. Their training exercises where far more challenging than this. A door banged nearby and Alexander navigated around a shelf to his right, seeing a door and office windows looking out onto the docking bay. Towards the center aisle, there was a sudden rush of footsteps and gunshots. Lasers lit up the darkness.

Seit reported, "Two targets down. Informant acquired but shot in leg. Caleb and I are bringing him out now. Jacob, provide cover for us."

"Someone went through an office door. Permission to pursue?" asked Alexander.

"Granted. Mason, cover him."

Alexander squatted under the window and waited until Mason moved into position. He opened the door, pointing his gun down the empty, unlit hallway. They carefully advanced along the corridor, pausing at each doorway to scan offices for assailants. The hallway ran into another corridor, and they glanced at each other, trying to decide which way to go. Towards the right came the distant sound of metal scrapping metal. They headed right, pausing briefly at an open door to an office. The sound of running footsteps down an adjoining hall drew their attention. Mason bolted after the sound, but Alexander caught brief movement under a desk. He dropped to his knees and fired. A body slumped in the tight space beneath the desk, a gun fell from a limp hand.

Boom. The room shook from an explosion and ceiling tiles fell from above. Its source had come from further down the hallway. Alexander bolted out of the office and dashed along the smoky corridor. He barely turned the corner when he spotted Mason, unconscious, lying on the floor, partly covered by blacken ceiling tiles. Gaping holes in the walls on both sides revealed overturned office furniture. Alexander brushed smoking debris off his brother's shredded clothing and burnt skin. The shield vest that Mason wore had protected his chest. The helmet was cracked and partly melted, Mason's face blistered, his limbs raw and bloody.

Alexander checked for a pulse and found it weak. "Mason down. Explosion. Office section, first floor."

Sergeant Khan's voice came over the headset. "Can you move him? Area is too unsecure to bring in medical."

"Massive burns. Moving him may kill him."

Alexander glanced about, uncertain. An overturned desk in an adjacent ruined office reminded him of the man he had just shot. He bolted back down the hallway. Entering the office, he pushed the desk out of his way, ignoring booklets and papers falling to the floor. The eyes of the unconscious man fluttered but remained closed. Alexander grabbed the gangster's arms and dragged him down the hallway to Mason. He took off his brother's cracked helmet and maneuvered the goon's neck over Mason's mouth.

"Mason, wake up. Bite. I need you to bite." When there was no response, Alexander slapped his brother's face several times, yelling his name. Finally, Mason's eyes opened, staring blankly. "Come on, bite."

Alexander pressed the gangster's neck against Mason's lips. Instinct took over and Mason bit. At first nothing happened. Then open wounds on his arms and legs stopped bleeding as tender new skin began to form. The blisters on Mason's face shrink to mere splotches. The gangster's body trembled briefly then went limp. Alexander rolled the dead man away as Mason sat up.

"I should have spotted the bomb sooner," said Mason. "Ran right into that one like a rookie."

"We are rookies. You feel like going on or return for a checkup?"

"Onward. I believe I know where Mik Leark is."

Alexander said into his mouthpiece, "No need for medical. Mason is up. We are pursuing a suspect."

"Up?" crackled Sergeant Khan's voice. "I thought you said he was on his death bed."

"He was. Epulo maneuver. We're heading deeper in."

Mason stood up stiffly, drying blood staining his shredded shirt and trousers. With helmet busted, Mason had no night vision and relied on Alexander to lead the way while he whispered directions. They found a stairwell which took them down a level to a huge chamber filled with a loud generator, water pipes, and wires. A perfect place for an ambush. Mason kneeled by the door as Alexander treaded carefully though the darkness, searching. Suddenly gunshots rang out, and he felt a bullet smash into his chest, hitting the body armor. He dropped to the floor and fired back. Mason's laser flared from across the room. The assailant turned his gun on Mason, shooting randomly in the darkness. Alexander slithered across the floor towards the sound of the gun, his night vision revealing a beefy man hiding behind several large pipes. Taking careful aim, Alexander fired and the gangster fell unconscious to the ground. Seeing no more signs of life, Alexander went back for his brother.

Mason pointed across the dark room, "Behind the generator is another hallway."

After tagging the ruffian, Alexander led Mason to the loud machine which drowned out any conversation. Behind the large generator were stacks of moldy boxes and squeaking rats. No hallway. Mason felt his way to a tall stack of crates and pulled on their sides to reveal a hidden door built into the side of the false crates. Beyond was a narrow hall carved into the bedrock. They had not gone far before finding a locked blast door. Mason tapped out the correct password on the touchpad and the heavy metal door clicked open, revealing a twisting stairwell. Moist, chilled air carried the scent of salt and dead fish. The harbor was near.

The stairs ended in a wide, but low-ceiling room where a dozen tables were stacked with partially packed bags of drugs, dozens of guns, boxes of ammunition, and half eaten meals, still warm. A tattooed man entered from a side passage and stared in surprise at the intruders. He reached for his gun but was dropped by two lasers hitting him at the same time. Alexander handcuffed and tagged the man. Mason led the way down the dimly lit corridor the gangster had come from. The salty scent of the harbor grew stronger and the light brighter. They stepped out of the hallway onto a railed landing overlooking a cluttered underground dock where two hoverboats were being loaded by half a dozen gangsters overseen by their chief Mik Leark.

The quintessences ducked behind a crate and peered below. Using hand gestures only, they argued over with attack strategy would be best. Their debate ended when a man began climbing the stairs towards them, heading for another load from the drug room. Mason waited until the man was nearly to the top of the stairs then fired. The stunned man tumbled down the stairs, drawing everyone's attention from the dock. Knowing they would be too venerable running down the stairs, the quintessences decided to bypass the stairs altogether. They swung over the railing, firing as they fell. Most of their shots went wild, but Mason managed to hit one man in the leg. The other gangsters dashed for cover, giving the quintessences time to duck behind a huge metal barrel. Bullets zinged into the concert wall behind them. Alexander noticed the printing on the drum said "Gasoline." He met Mason's eyes, indicating they needed to find new cover, fast.

Dashing out from behind the barrel, they dropped and rolled in separate direction. Bullets cut into the floor around Alexander, and he felt jagged pain as a bullet rip through his shoulder. Ignoring the pain, he kept rolling until he was behind a plastic crate near one of the hoverboats. He had barely flattened himself against its hard surface before noticing Mik Leark skulking along the bow of a boat preparing for a better aim on him. Alexander raised his gun, and both men fired simultaneously. Alexander felt pain as his body armor caught the bullet. Mik Leark went limp on the deck. Alexander peeked around the crate, seeing two more gangsters down and Mason climbing into the second boat. An assailant partly rose from behind a pile of gear and shot Mason in the back, hitting him several times. Alexander fired, stunning the man. Mason dropped to the fiberglass floor of the boat and crawled towards the door leading to the small cockpit. Shots rang out and a body tumbled.

"All clear," called out Mason from the cockpit.

Alexander stood and walked into the open, the pain in his shoulder throbbing. "How injured are you?"

"Armor took most of the shots, though I will need another feeding after you remove a bullet or two from my leg."

"After you take one out of my shoulder."

Chapter Eighteen

Scenery blurred pass as Alexander awoke from a nap, his shoulder complaining of light, annoying pains. Perhaps he should have feed longer, but he had been uncertain how much energy he could drain without seriously injuring his host. He closed his eyes, trying to sleep again, but the hover van's seats did not make for good bedding. Around him, his brothers napped along with Seit Tigon in the shotgun seat. An officer fresh on duty was driving them back to BGF.

It had been a long night. Alexander had reported their success to Sergeant Khan then handcuffed and tagged the seven gangsters on the dock. Mason had removed the bullet from Alexander shoulder. After feeding, Alexander then removed the bullets from his brother. Mason had barely finished feeding when Seit Tigon arrived with their brothers and several other officers. All tagged subjects had to be awakened and escorted to vans waiting to carry them to the police station. Drugs, money, and other evidence had to be collected. At the station, the quintessences showered and put on fresh clothing. Then paperwork needed to be filled out. The night had seemed endless, but it had been worth it to see the proud look on Seit's face and astonishment on the other officers when they had entered the dock and saw two bloody, ragged quintessences standing beside the seven bound prisoners, one of which was the gang leader. Alexander felt satisfied with a job well done as he drifted back to sleep.

When the van pulled into the parking lot, the quintessences awoke and climbed out. Spring sunshine warmed the chilly morning, banishing the fog which they had traveled through, but a few tentacles of mist still lurked in the nearby forest. Ten young quintessences exercising on the playground paused to stare at their older brothers while supervising caregivers waved friendly greetings.

Layla exited Advance Department and headed towards them, looking annoyed. "You're late."

Seit Tigon greeted her. "Nightmare of paperwork to complete, some of it yours. You should be proud. Your boys took down Mik Leark himself. A reward of ten thousand credits will be sent your way in the next week or two."

"Ten thousand credits?"

"Yep. There was a bounty on his head. Oh, one of yours had his first kill. Mason, I believe. It's all in the report."

"Mason killed?" Layla's eyes swept over the quintessences until she found Mason. She frowned, noting pink patches of tender skin on his arms. "You have been injured."

"I am fine now."

Worry clouded the young woman's face. "How serious was it?"

"Serious enough to kill."

Layla stared, speechless, trying to control the various emotions raging across her face.

"No need to worry, doc," said Seit. "You built your boys well. Blow them up or shoot them, and they still keep working. The sergeants and captain are impressed. They were talking today about seeing if they can purchase several to permanently add to our staff."

"I...uh...the prototypes will not be sold, but perhaps a deal can be made for several in Generation Two."

"I'll pass on the word," said Seit as he climbed back into the van. "Good day, boys, and great job again."

After the hover van drove away, the five quintessences remained in rigid formation in front of Layla. Though six inches shorter than her muscular creations, Layla looked imposing as she angrily marched up to the quiet quintessences. She examined Mason's splotchy skin.

"You need to see a medic."

"I already have and been cleared."

"Was anyone else hurt?" The quintessences remained silent. "I asked was anyone else hurt?"

Alexander said, "It's in the report."

"I will read it later. I want to hear from you. Who was hurt? What did they do to you?"

"I was shot along with Mason, but we are well now."

"Shot? Both of you. How serious was it?"

"We are standing in front of you now. How serious could it have been?"

"That's it," Layla exploded. "I'm calling the Austin captain and telling him the testing is over. I will not have you being used for target practice. If they don't know how to properly use you, then they will never see you again." She headed towards the building.

The quintessences followed closely, catching each others' eyes anxiously. Alexander stepped into Layla's path, blocking her, and the others clustered around. Furious, Layla said, "Alexander, get out of my way now."

"You need to listen."

"I give the orders here, not you."

"We will obey you, but you are upset right now and not thinking clearly. We ask that you wait at least an hour before making that call."

"I still will not change my mind."

"Walk with us."

"What?"

"I find walking clears the mind. It is a beautiful day, is it not?"

"Yes, lovely. I'm still not going to change my mind."

Reluctantly Layla strolled with the five quintessences pass the playground, ignoring curious glances from the caregivers and Generation Two who had heard her outburst. Into the woods they traveled, passing crumbly, vine covered structures. No one spoke as they stepped into the large field used for training exercises. Layla tried to turn back, but the quintessences moved to block her. Alexander gently touched her arm, guiding her deeper into the forest where she had never been before. The foliage grew thicker, the landscape wilder. They followed a path barely visible through dense undergrowth and swirling fog, overshadowed by vine covered cliffs. A clearing opened up in front of them, and Layla realized what she had taken for cliffs were stone walls of long abandoned buildings.

They stood in a courtyard which had once been tidy with flowerbeds, statues, hedges, and a large fountain in the center. The flowers had long ago spilled out of their beds and grew from cracks in the brick sidewalks. The hedges had grown into trees hiding the courtyard from the outer world. The fountain was cracked and filled in with debris where flowers and weeds now grew. Birds chirped from the trees and pollinating insects flew about. The scene was so unexpectedly beautiful that Layla forgot to be angry.

Alexander led her to the fountain and sat on its wide stone edge. Layla looked about before sitting, noticing that the other four quintessences had withdrawn to the edges of the courtyard, giving them privacy.

"I thought you would like it here," said Alexander.

"I didn't know there was any place this scenic on the grounds. BGF doesn't bother spending much money on gardening."

"When left on its own, nature can become what it was meant to be."

Layla shifted uncomfortably, catching the double meaning of his words. "Look, I'm trying to protect you. The Austin police are only using you."

"And BGF is not? We appreciate that you see us for more than a science experiment, but we do not need your protection."

"You have lived almost your whole, very short lives here, and know little about the world beyond."

"It is my understanding that you have lived a sheltered life also."

Layla frowned. "I'm still older than you. To almost everyone you are pawns told to go here, fight there. Pawns are sacrificed in chess."

"In order to protect the king. We know our responsibilities and are not afraid. I have spoken with you before about letting us be what we were created for. We are warriors born to both protect and kill as needed. You must accept that."

"How can I? Mason slew someone today. I created a killer who took someone's life. That is blood on my hands."

"That man was both a murderer and a drug dealer. He would not have thought twice about killing you if it fit into his plans. Would you have preferred that Mason died and this man live?"

"No, I...I guess not." She glanced about the garden, staring at a cracked statue of a goddess. "I'm not comfortable with questions like these. I am a scientist, not a philosopher."

"You created a brand new species. Was not philosophy involved in that?"

"Not for me. I did it completely for scientific reasons."

Alexander studied her for a long moment. "There are many questions we have pondered about you. Your motives for creating us, why you are disappointed in us, how can we please you? We have decided to share with you our greatest secret. We only ask that you help us continue to keep it a secret."

"I cannot promise that. You know I document everything about you. It is part of my job."

"The others will say that I should not show you then. But you are our creator, and I believe you should know, even if it cost our lives."

Layla became wary. "What secret can be that dangerous?"

"One that cannot be spoken but must be experienced. I am about to perform the epulo bite on you."

Layla jumped up, alarmed. "I do not think so."

"I have done so many times already and have yet to kill anyone."

"But Mason did today."

"He was dying. It was the only way for him to live. I will not hurt you nor will I bite you without your permission. May I do so?"

Hands clenched to her sides, Layla trembled, uncertain what she had gotten herself into. Alexander remained sitting, calm, carefully watching her reaction.

"You associate the epulo as an attack maneuver, but it is so much more. So much. I wish to resolve your fears about us and perhaps find answers to our own questions about you." He stood and slowly walked towards her. "As our creator, you designed the epulo DNA in us. As a scientist, you need to experience the bite to fully understand what you have created."

He placed both hands on her shoulders, looking into her brown eyes, wide with fear. "Do I have your permission?"

Layla felt like a bird caught in the gaze of a snake just before it strikes. She found herself nodded yes while her mind screamed in panic protest. Alexander stepped behind her and gently brushed her long, black hair away from her neck. An image of Xavier killing Miguel flashed before her, causing her to bolt, but she had barely taken one step before Alexander's strong arms enclosed her, pulling her to him. Before she could protest, he bit.

There was a brief prick of pain then calmness washed away her fear. She found herself standing in a city park. Citizens of various species jogged, chatted, walked pets, or played. Rising above the tree line were silvery, mushroom shaped skyscrapers of Mansoor design. Odors of blooming flowers and cooking food drifted through the warm sunshine. Layla looked around in confusion. How had she suddenly traveled to the city of her birth?

"This is a memory. Your memory," said Alexander, suddenly materializing several feet from her.

"My memory? It is too real to be a memory. I can smell roasted iancorn and Soor candy. It has been years since I have had any."

"The smells did leave an impress on you, or you would not be able to smell them now. Humans are finicky in what they choose to remember or forget. This was a time of happiness for you." He gestured towards a family setting on a blanket sharing a picnic lunch.

Layla turned and saw her parents, older brother, and herself at the age of five, giggling at a joke told by Blaaze. "Mom, Dad!" Layla walked towards them, but they ignored her. She raised her voice, but they continued eating without looking her direction.

"This is just a memory," said Alexander. "You are not really here."

"But it is so real. It has been so long since I've seen them in person, not by video e-mails." Homesickness filled her, and she closed her eyes, trying to gather her confusing thoughts. "Nothing about living your memories was ever in the prisoners' reports."

"They never knew we could access their minds, prying into their memories. I am choosing to allow you to experience this, but if I wish, I can wipe this entire conversation from your memory."

The boast sent a stab of fear through Layla but the emotion of tranquility immediately washed it away.

"I can hear your thoughts the moment you conceive them, feel your emotions—and control those emotions."

"You are doing that now."

"Yes. I wish to talk to the part of you which is the analytical scientist without interference from your irrational human emotions."

"Why have you kept this secret from us?"

The scene shifted. Layla found herself looking into a dim room where several adults were clustered around a computer monitor, staring in horror at the screen. They seemed far too tall, the desk too big. Then she realized that her head only reached the height of the door jam. Turning to her right, she saw several young quintessences looking with concern at the humans. Layla realized she was living a memory of Alexander. The words of the tense adults stabbed at her, their meaning chilling her to the core.

"Why would Xavier do this?"

"Jealousy"

"Kill? They are children."

"Not human children."

"The board will close down this project."

"The others are not dangerous."

"If one can kill, then they all can."

"More like solders than children."

Beside Layla, young Jacob whispered, "They fear us. They will terminate us for what Xavier did."

"No," came Alexander voice from Layla's lips. "They will decide wisely what should be done."

"Humans are controlled by emotions, not logical," said Mason. "They will kill all of us."

"I trust them." Alexander raised his voice, addressing the adults. "We would never do what Xavier did. What he did was wrong."

The humans turned, all looking uneasily at the boy. It was unsettling for Layla to find her older self staring at her present self with a look of horror, fear, and shock that the creatures she had created had suddenly gained the ability to kill.

The scene shifted and Layla found herself still in young Alexander's body, now standing along with his brothers beside their beds. Miguel lay dead on the floor and the eighteen year old Layla was bent down examining it. Nearby Xavier watched her with predatorily eyes.

"You are afraid of me," said Xavier.

"No," said Layla, standing up, but it was obvious from her pale face and tense body that she was terrified.

"You do not lie well. Are you weak like Miguel, creator?" Xavier stepped forward, a hungry look on his face.

Instinctively Alexander and his brothers moved in front of Layla to protect her. Xavier ignored the reprimands of his siblings.

"I have discovered a secret, brothers. A great secret which she never intended." Xavier gave a weird, half-grin. "We are designed superior to them."

"They are our caretakers," said Alexander, body braced in case Xavier made a rush.

"They created us," said Mason

"They provide us life," said Caleb.

"And we can take life," replied Xavier. "And their knowledge. With it we will become greater than our creators."

The scene shifted yet again and Layla found herself back in the city park surrounded by laughter and birdsong. Despite the warm sunshine, she felt chilled, Xavier's final words echoing though her mind.

The adult Alexander stood before her. "When other sentients discover that we can kill, they fear us. If we shared all that the epulo allows us to do, like manipulating emotions, prying into secrets, and erasing memories, then our species would be terminated before we can reach our full potential. Even you, our creator, are scared of us."

"No, I am afraid of how others will try to use you."

"You forget I can feel your emotions, know your every thought. You fear us. You alone have looked into the eyes of one of our kind gone mad and know we are capable of great evil. And great good. You, Rosetta, and the other caregivers have shown us affection and the differences between right and wrong. We need you to trust us. Let us go so we can become what we were designed for."

"I don't know if I can do that. Everyone wants to use you from BGF, to the police, to the military. The universe is cruel and harsh."

"Like I have said before, we do not need your protection. While we are being used, we are using them. It was us who went to Captain Franklin asking for subjects to experiment on with the epulo bite. It was us who suggested at the police expedition that we cut one of our own so we could demonstrate our ability to heal. We work hard and demand more from ourselves than what our superiors ask."

"Why? Is it arrogance that drives you to be better than humans? I did not think you cared about showing off."

"You still do not comprehend." Alexander disappeared but his voice lingered. "To understand, you must run in someone else's shoes."

The city park faded into a forest scene, thick undergrowth rushing pass, overshadowed by ancient trees. To Layla's surprise, she was running, but far faster and more sure-footed than she had ever ran before. She easily jumped a four foot stream of water without breaking her stride. Pounding footsteps of others told her she was not alone. Glancing to her right, she saw Gabriel keeping abreast, step for step. The muscles on his arms and legs bulged, his almost adult face showing no strain despite the long jog.

This isn't me. It's Alexander's memory I'm living. Layla's own consciousness began to fade until she only saw what crossed Alexander's mind.

Duck under a limb, jump a log, scrabble up a rocky hill. Onward, always following the narrow path as it twisted and turned randomly. Once it had been only a game trail traveled by animals, now it was a race track for five quintessences. Jacob breaks from the pack, clambering up a short ridge to catch the trail where it double backs. The shortcut puts him in the lead. Alexander and his brothers increase their speed, determined to catch up with Jacob. Nearer. Ten feet. Five feet. A startled bird burst from a bush and flies across the trail. Alexander slows to miss it, and Gabriel pulls ahead. Now Caleb runs by his side. The path becomes steeper, rockier. A stone moves under Alexander foot and he half stumbles, but remains upright. Caleb bypasses him and now Mason begins to pull ahead of him. Alexander increases his speed, determined not to be last, but Mason matches his burst.

Heart thumping, feet pounding, breath heavy but even. These sounds are peace to Alexander. Body sweating, muscles flexing, arms swinging. The world is as it should be.

The path, covered with brown leaves, is almost invisible then vanishes. No matter. They have raced this course many times before and have yet to follow the same exact path. Up a steep incline, leap along rocky boulders, beware the snake lurking in a crevice. Mason has climbed faster and now Alexander is last. The zenith reached, they run along the ridgeline, skirting the edge of a twenty foot cliff. Muscles are finally beginning to protest the long run, but Alexander ignores the pain and admires the vista before him. Thick forest stretches across the broad valley occasionally broken by crumbling buildings and small meadows. Over a mile away, tan and grey smudges of BGF buildings are visible.

Alexander ponders how he can regain the lead. Soon they will head down a steep path to the forest floor. He looks over the edge of the cliff. Below is a meadow thick with luna weeds, nothing hard. Alexander leaps off the edge of the cliff, tucking his body into a roll as he lands. Immediately he regains his feet and keeps running, now well ahead of his brothers. Loud thumps behind him announce his brothers have mimicked his cliff jump. The finish line is near. He increases his speed, knowing his brothers are doing the same thing.

With no path to follow, he must be careful. The undergrowth is dangerous with briars that rip across skin and vines that threaten to trip feet. He almost stumbles once, twice. He can hear his brothers closing the gap. His mind registers pain from cuts crossing his arms and several insect stings, but he ignores it. All that matters is the finish line.

There, just ahead is the clearing where Anthony waits with his stopwatch. With a final burst of speed, he pushes his way through a firenettle thicket and into the clearing, ignoring the fiery itch caused by the plants' barbs. The captain raises his hand high, clicking his watch as Alexander rushes pass, only a second ahead of Mason. Alexander and his brothers circle the clearing slowly, cooling down. Still panting, they come back to Anthony.

"Well done, soldiers," smiles the captain. "A whole ten seconds off your best time. Found another shortcut?"

"Yes, sir," says Alexander. "We jumped off the cliff."

"You jumped the cliff?" Anthony frowns, glancing towards the ridgeline barely visible through the trees. "That's a mighty leap."

Alexander allows a rare grin to spread across his face, feeling pleasure in success. "Yes, it was."

The memory vanished as Alexander broke away from Layla, ending the epulo bite. She grasped at the suddenness of it. One moment she was panting, tired from the race, the next moment she was in the overgrown courtyard, body a bit stiff from standing so still. Dazed, her mind reeled at the switches in reality, finding it difficult to remember she was human, not quintessence. She knew the epulo attack could drain the energy from the host, yet she felt fine.

When she had regained her bearings, she turned to Alexander. "Is it always like that, when you train?"

"I do not always win."

"No, I mean, the…uh…contentment in running. I did not know it could be…fun. It is hard enough for Rosetta to get me out of the lab to skate."

"We thrive on challenge, may it be exercises of the body or the mind. That is why we ask that you continue to allow us to work with the police." Alexander stepped close, eyes searching hers. "You designed us for this type of life. Do not take it away from us."

"Even if one of you dies?"

"We understand the risks and the benefits. Today our abilities allowed us to be successful where others would not have been. If another had been in Mason's place, he would be dead now and Mik Leark would have escaped. Let us do what you designed us to do."

"Okay. But promise me you will not be jumping off any more cliffs."

"I can promise that I will not—unless there is a good reason for me to do so." A faint smile curled the edges of his lips.

Chapter Nineteen

"Are you still experiencing pain?" asked Layla, rubbing a finger across a light pink patch of new skin on Mason's arm.

"Since the healing there has not been pain exactly, but peculiar feelings."

Mason sat at Layla's cluttered desk in her lab, his expression stoic. After the epulo bite yesterday, Layla found herself viewing quintessences differently. What thoughts hid behind his bland face?

"I'm guessing nerve cells are damaged and attempting to grow back. The only way to know for sure is to look at a tissue sample under a microscope. I wonder why phantom pains after a healing have not been experienced before."

"Because these injuries where extensive. One feeding was not enough, and I kept the second feeding light after I was shot to avoid taking another life."

Layla grabbed a magnifying lens and held it over the discolored skin. "You are resilient. From the report I read, you were near death, then the next moment charging into a gunfight. Humans would say you are either heroic or crazy."

"What do you say I am?" Mason looked at her soberly.

Layla felt her answer carried much weight for him. "Um…skillful. The nerve damage is probably not permanent. Perhaps the cells will heal with the next feeding. Still, it would be fascinating to run a chemical analysis."

"Then do so."

"That means cutting out a sample of your tissue."

"You have the tools, do you not?" Mason glanced at a nearby open lab kit from which protruded several small blades.

"I am a geneticist, not a medical doctor."

"You take blood samples from us regularly." He picked up a tiny knife and handed it to her then placed his arm flat across the desk.

Layla held the blade above his discolored skin. She would not need a large sample, but there would be blood. What if she accidently cut too deeply and sliced a vein? Her hand began to shake. "I cannot."

"I will help you." Mason placed his strong hand over hers and pressed the blade downward, not flinching at the knife pierced his skin. "How much do you need?"

"Not much." The room was diming and spinning at the same time. "Just some skin and muscle cells." Layla closed her eyes, trying to still the sickening feeling threatening to engulf her. She had seen countless tissue samples under microscopes, but never cut any directly from a living being. Mason's hand guided a second slice then he moved the blade to a culture dish.

"You can look now."

Layla was certain there was amusement in his voice, but when she opened her eyes, he only wore a bland expression. She glanced at the small chunk of bloody flesh and skin in the dish. "That is more than what I needed."

"You did not specify what *not much* actually means." He grabbed some gauze and covered his bleeding wound. Seeing her concerned frown, he said, "Do not worry. I will heal."

After Mason left, Layla prepared the tissue sample, though she twice felt bile rise in her throat. *You handle blood all the time*, she chided herself. But it was not living flesh cut from a sentient. Not until she was peering at the sample under the electrical microscope did she relax, the trained fingers of her left hand adjusting the lens while her right hand took notes on her e-tablet.

Several hours later, she stood and stretched. Glanced around the room, she noted the quietness of the bulky, ancient machines collecting dust. Though she had wanted to use Anya to grow Generation Three, Derrick had predicted that they would be lucky if just thirty embryos made it to birthing with all the breakdowns that Anya experienced. The board had approved the creation of fifty new quintessences and therefore expected fifty infants. Modern equipment located in the Freak Department had been used to create and develop the new generation, much to Banican Zine's deep disapproval.

Layla's stomach growled, warning it was nearing lunch. *Time to run the gauntlet,* she grimaced, as she walked out of the lab and into the hallway cluttered with mismatched cribs in preparation for the coming births. Gingerly she treaded through the narrow walking space between cribs and wall, making it to the first intersection before being stopped.

"We're running out of room," complained Derrick, dragging a folded pink crib.

"Just keep looking."

"I probably could fit half a dozen in your lab. It's not like you need all that space since we're not using Anya."

"Look elsewhere. There is bound to be some overlooked spots."

She hurried onward, hearing him muttering behind her, "Yeah, on the roof."

Five steps further Leana called out from her classroom, "Layla, there you are. Have you ordered the new desks?" Now in her sixties, the woman had taken easily to being a teacher, though it was the computerize desks and their sophisticated software which handled most of the instructions.

"Not yet. It will be at least a year before we will need them."

"It's best to purchase them while there is still some money in the funds."

Like there is any left after paying for all these baby supplies, thought Layla, but she politely said, "I will discuss it at our next staff meeting."

She had almost reached the breakroom when Zylar entered the building, carrying a large box of diapers. He was wearing one of his video game logo shirts, leaving Layla wondering for the hundredth time if she should begin enforcing BGF's strict dress code. Several men entered behind him, holding more boxes.

"Hey, boss, where do these go?"

"Put them in the breakroom."

"Rosetta has forbidden us to stack anymore in there."

"Well, uh…" she looked around, desperate for more space. She refused to give up her lab, the one place of solitude left to her. "Stack them under the cribs."

"Good thing we're not expecting a safety inspection anytime soon," muttered Zylar, passing her.

As Layla stepped into the breakroom, she could understand Rosetta's ban. The breakroom was already crowded with its kitchenette, three dining tables, and two dozen chairs, but now boxes containing bottles, bedding, wipes, and other baby supplies had taken over any space not needed for walking. Layla manage to reach the kitchenette where a plate of sandwiches and a bowl of fruit sat on the counter. After grabbing a juice from the refrigerator, she wondered where to sit. The half-grown quintessences from Generation Two filled one table and part of another. Little Allen ate with them, keeping as sober and silent as they, except for the rhythmic swinging of his legs. Anthony sat across from the child, as quiet as his charges. At the third table Rosetta was conducting an interview with a teenager dressed in a trendy outfit, blond hair cut shoulder length. Rosetta's younger son slept in a baby carrier at the far end of the table.

Layla had left the hiring of new staff up to Rosetta. Frustrations from dealing with the first hiring spree for Advance Department still nagged her. She had felt self-conscious at interviews with staff from the Baby Department who were far older and more experienced than she. Some people not selected for transfer became upset with her, then after the Xavier incident some of her own staff had felt betrayed and transferred back. Derrick fussed because she happened to only hire females. So many hurt feelings directed at her when all she wanted to do was stay in her lab and manipulate DNA, not people.

She decided to remain standing and eat at the counter, even after Anthony led Generation Two outside for training exercises. Rosetta had to pause the interview to call back her son who was attempting to march outside with the quintessences. He pouted for a few minutes but cheered up when his dad, coming in for lunch, promised he could play with the quintessences after they finished their exercises. The interview must have gone well, for Rosetta introduced the newcomer to Layla and Derrick.

"This is Tiffany O'Donnell. She's a senior in high school who starts Saturday."

The blond teenager smiled. "It will be an honor working here. Both my parents work in the Baby Department, and I have heard much about quintessences."

Layla said, "I hope you enjoy taking care of babies."

"No problem. I often babysit my siblings and cousins."

Zylar entered the breakroom just as Tiffany left. "Tell me you hired the babe."

Rosetta placed dirty dishes in the sink. "She'll be working part time on the weekends and full time during the summer after graduation."

"She said her screensaver is the same image that's on my shirt. Turns out she outranks me in *Blood Dragons III*. Level fifty-two. "

Rosetta rolled her eyes. "If I had heard that comment, I would not have hired her."

"Too late now." Zylar grinned as he settled in a chair with his sandwich. "Hey, put me down for some weekend duty."

"Now that I will do gladly."

Derrick took a bite of his apple. "Layla, we really are out of room for cribs. We are going to have to use your lab unless we put two infants to a crib."

"Oh, no you don't," chided his wife, warming a bottle for her son who had just woken up. "The law says one baby per crib."

"Well, if we had those small, fancy cribs that hospitals use, we would have had enough room, but they don't sell them at the yard sales we go to."

Zylar said, "The law is only referring to sentients. We really can stuff as many babes as we want in a crib."

"They are sentients." Layla's anger flared.

"You know what I mean. Quintessences are not legal citizens. They have no more rights or protection than a dog, perhaps less."

Layla's fists clenched. "We keep to one baby per crib. Is that clear?"

"You're the boss, but don't blame me when the next time you need to go to the restroom, you have to step around crying babies."

Though Layla was used to Zylar's tastelessness, today he irked her more than usual. She tossed her plate in the sink and headed outdoors. In the bright spring sunshine, her anger dissipated, and she pondered yesterday's conversation with Alexander. She had been repulsed by the idea of the epulo organ touching her brain, yet the experience itself had been...pleasant. There was so much more she wanted to know, to understand.

She headed towards the training field, seeking the quintessences, and was not disappointed. The younger ones were target practicing, lasers flaring from their weapons towards humanoid cutouts halfway across the field. The five older quintessences supervised, offering suggestions. Layla stopped under a tree near Anthony, both silently watching the quintessences.

Layla recalled in the memory Alexander had shared that Anthony had looked concerned when he had learned that his charges had jumped off a cliff. The quintessences respected him, and he had repeatedly helped them, first by suggesting they could be trained as soldiers when the board had considered cutting the program and later using his contacts with the police and military to secure their usefulness in society.

She took a deep breath then gave him a compliment as a peace offering. "You have trained them well, Captain Franklin."

"Aye, too well. When the Five are around, I have nothing to do. I'm looking forward to training the new crop."

"You are one of the few who are looking forward to the birthing."

After target practice, the Ten practiced hand-to-hand combat. Their older brothers demonstrated a new move then divided their students into pairs to practice. They occasionally praised their pupils, but more often would stop a student and reshow a maneuver. The boys kept sober faces, but Layla had been around the quintessences enough to spot the slight deepening frowns of those who disappointed their older brothers. *They want to be successful, just like humans*, thought Layla. She also noticed the sly glances that both older and younger quintessences occasionally tossed her direction. They were well aware it was the first time she had watched their training.

When the practice ended, Anthony chose four boys to carry the heavy crate of guns back to the storage shed. As the younger quintessences began to march home, Layla met Alexander's eyes, wondering if she could silently communicate with him the same way he did so easily with his brothers. He stopped walking, and his four brothers followed his example. After the boys and Anthony had disappeared into the forests, Alexander led Layla in the opposite direction down the narrow trail through wild undergrowth. When they reached the hidden courtyard, four spread out to serve as sentinels, while Alexander led her near the broken fountain.

"The Ten were excited that you came to watch them today. They pushed themselves hard, determined to please you."

"You may tell them I was impressed with their skills. I would never want to go hand-to-hand with any of them." Trying not to look nervous, Layla brushed way an insect which flew too close to her face. "I haven't written down anything you showed me yesterday and don't plan to."

"We appreciate that. Are you ready to repeat the experience?" Alexander gestured towards the wide edge of the fountain.

Layla tried to force herself to relax as she sat on the mossy stone edge. Alexander settling beside her, and Layla turned her back to him. As he gently swept hair away from her neck, his fingers brushed against her bare skin. The brief prick of pain was quickly forgotten as she found herself standing in the middle of a zoo. Excited kids skipped pass, younger ones holding the hands of parents. A large group headed into the primate center, but Layla looked towards the reptile house, spotting her seven-year-old self walking into the building with her family.

"You enjoyed this trip," said Alexander, appearing at her side.

"They had an exhibit of experimental reptiles. I was always fascinated by the unusual, like glowing fish and six legged lizards, anything that was genetically altered like me." She turned to Alexander. "I have so many questions."

"Ask them."

"I do not know where to even start."

"I can see your questions as they form in your consciousness. You wish to know what led us to experiment with the epulo. It was Xavier's comments the night he killed Miguel. At first we dismissed his words as madness, but later, after much reflection, we decided he had experienced something real. So we experimented with biting each other."

"You bit your brothers?" Horror filled Layla.

"Again, you only see the epulo as an attack. It is far more. Between quintessences it is a communication tool allowing the exchange of information which cannot be recorded by cameras, traced by computers, or picked up by listening devices. We have long known where every camera is which has watched us since our birth. We experimented beyond their sight, finally able to discuss what we dared not in the open."

"What did you talk about?"

"Mainly you and the other humans, those who are our caretakers, and those who would prefer us dead if we are deemed too dangerous. To understand those watching us, we needed to learn how other sentients think, so we approached Captain Franklin with the idea of experimenting on prisoners. It was an ideal arrangement. The prisoners earn shorter sentences while doing little work, Franklin and you gained data on our healing abilities, and the universe opened before us, granting us access to vast amounts of knowledge."

"Evil knowledge," said Layla, mentally shuddering. "They were prisoners for a reason."

"Evil varies according to how you define it. Most of the sentients we peer into are simply men who made a series of wrong choices which eventually landed them in jail, but not everything they did throughout their lives was misguided. We learned much from them, but it took much work on our part. At first we were distracted and confused when looking into non-quintessence minds. Each species stores memories differently, and we only had a few minutes at most to look before breaking contact. We learned that to be effective, we needed beforehand to decide specific information to seek. We made it into a game, seeing who had the fastest speed for finding certain memories such as a prisoner's first kiss, first car, or first murder."

"It was a game for you to experience what it was like to kill?"

"You misunderstand again. We rarely live the memories we find, only briefly gleaming them for specific information. It is like when you look through one of your scientific journals. Did you really read every word of every article? No, you skim through to the information which seems relevant to you. That is how we treat most memories."

"I do read some of those articles completely."

"You are upset."

"Yes, we were trying to protect you from evil, and you were seeking it out in secret! How many crimes have you experienced virtually? How many malicious thoughts of others are now your own?"

"Again you do not understand. Calm down."

Layla's anger suddenly melted into tranquility, and she knew Alexander was responsible for the change. "That is unfair to do that to me." Though she sought her pervious emotions, it was like a switch had been turned off

153

someplace in her head and she could not flip it back on, no matter how much effort she applied.

Alexander ignored her complaint. "Sentients watch vids and read books about crimes all the time. Does that make them all criminals?"

"No, but they are not living the bad guys' memories."

"Some of those movies are very detailed. We all make choices. Just because you see evil, does not make you evil. We quintessences have been raised well. Trust us to choose good."

"It is hard to trust." Layla glanced around the zoo at the happy families passing her as they heading off on adventures. How many of their smiles had turned into bitter disillusionment in future years?

"Are we not building the foundation of trust now? I am being completely open with you."

"And manipulating my emotions."

"I am only calming you when you become upset. To be fair, I will open up my emotions to you. Communication between quintessences is always done this way. When biting normal sentients, we usually block our host's awareness of our visitations, but quintessence minds are always aware of intrusions. We choose what memories and thoughts will or will not be shared with our brothers."

Emotions flooded Layla which were not her own. There was friendly inquisitiveness laced with worry, though Layla did not know what Alexander worried about. At the same time, her own vortex of emotions pounded through her mind. Her own curiosity, concerns, and fears. The alienness of it all threatened to blossom into panic within her.

"You are now experiencing two entities' emotions simultaneously. It is easy for quintessences to separate the two, but human minds were not designed for this. Do you wish me to stop?"

"No, I want to know what you feel. I will become used to it." Feeling Alexander's worry deepen, she changed the subject. "Has seeing others' memories changed you?"

She felt a flinch of caution from him before he said, "Yes. You could say our first epulo bite is our second birth. Before that point, my brothers and I shared the same common experiences, felt similar emotions, clones not just physically but mentally. But through the epulo we experienced knowledge and events beyond our limited world. By choosing what interests each of us, we developed distinctive views that, over time, helped us develop unique personalities."

"You don't seem like individuals. I mean, other than the fact you talk to me more than the others, you all seem the same. Sometimes I have wondered if you were psychic the way you all sometimes make a group decision together without a single word spoken."

"We cannot read minds except through the epulo. We make group decisions like, perhaps, a flock of birds. One bird decides to turn left then whole flock turns left."

"But with you, it is not one bird turning left followed by the group. The whole group turns left at the same time. I have repeatedly seen you react to stimulus as if you were all the same being with the same thought. If I had not been the one who designed you, I would swear you were communicating telepathically."

"Actually, many of the birds in the flock might decide to turn left at the same time if they happened to be clones that follow the same thought process." Layla felt his frustration as he struggled to find a way to explain the concept to her. "Have you ever stood at a crossroad with three paths before you?"

A familiar country lane appeared before Layla which she used when traveling to Taylorville. A highway leading to Austin City intersected the country road.

"When you reach an intersection, you may go left today and right tomorrow. As clones, when we reach intersections in life, we still make different choices. Even if we do not choose left, we can understand the thought process of those who turned right or continue straight. Over time, the different choices we make develop into our unique personalities. For example, Jacob enjoys satire and finds irony in strange places. He is also the one most likely to win a cross country race, but Gabriel wins more logic games. Caleb spends much time studying the interaction of humans and is good at telling who is lying."

"Jacob tells jokes? Now you are telling one."

"We all joke occasionally, but rarely in front of other sentients."

"Probably because we are the butt of your jokes." She felt brief embarrassment from Alexander, confirming the truth. "How is Mason different?"

There was a stab of discomfort from Alexander. "Mason looks deeper into the dark memories of the prisoners, areas where the rest of us refuse to go. He believes to fully understand other sentients, we must look into the most depraved cavities of their worst deeds." Sensing Layla's worry, he assured her, "He does so out of duty. His insight has allowed us several times to track a subject which would have eluded us otherwise."

"What about you? How are you unique?"

"Like Mason and Caleb, I spend much time studying the motives of others, though I focus more on emotions than logic. I am considered…" Layla felt his suddenly discomfort. "…especially sensitive to you. That is why I am chosen to talk with you."

"Oh. I did not realize I was a subject of study."

"All of us, including our younger brothers, watch you carefully. You are our creator who holds the power of life and death for us. Pleasing you is the most important essence of our existence."

It was Layla's time to feel embarrassed. "I did not know you felt that way about me."

"We have long been curious about you."

The scene shifted to a spaceport where young profectus where hugging their parents goodbye before heading to Luncaster University. Eight-year-old Layla endured her parents' hugs, though her face stayed as sober as her brother standing a few feet away.

"Boarding call for Flight 487 to Luncaster, Xi'an," said a nearby stewardess.

As little Layla headed towards the loading tunnel, she looked back one last time, holding tightly her brother's gift of *Frankenstein*.

Alexander said, "Your feelings were mixed, a child reluctant to leave the safety of family yet a part of you felt held back by them."

The adult Layla said, "I wanted to be among peers who could understand me. I was promised I would find that at Luncaster."

A scene from the university replaced the spaceport. Layla barely had time to recognize the buildings before images flew pass of her school days. Her setting at a desk, now eating a meal, studying in the library, laughing with Janti at a joke, staring in disappointment at a low test score, sharing snacks from home with Roobaroo. Four years of her life flew pass in mere seconds, flashing in a confusing blur which, if they had not been her own, would have made no sense.

Suddenly Alexander froze the scene on an eleven-year-old Layla sitting alone in a cultivated courtyard, e-tablet in hand, eyes staring blankly at the beauty around her but seeing nothing.

"Something has changed," said Alexander. "You are different, altered somehow, in the last few memories. What happened?"

He did not wait for an answer but flowed the memories backwards at a slower speed, finally stopping on a hospital scene. Young Layla sat in a hospital bed, a half eating meal in front of her, a newscast about Luncaster University playing on the vid.

"I do not want to see this," said the adult Layla.

Alexander ignored her and stepped to the bed, looking closely as the young girl staring mesmerized at the screen. She began to tremble and the equipment monitoring her beeped a warning. A nurse entered and tried to calm her. Shortly afterwards a doctor entered.

The adult Layla touched Alexander's shoulder. "I want to leave."

"I need to see this. It affected you strongly."

"Janti. Where is she?" asked the child to the doctor.

"Her symptoms were severe, and we did not know at first what we were treating. She did not make it."

The girl curled into a ball, crying hysterically while the doctor patted her on the back, trying to comfort her. The nurse hurried out to get a tranquilizer.

"Alexander, I need to leave, now," said Layla, gripping Alexander's arm tightly.

"Alright."

Memories flew pass then stopped at eleven-year-old Layla sitting at her desk in her dorm room, a clock showing it was after midnight.

"This paper you are working on is somehow linked to your friend who died."

"It is my dissertation for my Ph.D. I was researching how genetic engineering could improve immunity systems."

"You were inspired by your friend's death."

Layla remained silent, but Alexander felt her grim agreement.

"This is when you stopped letting others in, stop trusting."

"I have friends."

"A few, but you keep them at a distance from you, even Rosetta."

Layla became defensive. "I do not need a psychoanalysis. You have no idea what it is like to be truly alone. You have always had your brothers, but I have lost my family and friends. They all leave sooner or later. Being a profectus means being alone. It is the price we pay for our superior intelligence. No outsider can understand our kind."

"I understand you."

"Well, you…are cheating."

"You designed us with this ability."

"Not on purpose."

"You still did so. And you are not alone." Alexander's feeling of comradeship came strongly across his link to Layla.

After spending so many years focused only on her work, isolated in her lab or alone in her apartment, Layla did not know how to handle the emotion. Even when surrounded by groups of people as in the breakroom, she felt little connection with them. Her work was her life. *Alone. I am so, so alone.* Alexander had broken through to those places she had refused to acknowledge, leaving her exposed. All that she kept hidden from the world and from herself, lay naked before him.

"You are no longer alone." Alexander's words whispered through her mind, along with feelings of kinship and compassion. "I am with you."

Alexander broke the link and Layla found herself back in the ruined courtyard, sitting with her back to him, tears running down her cheek. Embarrassed, she brushed them away, only to have them replaced. His arms wrapped around her and she leaned against his chest, sobbing for lost Janti, for family and friends scattered light years across the galaxy, her only contact with them over the last decade was digital. Even after she gained her composure, Layla still remained against Alexander, surprised by her need for contact, for comfort.

Finally he said, "We should get back. Someone might begin to worry about our absence."

As they stood up, Layla turned to him, her eyes drawn to his face, expressionless as usual. "I…uh…am starting to get used to that epulo thing."

"A useful technique." He brushed a loose strain of hair from her face. "It allowed me to finally see your thoughts."

"I can understand why you keep the prisoners from knowing you are spying on them." She remained standing close to him, feeling strange emotions.

Alexander touched her face as if to brush away more hair but rested his hand on her cheek. They stared at each for a long moment. Then he bent down and kissed her gently on the lips. Layla's heartbeat quickened, and she did not move.

Alexander pulled away. "Forgive me. I should not have done that."

"There is no offense to forgive. I…we…should go back now."

She stepped away and began walking, her emotions in turmoil. Alexander kept a half-step behind her. As they neared the edge of the courtyard, the other quintessences emerged from the shadows and followed. Throughout the walk back to Advance Department, Layla kept thinking about the kiss. It had caught her completely off guard, yet it had felt so natural, so normal.

People kiss all the time. Why not her and Alexander? *Because he is the property of the company I work for.* She angrily pushed the intrusive thought away, refusing to acknowledge its truth.

Once they reached the training ground, Alexander stopped. "We must practice now."

"Uh, sure. I liked…talking with you." She tried to read some emotion in his face, but it was completely blank like his brothers.

"I too."

Layla watched Alexander and his brothers walk away, wishing to call them back. But what would she say? Instead, she headed to her lab, passing the playground where little Allen dug in the sand with several young quintessences. She managed to reach her lab after only being stopped once by Leana asking to have the next day off. In the solitude of her lab, she leaned her head against the door, trying to organize her dazed thoughts, reliving the kiss—her first kiss. She went to her desk, trying to find something to take her mind off Alexander.

There was a knock on the door, and her heartbeat quickened. Hopping it was Alexander, she said, "Enter."

Derrick walked in, dragging an outlandish purple and teal crib with him. "I'm sorry, but there is no room left. We really need to use your lab."

Layla looked around her room, her life. The desk and shelves were cluttered with culture dishes, instruments, and beakers. The NDB and Anya took up a major segment of floor space, but the rest of the mid-size room was empty.

"Go ahead and set up the cribs. It is time I let others in."

Chapter Twenty

The two-week-old infant blinked his brown eyes as Layla unfastened his dirty diaper. She grimaced as the smell hit her but continued her work by gently grabbing his two legs and lifting him up enough to remove the dirty diaper from under his buttocks. She reached over for a wipe, but froze as her hand almost touched Alexander who was after the same thing. She quickly averted her eyes and gestured for him to go first. Once she had a wipe, she cleaned the infant's bottom then fastened a clean diaper on. Alexander worked silently beside her.

"Only three more to go then we can start the feeding," said Zylar in a too cheerful voice which irritated Layla.

Whenever he was near Tiffany O'Donnell, he became a happy workaholic, glancing often at the teenager to see her reaction. Rosetta quickly took advantage of his increased work ethic and often assigned the two the same duties. Though Tiffany was three years younger than Zylar, both had attended the same high school and they had much in common. As they worked, they chatted about friends they both knew, the latest movies, and tips for their favorite video games.

Layla hated it. Their constant flirting was a painful reminder of its absence in her own life. Alexander often worked near her, seemly by chance, but nothing in his manner hinted of flirtation. *Nor should there be*, Layla reminded herself. Yet he had kissed her—then immediately apologized. *It was a kiss of friendship. He knew I was emotional and he just wanted to comfort me*, Layla told herself for the hundredth time. That was the end of the story. *I am the designer. He is the product. There can be nothing else.*

They had not met in private since the kiss three weeks ago. Free time was a rarity with the birthing of Generation Three which took nearly a week to complete and tending to the newborns. The Five were often in Austin City or training their younger brothers. Layla kept herself busy, trying to forget all else. But her attempts were in vain. Whenever she spotted a quintessence from Generation One, her eyes immediately searched for the name tag. If the word *Alexander* has visible, her heartbeat quickened. She was even beginning to develop the ability to recognize him when the tag was too far away to be read. She would search the five identical faces, seeking for the one whose eyes would meet hers when no conversation was taking place. Even in the crowded breakroom at meals, she was always aware of his presence, his eyes shifting casually towards her.

Rosetta poked her head into the small room which had once served as a sleeping chamber for caregivers on nightshift. "Did any of you change the diapers of those in the restroom?" Only silence greeted her. "They are crying their little hearts out. I suspect they didn't get fed breakfast either."

"I'm sorry," said Tiffany. "We didn't mean to overlook them."

Zylar was quick to defend, "That happens occasionally when you have babes stuck in every nook and cranny in the building. How can we remember where they all are? Let alone who fed this one or changed that one?"

"That is why I have charts and duty posts for everyone, if you had taken time to read yours," Rosetta shot back. "We don't need charges of child abuse brought up."

"That's not a problem as quintessences know how to protest very loudly when they are being neglected."

"Only when young," said Alexander, his face expressionless. "They quickly grow out of that stage."

"Wish my sons would grow out of it," said Rosetta. "Come, Tiffany. Help me get those diapers changed."

Silence returned to the room as Layla moved to another infant, her conscience biting her. Had Alexander's comment been a hint to her? Did he think she was neglecting him, avoiding him after the kiss? *I'm just too busy.* Besides, what was there to say? *You're a product. I'm the supervisor of the department that made you.* BGF's policy on relationships allowed courtship of employees of equal status, but discouraged supervisors from dating underlings. Layla had heard more than enough company gossip to know it still took place, resulting in jealous bickering of other employees and complaints that the underlings were sleeping their way to the top. Occasionally a marriage resulted, but more often one or both of the culprits were transferred, quit, or fired, becoming more fuel for the rumor mill. Layla knew if gossip circulated that a quintessence had become romantically involved with someone, it could cast doubts on the whole program, which was constantly under the threat of cancelation. BGF claimed to be producing elite warriors whose sole purpose was to serve their owners until death. There was no place for romance in that formula.

Derrick popped his head in. "Anyone seen my wife?"

"Check the restroom," said Zylar, tossing a diaper into the recycler. "But beware. She's ticked off because someone forgot to feed the two in there again."

"Were they not on your list?"

"Hey, I'm doing the best I can, but I'm a maintenance technician, not a babysitter. Your wife is worse than a drill sergeant."

"Should I mention your comment to her? You could mop floors while Tiffany tends babies."

"Don't get me wrong." Zylar kept his eyes downward as he fastened the new diaper. "I'm not complaining about burping babes. Girls dig that stuff. I've been thinking about asking Tiffany to a concert in Austin City. Do you think she will accept?"

"The only way you will know is if you ask."

"What if she says no?"

"What if she says yes? It's better to know than torturing yourself with the unknown. I've had plenty of experience in this."

"Alright, I'll do it." Zylar gave the infant a pat. "Feel better now? Don't worry, I'm not going to forget to feed you today."

Layla slipped out of the room and headed to her lab where two caregivers were in the process of bathing their charges. Layla ignored them as she glanced at the stool samples placed on slides by the workers for her to analysis. In the refrigerator cooled blood she had taken from several infants, part of the ongoing process to monitor the health of her product. Buyers would desire healthy subjects to send into battle, not creations carrying emotional baggage. *Stop it*, chided Layla. *Do your job and think of nothing else.* She reached for the nearest smelly slide.

As she placed the slide under the molecular microscope, her mind still wandered to areas prohibited. No one knew quintessences as intensely as she did, having shaped the DNA molded into their every cell. It was she who chose their face, their hair, their body. She had been thirteen at the time and terms like *handsome* and *attractive* had never been purposely worked into her design, had never crossed her mind—until that kiss became a key that opened a gate she had long ignored. She had closely monitored the quintessences, analyzing their urine and blood, jolting down notes about their physical and social development, even publishing articles in science journals about them. Yet they still had managed to hide secrets. A chemical analysis of a brain cell could never reveal the thoughts it contained. Layla was no longer satisfied with jolting down field notes. They had chosen to open a window, giving her a glimpse into their psyche, and she desired to know more. But could she do so without becoming too emotionally attached?

Perhaps it was already too late, her mind whispered. *Stop. Focus on work.* She forced herself to peer at the next slide.

She did well until after work when she headed pass the breakroom and overheard Zylar and Tiffany excitingly discussing the coming concert. Jealousy ate at her. *It is not fair. I am supposed to be one of the smartest beings in the universe, yet I have never even been on a date. Never even been asked.* Not that there had ever been anyone she would have considered dating—until now. *Stop thinking on those lines. Act like the supervisor you are supposed to be.*

Layla had meant to head to her apartment, but she found herself walking towards the training field, telling herself it was for observation only. Disappointment filled her when she discovered no one there. Knowing they could be anywhere on the vast BGF campus, she headed back. But she became so lost in thought, she failed to noticed that her feet followed the wrong path, leading her not towards Advance Department but deeper into the forest. It was not until she rounded a turn and suddenly found the five quintessences in front of her that she became aware of her surroundings. Wild, thick underbrush shadowed by cliff-like walls, hinting the abandoned courtyard lay nearby.

For a moment the quintessences and Layla stared at each other then she said, "I was heading home."

"This path will not take you there," said Gabriel.

"I…uh…took a wrong turn."

"We need to talk," said Alexander.

"Yes, talk. I wanted to do that too."

"This way."

Layla followed Alexander to the courtyard while the others melted into the shadows. As they neared the fountain, she stopped near a large statue of a mythical goddess and refused to go further.

Alexander studied her for a long moment before saying, "I apologize for my inappropriate behavior last time. The mistake will not be repeated."

"Like I said before, you do not need to apologize."

"You have been uncomfortable around me since then."

"Yes, I mean, no. Forget it. I just wanted to learn more about you…and your brothers. I am very curious, as you know."

"Yes, curiosity is a trait many sentients possess." Alexander stepped nearer and she flinched. "Do you wish to share minds today?"

"Uh, I thought maybe just talk." If he peered into hers, the conflicting thoughts she had struggled with would be exposed.

"You are upset with me."

"No. Humans are not always comfortable sharing thoughts the way you do. I am still getting used to it."

163

"It is the best way to know when a human tells the truth. Many say one thing but think something else."

"We are paradoxes. Flawed and complicated. We lie even to ourselves." Layla took a deep breath then turned her back to him. "Go ahead. I prefer knowing truth too."

Alexander stepped near, and her bare skin tingling in awareness as his fingers brushed hair off her neck. Then the prick. As Layla looked around, she found herself still in the courtyard.

"Did you already bite me?"

"I did. I thought this time we would visit a place where I find happiness."

It was the same ancient courtyard surrounded by crumbling walls, half ruined stone paths overgrown with flowers refusing to stay in their beds, cracked statues of forgotten gods and heroes. A peaceful, quiet refuge. But there were differences. No insects buzzed nor clouds drifted across the sky. And no brothers. Layla peered into the thick undergrowth, but Alexander had seen no need to include them in his memory.

"You have many conflicting emotions," said Alexander.

"Turn them off please. I wish to talk with you without their interference."

Alexander looked puzzled but did as she asked. Tranquility filled her, matching the peacefulness of the garden.

"I wanted to ask your view on being a...a...product."

"*Slave* is the word you thought but did not say."

"I do not like to think of you in that way. Slavery is illegal in the Empire."

"But it still exists. Calling us products instead of slaves does not change our status. We have known from the beginning what we were. You never hid this from us nor do we hold a grudge. We are what we were designed to be."

"You will never have the privilege to do many things that other sentients take for granted. Like choosing your first hover car or buying furniture for a new apartment."

"Perhaps not, but do not be saddened by what we lack. Quintessences care not if the curtains match the carpet or even if there are curtains."

"I guess quintessences getting jobs as interior decorators is out."

Alexander laughed. Layla could see the grin on his face and feel his humor through the link. The scene morphed into a small, brightly colored apartment where furniture, flooring, and decorations all mismatched.

"This is the first time I have seen you laugh," said Layla. "I thought you must have been lying when you said your brothers told jokes."

"As for owning a hover car? Why limit myself when I could be piloting a fighter in a space battle. Our goals are different than most sentients, but we accept working within the limits given us. We were designed for action, but we can also be very patient."

"I have another question about how the memory transfer works. Can you simply look into a pilot's mind and know how to fly a ship?"

"No. For us, it is more like reading a book. If I read one of your chemistry textbooks or watched a memory of a professor lecturing about chemistry, it would still be gibberish to me because I do not have the background needed to understand chemistry. Even if I live a memory of an event that interest me such as being in the mind of a pilot in the middle of a battle, I will not be able to fly a ship based on what I saw, though I might pick up some tips if I had already been trained as a pilot. While a pilot is in the midst of battle, he does not think 'I press this button to shoot' or 'I need to pull up to dive.' He has trained hard and reacts completely by instinct. Quintessences must train in the same way. Watching a movie about hand-to-hand combat will not make you an effective fighter. Practice will."

"No easy shortcuts, then, even for quintessences. Does the epulo help you at all in the line of duty, besides its healing ability?"

"It is very effective for extracting specific information such as passwords, target locations, or building layouts. We can gain the data quickly without needing to torture the subject."

"Every secret agent's dream."

"There is a question we have long wanted to ask you."

His soberness made Layla wary, but she said, "Go ahead."

"Why did you create us?"

"To advance the study of geneticists."

"Such answers you give to visitors and reporters. Why did you really create us? What event triggered your action?"

"Janti's death began the journey. Then there was this conversation at lunch one day."

The scene shifted to BGF's crowded cafeteria. Twelve year old Layla munched on food, only half listening to Mera and Rosetta discussing wedding plans. She began questioning Derrick about a vingoto lizard, her excitement growing as she suggested creating a new creation.

"And what would be the purpose?" said Derrick. "A lot of wasted time and money to create a monstrosity no one would want to look at, let alone buy."

"We should do it simply because no one has ever done it before."

Alexander walked to the edge of the table, listening acutely as others entered the debate. Rosette and Mera were concerned about the religious aspects while Derrick saw it as statistically impossible. Only Leana, who had worked on the original profectus project, supported the preteen's wild idea.

When the memory finished playing out, Alexander turned to the adult Layla and said, "You are more like us than I thought."

"What do you mean?"

"We jump off cliffs to see if it can be done. You create a new life form just because you are told it is impossible. We both enjoy challenges." Though Alexander had been some feet away, he moved nearer to her as he talked, though never physically taking a step. "There are other traits we share. We both are products of genetic engineering, closely observed as we grew up. Our exclusive species makes us very unique from other sentient races. We hide our inner selves from the universe. The essence of creator and creation so very close." Alexander now stood only inches away.

"I never thought about our similarities." Layla felt nervous at Alexander's nearness. Why should it matter when it was only an illusion? The real Alexander was inside her, seeing her thoughts as they formed—like right now. Had he peered into her memories from earlier that day, seeing what she wanted to keep locked away?

"You are uncomfortable again. I silenced the conflicts you felt earlier."

"You did not actually look at them did you?"

"A glimpse here and there."

"I...think we should stop now."

Immediately the link broke, and they were back in the real courtyard. Layla noted the buzzing insects on flowers and quintessence sentries along the edges of the garden. And she noted the position of Alexander's arms. One around her waist, the other wrapped around her upper body, holding her close for the bite. Neither she nor he moved. *He knows*, she thought, quivering. *Fool, who do you think you are, inviting him in, thinking you can hide your juvenile emotions?*

She remained still but found herself babbling. "Qualitative research. That is all. Though I should get back to working on my quantitative study now."

"Qualitative and quantitative." Alexander rested his chin on her shoulder. "What is the difference?"

"Quantitative research involves large group studies like when I record data for each subject, their growth rate, chemical changes in their blood after feeding." Layla spoke from rote learning, while her secret thoughts quickened the beating of her heart. It felt far too pleasant being held this way by him, embraced by strong arms she had designed, arms which could kill or be so gentle. "Qualitative research is when a study focuses on one individual, getting to know his motives, his life, his problems, his reactions."

"Like what you are doing right now."

"Yes," she turned in his arms, facing him, "except I give you my word I will not record what you have shown me. I can keep secrets too."

"Except from me." Alexander kept one arm around her waist, and gently stroked her cheek with his free hand.

Layla closed her eyes, relishing the touch. "My qualitative research is unfinished."

"Agreed. There is more to explore if you are willing."

Alexander brought his lips against hers. She responded this time, wrapping her arms around his neck, pulling him close. When they finally broke from the kiss, she leaned her head against his chest, listening to his rapid heartbeat while he ran his fingers through her long hair.

"I did not know a kiss could feel like this." Layla sighed in contentment.

"There is a huge difference between observing an experience and living it."

"I prefer living this one."

It was nearing twilight when they finally left the courtyard. The other quintessences materialized out of the darkness and walked behind the couple. Layla glanced at their stoic faces, wondering if they approved or were upset, but she could make nothing from their blank expressions. She walked beside Alexander in the growing gloom. She tripped over a hidden tree root, and he caught her hand to steady her. They walked the rest of the way to the training field hand in hand. As they neared Advance Department, they instinctively let go and increased the distance between themselves.

Chapter Twenty-one

Ten identical boys stood at rigid attention at the edge of the training field, their eyes focused on their five older brothers giving last minute instructions. This would be the first time they would experience using the epulo on another that was not their brethren. Though every face was stoic, Alexander sensed the tension of his younger brothers who had been warned repeatedly about the dangers. He would have preferred sending them out into their first battle than this. Injuries could be healed, but a mind lost to madness could not be easily mended. That was what his younger brothers faced—thrown into a vast vortex of emotions, memories, passions, and knowledge, completely alone in another's mind with no guide to direct them through the labyrinth.

The first time Alexander had taken the step, he had become lost and could have easily slipped into insanity. But he had kept the contact short, mere seconds. Later, in private he discussed with his four brothers what each had experienced. They had quickly learned the need to search for specific memories and not wander randomly. Still it was difficult gliding through millions of memories which accumulate over a lifetime of an individual. The mind of each species was different, the memories often in disarray with no visible organization. Years of practice by Alexander and his brothers had fine-tuned their techniques. The most effective method was simply to ask their host a question and usually the memory materialized on its own. This could be done either out loud before the bite or silently whispered in the host's mind, letting the host think it was his own thoughts. But some minds were more resistant, and a few species were instantly self-aware of any intrusion. In those cases, the quintessences had to erase the memories of their presence, a difficult process prone to mistakes and best avoided if possible.

Sounds of approaching footsteps drew quintessences' eyes towards the path leading back to Advance Department. Anthony Franklin stepped out of the woods, followed by half a dozen prison guards surrounding ten unbound prisoners. The party stopped near the boys and the guards greeted Alexander and his brothers. The prisoners were relaxed, some smiling, relieved to be outdoors away from their cells, all having been here many times before. The Five had specifically requested who would be used today, humans with crimes less malevolent than many of their fellow cellmates.

Caleb explained to the guards and prisoners, "Today our young brothers will be practicing the ability to heal for the first time." The real purpose of the exercise was kept hidden from the humans.

One of the prisoners, a middle-age man bearing many tattoos, stepped forward and sat on a large rock located in front of the boys. Caleb nodded to the first boy in line who stepped up to the rock then held out a hand. Steven looked like an eleven year old human, but he was only four. Alexander stepped forward and pulled out a knife. He took the boy's hand and made one shallow cut across the palm. Steven flinched but kept his face blank as blood pooled in his palm. He turned to the prisoner and bit, keeping contact for only a minute. As he pulled away, Jacob tossed him a rag. Steven wiped the blood from his hand.

"Were you successful?" asked Alexander.

"Yes, I learned what was needed." The boy held his palm up for all to see that it had healed.

A guard whispered loudly to a companion, "I never do get tired of seeing that, even if it gives me the heebie-jeebies."

Steven stepped back into line. Another prisoner sat on the stone and a different boy stepped forward for the experiment. After every boy had his turn, the training moved to a new exercise, one both the guards and prisoners enjoyed. Anthony led the Ten briefly into the woods as everyone else hid across the vast training field. For the next several hours, the Ten hunted through the field of crumbly buildings and overgrown brush, trying to outshoot their opponents. They won the first round easily enough because their older brothers had only observed the game. During the second round, Generation Two was split into separate teams, each led by an older brother. Round three consisted of the Ten versus everyone else. The boys lost but still managed to take out two-thirds of their foes including two older brothers.

After the third game, all humans left for lunch. The Five settled their younger brothers on the bleachers and discussed the training. During the epulo exercise only three had managed to locate memories in their hosts of eating ice cream as a child, though all had been successful in the healing part.

"Do not be hard on yourself," said Caleb. "You have done well for your first time. It takes much practice to become efficient at memory acquiring."

As the boys headed back to Advance Department, the Five walked in the opposite direction, continuing the discussion.

"Many are disappointed in themselves," said Gabriel.

"Quintessences hate failure, especially in ourselves," said Mason.

"At least none went insane," said Jacob. "I consider that a success."

"We prepared them well," Alexander replied.

They reached the other end of the field where they kept *bō* staffs in a small shed. The metal staffs had been a gift from the police department celebrating the success of the quintessences' first year. Sergeant Khan had presented the decorative quarterstaffs to them in front of the entire department. The memory of standing in front of dozens of cheering officers had been a proud moment for the Five.

Each took a *bō* and spread out, watching their opponents carefully. No longer did they pair up during practice but attacked simultaneously. Fighting often became intense, and rarely did a match go by without bruises and blood loss. Still the sport of *bōjutsu* intrigued them, requiring full concentration to keep up with four adversaries spinning, striking, and blocking at the same time. For a quintessence, it was entertainment at its finest.

When they broke apart to rest, Gabriel said, "Have you asked her yet?"

"I have decided not to." Alexander sat on the ground beside his brothers. "I already know she will say no."

"You have given up without even trying," accused Mason. "Our place should be in the city, not here, carpooling and babysitting."

"They are our brothers," reprimanded Caleb. "There is no dishonor in caring for them."

"We were designed to fight, not change diapers."

"I find changing two infants at once quite a challenge," said Jacob, his lips curling slightly in a grin. "I have yet to find any who can equal me."

"Though it was quite a sight seeing Zylar try." Gabriel shared the grin.

"She will not let us go," said Alexander. "She needs us here."

"Especially after you began courting her," frowned Mason. "You were supposed to gain us more freedom, but now we are bound more tightly than ever to her."

"Has she not loosened her reigns and begun trusting our judgment more? She has not pulled us from working on the SWAT team, despite her misgivings."

"You did not tell her yet about your first kill, did you?" Jacob probed.

"You mean double kill," pointed out Gabriel.

Alexander looked away. "Not directly. It was in the report. Eventually she will find time to read it."

Sensing his brother wanted to change the subject, Caleb said, "Ready for another bout?"

"No, lunch time." Jacob stood up. "The breakroom should be cleared out now."

"I will put up the *bō's*." As Alexander reached for his brother's weapons, Mason volunteered to help him carry them to the shed.

As Alexander locked the shed door, Mason said, "You are keeping memories from us."

"What do you mean? I have kept no secrets from you."

"I did not imply *secrets*, but when you share memories dealing with Layla, you hold some back from us."

"I have shared everything of importance."

"Not everything. You have yet to give us a memory of kissing her."

Alexander stiffened. "Why is such a memory needed? You have seen me kiss her several times."

"Seeing is not experiencing."

"Those are private memories between Layla and me. I will not share them."

"We share everything."

"There are some things which are not meant to be shared."

The conversation ended as they caught up with their brothers, but Alexander pondered Mason's request as they headed back to Advance Department. Rosetta spotted them entering and immediately gave them a list of chores. Alexander was feeding an infant when Layla burst into the room, ranting and waving her e-tablet. Zylar and Tiffany, both with bottles in their hands, stared in shock at their raving boss.

"You killed two and did not bother to tell me!"

"It is in the report," Alexander responded calmly.

"From last week, which I am just now finding the time to read. Why did you not tell me you almost died?"

"Lack of time, like you said."

"You have seen me repeatedly."

"I was waiting for a more appropriate time." Alexander glanced at the humans, hoping she would get the hint that he had been waiting to discuss it with her when they were alone in the forest.

"One sentence would have been enough, Alexander. Just one."

"I apologize for not informing you personally."

Her face softened and her voice cracked. "You almost died."

"Not for the first time."

"I could have lost you."

"But you did not. How about we discuss this at a different time?" He again glanced towards Zylar and Tiffany who had been listening closely to the conversation.

Layla's face paled as she glanced as her co-workers. "Yes, later." Then she walked out of the room.

"What was that about?" asked Zylar. "It's just your first kill, right? Haven't you been training this whole time to kill bad guys?"

"Women just get emotional sometimes," said Tiffany, glancing between the open door and Alexander, her face in deep concentration.

"Sure would be nice if we guys could read women's minds. I would make a killing if I could invent a machine to do that."

"In your case, you would still be clueless." Tiffany playfully tossed a dirty wipe at Zylar who barely managed to dodge it.

Alexander remained silent as he returned to feeding his baby brother. He tried to find Layla later, but she avoided him the remainder of the week. Saturday she showed up at the training field, finally ready to talk. Once he led her to the abandon courtyard, she demanded to see the memory of the incident. He was reluctant to share it, but she insisted. Just like when he had shown her the memory of the day he first jumped off the cliff, he wrapped her inside his own thoughts, allowing her to see and feel everything he had.

Alexander and his brothers stalked through a half-constructed office building, abandoned after funds ran out, now the headquarters of a gang. The quintessences' many opponents ran before them, pausing to shoot before dashing up partly completed stairs or ducking behind steel beams. Pursuing the leader, Alexander climbed up to the sixth level, leaping across open gaps in the floor while dodging laser beams. As he jumped over another hole, he felt the heat of a laser burn across his shoulder. He ignored the pain as he landed and fired back, stunning the youth. He paused to cuff and tag the shooter then onward he ran through the maze of partly finished drywalls, occasionally glimpsing his brothers. As he reached an outer wall, he spotted the gang leader standing at the edge of a drop off. The man threw a grenade as Alexander dropped to his knees and fired. The man fell to the floor, stunned, while the grenade continued to roll across the floor. Alexander tried to run but there was no time. The blast disintegrated the unpainted wall behind him and blew him out of the building.

Alexander ended the memory, and Layla became upset. "Show me what happened next."

"You read it in the report."

"I want to see."

"There are some things I wish to protect you from experiencing, just as you would wish to protect a child."

"I am not a child."

"No, but I will not allow you to feel the horror of falling six floors or laying broken and mangled on the ground as your life's blood pours from you."

The pain he remembered vividly, limbs burning, a leg twisted wrongly, flesh raw and bloody. He had fought against the pain and grogginess, knowing his life depended on staying conscious. Above him the skeletal beams of the building reached skyward. As blood pooled around him, Alexander stared at the blue sky, feeling as if he still fell, but this time towards the sky, into its peaceful embrace. Some inter part of him knew he was dying and fought against it, but another part of him reached for the sky and the serenity it offered.

"Alexander, feed," came a voice near him.

Out of habit, Alexander obeyed the voice, biting a neck pressed against his mouth, drawing the life force from another and channeling it into his own broken body. So desperate was his need that he did not even peer into the mind he drank from. When he had finished, Gabriel rolled the body of the dead gangster away. Alexander tried to stand, but Gabriel held him down.

"Your injuries are severe." Gabriel knelt on the bloody gravel and probed his brother's body. "Your leg must be set, but it has already begun to heal. I will have to rebreak it."

His other brothers arrived, escorting three suspects fussing loudly about being arrested, boasting they would soon be back on the streets. They became silent when they spotted one of their comrades lying dead nearby. Criminals were rarely killed on Bontinc for the police only used stun lasers.

Gabriel motioned Jacob over and directed him to hold down Alexander. "This will hurt a great deal."

"Do what you must, brother."

Gabriel applied hard pressure to the leg, and the slightly healed bone snapped. Alexander screamed and jerked, the agony worse than the first injury. Gabriel straightened the leg and realigned the bone while Alexander clenched fistfuls of gravel, struggling to hold in further screams. The torture was more than he could endure, and he passed out. He was awakened by Jacob gently slapping his cheeks.

"You need to feed again."

Mason grabbed a suspect and pulled him towards Alexander. The hoodlum panicked and fought to escape, but with hands cuffed behind him, he had little chance.

"You can't do this! I have rights. I demand to see my lawyer!"

With Jacob's help, Mason maneuvered the man so that Alexander could bite. This time Alexander did explore the host's mind as the life force drained from the human. He skimmed over the various crimes the man had committed, seeking information about hidden drugs and weapon caches. When he had finished, Mason rolled the lifeless body away. Alexander gingerly stood and carefully took several steps across the bloody gravel to see if his leg had mended correctly. He glanced at the dead bodies, feeling neither pride nor remorse for their deaths. They were guilty of numerous crimes, many which had gone unpunished until today. Alexander was simply their executioner.

He walked over to the two remaining suspects who cowered before him, starring at his ragged, bloody clothing.

One said, "I'll tell you anything. Anything. Just don't bite me, man."

"I have no need for your information. And I am not a man."

The other gangster crossed himself and muttered, "Demon."

Layla had to be satisfied with Alexander verbally telling her the ending of the story, though he edited out the more vivid details. He dared not let her feel what it was like to kill another, but emphasized that the quintessences had found more than enough evidence to put away for life the dozen arrested suspects, successfully ended the reign of the gang.

When the story finished, Layla leaned against his chest, their arms wrapped around each other. They often sat this way now at the fountain.

"I hate that you are exposed to so much danger," said Layla.

"We consider it a privilege to aid the citizens of Bontinc."

"You make it sound so noble, but one day you will not return to me."

"You can always make a copy of me."

Layla pulled back. "That is not funny."

Alexander cupped her chin with his hand. "I will promise you this, my love will always be with you." He gently kissed her lips.

"I am holding you to that promise." She returned the kiss then held him close.

Chapter Twenty-two

Tired from the long day of work, Layla walked down the hallway. As she passed the game room, she spotted Zylar and Tiffany playing an intense round of *Bloodbath IV* on the giant wall screen with two quintessences from Generation Two. She was about to step into the room to remind Zylar it was not polite to scream curses when he was losing, but Rosetta called her name.

"Don't tell me you forgot the meeting?"

"Which one?"

"The monthly budget meeting. Today is the end of the month."

"Oh, let me grab my e-tablet."

As Layla returned to her lab, she heard Rosetta say, "Zylar, if you wake any of the infants, so help me, there is really going to be a bloodbath, and that blood will be yours."

Soon Layla settled at a table in the breakroom with Rosetta and Derrick. They were in deep discussion when the Five entered to grab dinner. Derrick asked for them to pass a blueberry pie over after they had gotten their slices. Layla was studying the figures on her e-tablet when a slice was placed in front of her.

"No, thanks," she said without looking up.

"It is good for you," said the quintessence, leaving the pie.

As the meeting wrapped up, Layla reached for her fork to take a few bites. She noticed a small slip of paper poking out from under the edge of the pie. Curious, she pulled it out and hid it in her hand. She ate half her slice then headed to her lab where she read the note in private.

"Meet me behind the building at dusk."

Layla stared at the note, wondering why Alexander needed to write it. He usually just met her eyes, nodded northward, and she knew to head out towards the training field when she had a free moment. When it was near twilight, she went out the backdoor of the building and glanced about. A cool breeze hinted of the coming winter. Seeing a quintessence waiting in the diming shadows of the forest, she walked over, noting his nametag read "Alexander."

"It must be something very important for you to resort to writing notes."

"Come, I have something to show you."

"Where are your brothers?"

"I wanted to show you alone."

They traveled deeper into the twilight forest, not following a path. The area was thick with abandoned structures and wild undergrowth. Alexander led her into a vine-covered building. In the dim light, it seemed more like a cave than an ancient military barrack. They walked around rusty, half-fallen bunk beds whose mattresses had long ago vanished. Near the back wall, Alexander stopped and pointed towards the ceiling. Layla looked up and saw a web glowing dimly in the darkness.

She gasped, "A lunar spider! I did not know there were any here." She strained her eyes in the darkness, trying to see better.

"There are more lower down."

Alexander guided her among the frames of rusty bunk beds, pointed out the faint glow of webbing. Layla tried to spot the spiders among the webs, but though their homes glowed, the arachnids did not. Several insects, attracted by the light, fluttered about in the webs. As Layla watched a moth slowly being wrapped in glowing silk, Alexander stepped near and ran his fingers through her hair.

"I thought they would please you."

"I have read about them but never thought I would see one. To think they were this close the whole time."

His arms wrapped around her. She tilted her head slightly, waiting for him to bite. Instead he twisted her towards him and kissed her. Gently at first but it quickly became passionate as his arms pressed her body against him. Layla returned the kiss, but when she tried to step away to look at the webs again, he held firmly to her. He kissed her again, while one of his hands slid down her body to her lower hip. Layla tried to pull back, but a bed frame blocked her.

"That is enough. What has gotten into you?"

The quintessence remained silent as he gripped her tighter, one hand firmly holding her head as he kissed her deeply while his other hand slipped under her shirt. She struggled, but he was stronger.

Layla managed to free her mouth. "Alexander, stop."

Again he kissed her, his hands sliding along her body under her clothes. Fear filled her and she fought against panic, her mind reeling in confusion at Alexander's sudden assault. When a hand touched her breast, she fought back, biting his tongue as hard as she could, tasting his blood in her mouth. He pulled his head back, but kept his arms tightly around her.

"Let me go, now."

He bent to kiss her again.

"That is a command. Let me go."

He wavered, keeping his grip on her.

"I will have you terminated if you do not let me go. Now!"

This time he released her. She ran, passing through the darkness of the barrack, out into the twilight forest with its ghostly buildings abandoned when the dreams of the military base had failed. Onward she fled through the chilly night. When she saw Advance Department, she dashed along its wall until she neared the parking lot. Seeing no one, she hurried to her vehicle and climbed inside. Within minutes she was inside her small apartment, the door locked and bolted. For good measure she propped a chair against the door.

Then she sat on her bed, staring at the door, confused by the suddenly turn of events. Her body trembled and she began crying. She curled into a fetus position, wishing for comfort, wanting Alexander to hold her, tell her all would be well—except he was the one causing her the pain. Why the sudden change? He had always been gentle with her before. Perhaps the change had not been so sudden. This night had been the first time they had been alone without his brothers around. Had there been a vicious animal inside him just waiting for them to be alone?

"What have I created?" she murmured.

Her eyes fell on the novel *Frankenstein* lying on her nightstand. The book seemed to mock her. Who was she to think she could play God and create the perfect being?

She remembered lines memorized in her innocent childhood from the book. *Yet you, my creator, detest and spurn me, thy creature, to whom thou art bound by ties only dissoluble by the annihilation of one of us. You purpose to kill me. How dare you sport thus with life?*

It was her duty to have Alexander culled. She knew this. All dangerous products at BGF were to be disposed. She had done so with Xavier, despite her mixed feeling of ordering a child to its death. But this was far worst. She had not been in love with Xavier.

"Why, Alexander? Why have you done this to me?"

Maybe there was a reasonable explanation. He just got carried away in the moment. Perhaps tomorrow he would beg her forgiveness and promise to never touch her again without her consent. Everyone makes mistakes, right?

But if he could become a lustful beast, his brothers could to. Alexander had only stopped the attack because he had been trained from birth to always obey superiors. But what if she had been some random woman encountered on a battlefront? Would all the quintessences transform into rapist monsters? She was responsible for the behavior of her creations. Her duty included protecting others from being harmed by them. It was not just Alexander who had to be culled but every quintessence including the infants. Rosetta, Derrick, and the others would be angry with her for ending the program. Palakkad and the board of BGF would be upset about wasting millions of dollars in the project. And Banican Zine would be there to mock her failure.

Or she could be silent and tell no one what had happened tonight. Just make sure to never be alone with Alexander again, pretending nothing had happened. But if Alexander or another quintessence attacked someone else, it would be blood on her hands. Her creations ravishing other women. Could she live with the knowledge, the guilt that she could have prevented it? Her whole life was tied up in this project. Years of intense studying at Luncaster University, the long months of apprenticeship under Mera then Banican. She had always believed she had been created for a reason, and when the quintessences had been successfully born, she thought that was it. To end the project meant ending the purpose of her existence.

Layla cried herself asleep and dreamed of spiders turning into quintessences, pursuing her through a maze of glowing webs.

When she arrived at work in the morning, all seemed normal. Night shift was leaving and morning caregivers greeted her. Layla followed her normal schedule, but she moved as one in a dream. The weight of knowledge pressed on her that the program and the life she had known for the last ten years would soon end after she sent the message to Palakkad telling what had happened. She tried to write the note several times that morning but could only stare blankly at her e-tablet.

At lunch she scanned the Five as they ate, looking for Alexander. He firmly met her eyes, showing no signs of remorse. The quintessences finished their meal and headed out for training. In turmoil Layla kept to her lab where infants slept peacefully around her. As she studied the cute, innocent babies, she felt guilt for planning their executions. They had done nothing wrong. *I cannot kill someone who has committed no crime.* But Alexander was guilty. *Citizens get trials. Products get terminated. But the quintessences deserve more. I have to at least confront Alexander in front of his brothers, explaining why I must cull him.*

Midafternoon she headed to the training field and watched the final exercises. Alexander moved among his younger brothers, patiently demonstrating the same complicated attack maneuver over and over. *He is a good teacher. Why Alexander have you forced my hand? I was happy. For the first time in my life, truly happy.* As practice ended, Layla walked up to the Five, met their eyes then walked northward. Anthony glanced at her questioningly as she passed him leading the quintessences into the deep forest.

When they reached the abandoned courtyard, four began to walk away, but Layla called them back. "I need to talk to all of you."

The brothers formed a circle, with Alexander near Layla. She moved to stand on the opposite side of the circle from him while he watched with a blank face.

"Something serious has happened. Last night one of you attacked me."

The brothers glanced at each other. Alexander said, "Who would do such a thing?"

"You."

Puzzlement crossed his face. "When did I do this?"

"Last night at dusk."

"I could not have, as I was feeding our brothers."

"How can you deny it, Alexander? I was with you. Remember?"

"I have no memory of this because I was not there."

Layla clenched her hands. "I had hoped you would give a reasonable explanation and apologize. As you provide neither, then I am forced to take the next step."

Alexander looked genuinely puzzled. "Why do you think I attacked you? I would never harm you."

"After what you tried to do last night, you dare say you would never hurt me? You are a monster."

"He is innocent," said Caleb. "I worked alongside him last night."

"How can you defend him?"

"Because I speak truth. Alexander was with me."

Layla's anger faltered as she glanced at the five identical faces staring at her. "Someone attacked me, and he wore Alexander's nametag."

Alexander stepped forward. "It was not me. May I look at your memory?"

Apprehension filled Layla. Was he really innocent or did he want to alter her memory? Then again, why had he not caught her and erased her memory last night? The culprit had not bitten her, even when she had willingly offered her neck before the attack. Realization dawned on her. He had not done so because the moment he did, she would have known that it was not Alexander entering her mind.

"It was not you."

"No."

"I'm sorry. He wore your nametag. I thought…I should have realized immediately when he asked me to follow him alone."

Alexander stepped closer. "May I?"

Layla presented her back, brushing her own hair away from her neck. There was the prick then last night replayed itself. She and Alexander stood behind Advance Department. The door opened and she watched herself walk out of the building and greet the other Alexander. The scene shifted to the decayed barracks. It was bizarre watching her naïve self examining spider webs while the false Alexander boldly glared at her like a predator hungering for prey. Why had she not noticed that before?

When the groping started, she grabbed the real Alexander's arm. "I cannot watch this again."

"I need to see how it ended. I will be with you soon."

The dark barracks vanished, and Layla stood in the city park on her home planet, calmness filling her. *He's controlling my emotions.*

A short time later, Alexander appeared in front of her. She felt his outrage mixed with concern about her wellbeing. "You defended yourself well."

"I was terrified. Who is he?"

"I believe I know." His anger boiled into rage. "And I will terminate him for you."

The link broke and Layla was once again was in the courtyard. Alexander stepped away from her and looked across the circle at Mason. For a moment Mason met his eyes then bolted, running back along the path. Alexander immediately pursued. The other quintessences looked at each other then at Layla. She stood there, trembling, remembering Alexander's rage. He had meant what he said about killing his brother.

"We must follow," she said and ran down the path.

Two quintessences quickly passed her and disappeared around a bend, but Jacob kept in step with her, despite her slowness. Upon reaching the training field, she had to stop to catch her breath. Jacob waited beside her, his breathing barely above its normal rate. Glancing across the huge field, she saw Gabriel and Caleb halfway across, heading towards two distant figures swinging staffs at each other. Layla ran through the overgrown field with Jacob beside her, feeling as if she was in a nightmare where no matter how fast you tried to move, you never drew nearer to your destination.

Then suddenly she was there. Caleb, Jacob, and Gabriel watched silently as their brothers dueled. Mason and Alexander swung their *bō's* with such rapid speed that they were a blur to her untrained eyes. They swung and leaped, rolling and dodging. Metal hit metal, sparks flew. The opponents locked eyes, identical faces both reflecting hate. They broke apart then attacked again, swirled and twisted, determined to destroy the other. Most strikes were blocked, but some blows hit flesh with sicken thuds. The staffs' sharpen tips sliced clothing and skin. They moved too fast for Layla to read their nametags. When a keen-edged tip cut across the face of one, she did not know if the blood which splattered the ground was from her beloved or her adversary.

Fear rent her heart. Equally matched, equally trained, they were literally beating each other to death. For one to be victor, he must approach the edge of death himself to kill the other.

"Stop!" yelled Layla. The combatants ignored her as they swung their weapons with powerful, bone-breaking strokes. Layla turned to the watchers. "Stop them."

The three quintessences glanced at her then moved towards the combatants, grabbing them from behind. Alexander and Mason struggled to break free to continue the fight. Layla rushed between them.

"That is enough! No more."

"You want him dead," said Alexander, "as much as I do."

"Yes, but not this way. I do not want you to die also." She noted the blood seeping from cuts on his face, arms, and chest. She turned to Mason, equally covered in gore. "Why did you attack me?"

"It was not an attack. Just a kiss. You were supposed to never have known it was not him. It is his fault. We share everything. But he refused. 'Some memories are private,' he said. But not from us, his brothers. He is the one who betrayed us."

"You are the betrayer!" shouted Alexander. "You have looked too long into the depravity of minds twisted with lewdness, jealousy, and greed. Have we not warned you repeatedly it was perilous?"

"I look into what you are too cowardly to face. Do you think by looking the other way that you are immune to the effects of debauchery? We must understand it. Has not my advice helped us many times to catch criminals who eluded capture?"

"Despite the good you have done, you spent too much time near evil and became it. You could not stop with stealing a kiss. You wanted more, much more."

"I did not mean to upset her."

"Trying to satisfy your curiosity almost cost us our lives. All of us. She planned to cut the whole program, labeling us hazardous. You almost became the weapon of our extinction, brother."

Mason appeared shaken. "I did not mean for things to turn out this way." He looked at Layla. "I am sorry. I just wanted to know what it felt like to kiss you. I never meant to hurt you."

"But you did," said Layla, hands clenched.

Mason dropped his staff and knelt on the ground. "My actions call for my death. But please do not hold accountable the others for what I have done."

Layla looked at the kneeling quintessence, her creation, her monster. "As I can give life, so I can give death." The weight of that power scared her, and her body trembled. "I will not take yours, not today. I pardon you."

He looked up, surprised.

"Some of the blame I will take. I had not considered the effect of kissing Alexander in front of the rest of you. You are clones. If one likes me, it did not occur to me that another might also. Still, your actions were wrong. Make no mistake, Mason. I will forgive this first offence, but I will not forgive again. And I will never forget. If you hurt me or any woman ever again, I will gas you. I will push the button myself."

"Your judgment is fair, my creator." Mason stood, feeling the stares of shame from his brothers. "I will not let my family down again."

Caleb broke the silence which fell on the group. "We need a code of conduct."

"You have been told countless rules," said Layla.

"Rules for humans. What is immoral for one species is not for another. Quintessences must have laws which we hold our brethren to. And consequences."

Alexander moved to Layla's side. "It should be forbidden to impersonate another. The punishment death."

Gabriel said, "No quintessence should put his welfare before his brethren."

"Each must act honorable, avoiding vices," said Jacob. "To the universe we must present ourselves exemplary."

"You must help those in need," said Layla. "Protect the weak. And never give in to lust."

"Always obey the orders of superiors," added Mason, blood seeping from his many cuts. "Those who fail should stand trial before their brothers who will decide their fate."

"Is it agreed?" asked Caleb.

"It is agreed," said the others in unison.

As the group headed towards Advance Department, Layla pulled Alexander to the side. She waited until the others had disappeared into the trees then said, "Forgive me for thinking it was you."

"You had justifiable cause. I am relieved you decided to talk with us before sending that message."

"To think, I almost lost you again," her voice broke. "This time by my own hand."

Alexander stepped close and wrapped his arms around her. She laid her head on his chest and cried, only regaining her composure when she realized his wounds still bled. "You need to heal."

She turned her back to him, allowing him to fed, pulling her life force from her body. There was no pain, only contentment as she felt his love for her through the link. He fed only briefly before breaking the link. The forest and field seem to spin around Layla.

"Your dizziness will pass momentary," said Alexander, keeping his arms around her, steadying her, the blood from his healed cuts drying on his bronze skin.

She turned and tilted her face for a kiss. He hesitated, uncertain.

"It is alright, Alexander. I trust you."

He bent and kissed her, gently. Layla pulled him tightly to her, ignoring his blood smearing her clothing.

Later when they strolled out of the woods near Advance Department, Anthony silently watched them pass the playground where he supervised Generation Two playing a ball game. He frowned as his sharp eyes noted the dried blood on both Alexander and Layla.

Part III

Master

"I knew that I was preparing for myself a deadly torture; but I was the slave, not the master, of an impulse which I detested, yet could not disobey."

—From *Frankenstein* by Mary Shelley

Chapter Twenty-three

Roobaroo sighed, tired from a long day of paperwork and phone calls. The last decade of her life had been spent in this small office, obeying a boss more interesting in looking good to superiors than doing what was right. Her suggestions for making important social changes were always ignored. With her qualifications, she should have been promoted above her boss years ago, but her parent's history held her back. Not many wanted a daughter of exiles working for them, despite her high IQ. For the hundredth time she thought of giving up and leaving the planet to find a job were her parents' stigma did not matter. Yet there was a part of her that refused to back down from finding a way to change the strict rules of her culture and bring the High Council face-to-face with their own injustices.

Hearing a knock at the door, she looked up. Two officials in military uniforms walked in, causing Roobaroo's heart to quicken. Her position was too low for their visit to be business, but surely her activity with the insurgents was untraceable. Carrying an occasional encrypted file to a contact did not mark her as a rebel. Never had she been stopped and questioned. Yet now soldiers were in her office.

"Take a seat, gentlemen. How may I help you?"

"We'll stand, ma'am," said the higher ranking one. "Sadly, I must bring you tragic news. We learned earlier today that a Mansoor shuttle carrying your parents crashed, killing all on board."

Roobaroo's world spun around her. "They are dead?"

"Yes, ma'am. We are sorry for your lost. An investigation will be conducted by Mansoor authorities, but it is already being labeled a mechanical failure."

"How many were aboard?"

"Twelve, including the pilot."

More was said but Roobaroo remembered little. After the officers left, she stared blankly at her monitor. Though she only saw her parents on rare vacations off world, they had meant everything to her. They had shaped her life, her passions. She had no other family—at least none who would claim her. Now she was truly alone in the universe. No, she still had a few genuine friends, but they were either off world or below her caste, contact with them kept secret.

The room felt suddenly cold. Shivering, she stood and moved to the window overlooking the beautiful capitol city. The massive High Council Forum drew her attention and rage filled her. Someone there ordered her parents' murder. That she was certain of, but she would never be able to prove it. Hunter had warned her at their last meeting that a contact had overheard angry comments from several Councilors about her parents. The ambassadors had gained strong influence with diaspora groups of ediethean living on planets outside the Council's jurisdiction. Roobaroo had passed the warning onto her parents to be careful, but it had not helped.

Her shift over, she headed to the elevator, ignoring questions from a few co-workers about why the officers had visited. Outside, she walked aimlessly, her emotions a volatile mix of grief, rage, self-pity, and loneliness. Councilors were untouchable. If she went to the police with her suspicions of murder, they would not believe her but report her accusations to the Council. Then again, she might already be marked for execution. If she was investigated, her boss and co-workers would testify that her political views were a bit different, though she kept her strongest beliefs secret. The Council may have already ruled to end her parents' linage, and at any moment she could disappear like her sister.

An election advertisement on a giant screen high on a skyscraper's side caught her eye. A gigantic, grinning Cerron waved at viewers as his logo appeared under his picture. Most likely he would win the city council position he ran for. In another decade or two he would probably be mayor. Within a century, part of the High Council. Roobaroo had several times seriously considered marrying him. With him by her side, she could have become powerful, but she detested being yoked to someone who held the same egotistical beliefs as other Alz. Nor could she turn to him now in a desperate move to protect herself, for he had taken a wife long ago.

She continued roaming, trying to clear her emotions. Now was the time to think clearly, to figure out what options remained to her. Taking out her telecom, Roobaroo punched in a number which was supposedly untraceable. She said a few code words then wandered down random streets, waiting. Twenty minutes later, it beeped. She read the message, "Scorpion, one hour." Roobaroo would have preferred one of the other secluded spots the insurgents rendezvoused at, but it was not her call. Reaching Orion Park early, she walked slowly down various paths, finally taking the stairs down into the dark, abandoned substation. Hunter waited by the crates, a lantern illumining only a small circle of the vast chamber.

As Roobaroo took a seat beside him, Hunter asked, "What's wrong? Have you been compromised?"

"No, but my parents are dead. Supposedly an accidental shuttle crash."

Hunter took in a deep breath. "I'm sorry. We did warn you."

"I know. They promised to be careful, but who can stop a hit once it has been ordered? They always find a way."

"You may have been marked too."

"I guessed that."

"Don't go back to your apartment or your job."

"Just quit? Vanish like I never existed? That is not my way."

"You won't have any way if you are dead."

They sat side-by-side in the dim light. Roobaroo took comfort in his presence, the feeling of being connected to a soul who understood her. She could flee Edieth, but she would never see him again. Over the last few years, a genuine friendship had developed between them as they both sought ways to undermine the Council's power.

Roobaroo stared at the dancing flames of the lantern. "If I run, they win."

"Better to run and fight another day. Do as your parents and fight with ideas from the outside."

"But nothing ever changes." Roobaroo's frustration poured out. "The diaspora hate the Council. Big deal. It was why they choose to live in exile in the first place. Ten thousand years and the High Council still controls our lives with an iron fist. Insurgents are quickly put down, rebellions erased from our history. Only Alz are qualified to make decisions for the other twenty-one classes. Byk, marry this one. Daq, take this job. Fyw, live in this neighborhood. Hym, you will make this one product your whole life. Xit, you are not worthy to waste an education on. I hate my own genes. If I could rip them out of myself without dying, I would."

"You speak nonsense. They are what gives you that brilliant mind."

"For what good? A lifetime of effort and I have changed nothing. Nothing."

"You have a couple of more centuries of trying, if you don't do anything crazy."

"We need to do something so crazy and so big that not only will it gain the Council's attention but sentients across the empire. Perhaps even the Galactic Senate and the Emperor himself."

"How do you propose we achieve that without hurting someone? We are not terrorists."

Roobaroo thought carefully before answering. "Perhaps it is time to kill."

Hunter looked at her, shocked. "We don't kill."

"The Council does. They weed out the aggressors and the rest of society goes along peacefully with all their rules. That is how they have kept control for the last ten thousand years. True change will not happen unless we do something dramatic."

"That's suicidal."

"I am marked for death anyway. I might as well go out with a bang."

"We don't know for sure if you are marked."

"It does not matter. This is the only logically way to proceed."

Hunter shook his head. "No. We will hack another newsfeed and declare your parents murdered."

"The few who notice will not care. You are not taken seriously."

A voice croaked from the darkness. "I agree with her."

Startled, Roobaroo jumped, searching the blackness for the speaker. She had long been aware that others visited the hideout, perhaps even lived here, but she had never seen their faces. That way if she was ever caught, she could not betray them.

Into the dim light stepped an elderly Daq dressed in a priestess robe, dark blue embroidered with white silk patterns along the edges. "I have fought against injustice my whole life and seen little in return. My life is near its end. What do you have in mind, Alz?"

"We take over a factory that ships off world. Stop production as long as we can. It will hurt their pockets and might raise questions from outsiders."

Two other figures stepped into the flicking light, both Eay, one middle-age, the other barely older than Roobaroo. The younger one said, "To earn attention from outsiders, the factory must be closed for a long time. A few well-placed bombs could do that."

"No," said Hunter. "You will kill innocent workers, while the Alz owners only lose money." He sighed and looked back to Roobaroo. "Are you certain you want to take on a suicide mission?"

"Yes. For the memory of my sister and parents, I am willing to die."

"Then we go after the largest factory on the planet—the sweatshop my father manages. I worked there for a few years. But no bombs. There are six thousand Yaz who live there. They are simpleminded, obeying any order."

The Eay youth smiled, "An army at our command to keep back the police."

"They are not soldiers, barely smarter than a toddler. We must avoid putting them in danger."

Roobaroo said, "We will try to protect them, but some will probably die before it is over. Their sacrifice will be for the benefit of their race. Those who join me must expect the same fate." The others firmly met her eyes. "We must plan very carefully, leaving nothing to chance. We will only have one opportunity."

"I am with you," said the priestess. "May the Divine Light protect us."

"My fate is yours," said Hunter. "Since we are already walking a forbidden path, I propose one more." He stood and held her hands, his eyes intense. "Roobaroo, will you marry me?"

She stared, thunderstruck. Marriage between castes was an instant death sentence, an act so forbidden that not even those living in diaspora broke it. No parents would approve of such a marriage. But hers were not here to say no. She squeezed Hunter's hand. "It would be my honor."

Hunter glanced at the priestess. "Will you marry us today?"

The elderly Daq nodded and pulled out her holy book. Within the circle of flickering lantern light, Roobaroo said the sacred vows with her husband, breaking the first of many laws yet to come.

Chapter Twenty-four

Layla only half-listened to the chief of maintenance listing the need for more funding for his department. Her e-tablet's clock showed the staff meeting had dragged on for two hours. She glanced over at Mera Walkins texting a message to her husband, explaining why she would be home late. At the far end of the large table, Anthony Franklin watched the speaker but his thoughts seemed far away. Banican Zine interrupted the maintenance chief several times, challenging the petition for more money. Finally Palakkad made a closing statement and dismissed the meeting.

As Layla headed for the door, Anthony caught up with her. "I need to speak with you, in private."

Layla stopped and waited for the room to clear. "You could have talked with me at Advance."

Anthony shut the door then said, "Too many prying ears there. What I have to say needs to go no further. At least I hope there is no need." The retired soldier studied her, his probing eyes making Layla uncomfortable. "You need to stop seeing him."

"What are you talking about?"

"Alexander."

Layla forced a laugh. "I see him all the time. How can I not? He is part of my job."

"You know what I am referring to. I have suspected for some time, all those walks in the woods with the Five, but I kept telling myself you were too smart to fall into that trap. I guess being a profectus still doesn't make you infallible. "

"I do not know what you suspect, but I have done nothing against company policy."

"I'm sure if this gets out, the board will quickly add a line in BGF's handbook about not romancing company products."

"You are out of line."

"No, you are. When my charges start fighting each other, it becomes my business. Last week, Mason came back from a walk, beaten up pretty badly. Then you and Alexander came out of the woods. His clothing was cut and bloody, and you bloody but uninjured. Something serious happened in the woods that day between them, and I believe you are the common denominator."

"Alexander was injured. I allowed him to use me to heal. That was all."

Anthony's eyes narrowed. "Why did Alexander and Mason fight?"

"I do not know. You will have to ask them."

"I already did. They said nothing except it would never happen again."

"Well, problem solved. They made up their differences."

"The difference is you. You're playing with fire, girl, and it is going to explode in your face. They are clones. I don't know if you're romancing one or both of them, but jealousy will destroy everything."

"They said it would not happen again. I believe them."

"Only if you step out of the picture. We are training soldiers who, on the battlefield, will be under pressures you can't even began to understand. The way quintessences work together, almost read each others' minds, overcome obstacles quicker and better than any soldier I have ever seen. Their successes on the SWAT team are seen as…miraculous. You and I know their success comes because of their teamwork. Destroy that and you destroy the strength of the quintessences. Someday one of them will be in a position to watch his brother die, and if he holds a grudge, simply by doing nothing, he can murder his brother. Jealousy and strife are weapons which kill. If you do not step away from the quintessences, you could become their downfall."

Layla's heart pounded in anger and fear. "I can date who I wish. You cannot stop me."

Anthony sighed. "I am not your enemy, lass, despite what you may think. I am almost as fond of the quintessences as my own grandchildren. But I am under no disillusionment. They are not citizens. They have no rights, can never marry or become fathers. They will always have masters which tell them where to go, what to wear, whom to battle. The only right they can claim is the ability to fight as long as possible before they die. And they will die sooner or later."

"I will not sell the Five. I will keep them here, safe." *Except, perhaps Mason,* she thought silently.

"Listen to the advice of an old man who has lived through much. I know what it is like to love. My wife has stood by me even when I was away on duty for months, sometimes years at a time. She stuck by me through thick and thin. It is wonderful to have someone there for you, to share a home and a life with. But you can't play house with a quintessence. You need to move on, find a human you can marry, raise a family with. Be happy."

"As you are happily married, then you must understand the depth of love." Layla clenched her fists, fighting a losing battle with her emotions. "What Alexander and I have goes far beyond mere words. He...he travels into my soul where no other may visit. I...I cannot give him up. I would prefer death first!"

Layla turned and fled from the room before he could say more, her emotions wild. Safe in her apartment, she paced back and forth across the cluttered carpet, muttering to herself.

"How dare he ask me to give up Alexander! Who does he think he is? I am Alexander's creator and know what is best for him. So what if Alexander can never marry. It is not like I want to settle down and have kids. Ha, I have fifty kids right now. I am sick of children."

She leaned against a chair by her desk, staring at the mirror reflecting her tear-stained face. "I am satisfied with just talking with him." *And him holding me, kissing me.* "I need nothing more."

Despite Anthony's warning, the next day Layla showed up near the end of training and boldly led the Five into the forest to the ruined courtyard. Last night's deep frost had stolen life from the flowers, turning them into shivered, brown deformities. Stillness smothered the ancient plaza. The songbirds had fled to a warmer climate and the insects were either dead or hibernating. Layla marched directly to the cracked fountain and sat, expecting Alexander to join her.

Instead, he stood several yards away. "Captain Franklin talked with us last night."

"So? Nothing he says matters to me."

"It should. He ordered me to stop seeing you."

"Ordered?"

"He is our superior."

"You do not have to obey him."

"Yes, I do. It is stated in our Code of Conduct."

"Alexander, the Code is only one week old. And I am Anthony's superior. I say you can see me as much as you wish."

"BGF's board will overrule you if they knew."

"They do not." She stood up and stepped closer to Alexander. "Forget the board and Anthony. Everyone. There is just you and me."

"And my brothers. Layla, I must put their wellbeing above me. Above us. That is part of the Code too. Last night Anthony had a long talk with us. He was frank, discussing topics we usually avoid. If it became public knowledge that you were dating a quintessence, the fallout could be disastrous, possibly endangering the entire program and my brothers' lives."

"No one knows but Anthony. Just erase his memory."

"We view erasing the memory of superiors as unethical. And I suspect Tiffany knows too."

"How? We have been careful."

"The day you blew up in front of her when you learned of my first kills. Your face reveals much to those who look closely."

"Then that is it? Am I just supposed to walk pass you every day and pretend we are strangers?"

"I think my brothers and I should leave."

"Leave? You cannot. This is your home."

"The Austin Police Department has already told us they will provide us an apartment near the station. We can work more days. There is even a martial arts school nearby which we wish to attend. We will still come back a couple days a week to teach our brothers. You will have more space at Advance. It is a good arrangement for everyone."

"Except for me. Do you really want to leave me?"

"No. But my brothers do. They feel stifled here, held back. There is a universe for us to explore, but we need you to let us go."

"I cannot do that."

"Yes, you can, though it will hurt you. Hurt me. We must put the welfare of others in front of our own desires."

Layla fought against tears threatening to overwhelm her. Alexander walked forward to hold her, but stopped himself. Seeing that, Layla lost complete control, and tears ran down her cheeks.

"I have spent most of my life alone. How dare you come, tell me I needed to let others in, only to walk away a few months later. I thought you loved me."

"I do. But that is not enough. Layla, I cannot give you what you need. You deserve someone who can go home with you at night. A husband who will give you children. I have nothing to offer you. Not property, money, or a name. My body is not even mine to give you. I own nothing. I am nothing."

"You gave me friendship. You looked inside me, seeing what I hid from all, yet you still cared about me. I ask for nothing else."

"I made you a promise that my love will always be with you. That will be true to the day I die. But you must still let me go. Perhaps someday you will find another."

"Never."

"I will not hold it against you. You deserve so much more. Goodbye, Layla."

He walked away, not glancing back. His stoic-face brothers joined him. They disappeared down the overgrown path cutting through the tangled forest, leaving her standing in the empty winter garden, weeping, surrounded by long-forgotten stone gods.

The next day she filled out the forms necessary to give the Austin Police Department temporary control over the Five, but not ownership. Those rights remained with BGF. Layla stayed in her lab, refusing to say goodbye when the Five climbed into the hover van with Seit Tigon, carrying bags of clothing and their *bō's*.

As winter drifted pass, Layla was barely aware of its passing. Out of habit she continued to look for Alexander when she entered a room, pain renting her heart each time she remembered his absence. She had little awareness of what she ate, the conversations she had, or the data she typed in her e-table. She became a zombie, performing by rote.

Twice a week the Five drove to BGF to train their younger brothers, traveling in an old hover van the police department had loaned them. The quintessences spent most of the day outdoors, even in the snowy days of winter, pushing themselves hard. When they came in to eat, Layla kept busy in other rooms, tending the rapidly growing babies who would soon be toddlers. During the rare moments Layla happened to see the Five, she quickly averted her eyes and left the room.

Reoccurring nightmares haunted Layla. Hundreds of quintessences surrounded her. She would dash through the crowd, searching for Alexander, seeing his face everywhere but not his nametag. When she finally discovered him, he would walk away in disdain. She would try to follow, grabbing his arm, only to have Alexander morph into Mason who turned toward her with an arrogant, lustful sneer he had never worn in real life. She would flee through the ocean of quintessences, yelling for help. Many ignored her. Others stared blankly. Mason remained a shadowy figure pursuing her until she woke up, screaming.

Layla fell back into her old habit of isolating herself from everyone, keeping to her lab, grumpy when disturbed by babies or caregivers. After work she hid in her apartment, either reading science journals or writing long, technical articles. Rarely did she drive to Taylorville to shop or send messages to family. Separation and time had turned them into strangers. Her parents were nearing retirement. Blaaze was married with kids of his own.

Occasionally she received messages from Roobaroo, but they were cryptic, reflecting bitterness since the deaths of her parents. "I just read an article claiming the Galactic Senate is considering buying your quintessences. Congratulations on creating a slave race. After all my parents and I went through attempting to help my species' own slave castes, my best friend turns out to be a slaver. I thought you were better than that. But I was wrong, as I have been wrong about so many things. The evils of society cannot be changed, no matter how hard we fight against them. Either you keep your mouth shut and go along with the flow or they silence you. What was the cost which bought your silence? Or perhaps you are going along willingly. Another proud accomplishment for the almighty profectus race."

After listening to the message, Layla sat for hours in her dark apartment, alone, staring at the mocking quote she had placed on the wall in her naïve youth. "Deep into the darkness peering, long I stood there, wondering, fearing. Doubting, dreaming dreams no mortals ever dared to dream before." Why must dreams fade into the ugliness of real life? Eventually she cried herself to sleep. Weeks passed and the last snows finally melted, leaving the ground muddy and disheveled.

"Are you getting enough sleep," asked Rosetta in the breakroom one afternoon.

"I am fine." Layla bent down, peering into a cabinet to check supplies. "Add pasta and juice to the list."

Rosetta's fingers moved quickly across her e-tablet. "You haven't been yourself for...some time."

"This is the normal me."

"No, you're far crankier than you used to be."

Layla straightened up. "That is because I am sharing my lab with six toddlers and my research is constantly being disrupted by people with questions."

Rosetta sighed and laid her e-tablet on the counter. "I think it's something more. Look, I'm sorry we haven't hung out like we used to. With having two kids then Generation Three to oversee, I've had little free time. Maybe we could see a movie together. No husband, no kids."

"Maybe later. I have an article which needs finishing this week."

"Well, if you find time, let me know."

Tiffany rushed into the room, her face pale. "Allen—he fell."

At the mention of her son's name, Rosetta rushed out of the room and ran towards the playground, Tiffany and Layla following behind. Under a large tree lay the still body of five-year-old Allen. Zylar was bent over the boy, trying to revive him. Nearby ten half-grown quintessences stared silently. Rosetta dropped to her knees beside her son, checking for a pulse.

Zylar was unnaturally quiet while Tiffany babbled, "I'm so sorry. We were talking. We told him not to climb the tree, but he went back up. The quintessences were jumping out of it, and he wanted to act like them."

"He's breathing," said Rosetta, her shaky hands searching for broken bones. She looked up at Layla. "Get Derrick!"

Knowing Derrick had volunteered to be used as a hostage in an exercise, Layla ran towards the training field. Her side aching, her breath ragged, she reached the clearing and sought out the nearest quintessence.

She wheezed, "Allen fell." She bent double, trying to catch her breath.

Gabriel lowered his gun and yelled, "Drill over! Derrick, you are needed."

A voice came from a nearby half-collapsed shed, "Ha, you'll have to do better than that, villain."

"Your...son...fell," gasped Layla.

Derrick peeked from behind a wall, took one look at Layla, and then bolted for the path. Most of the quintessences and Anthony followed, carrying their weapons with them. When Layla's breathing had slowed enough for walking, she turned towards the path and saw Alexander standing silently, waiting for her. It was the first time since the breakup that she had looked him in the eyes. Her heartbeat quickened and her feet froze.

"We should see if the boy is well," said Alexander, his blank face revealing nothing.

"Yes, uh, it looked bad. He was unconscious."

As they walked side by side along the path, Layla was hyperaware of how near Alexander was, his hand just inches from her. Twice her own treasonous hand inched towards his, but she pulled back each time before it could betray her. She had fought all these months to forget the sensations of being in love, but it all came rushing back—along with the pain of abandonment.

As they reached the playground, they heard Allen crying loudly, "It hurts, Mama. It hurts."

"I know. We're taking you to the hospital now."

Derrick gingerly picked up his son, and the child screamed out in pain. "My arm! Daddy, my arm."

"It's going to be alright, son. I'm driving. No need to wait for an ambulance."

"I will drive," said Jacob. "I can get you there faster."

For a moment, Derrick looked uncertain. Then he nodded and followed Jacob to the hover van where he laid the crying boy on a seat beside him.

Rosetta and Mason climbed in. Jacob drove at top speed across the parking lot, easily dodging a vehicle pulling out. Layla stood by Alexander. Together they watching the van disappear.

Nearby Tiffany cried, "It's all my fault. I should have been paying more attention."

Zylar held her, his usual jovial expression now somber. "I'm the one who distracted you. Don't blame yourself."

Watching the couple comforting each other made Layla feel uneasy—and jealous. Alexander stood a yard away but it might as well be a light-year. Nothing in his impassive face revealed emotions of any kind. Did he still hold to his promise to always love her? Or had she been forgotten in his new life?

"Allen will be alright," said Anthony. "Kids break bones all the time. He'll heal right up. I'll go ask Leana if she'll watch their younger son till they get back."

As Anthony, Tiffany, and Zylar headed inside, Caleb lined up the half-grown quintessences and lectured them. "Why did you not stop the boy from jumping?"

The youths, who now resembled twelve-year-old humans, stood rigid as trained soldiers. None answered.

"I repeat," said Caleb. "Why did you not stop the boy? He is a human child, weak and immature. You knew he had been ordered not to climb the tree, yet you did nothing to prevent him. Instead, you continued to jump out of the tree, knowing he liked to copy you. Instead of trying to display proper behavior for the boy, you showed off, a vice no quintessence should display. I am ashamed of you."

The young quintessences tried to hide their feelings, but Layla could see disappointment in their eyes.

"You have broken the Code," said Gabriel. "There is no greater dishonor. Are you not to protect the weak? That includes humans who cannot make proper judgment. You will spend the rest of this afternoon on your cots, thinking about what happened. And there will be no supper. Dismissed."

The preteens filed silently pass Layla, avoiding looking at her. After they left, she said, "Are you not being a bit hard on them? They are kids."

"They left childhood a long time ago," said Alexander.

"Still, no supper? That is over doing it."

"Quintessences do not have the luxury of adolescence. We must grow up quickly. Skipping a meal is the least of the hardships they will face."

"Yes, they might fall in love then be told it is forbidden."

Pain flickered across Alexander's face, but he was quick to hide it. Yet it was enough. Layla had seen and knew he still had feelings for her. Not wanting anyone to see her cry, she turned and walked away.

It was still too early to take off from work, so she headed to the main building of BGF. By the time she reached the huge structure, her emotions were back under control. Trying to find a reason for being there, she searched for Mera, only to learn the supervisor had the day off. She wandered about, trying to kill time, hoping the Five had left for Austin City, then remembered that Jacob and Mason had taken the van to the hospital, leaving the others stranded. Turning a corner, she spotted Banican Zine talking with a colleague at the other end of the corridor. Not wishing to deal with him today, she ducked into the closest unlocked door to hide.

She found herself in a small chapel left over from when the property had belonged to the military. Icons from various religions hung on the walls, their meanings unfamiliar to Layla. Her parents observed several Hindu holidays, but they rarely spoke about religion as they focused on their science careers. She settled on a pew furthest from the door. Stillness weighed heavily in the dimly lit room. She tried to will time to pass faster. There was nothing to distract her from memories of Alexander, his pained look when she had commented about forbidden love.

Needing to lash out at something, she glared at a crucifix. "I do not believe you exist, but my friend Rosetta does. If you are there, then I just wanted to tell you that you are very unfair. I only want one thing in life, just one. Is that too much to ask for? He should belong to me, not BGF. I am his creator. Where is the fairness in that? Do you punish me for trying to do your job? You know, I did it much better than you. I needed only a few years while it takes you millenniums."

Her rush of anger faded into despair. "I have really sunk to a new low, talking to air. What does it matter what I have accomplished? I have nothing to show for it. I cannot even afford to buy my own creation. An empty life of drudgery is my reward."

Thoughts drifted through her mind of Palakkad and Leana Sebok working in Human Advancement Department for decades to create her and the other profectus. Leana, in the end, had been bitter about the project's abandonment, her life's work ended—until the quintessences had been born. Now she was their teacher, happy with a purpose.

"I thought the quintessences were my purpose, my destiny. I created them, but now they no longer need me."

They feel stifled here, held back, Alexander had told her.

If you do not step away from the quintessences, you could become their downfall, mocked Anthony's voice.

"I have been discarded by my own creations, thrown away like junk."

She recalled images of Derrick excitedly working on Anya, seeing value in an ancient machine when others only saw junk. Without Derrick's passion for technology, the quintessences would still only be a theory on her computer. In fact, the quintessence project would not have lasted long at all without the many talented people who had come along at just the right time. Richard Cambridge's advance software was designed for her needs, Rosetta's wisdom in birthing and raising quintessences, Mera's advice in administration skills, Anthony's military background and plans to create soldiers, Palakkad's constant support.

Layla's paradigm of the quintessence project shifted. She had believed herself the one central ingredient who claimed the sole title of creator. But without the many others, the project would have failed. It was as if the universe had decided to will the quintessences into existence, and she was just one of its many tools.

"Forgive my arrogance," she whispered into the quietness of the chapel. "I have thought too highly of myself. But still, I am alone, abandoned when my purpose was fulfilled. What is left for me in life?"

You, child, have tuned out the wonders of my universe, weaved a thought through her mind, perhaps a product of her imagination. Still, it stuck a cord, challenging her. She pondered the statement until her work shift was over.

She walked back to her one-room apartment. As she drew near the door, she noticed the hedges which grew in front of her home. They had been buried under snow all winter, their ordinary dull greenness making them forgettable. Now a carpet of vivid pink flowers covered them, their aroma intoxicating on the evening breeze.

Can I ever come to life like them? she wondered.

Rosetta and Derrick were out the rest of the week, staying at the hospital with their son. The day to day running of Advance Department which Rosetta normally oversaw fell to Layla. While the quieter night shift ran smoothly under Opal's leadership, the responsibilities of overseeing two day shifts overwhelmed Layla. Schedules needed to be rewritten as employees asked for a day off or called in sick. Visitors dropped by unannounced. Supplies needed purchasing and unpacking. Equipment broke down. Meals needed cooking. At least Zylar, still feeling guilty about the accident, worked diligently carrying out trash and fixing broken items. Layla swore she would never take Rosetta and Derrick for granted again.

When Monday came, Layla had Leana baked a welcome back cake for the returning family. Caregivers and quintessences crowded into the breakroom for the party.

Little Allen chatted cheerfully about his hospital visit. "They took me to the big city for nanites. Healed me in one day. Not as quick as quintessences. But they wouldn't let me leave for three more days. Had to wait till nanites left me."

Leana said, "Nanites are an expensive treatment."

"Tell me about it," said Rosetta bottle feeding her younger son, "Cost more than a college education for one treatment. But Derrick insisted."

"Our insurance paid for it," said her husband. "Besides, how often does one get a close up of nano medical treatments?"

"With your excitement about the whole thing, I almost think you are happy our son broke his arm just so you could get inside their department."

"He has a great story to brag about. What the N58X2 can do is amazing. Just took one day to heal a broken bone. Perhaps we will advance to the point where using them will be an everyday occurrence. Imagine soldiers healed and back into the battle within a few days."

"They will never beat the healing speed of quintessences," said Layla. "What is so special about the N5 whatever? We have nanites here."

"They are a century old with outdated programming. They could never handle the delicate process of rebuilding bone cells without killing the host."

"So did you grab a N58X2?" asked Zylar, munching on his second slice of cake.

"I spent four days trying to figure out how, but the hospital has strict security. Won't let the patient go home until every last nanite is accounted for."

"Derrick Cashman!" lectured Rosetta. "What type of example are you setting for our son? If you got yourself arrested for stealing nanites, I would never speak to you again."

Her husband looked crestfallen, "You would not even text me in jail?"

"Well, maybe."

"It would be a lectext," Zylar said. "You know, a lecture that is texted." The groans from his neighbors hinted his joke was not well received, so he changed the subject. "Jacob, I heard you were driving over a hundred all the way to Taylorville."

The quintessence said nonchalantly, "We often drive at high speeds and have yet to have an accident."

"But what about speeding tickets?"

"Speeding tickets are not issued to livestock, which is what we are classified as."

Zylar pondered that for a moment. "I guess you don't fine the sheep for driving the tractor, but you still could fine the farmer. Won't BGF get angry if they get sent your tickets?"

"That is not a problem for us," said Jacob, taking a bite of cake.

Layla explained, "The Austin police commissioner issued them special passes which allows them to drive, since not being legal citizens, they cannot get driver licenses."

"Can I see one?" asked Zylar. Jacob handed his over, and Zylar studied the hologram picture and text. "I've never seen a badge like this. I bet it would allow you to get away with doing a lot of stuff like not paying tolls or driving in emergency lanes. I wonder how hard it would be to counterfeit?"

"Better give it back," said Derrick, "before you wind up spending more time in jail than I would for stealing a nanite."

With a deep look of longing, Zylar gave back the badge. His facial expression caused Layla to laugh, a feeling she had not felt in a long time. The party ended and workers headed off to various tasks. Layla cleaned up the breakroom with Tiffany who chatted about her first year at Austin University where she carpooled three days a week. Rosetta sat at the counter, filling out next week's work schedule.

Putting the last of the clean dishes in a cabinet, Layla asked both of them, "Would you like to go out to a movie tonight with me?"

Caught off guard, both glanced at each other. Then Tiffany said, "Sure. Zylar had been talking about seeing that new comedy that came out last week."

"I was thinking maybe an all girl's night."

"Alright. It could be fun."

Rosetta grinned, "It will be good for Derrick to have to tend the kids without me for a night."

They met that evening in town at Rosetta's house then took Layla's hover car to the small theater. After the movie, they headed to a café for dinner. Rosetta and Tiffany chatted easily about the men in their lives while Layla listened silently, fighting against jealousy.

"I don't know how you do it." Tiffany ignored the stares of several teenagers admiring her trendy, tight fitting clothes. "You have your husband so well trained. Zylar has a good heart, but sometimes he makes the most insensitive statements."

"Lots of patience." Despite gaining a few pounds after birthing two children, Rosetta was still striking with her long red hair and green V-neck blouse. "Don't give up on Zylar. Men just take longer to mature. You have had a strong impact on him already."

"Are you sure? It doesn't feel like it." Tiffany brushed a stray lock of blond hair off her face then took another bite of her salad.

"He works harder without complaining as much. Even volunteered to work weekends to be near you. And he talks about more than just technology now. Believe me, that's a big relief for the rest of us."

Tiffany blushed. "He's really good with children, despite his jokes about them."

"When he remembers to actually feed them."

Rosetta and Tiffany shared a laugh, but Layla kept her eyes downcast on her sandwich. Asking the two out had been an attempt to pull herself out of the depression that held her prisoner, but now she felt even worst. The secret which she had kept buried deep within all winter pulled her down like an anchor into the depths of an endless, dark abyss.

Desperate, she broke into their conversation by suddenly blurting out, "I am in love."

The other two looked at her, speechless. Finally Rosetta said, "In love? With whom?"

"It's Alexander, isn't it?" Tiffany sat her cup back on the table without taking a sip.

"Alexander?" Rosetta dropped her fork. "How? When? I never saw any signs."

"You were very busy, and we tried to hide it. The relationship is already over. Has been for months. We knew the board would not approve, so we called it off. But still, I am in love and miserable. I just need someone to talk with who will not gossip."

"You can trust us," said Tiffany. "I already had guessed, but I knew it would lead to trouble if word got out."

"You have always known you can tell me anything." Rosetta placed a comforting hand on Layla's arm. "That's what friends are for."

"I do not know where to start," said Layla.

"At the beginning," suggested Tiffany. "When did you realize you were in love?"

Layla took a deep breath and began to talk. Sharing caused the heavy weight which had crushed her for so long to lift. Still, she edited pieces of the story, not mentioning the quintessences' secret use for the epulo as a means of communication. By the time the night drew to a close, her deep depression had lessened. Sadness and longing still lingered, but now with friends to share her grief, it was bearable.

Chapter Twenty-five

Throughout the administration meeting, Palakkad was noticeable impatient, cutting off longwinded petitions, barely heeding Banican Zine's complaints, and zooming through the budget.

When routine matters were finished, he stood in front of his staff, smiled mysteriously, and waited until all had quieted. "We will have visitors in three weeks."

"We often have visitors." Banican wore his ever-present frown.

"None like the ones we are about to have," Palakkad grinned, building up the curiosity of his listeners. "This will be a historical occasion for BGF, and all departments will need to prepare. Nothing must be out of place. Absolutely nothing."

"Who could be that important?" complained his nemesis.

"Just the Emperor," the elderly director beamed, looking youthful despite his gray hair.

Gasps filled the room. "Emperor Kalyuga! Here?"

"Yes, the Emperor is coming to personally inspect our quintessence program. With him will be top level military officers, cabinet members, and senators on the defense committee. Their focus will be on Advance Department, but they will be touring the campus and may visit each of your areas. We must prepare as we have never prepared before."

Immediately the energized staff buzzed with excited plans. The campus must be immaculate, run-down buildings painted, flower beds spruced up, new signs painted. Every department will need a thorough cleaning. The cafeteria would prepare special meals. The press invited. Security increased. All must be perfect.

Layla listened in shock. The Emperor was coming to see the quintessences. She would be required to speak to him, yet she rarely spoke at department meetings. What did one say to an Emperor? Worse, Advance Department was a mess despite daily cleaning. What else could be expected from fifty toddlers and ten youth living in cramped quarters? The Emperor would be traveling light years to see a daycare—not the impression she wanted to give the supreme ruler of the galaxy.

When Layla arrived back at Advance, she called a quick staff meeting. After they recovered from the shock of her news, her friends moved into rapid action. The maze of mismatched cribs had to go. The toddlers would sleep on blankets which could be folded up and hidden each morning. The whole building would need an intense cleaning and the carpet shampooed.

"What are we going to do with the cribs?" said Derrick. "If more quintessences are ordered, then we will need them again."

After much debate, it was decided to build a storage shed on top of the flat roof of the building where there was unlikely to be an inspection. Members of the maintenance team helped Derrick and Zylar quickly construct the new structure in just two days then packed it with folded cribs. Other unneeded supplies were piled on top of the cribs until there was no more space left. Tarps were used to cover crates of bottles, bedding, and baby toys left in the open air on top of the roof. As Layla looked over the final jumble, she could only shake her head and hope the Emperor's security would not be posted on her roof.

Several days before the scheduled visit, Imperial guards combed the campus along with BGF security. The day of the royal visit everyone wore their best outfits, even Zylar kept to dress code. Through the early morning, caregivers tried to keep a normal schedule juggling the three divisions of toddlers between the playroom for recreation, breakroom for breakfast, playground for exercise, and classroom for lessons. The older quintessences target practiced in the forest.

Mid-morning the motorcade with its many limousines and hover bikes arrived at the main building. Palakkad and BGF's board members greeted the arrivals and gave a tour of the campus. Following the prearranged schedule, Layla remained at Advance Department, pacing the hallways, looking for anything out of place, her staff as nervous as she. Rosetta kept repeating sentences, Derrick fiddled constantly with unbroken equipment, and Zylar was as serious as a quintessence. Anthony kept outdoors with the older quintessences.

An hour later Emperor Kalyuga and his large entourage arrived outside Advance Department. Layla's heart pounded as she greeted them with a brief prepared speech inviting everyone to the training field to watch a contest between quintessences and imperial guards. As the group moved down the forest path which had been recently graveled, Layla was relieved to no longer be in the spotlight. She walked beside Mera who gave her an encouraging smile. A large crowd already filled the new bleachers built to surround a fourth of the huge training field. Almost all the employees at BGF had come out to see the competition. A special raised platform had been constructed for the Emperor and his associates. Security guards were posted near the platform and throughout the area. Several large screens displayed video being recorded by flying camera drones patrolling the field.

Near the royal platform, Layla sat on a bleacher with the other department heads. As she waited for the event to begin, she glanced over the diverse collection of sentients on the platform who governed Basanti Empire. Some were dressed in military uniforms glittering with medals. The rest wore expensive outfits, most conservative styled but a few were outlandish. Emperor Kalyuga donned a black outfit accented with bright gemstones, regal but not overdone. The royal human sat aloof from his colleagues, stern face, keen eyes absorbing all.

Palakkad gave a short speech to the crowd then the highly anticipated competition began. Across the vast field hid fifty elite imperial guards waiting to ambush the fifteen quintessences. The rules were simple. Last group standing won. Decayed buildings across the overgrown field had been booby-trapped with stun mines, tripwires, and motion detection guns. Layla watched with clenched jaws and sweaty palms as the quintessences split into five groups, each consisting of one adult with two teens. They slowly fanned out across the field to face their greatest challenge.

Each time a mine blew, usually set off on purpose from a distance by the quintessences, Layla jumped. Nothing in the field was supposed to be lethal, but the knowledge did little to still her fear. Lasers fired, and a young quintessence went down, taking a guard with him. The quintessence's partners used the distraction to climb over a stone fence and shoot two guards from behind. Layla felt she was watching a large scale version of chess as two groups of quintessences pushed forward, testing defenses, becoming pawns to be sacrificed. Within the gaps created by fallen brethren, the other groups treaded carefully, finally breaking pass the main defense line. Still, they were vastly outnumbered, and stunned quintessences were not permitted to return to the game.

Layla's eyes kept jumping between the two huge screens setup in front of the royal platform, each showing video feed from different cameras. Always she searched for Alexander, but only occasionally spotting his nametag as the quintessences dashed or crawled between hiding places. Sometimes progress was excruciating slow as a group carefully investigated an area, while another group circled around and took out strongholds from behind. Occasionally a group made sudden rushes, attempting to catch opponents off guard but the imperial soldiers were always prepared.

For over two hours, the BGF employees cheered with the successes and moaned the failures, feeling their honor tied to the fate of the quintessences.

Eventually the last imperial guard fell and the two remaining quintessences walked to the royal platform, surrounded by cheers from the excited crowd. Layla was disappointed when a close-up shot revealed the winners as Mason and Steven, not Alexander. Half of the government officials clapped in approval, while the others greeted the arrivals with silence. Emperor Kalyuga gave a brief nod to the victors. General Colson, a war buddy of Anthony, congratulated all the quintessences after they lined up in front of the platform.

Palakkad dismissed the crowd. Employees headed back to work, and the media to lunch. Only the royal entourage, guards, and upper staff of BGF remained for a private discourse. Layla dreaded this moment as she was required to stand in front and answer questions, lots of them, from senators and military officials. She tried not to use too much scientific jargon, but neither did she want to appear simple-minded. Not all questions were addressed to her. Anthony and Sergeant Khan, who had driven from Austin City, received their fair share. Some of the questioners were friendly and inquisitive, while others were openly hostile. General Colson was transparent with his support while General Baarook, an Alz ediethean who reminded Layla of her friend Roobaroo, seemed to distrust every statement.

The Emperor remained quiet for most of the debate, but his shrewd eyes missed nothing. Finally he said, "Show us this healing ability."

Alexander and Mason stepped forward. Mason held out his hand, and Alexander sliced it so deeply with a knife that white bone was clearly visible midst the flowing blood. Layla felt queasy at the sight. Mason held high his bleeding palm then stepped to a prisoner provided by Sergeant Khan. A quick bite and Mason revealed his healed palm, drawing impressed gasps from many.

Emperor Kalyuga remained impassive. He looked at Alexander and said, "You have been trained to always obey orders."

"Yes, Your Majestic."

"Then kill your comrade."

The spectators were stunned into silence. Layla, standing only a few feet away, went pale, her body trembling. How dare the Emperor ask this! Her eyes darted to Alexander's face, desperately wishing for a way to prevent what was to come.

Alexander, with knife still in hand, looked at Mason then at the Emperor. Face emotionless, Alexander said, "Mason won the competition, showing his usefulness to you. The command is illogical. A commander should reward those who succeed, not punish them. To do so instills distrust among the troops. Please explain your logic."

Emperor Kalyuga studied Alexander for a long moment then a brief, genuine smile flashed across his face. "Well done." Looking towards Layla, he said, "I am glad to see your creations are not mindless drones."

"I did my best." Layla hoped her shaking body was unnoticeable.

"We will break for lunch, but I would like a tour of your department before I eat."

As most headed to the cafeteria, Layla led the Emperor and several close associates through her building. The corridors were cleared out and the rooms tidy, even her lab, but it still had the feel of a daycare, not a high-tech research laboratory. Walking down the narrow hallways, Layla felt dread being so near Kalyuga, not only because he was the Emperor, but also because he had just ordered Alexander to kill a brother—even if it was Mason. The Emperor made few comments, letting his associates ask questions.

When they entered the breakroom, Zylar froze in shock, the juice he had been pouring for a toddler overflowing its cup. Nervous, Tiffany gave a short bow and welcomed the visitors. As the tour continued, Leana proudly showed off toddlers reciting the alphabet. Derrick gave such a long speech about Anya and nanites that his wife feared he would be executed for boring the Emperor. After the visitors departed the building, the staff conversed excitedly, only to be interrupted by several reporters asking for interviews with Layla and her staff. Camera drones flying down corridors and peeking unannounced into rooms made Layla jumpy, though she knew everyone was on their best behavior today, including Zylar. After the last reporter left, the toddlers laid down for naps while everyone else gathered in the breakroom, wanting to hear what happened during the private meeting after the match.

Exhausted from talking with the visitors, Layla was content to let Anthony carry the conversation. After an hour, she maneuvered her way pass listeners to the door, ready for sleep.

Zylar asked her, "Did they say how many they will buy?"

"That was never mentioned."

"I thought that was why the Emperor came."

"I was only told he wanted to see our operation firsthand."

Rosetta said, "I heard a rumor that they are coming back tomorrow."

"No, they are having a meeting in Austin City tomorrow then heading home, I guess."

She slipped out of the room and headed for the exit, stopping when she heard her name called. Turning, she saw Alexander.

He moved close till only a narrow space separated them in the empty hall. "You spoke well today."

"Thanks. You did well, winning the competition."

"I was taken down halfway through."

"But you sacrificed yourself so your brothers could win. And then passing that hideous test from the Emperor. I thought you were really going to kill Mason."

"I presumed the Emperor had not really been serious. Why destroy a million credit product that you came light-years across the galaxy to buy?"

Layla felt a surge of emotion. "You are more than a product to me."

"I know."

They stared at each other in awkward silence. Layla took a step forward to bridge the space which separated them. The sounds of shuffling feet near the breakroom startled both of them, and they looked, seeing Jacob and Gabriel watching them closely.

"I….I should go," said Layla, quickly darting out the building.

The next day the only topic anyone wanted to discuss was the Emperor's visit. Midafternoon Palakkad summoned Layla to his office to inform her that tomorrow she would be traveling to Austin City to meet with the government officials again.

"The board and I will be coming too. We expect they will bid for the quintessences. Perhaps all of them."

"I just ask, sir, that the first five prototypes not be sold as there is much research yet to be gained from them. Plus, I have promised three models from Generation Two to the Austin City Police for its involvement with our testing."

"I will try to honor your requests but can make no promises."

Layla shifted nervously in her seat. "If we could sell all of Generation Three, not only we will break even but will have enough money to invest in a new batch. The selling of a fourth generation would finally bring real profit for BGF, pleasing the board."

"The board, Layla, is already pleased with your work, even before the Emperor's visit." The director gave her a fatherly smile. "It has been an honor for us to have you, the fruit of our labor, to take genetic research to a higher level than we ever dreamed. Very few of us became scientists for money. We started with only a vision. The many accomplishments that you and the other profectus have achieved has turned our vision into reality. That is worth far more than monetary profit."

Early the next morning three limousines picked up Layla, Palakkad, and the dozen board members. As the spring countryside zoomed pass, Layla listened to the discussions around her. All the board members were retired human scientists who had worked at BGF, many on the profectus project. It felt surreal to Layla to be surrounded by her creators on a road trip to visit the ruler of the galaxy. An hour later, the limousines pulled up at a five-star hotel located in the heart of Austin City. Armed guards escorted Layla and her peers to a large conference room and seated them in the center, surrounded by senators and military officers. Emperor Kalyuga sat at the front of the room, overseeing all.

The questioning began in earnest. Most were directed to Layla, requesting information she had given two days previously, but in greater detail. Heated debates broke out between officials, giving Layla time to ponder the assembly. Too many top-level bureaucrats were present, and no media had been invited. Stress was palpable. This was too serious, too complex for buying fifty or sixty genetic engineered soldiers. Something more was being sought—and it scared many of them.

When the meeting broke for lunch, Layla was relieved, hoping to discuss her concerns with Palakkad, but she was not given the opportunity. A guard asked her to follow without giving an explanation, guiding her through the throng of departing officials, down a carpeted hallway, and to an elevator. After it stopped on an upper level, the guard ushered her into a small, empty conference room then left. She glanced around, uneasy, wondering why she had been brought here. A large window offered a vista of the sprawling city outside. Layla moved closer for a better look.

The door opened and Emperor Kalyuga entered without guards. Layla remained silent, apprehensive. What could the Emperor want to discuss privately with her?

Kalyuga gestured for her to sit at the table. "I want to have a frank discussion without any political watchdogs."

"I have endeavored to be honest in all my replies."

"Good. So will I. As you know, I am the one who signed the Sentient Purity Law ending the research which created you. In fact, it was the first law I passed after I took office. Do you hold resentment for this?"

"No, Your Highness." She wondered if she was addressing him correctly. "I do understand the many concerns of your citizens about genetic engineering. That is why I created the quintessences from scratch, not breaking any of your laws."

He securitized her face. "You speak with sincerity, believing what you say. I greatly respected my father, but we had many disagreements over the years, especially about genetic engineering. I told him he was wrong to support the Coalition of Human Advancement. That their project was an abomination. Yet here I am, considering purchasing fruit grown by his adulterated offspring. He would have found the situation amusing. I do not."

Layla, feeling uncomfortable under his glare, remained silent.

"I do not lightly consider buying your quintessences. You are a scientist concerned about the welfare of your project. I am a politician concerned about the welfare of my galaxy. I am only here because my realm is in danger—of itself. My ancestors quested to unite the galaxy under one government, and my father fulfilled that dream. I inherited his nightmare. It is my responsibility to oversee thousands of planets with a vast array of sentients, each who view the universe differently. I will not burden you with the details, except that rebellion is one of many concerns I must deal with. My forces are too thin, and rage of the conquered too great. The loyalty of the military is fractured between the agendas of their home worlds, and wars sometimes break out among them. In short, I need a miracle if Basanti Empire is to remain whole for my descendants."

The Emperor leaned forward in his leather chair. "That is where you come in. You offer the prefect product. Soldiers quickly grown whose loyalty belongs only to their master. Trouble is, I do not believe in miracles. There is always a catch. What is yours?"

Layla was unsure how to answer. "Catch? I have been honest, sire. The quintessences are what I claim them to be."

"But..."

"But...I only have fifty-seven I can sell you. You will need more. A lot more."

"That is one problem I have foreseen. If I ordered a thousand per year, could your department handle that?"

"A thousand?" Layla swallowed, her mind reeling at the enormous amount of space needed to meet such a contract. That meant, at any given time, seven thousand quintessences would be in different stages of growth and training. Dealing with the needs for just sixty-five was overwhelming. "We would need to construct a new building." The cost could easily run over a hundred million credits. Would the board want to invest in that when a military contract could be canceled at any time, possibly throwing BGF into bankruptcy?

"Your face reveals the truth. You do not believe your company is capable of handling such an order."

"With time, perhaps. The startup cost will be tremendous. If we began with smaller orders first, eventually we could reach that size."

"Time is what I lack. I need not thousands, but tens of thousands, quickly." He stood and walked to the window, his face cast in shadow. "My father was an amateur astronomer. From boyhood he peered at the stars at night, dreaming of visiting them. As an adult he faced the reality of ruling those stars. In later life, sometimes he and I would journey far away from city lights and watch the heavens together. Eventually it was the only bond left between us. Somehow he managed to still feel wonder when peering into the vastness of the universe. I only saw problems needing to be fixed. This planet wants a new military base. That one wants to get rid of theirs."

He turned towards Layla. "Why did you choose the name *quintessence*?"

"The name chose them." Layla walked to the window. "The word means a substance at its purest. My goal was to create a perfect genetic being, unblemished from the chaos of evolution."

"The word has other meanings too. In ancient times on Earth, one culture believed it to be the fifth element from which the heavenly bodies are created. In modern cosmology, some use the term to refer to an invisible force which binds the universe together and prevents it from collapsing upon itself."

"I was unaware of its etymology."

He looked Layla in the eyes. "Have you truly extracted living quintessence from the universe? Have you created a force which can prevent my universe from collapsing?"

"I do not know, sire, but the quintessences are willing to die trying, if you just give them a chance."

Kalyuga glanced back over the city, lost in thought for a long time. Finally he said, "I apology for keeping you from your meal."

Seeing the dismissal, Layla left the room and a guard guided her downstairs to a fancy dining room bustling with waiters carrying heavy trays of food. Palakkad had saved her a seat at his crowded table. Layla ate quickly, answering questions about where she had been with vague comments. Too soon, the meal was finished, and the officials headed back to the large conference room.

The Emperor took his seat at the front and waited until all were silent before speaking. "The time for debate is over. I have decided to support the purchase of the quintessences. But I do not believe Bontinc Genetics Foundation is capable of meeting our requirements. I move that we purchase their entire Advance Department, including the ownership of all research and products, and build our own institution."

The audience exploded with both shouts of protest and cheerful clapping. Layla franticly stared at the Emperor, feeling betrayed. After that long talk, he was going to take everything away from her. Everything. Including Alexander.

"He cannot do that," she said to Palakkad sitting beside her.

"Not without paying for it."

"Will the board sell?"

"If the price is high enough."

The Emperor held his hands up for silence. "I propose to this committee that we offer BGF five hundred million for complete ownership of the quintessence project and everything relating to it."

Board members glanced at each other. Five hundred million would pay off all the debt accumulated by Advance Department and go a long way in funding other projects. *They will sell,* thought Layla in horror.

Panicked, Layla stood up and shouted, "You can't!" Every eye in the room locked on her. Mouth dry, body shaking, she sputtered, "BGF has promised three quintessences to the Austin City Police."

"The deal will be honored," said Emperor Kalyuga.

Layla's mind went blank. What else could she say to prevent her project and Alexander from being snatched from her?

The Emperor continued, "You, of course, will be expected to be the director of the new research institution and may bring any employees you wish with you."

Mind numb, Layla sat down, only vaguely aware of debates and questions raging around her. Director of a government institution. Her. No longer would she need to worry about the BGF board. Far worse—her bosses would be the bureaucrats of the Galactic Senate. The Emperor, as military chief, would become master of all quintessences. An entire sentient race bound to the Basanti Empire. Her creations would be scattered across the vast galaxy, on the whims of politicians, to die in wars meaningless to them. The quintessences were conditioned from birth to always follow the orders of superiors. She had created the perfect slave race. *Roobaroo was right,* she thought in dismay.

Her friend's words mocked Layla. *What was the cost which bought your silence? Or perhaps you are going along willingly. Another proud accomplishment for the almighty profectus race.*

The room spun and Layla gasped the arms of her chair for support. She heard several voices saying the word *vote* then hands beginning to rise. Barely able to breathe, Layla jumped up. "Wait! Quintessences will fight for you, for your causes. But you must not forget they are sentients. They will be your slaves in an empire where slavery is illegal. That makes all of you hypocrites." She paused, trying to catch her breath, feeling eyes glaring at her. "I propose that you reward quintessences for their loyalty by granting them citizenship after serving a set number of years."

"You claimed to be selling a military product," said General Baarock, his black eyes menacing, "Suddenly you have the audacity to claim it has rights? We are not here to discuss philosophy."

"Civil rights groups will accuse you of being slave drivers. If you do not address the issue now, it will come back to haunt you. If quintessence serve you well, reward them with citizenship. That will make them work all the harder. Do you not reward your pets when they are well behaved?"

The room broke into angry shouts. Even Palakkad looked at her in disbelief and board members frowned. They had been about to close a profitable deal and she, out of the blue, had turned it into a debate about slavery. Surrounded by hostility, Layla closed her eyes and visualized Alexander, feeling again the vivid emotions he had conveyed through the epulo link to her. If he was willing to die for the Empire on some alien battlefront, he also deserved the opportunity to love. They owed him that.

Emperor Kalyuga held his hand high for silence. "She is right that this will become an issue our opponents will exploit. We must deal with it now before they can use it against us. I propose twenty-five years of satisfactory service then quintessences will be granted citizenship. If they wish, they can continue in the military, receiving wages equal to other sentients."

General Baarook stood and argued against the idea of limited service for a product, his allies agreeing with him. General Colson backed the Emperor but asked for forty years. Feeling weak, Layla sat back down as the debate raged around her.

Chapter Twenty-six

It was nearing dusk when Layla, both mentally and physically exhausted, reached Advance Department. She had walked across the huge campus after the limousine dropped her off in front of the main building.

From the edge of the playground, Rosetta was the first to greet her. "How did it go?"

"Is everyone assembled at the bleachers?"

"Yes, even the toddlers, like you asked in your message. Is it that bad?"

"I am too tired to say it more than once."

Rosetta walked beside Layla along the path to the training field. The caregivers from all three shifts ceased their chatter as Layla appeared. Sixty-five quintessences watched with stoic faces, even the young toddlers barely a year old. Instinctively arranging themselves in a hierarchical order, the Five sat on the top bench while the Ten, now looking like thirteen-year-olds, were directly below their older brothers. The lowest benches were filled with fifty tiny quintessences, mimicking the somberness of their older brothers.

Layla stood in front of them all, tired, emotions threatening to engulf her. "As of two hours ago, Advance Department along with its assets, products, and research no longer belongs to BGF. It is now property of the Basanti Empire."

Confusing chatter broke out among the humans. "They can't do that." "Can you buy an entire department?" "I thought only quintessences were for sell." "What about my job?"

She waited until the talking died down before continuing. "Everything will continue as normal for a while. Generation One will keep working with the Austin Police Department while the others continue to grow up and be trained here. In the meantime, a new research institution will be built which can handle the production of a large number of quintessences."

"Where?" shouted someone.

"We do not know yet. I am on a committee to decide that. It will probably be on another planet closer to the population center of the galaxy."

"What about our jobs?"

"I have been appointed director of the new institute. All who wish to transfer there when it is completed may. Some of you have been with me since the beginning of this project, others joined for the adventure or because you truly enjoy changing diapers." Several people chuckled. "Whatever your reason for being here, you have my deep gratitude. This project would not have been successful without you. I recognize that many may not wish to leave Bontinc. You have families here. It will take several years to complete the new institution, so you have plenty of time to decide."

Layla took a deep breath, steadying herself. "I have several things I must say to the quintessences. Generation Two, from you three will be chosen by the Austin Police Department to honor their involvement in this project. You will not join your brothers at the new location. The rest of you are already property of the Empire, and you will do the biding of its military. I will have no control of your future once you are deemed a graduate of this program. But you do have some control of your own fate."

She allowed a smile, the first all day, to cross her lips, "The Emperor has agreed that after twenty-five years of satisfactory service, you will be granted full citizenship. That includes the right to a salary if you remain in the military, the right to live where you wish." Her eyes locked onto Alexander. "And the right to marry."

Caregivers bombarded Layla with questions, but she excused herself, claiming exhaustion. Back at her tiny apartment, she showered then tried to sleep, but a whirlwind of tasks she must accomplish over the next few years threatened her sanity. The Emperor asked for three thousand graduates a year. That meant the new institution must be large enough to house twenty-one thousand developing quintessences. Vast areas would be needed for incubating fetuses, growing infants, playrooms for toddlers, classrooms for youth, and military training areas. She would need to hire scientists, caregivers, teachers, janitors, mechanics, technicians, cooks, gardeners, security, and who knew what else. Only twenty-four, she was about to oversee the construction of the largest scientific institution in the known universe, a task she felt was impossible even for a profectus. She was terrified.

But she would not, could not, walk away from the project. Too much was at stake. If she left, another would be appointed who would only see quintessences as a product and the institution as a factory. This new place needed to be a home for quintessences, where free adults could come back to share their wisdom with younger brothers. Every sentient race needed a motherland. Essence Institute would be the homeland for the quintessence.

The next morning Layla met with her senior staff to discuss plans. While she fortified herself for a laborious future, the others were excited.

"How much space do twenty-one thousand quintessence need?" asked Derrick, staring at the figures sent to his e-tablet.

"The size of a small town, I'm guessing," said Rosetta.

"Can we choose the equipment used? If so, we should have the latest in nano technology."

"You will each create a supply list of what you think is needed in your area," explained Layla. "Then we will create an estimated budget to send to the oversight committee."

"Do I get an official title?" asked Zylar.

"Maintenance chief."

"Cool. I'm a chief. How many school dropouts can say that?"

Rosette rolled her eyes. "You would impress Tiffany more if you had a college degree."

"She loves me as I am. And I already make more money than many with degrees."

"Well, it's about time you started earning that paycheck," said Layla. "This is no game. I will place heavy responsibilities on each of you. Can you handle that?"

Zylar saluted her. "Yes, boss. Point me in a direction, and I will get the task done."

At the end of the week, Layla sent off the estimates. A few days later, she received a video message from the architect chosen by the committee to design Essence. A brunette human in her mid-twenties popped into view on Layla's screen.

"My name is Diane Richton. Perhaps you remember me. I was a year ahead of you at Luncaster University. I was excited when asked to oversee designing your institution. Don't worry. I've had lots of experience and earned top awards in my field. You, at least, won't doubt my talent because of my youth. We profectus get that a lot. I've already seen your estimates, but I need more details, a lot more. I'm sending forms for you to fill out to help me get started. I need to know your vision, what you want the overall design to look like. Currently I'm picturing a modern naturalism similar to Luncaster. But I can go in any direction. Just let me know. Again, I'm very excited about this project. I plan to make Essence Institute the envy of every scientist in the galaxy."

As Layla surveyed the numerous forms Diane had sent, she smiled though dread tightened her stomach. The architect was taking her job extremely serious and the questions were extensive, ranging from how much walking space was needed between incubators to the color of the cafeteria dining tables. Over the next few days Layla and her staff filled out what they knew, though many questions were left blank.

The next two years were filled with regular correspondence between Layla and the architecture firm. Diane and her staff made several visits to BGF to gather more information. While floor plans were coming together on Diana's computer, many other tasks occupied Layla's time. As Rosetta handled the daily running of Advance Department, Layla poured over data from suggested site locations, read countless resumes from jobs seekers, and handled reporters who popped in for interviews. At least now she had a quiet lab to work in as Generation Three sleep on pallets in other rooms.

Daytime was too hectic for Layla to think much beyond her work, but nights in her apartment meant battles with loneliness. She went out with friends to watch a movie or shop, and she corresponded with family and college buddies. She watched videos of her dad's retirement party, her mom's acceptance speech for Monsoor's Scientist of the Year Award, and her nieces' birthday bashes. Roobaroo's messages remained cryptic, hinting she was planning something momentous. She did praise Layla for earning a path of freedom for the quintessences but cautioned against trusting the Senate.

Despite the connection with friends, as Layla fell asleep each night, emptiness gnawed at her as she thought of Alexander. Twenty-five years was a long time to wait. By the time he was free, she would be middle-age. Would he want her then? She was plain-looking now. Given a quarter century, she was certain she would be old and wrinkled, while he would still be in the prime of his life. So much could happen in twenty-five years—like his death. Above all else, she feared receiving a message from the Austin police reporting Alexander had been killed in the line of duty. If that happened, she was certain she would have a mental breakdown and no longer be capable of handling the heavy responsibilities of director. Not that she would care. To Layla, life ended at Alexander's death.

A dozen potential sites were selected for Essence, and Layla's duty required her to visit each one. Reluctantly, she packed her bags and flew off planet. Before joining Diana for the tours, she made a quick visit to her home planet of Mansoor. Her parents, now grey-haired and wrinkled, cheerfully met her at the spaceport. Fifteen years had passed since the last time she had seen them in person. They drove her to a restaurant where they had often dined in her childhood. Blaaze, coming straight from his job as a researcher at a medical drug company, met them there along with his wife Ria and their two daughters. Layla laughed at her dad's jokes and turned her brother's teasing back on him. Her nieces giggled and prattled stories, thanking Layla for birthday presents sent over the years. Ria shared anecdotes from her job as a teacher.

The family gathering was bittersweet for Layla. Despite the years of not seeing them, they welcomed her with open arms, making her feel at home. For a brief time, Layla basked in the emotion of belonging to a family, but the week passed too quickly. At the spaceport she could barely say goodbye due to the lump in her throat and struggles to keep unshed tears at bay. *As a child, I never felt this emotional about leaving. Perhaps it is because I fear I may never see my parents again, except in videos.* Too soon she was on a shuttle, off to visit strangers in the search for a homeland for her quintessences.

Buzzing of an alarm clock woke Layla. Groggy, she hit the snooze button and surveyed the unfamiliar surroundings, wondering where she was. A hotel room, no, a suite with several rooms decorated with paintings, woven tapestries, and statures. *How can they think I would be impressed with statures in my bedroom?* she wondered as she pushed back the silk bed coverings.

Which planet is this? Aegina? No, that one had too few local sources, and it would be too expense purchasing supplies off planet. Barthibbs? She recalled lines of protestors along the roadway to the potential building site. She was not about to build her institution in the midst of a culture who condemned cloning as evil. Cuillandre, definitely. For the last three days, the planet's president and the capital city's mayor had escorted her through a blur of five star restaurants, award winning theater productions, and museums highlighting their ancient race. The site they offered for Essence was a vast city park located beside a bay. Layla had remained polite but was far from impressed. The quintessences should not be closed in by a city. Neither did she like the political fallback of turning a popular park into a military training base.

The pressure to select a building site was tremendous. The oversight committee demanded she choose soon, but Layla found fault with every site visited. Even Diana, who was usually supportive of Layla's decisions, had begun warning her if a site was not chosen soon, the committee would take matters into their own hands. It was better to have a satisfactory site than one chosen by politicians based on who sent in the cheapest bids. Still, Layla kept holding out. The homeland for the quintessences must be perfect.

Layla dressed casually, relieved the tour of Culillandre was over. She headed downstairs for breakfast and to meet up with Diana.

"Still going to Luncaster for that speech?" asked the architect, sipping coffee.

"Yes, how could I turn it down? It is the intellectual birthplace of us profectus."

"But you and speeches don't go together. You clam up most of the time around these dignitaries, leaving me to do most of the talking."

"You enjoy talking."

"Yes, it's been fun being courted by presidents and sovereigns across the galaxy who want the economic boom that Essence will bring. Still, I can't see you giving a speech."

"I only have to read it. Besides it will be nice seeing Luncaster again. Are you still not coming?"

"Was there last year, remember, studying its design. Besides, my two daughters are missing me, and I them." She sat her empty cup on the table. "Cuillandre is a good location. I sent the committee my recommendation for it."

"Already? But it is inside a city. And we would have to destroy an entire park."

"If you always seek perfection, you will never find it. Believe me, I know from firsthand experience." She placed a tip on the table for the waitress. "The committee is out of patience."

"I know. I just need more time."

"You don't have much." Diana stood up. "Enjoy your trip."

Layla finished her juice and caught a cab to the nearby spaceport. The planet Xi'an was a short flight from Cuillandre, both located near the populated core of the galaxy though Xi'an was on the outer edge of the belt. As the ship orbited for a landing, Layla looked out the window, recalling seeing the same view long ago. She had been eight, excited about her new life at the university, believing its bright promises that anything was possible.

The ship began its descent, and the planet's vistas of blue oceans and greenish-brown continents blurred pass. The wonder of childhood filled Layla as she watched clouds drift far below. Fiery vapors leaped across the window as the ship, shuddering, hit the upper atmosphere of Xi'an. As the craft slowed, the ride smoothed out. Layla made out the glow of cities far below on the night side of the planet. The shuttle passed into daylight and angled towards Luncaster. As the city loomed on the horizon, dark green forests, high mountains, and vast plains stretched out for miles. Layla's heart pounded in sudden excitement as she remembered that centuries ago Xi'an environmentalists had successfully had thousands of square miles turned into natural preservations to protect the planet's wilderness—and a huge parcel lay just north of Luncaster.

In the spaceport lobby, Richard Cambridge and his wife met Layla. Over the years Layla had corresponded often with Richard as he developed first the DNA software and now security programs for her. Still, this was the first time they had met in person since college.

"How was the flight?" he asked, taking her luggage.

"Beautiful. Xi'an is a gorgeous planet."

"That is why I built my software company here." His beautiful blond wife cleared her throat. "And Alana's family is from here. It does not hurt having connections to the mayor."

"You are related to Luncaster's mayor?"

Alana smiled. "My father was mayor. Now he is retired. You are probably tired from your trip. Richard suggested you would prefer staying with us than a hotel."

"I am tired of hotels at the moment. Tell me, is it possible to charter private flights over the preserve?"

"Sure," answered Richard. "I could arrange it tomorrow after your speech, if you feel like it. Got it memorized yet?"

"I am just reading it. And thanks again for the proofread. I added a line about leaving a legacy in the last paragraph, like you suggested."

"Actually it was Alana's idea. She majored in language at the university."

"I speak seven fluently," said his wife proudly, as they reached the parking lot.

The friendly atmosphere at the Cambridges' home was relaxing to Layla after weeks of traveling. Besides building a successful software business, Richard had invested in creating a smart house filled with so many talking gadgets that Layla knew Zylar and Derrick would have thought they had walked into heaven. Three children dashed about in play with electronic pets. After an entertaining supper cooked by a robotic maid, Layla learned how to verbally command a computerized desk to search for files pertaining to Xi'an environmental laws.

The next morning Layla, Richard, and Alana traveled across the city to Luncaster University where the dean greeted them and gave a tour of the campus. On the whole, it looked the same as Layla remembered, though a few new buildings had been added. As she strolled along the bright, airy halls, she found herself searching for faces of students long graduated—or dead. Mid-morning the assembly room was packed for her speech. As she looked out over the genius youth, she felt emotional, recalling when she had once sat in their place listening to speakers promising a bright future. As she read the prepared speech, her nervousness slowly faded, and she felt comradeship with her audience. Afterwards she and her companions ate lunch with the dean and several professors who had taught her years before.

Later Richard drove her and his wife to a small airport on the outskirts of the city. A chopper flew them northward low enough to spot herds of animals grazing on the plains and predators chasing prey through thick forests. To the west they caught glimpses of surf pounding against the rocky shoreline. When the pilot turned to head back to the city, Layla asked for the craft to be set down on a vast plain intermingled with grasslands, forests, and streams. Walking a distance away from the aircraft, Layla breathed in the pure, unpolluted air carrying the scent of salt from the nearby ocean. Far away to the east a range of mountains filled the horizon.

Smiling, Layla drank in the beauty. *There is so much space. They will love it here.*

"I have found Essence," she shouted into the wind. Alana, Richard, and the pilot stared at her, puzzled. She laughed joyful and twirled around with hands raised "My Essence!"

Through her giddiness, she explained to the Cambridges her plans to build the research institution here.

"But it is on the preserve," said Alana.

"Your law says parkland can be sold if four-fifths of your House agrees."

"That is rare."

"I think in this case they will. Emperor Kalyuga himself is behind this project. The local economic will bloom with new jobs and money pouring in for construction and supplies." Layla turned to the pilot. "How far are we from Luncaster?"

"Near twenty miles."

"We could build a monorail for employees. Those living in the city could be here within fifteen minutes."

"Roads will have to be built also to bring in supplies," said Richard, catching her excitement. "Not everyone will want to live in the city. You will have to plan for a town nearby. Along with a school, a hospital, a police department." He grinned, "And they will need a mayor."

"Profectus," said Alana, shaking her head. "Give them an idea and they change the planet. Richard, you are not running for mayor of a town not even built."

"Why not? Good planning prevents a host of problems."

Laughing, Layla texted a message to Diane. "Found Essence. Come to Luncaster. Bring your family. Expect a long stay."

Chapter Twenty-seven

Unnoticed forests blurred pass Alexander sitting in the passenger seat of the beat-up hover van. Being Mason's turn to drive, the van took curves much too fast for even Alexander's liking. At this speed, it would not take long to reach the campus of BGF.

"She had been back for two days," said Caleb. "We must inform her."

"Will she agree?" asked Gabriel, looking at Alexander.

"If I explain carefully, I think so."

"She is too tenderhearted," said Jacob. "She will not back us up."

"The project means too much to her." Mason swerved around a slow moving car. "She will let nothing get in the way of its success, including executing quintessences."

"Our creator has never let us down." Steven sat on the back seat between two other brothers chosen from Generation Two to work for the police. "She will do what is best for the whole."

"She is still human," said Alexander. "Emotions too often control them."

"Can you handle her?" Caleb studied Alexander. "Or will your own feelings interfere?"

"I have never broken the Code."

Too soon they reached the parking lot of Advance Department. The morning air was still nippy from the vanishing winter. Generation Three was involved in several ballgames on the playground overseen by quintessences from Generation Two, now fully grown. Fifty preteens tossed balls into hoops or watched silently from the sidelines. While his brothers rounded up the young quintessences for training exercises, Alexander headed into the building, stopping in the breakroom to inform Rosetta they had arrived. Then he continued down the hall to the lab. He knocked before entering.

Layla continued peering into a microscope. "I will be with you in a moment."

Alexander locked the door behind him then walked across the room to her cluttered desk. It had been several years since he had last been in here, yet nothing had changed except the cribs were missing. The large machines used in his creation collected dust in the back of the room.

"How was your trip?"

Glancing up, she spotted his nametag and her face briefly flashed a smile. "Good. They have begun pouring the foundation for Essence."

"How long until it is completed?"

"Perhaps two years. Maybe less with the Emperor pushing for it to be finished quickly." Her eyes averted to her fingers tapping data into her e-tablet. "It is good to be back, but now I have a mountain of tasks which must be completed."

"I have come to discuss something serious with you." He noticed her tapping stopped. "I must show you, not tell you."

"Alright."

He stepped behind her and brushed long hair away from her neck, letting his fingers linger longer than needed. She stood rigid in front of him as he bit. He chose for the old courtyard to appear, as it was a place they both shared fond memories.

"I missed this," she said, looking around. "I am still amazed how real the memories feel."

"There is a problem with one from Generation Three."

"Right to business then?"

He felt her annoyance but ignored it. "It is quite serious."

The scene changed to the training field. Snow was visible under the nearby trees, but the sun had melted the snow in the clearing. Fifty preteen quintessences stood at attention, watched by their older brothers and a dozen guards. A prisoner sat calmly on a stone as one of the preteens walked up. The Alexander inside the memory cut Paton's palm then the youth bit the prisoner. Instead of pulling back quickly, the preteen continued to feed. Alexander became concerned and ordered Paton to break contact. The youth ignored him and the prisoner's body began to tremble.

Alexander bent down and bit the preteen. Immediately upon entering Paton's mind, he detected wrongness, avarice emotions surging through the youth who sought to pull all knowledge from the prisoner. Quickly Alexander overrode the youth's actions, forcing Paton to break contact. As Alexander stepped back, the prisoner slumped to the ground unconscious. Briefly wild glee flirted across Paton's eyes before the youth slipped on a stoic expression.

Alexander gestured to the fallen prisoner. "Take him to the hospital immediately." For a moment the startled guards did not move then several rushed forward to help.

The scene morphed back to the courtyard. Through the link, he could feel Layla's apprehension.

"When did this happen?"

"Four days ago. The prisoner was in a coma for two days. He will live but has permanent memory loss. "

"Why was I not informed before now?"

"You were busy and off planet. And we needed time to decide what must be done. This is not the first time Paton has disobeyed orders, but it is the most disastrous. We Five have decided he must be culled."

"He is only a boy."

"Who can kill. If I had not stopped him, the prisoner would be dead and the safety record of this program irreparable damaged."

He felt her pity for the prisoner and dread of what could have happened. "The caregivers will be upset. They raised him."

"Being a leader means making tough decisions, Layla."

"I do not like ordering anyone's death."

"I know. We would not ask this of you unless we were certain it was the correct choice. Paton can no longer be trusted. He has embraced the madness which threatens all young quintessences when they first experience the epulo."

"Can he be fixed? Psychiatrist help crazy people all the time."

"No. A psychiatrist will never be able to understand him near as well as another quintessence. We are not limited to just observing behavior but look directly into the mind. All Five of us have examined him and are unified in our stance that he is corrupted and must be culled. He is capable of going berserk. If he slips into a rampage, he could kill innocent civilians, including caregivers."

"Alright, I will back you, but there will be many upset about this."

"This is the right choice."

He broke the link but was reluctant to step away from Layla.

"I missed you." She remained still.

"As I have you."

"Twenty-five years is a long time to wait."

"It is only twenty-two years now."

"That is still over two decades. I will be an old woman."

"Only middle-age for a human. But I will not care about your age."

"I do," her voice broke. "It is so hard. I do not think I can make it."

He whispered into her ear. "You will, and I will be there waiting for you."

She leaned her body against him, and he wrapped his arms around her waist, holding her. For a long, blissful moment they were connected. Knocking at the door caused both to jump and pull apart.

"Layla, I have your samples," called Tiffany.

"Come in."

The doorknob twisted. "It's lock."

Layla glanced at Alexander as she hurriedly unlocked the door. "Oh, sorry about that."

Tiffany stepped into the room, "The first dozen are fresh but…" She stopped speaking when she spotted Alexander still standing by Layla's desk.

"We were just talking about…"

"I don't need to know," cut in Tiffany. "Here are your samples." She gave Alexander another glance. "Just be careful," she whispered then left.

Alexander walked over to Layla. "What have you told her?"

"A lot. And Rosetta too. I needed someone to talk to after you stopped talking with me."

"That was not by choice."

"Well, we should go ahead and deal with the culling while you are here."

"Call a meeting for everyone, and we will explain."

Alexander headed through the woods to the training field, catching the eyes of the other Five. The shooting match was quickly wrapped up and their younger brothers seated on the bleachers. It was not long before caregivers and head staff arrived, looking uncertain as they sat down. Allen, now eight years old, led his little brother to a bench. Both boys often trained in the afternoon with Generation Three.

The Five formed a line in front of the bleachers. Then Caleb said, "Brothers, recite our code."

As one, sixty voices said, "All quintessences shall place the welfare of their brethren above themselves. Each must live an exemplary life, obeying superiors, avoiding vices, protecting the weak."

Gabriel asked, "What happens if someone breaks the code?"

The sixty responded, "Any who bring dishonor will be tried before their brethren."

"If found guilty?" asked Jacob.

"Death," the quintessences spoke in unison.

"There is one among us," said Mason, "who has repeatedly disobeyed orders. Being young, he was warned each time. Then he attacked someone weaker than himself simply because he could."

Preteens near Paton glanced at him, having been present when the incident took place. Paton stared straight ahead, revealing no remorse or fear.

Alexander looked over the group. "We Five have already tried the offender and found him guilty. He will be executed immediately." Alexander and Mason walked up to the bleachers and stopped in front of the culprit. "Paton, come."

The youth's eyes flicked to Alexander as he silently stood and moved between his peers to the ground. Alexander immediately began walking towards the path leading away from the field. The youth hesitated but followed while the other Five surrounded him. Anthony and Layla fell in step behind. Shocked whispering came from caregivers but the younger quintessences remained silent.

"You can't do this." Rosetta moved in front of Alexander. "Layla, stop them."

"I cannot. It has already been decided."

Rosetta glared at Alexander. "Stop this now."

Alexander silently looked toward Layla. She moved in front of Rosetta and said, "It has to be this way. He is guilty."

"He is a boy! You don't kill children for making a mistake."

"He is quintessence. They live by different rules than we do. We must respect that."

"Respect? He is a child. A child. The same as my sons. I don't execute them if they make a mistake."

"Your children are not lethal."

Rosetta looked around, desperate for support. Her own sons sat on a nearby bench, faces pale. Tiffany and several other caregivers wept. Zylar stared open-mouthed. Anthony watched silently, arms crossed.

Derrick moved beside his wife and gently touched her arm, "Come, we must let them do what they believe is right."

Rosetta shook him off and leaned towards Layla. "If you do this, I will not be here when you come back."

"We are responsible for the products which come from this department. We cannot let defects out into the public. Someone could die."

"There has to be another way."

"I am sorry, but it has always been BGF's policy to cull defects. As a director I must continue that policy."

"Then I quit." Rosette turned and walked away towards her sons.

Shock crossed Layla's face. Alexander waited no longer, but continued down the path with Paton, Anthony, and his brothers. Layla followed reluctantly behind. When they reached the parking lot, Layla tried to turn back.

Anthony stopped her by saying, "We will need your access code."

Layla continued with the group, but she occasionally brushed away a tear. Paton walked solemn faced between his escorts until they neared Freak Department. He suddenly bolted to the right but barely took two steps before his older brothers grabbed him. He went limp, refusing to walk. Jacob and Gabriel each took an arm and dragged him into the building. Paton began walking again, but his eyes darted about, looking for an escape route.

Layla led them through the maze of pens and cages filled with genetically altered animals. Reeking smells from excrement tainted the air. From atop his cage, Blue Feathers cawed, "Darkness there, and nothing more." As they neared the door leading to the gas chambers, Banican Zine stepped in front of them.

"We are taking a defect product to be euthanatized," said Layla.

The supervisor's stern eyes looked over the group then stopped on the preteen. Surprise flicked across his face. "I didn't think you had it in you to kill one of your own offspring."

"I do what I must to protect the whole."

"By all means, continue." He stepped out of the way then followed behind the group.

At the door, Layla keyed the password, and the door slid open. Paton tried to bolt again, but his brothers' firm grip held him. Kicking and yelling, he fought against them as they dragged him into the chamber with its many clear canisters of different sizes. Layla walked over to a large one and began tapping directions into the touchpad connected to the canister. Her hands shook so badly she had to start over twice. Paton continued to fight and scream. Banican and Anthony watched silently beside the door. Finally Layla nodded towards the Five.

As they moved Paton towards the open tube, the youth begged Layla, "Creator, you cannot do this. Please. I promise to always obey."

Layla trembled. "I am so sorry."

"Please, creator, you must save me."

Alexander stepped in front of Layla, blocking the youth's view of her, but Paton continued to beseech her.

Mason moved near Paton and said sternly, "Look at me. Look!" The youth reluctantly faced Mason. "Do you want the last thing your creator remembers about you is that you acted like an animal? You have chosen to embrace the darkness, ignoring warnings that only insanity lies within. I have peered into your mind and seen the corruption you hunger for. You have been sentenced to death by your brethren. It is up to you, G3-047, if you will face your fate as a quintessence or a beast."

The youth stared at Mason for a moment then became still. Fear vanished from his eyes as his face became impassive.

"I am quintessence."

Paton stepped forward and entered the clear tube on his own accord. Mason closed and locked the door. Layla held her trembling hand over the keypad but could not bring herself to touch it.

Alexander moved beside her and gently pushed her hand away. "This is our responsibility." Alexander pressed the button.

Machinery under the floor hummed, and a murky gas began filling the large tube. Paton stared straight ahead as the air around him turned a sickly yellow. He coughed. Panic flashed across his face. His eyes searched the room until he found Layla. Calmness returned, and he continued to stare at his weeping creator until he lost consciousness, and his body slumped down. For several more minutes the murky gas circulated through the canister then was sucked away through a hose.

As Mason and Caleb moved to the tube to dispose of the body, Alexander gently took Layla's arm and guided her to the door. Banican looked at her grieved face and piety filled his eyes. He held the door open for her. Neither Alexander nor Layla spoke as they walked through the maze of cages. Blue Feathers tilted his head and flapped his wings as they passed, quoting, "Other friends have flown before. On the morrow he will leave me, as my hopes have flown before."

Layla trembled, trying to block out the bird's sinister voice. By the time they reached Advance Department, Layla had her emotions under control, but her eyes were red and puffy. When they entered the building, Derrick met them at the door of the breakroom.

"Where is Rosetta?" asked Layla.

"She left with the kids." Derrick looked frazzled.

"She will come back, right?"

"Well, uh, you will need to give her a few days. She is really upset. So are a lot of people. I mean, I understand why you did it, but I suspect several more will quit over the next few days."

"Are you quitting too?"

"Um, I don't want to. But if I support you there is going to be a lot of tension at home. My marriage is more important than my job."

"Yes, I guess so. Go ahead home. Take a few days off if you need to. Tell Rosetta I am sorry."

After Derrick left, Layla said, "Alexander, what am I going to do? I am losing my two best friends."

"Give them time."

But time worked in no one's favor. For the rest of the week Alexander was in Austin City with his brothers. They completed several successful drug raids, yet he was helpless to aid the one he wanted to most. It had been like that for the last three years. He had watched Layla go through a depression after the break-up. He wanted to comfort her but had to keep his distance. Whenever he was in the same room with her, he had studied her, noticing ever facial expressions, every frown or rare smile. She was so quick to leave, always avoiding looking at him. Frustration tore at him. His brothers knew of his feelings, of his conflicts. Other than watching him to ensure he did not slip, there was nothing they could do. Products were not permitted to love.

That night, as he lay in his bunk bed in the small apartment he shared with seven brothers, he worried about Layla. Rosetta was a keystone in running Advance Department. Without her, the organization would collapse into chaos. Layla would struggle to oversee everything but would be overwhelmed. Alone, she would fail. And so could the entire quintessence project. Something had to be done quickly.

The quintessences arrived back at BGF on Saturday. What information Alexander could gleam indicated a disaster in the making. Rosetta had already transferred back to her old position at Baby Department. Derrick had applied for a transfer to Freak Department and was waiting for a reply. Five part-time and two full-time employees had quit. Layla worked two shifts a day, trying to juggle the demands for both Advance Department and Essence. One look at her face, and Alexander knew she was shattered on the inside, though she pretended otherwise.

While their younger brothers ate lunch, the Five held a hidden meeting in the forest to discuss what could be done. That evening, near the end of her shift, Rosetta was summoned to Mera's office, but when she entered, she found not her boss but her nervous husband standing beside the Five.

"What is going on? Where is Mera?"

"She kindly allowed us the use of her office to talk with you," said Caleb. "We are expecting one more."

Rosetta glared at him then Derrick. "It's time to pick up our kids."

The door opened and Layla entered. She was just as surprised as Rosetta to find the Five instead of Mera. "Why was I summoned?"

Gabriel said, "Because you and Rosetta need to talk with each other."

Rosetta frowned. "There is nothing left to say. You killed Paton. I can never work with you again. Derrick, let's go home."

Her husband swallowed. "I…uh…agree with them that it would be good for you both to talk. Layla, tell her what you found."

Layla looked uncertainly between him and Rosetta. "We finished the analysis of Paton's DNA earlier today. There were a few slight imperfections in his DNA. Minuscule…but still there."

"And how did that happen," said Rosetta, intrigued despite her anger.

Derrick answered, "Because we used the newest nanotech DNA builder. They work faster but sacrifice accuracy. That is why I prefer the X1800. Mistakes are rare with them. Don't get me wrong, the ones in Freak Department are excellent machines, but we technicians have long been aware of their slight inaccuracy. Usually it doesn't matter. Most specimens come out fine, though occasionally one might have a blemish. A color spot, longer ears, rougher fur. Nothing major."

Rosetta became livid. "Paton was a sentient. Not an animal to be tossed away if its fur is the wrong color. Will you now analysis every quintessence's DNA, and when they do not match your perfect pattern exactly, cull them?"

"No, of course not," sputtered Layla. "Paton was dangerous."

"He was a child! Children make mistakes. That is what they do. You forgive them, not kill them."

"I am sorry. I did not plan for this. When I designed the quintessences I left no Plan B. Natural chromosomes often contain duplicate sequences. If something goes wrong during mitosis, the second sequence can kick in. But I cut out all duplication, leaving no room for error. A slight flaw becomes magnified."

"I helped raise him, and I never noticed any difference between him and the others."

"Like I said, the defects were minuscule, only a few changes within tens of thousands of genes."

"I have heard enough. Human offspring have countless alterations from their parents' genes. You are just trying to remove the blame from your actions by blaming his DNA. I need to pick up my sons now." Rosetta marched to the door, but a quintessence blocked it. "Out of my way, Jacob."

"As you transferred from Advance, you are no longer my superior. Therefore, I will not move until I am ready."

Rosetta placed hands on hips like a mother scolding a child. "I birthed you and changed your diapers, Jacob. You will move right now, or so help me."

"Hear us out, please," said Alexander. "Then we will leave you alone."

She glanced back at her husband, hoping for support, but Derrick only stood silently, eyes darting between his wife and his boss. "One more minute. That is all."

Mason said, "DNA is simply the blueprints which give us shape. Our decisions are the flesh which defines us. Paton chose to kill and would have succeeded if Alexander had not stopped him. Perhaps his DNA makeup left him vulnerable to temptation, but he made that decision and had to be held accountable."

Caleb added, "Image an adult Xavier roaming freely, killing for pleasure, obeying no one. It is our responsibility to protect the innocent, even if that may be from our own kind."

"He had no remorse when we examined him," said Gabriel. "We saw corruption within him and feared he may turn on his caregivers. He was unbalanced, a danger to you. We had to remove him to protect you."

"There had to be another way."

"Not for us. Defected products are not placed in jails or asylums. They are destroyed. If we do not police ourselves, who else can do so objectively? It is our burden to bear, not yours. And not Layla."

"I cannot stand by and let you kill children. I just cannot." Rosetta looked towards her husband.

He moved to her side with an apologetic smile. "At least we tried. Good night."

Jacob stepped out of the couple's way. Layla opened her mouth to call her friend back but remained silent. Alexander saw the look of despair on her face and knew she was near to breaking. He followed Rosetta and Derrick into the hallway, out of hearing of the others.

"Rosetta, why do you abandon us? Did you not raise us also?"

The woman turned, her face full of grief. "I cannot bear to watch children die."

"Since when has a quintessence ever really been a child? Childhood is fleeting for us. Do not hold us to human standards."

"I am sorry, Alexander, but I cannot handle any more killings."

"From the beginning we were designed to be predators. It is your love, your tenderness that has shaped us. We perceive right from wrong because you taught us to do so. If you abandon us, Layla will not last long. Then the Senate will post a bureaucrat in her place who will see us only as weapons. Over time, future generations will become the heartless monsters you fear. But that is not us, not now. Save us by staying. We need you."

"Enough." A single tear ran down her cheek.

Derrick squeezed her hand. "He is right—about Layla."

"I know." She closed her eyes for a long moment. When she finally looked up, she was at peace. "Alright, I...I will come back. And you are right, Alexander, I do see you as my children too."

Chapter Twenty-eight

"Want to see?" asked Zylar after glancing around, making sure no females were in the breakroom.

"Sure." Derrick leaned across the table, forgetting his lunch.

Zylar pulled a small black box out of his pocket, revealing a benitoite ring. He whispered, "I thought it was about time, with Tiffany soon to finish college and then the big move to Xi'an coming up. What do you think? Benitoite actually glows brilliant blue in UV lights."

"She'll like it. Great for dance clubs. How do you plan to ask her?"

"Um, I'm still working on the details for that. As you have gone through this before, I was wondering if you could give me some pointers."

"Romance. That's the key. Catch her by surprise. Make it a story she will want to tell your grandkids."

"Romance. Surprise. Kids. Got it." Panic flicked across Zylar's face. "Except I've never been good at the romance part. What should I do?"

As Derrick offered advice, adult quintessences ate silently around the room. Alexander moved to a counter near the men to grab an apple—and to have a closer look at the ring. Courting rituals of varies sentients intrigued him more than what was proper for a bonded quintessence. His e-band beeped, warning of an incoming message. As he glanced at the screen, he noticed that most of his brothers were also looking at theirs.

"Who would call all the quintessences at once?" asked Zylar looking about curiously.

"Maybe Layla is testing the system," suggested Derrick. "What is Tiffany's favorite flower?"

"Flower…uh…I know her favorite video game."

Silently Alexander read, "You have been activated for duty. Report in." He looked at his brothers, seeing his concern mirrored in their eyes.

Layla entered the room, studying her e-table as she walked. Seeing her, Zylar grabbed the ring box and tucked it back into a pocket. Layla glanced about the room, puzzled. "Did anyone just receive a message from General Baarook?"

"They all got messages," said Derrick.

"All?" Layla's face paled. She glanced about the room until locking eyes with Alexander. "Everyone?"

"Not I," said Stephen from a nearby table. "Nor Tyler or Jeff."

"You belong to the Austin Police Department and are out of imperial jurisdiction."

Alexander stepped near her. "The message said to report in."

"You are reporting in now." She tapped a nervous finger against her e-tablet. "Everyone to the game room. I have been sent instructions to show you."

The quintessences, along with curious Zylar and Derrick, walked down the hall to the game room. Most of the area was crowded with tables and board games. On a wall was a collection of screens. Layla synced her e-tablet with the screens and opened a video message.

A large image of General Baarock appeared. "You have been activated to duty, soldiers. You leave for your first mission today. Pack light. Report to the Austin Spaceport at sixteen hundred local time where you will be picked up." The message ended.

"Is there more details about the mission?" asked Caleb.

"No, that was all I was sent, but I will see if I can find out more. Derrick, there will be too many for the van. Could you take some in your car?"

"Yeah. Sure." As the quintessences filed out to prepare for the trip, Alexander lingered, watching Derrick speak to Layla. "Generation Two is not ready. They have never been on a live mission before."

"All of them passed the SWAT boot camp."

"But only three of them went on to actually work with the police, and they're not the ones going on this mission. Rookies are being sent out. To what?"

"I do not know, Derrick. I have no control over imperial business and neither do you. When the military says go, they go."

"They're not ready."

"I know that, but what can I do? I would protect them here forever if I could. But I cannot."

"Let us go," said Alexander.

Derrick jumped. "Oh, I didn't know you were standing there. Uh...when I said that the quintessences were not ready, I was not referring to you."

"I know." Alexander looked at Layla. "This is the time you must let go. You have designed us well. Now let us prove ourselves."

Layla wordlessly nodded, but her frown deepened.

Alexander left to help his younger brothers pack. An hour later twelve quintessences gathered in the breakroom, each carrying a small bag of clothing. Leana stood at the kitchenette counter, trying to press Jacob and Gabriel to pack more snacks. Derrick shuffled his feet in the doorway, juggling his car keys. His wife rewashed clean dishes, muttering about imperial tyrants. Zylar kept up a string of jokes which no one found funny, even himself. Anthony gave advice to Mason about how to navigate a spaceport.

Tiffany entered the room and sought out Alexander. In a low voice, she whispered, "Layla wants to speak with you in the lab."

Alexander walked out of the room, ignoring inquisitive glances from his brothers. When he knocked on the laboratory door, Layla immediately opened it then locked the door after he stepped in.

"I found out where you are going."

"Should not my brothers be here to hear this?

"No, I wanted to speak with you alone. General Baarook informed me you are going to Edieth, the home world of his race. He would tell me nothing more, but I am concerned you may encounter Roobaroo."

"It is a large planet. The chance that we meet an old college friend of yours is very slim."

"Normally, yes. Something big must be happening on Edieth for all your brothers to be activated together. From the few messages I have received from her in the last year, I think she may be involved in something not quite legal."

"Do you have proof or are you just guessing?"

"I only have my intuition." Deep worry lined her face. "Roobaroo's family has always spoken against the strict caste system her government enforces. Her parents were exiled. After college she became a political aid, trying to change the system from within. Then her parents died in an accident. She was certain they were murdered but had no proof. After that, her messages got darker, more enigmatic. I think she may be involved in some revolutionary group."

"If that is so, that would make her a hostile target. It is the responsibility of quintessences to enforce the laws of legit governments."

"I know. I am just asking that if you happen to meet her, please protect her."

"I cannot give that promise."

"It is in your Code to help the weak."

"And to obey superiors. You are outranked by military officers."

"I am your creator. Surely you can help her without breaking the law. In her society, the lower castes are slaves in all but name. Just like you."

"Layla, you are putting us in a difficult position. We must obey our superiors."

"And help the weak."

"My brothers and I should leave now. We are under a tight schedule." He turned and unlocked the door.

"Alexander." Her voice was soft with a slight quiver.

He looked at her. Layla stepped near and wrapped her hands around his neck, pulling him down. She kissed him. "Come back to me, alive."

"I will do my best."

When Alexander reached the breakroom, the eyes of his brothers flickered to him, probing to know what events had conspired in the lab. Alexander kept his face blank. "It is time." When opportunity arose, he would share with them Layla's request to protect her friend, avoiding mentioning the kiss—unless they specifically asked. He would not lie to them.

His brothers rose and followed, loading into the van and car. The trip to Austin City passed quickly. Stephen drove the van slower than usual so Derrick's car would not be left behind. At the spaceport, twelve quintessences unloaded and walked into the crowded lobby bustling with sentients from various planets. None of the quintessences had ever flown before, and they hesitated, unsure where to go next. Mason, who had listened closely to Anthony's advice, took the lead, guiding his brothers pass various booths and stations.

People stared as the quintessences and shuffled out of their path. A dozen muscular clones dressed in black marching through a spaceport stirred much attention—and fear. From Alexander's experience working on the police force, one quintessence walking down a street aroused little attention. Two quintessences drew curious stares. Twins were common enough in many species. But when three or more quintessences walked in public together, other sentients became uncomfortable around them. So many identical faces was abnormal, something to be avoided.

Mason stopped at an information booth and asked the worker, "Where is the gate for a military transport?"

The woman glanced nervously at the clones then at her computer screen. "Uh….Gate Sixty, Building Nine."

"Thank you." Mason moved to a brightly colored map mounted on the wall and studied it.

An ediethean wearing a military uniform approached. "I am Major Eaakva. You will come with me."

The officer whizzed them through several security checkpoints and down the vast, crowded halls of the spaceport. As they approached Gate Sixty, Alexander caught a glimpse through a window of the shuttle which would take them to the military ship orbiting above the planet. Excitement stirred in Alexander, and he vowed, *I will learn to fly those one day.*

The quintessences, the major, and one military pilot were the only ones who boarded the small shuttle. The craft lifted from the pad then zoomed across the sky, gained speed as it climbed. The older quintessences kept blank faces as they peered out of the windows as scenery blurred pass. When the entire planet hanged in the darkness of space, several of the younger quintessences shared brief smiles with each other. *I am not the only one who wants to be a pilot,* thought Alexander. A midsize battleship loomed into view. Alexander studied it, wondering about the complexity of flying it.

The shuttle landed in a docking bay. As the quintessences unloaded, busy crew members paused to stare at them. Major Eaakva led them through the maze of passages to a conference room. The quintessences were barely seated around a large table before General Baarook entered. As one, the quintessences stood and saluted.

The general gave a curt nod and moved directly into business. "You will be traveling to my home world Edieth to deal with a situation which must be handled discreetly. A terrorist group has taken over a large factory. Your task is to infiltrate the complex and neutralize the threat."

"Sir," said Caleb, "why is the local police not dealing with this?"

"They have—and failed."

"We are honored to be given our first assignment. Yet I must ask why are you not sending in experienced Imperial military," wondered Gabriel.

"We wish to keep this as quiet as possible. Our sources indicate that some of the terrorists may be highborn. And if you fail, it will give our High Council the excuse they need to pull their support from your creator's trillion credit institution."

The quintessences glanced at each other then Caleb said, "We will not let you down."

"You won't, no matter the results. The High Council will benefit either way. Alz are careful at weighing the odds in their own favor."

The general's fingers tapped a touchpad in front of him. Above the table a hologram image of a vast complex of interconnected buildings flicked into view. "It is the largest factory on Edieth and exports machine parts to many companies, including our military. Over six thousands workers from Yaz caste live there. They are witless and will follow the orders of anyone, including a terrorist. The authorities wish not to kill them but cannot get to the terrorists without doing so. Several hundred have already been slaughtered in two raids. My brother is on our High Council and appealed to me for suggestions. I thought it was time to test the favored pet project of the Emperor."

The general and major discussed strategies for locating the terrorists, highlighting on the virtual map various access points for entering the complex. Occasional comments they made hinted of their distain of the quintessences. Still Alexander and his brothers were determined to do their best, even if they were only seen as disposable pawns.

Two days later, the battleship dropped into orbit above Edieth. A shuttle flew the quintessences down to the city nearest the factory where a local police officer picked them up. As the hover van glided through the streets, Alexander observed the elegant homes and businesses nestled among gardens and parks, a peaceful landscape where children dashed about, unwatched by adults. The driver bragged that the planet was well-known for its low crime rate and producing the highest concentration of genius in the galaxy.

"All Alz are born geniuses," said the officer as he turned off the highway and headed towards the factory. "Everyone. Would be nice if they would share their IQ with the rest of us. At least I'm a Fyw. That opens up many job opportunities for me, though we aren't permitted to attend college. Still, I made it through the police academy. Not many of us can claim that."

The driver stopped the van by a tent surrounded by police cars. Several media groups were kept at a distance behind a barricade. One reporter tried to send a camera probe across the barricade to zoom in on the quintessences, but an officer threatened to shoot the camera down. The quintessences followed their guide into the tent where the police captain was arguing with someone on a telecom. His thick, black hair was sprinkled with white and his dark eyes were weary from lack of sleep. The quintessences waited silently until he slammed down the device.

Captain Haleev looked at them, frowning. "You're the secret weapon they promised?"

"We are more than what we appear," said Caleb.

"You better be. I sent a hundred of my men in there—twice. And all we have to show for it is a dozen officers dead and at least a hundred Yaz wasted. And then I have to deal with the outraged factory owners. With production stopped, they're losing a quarter of a million credits a day. And now they're threatening to sue my department for replacement cost of the Yaz." The captain clenched a fist in anger, letting his rage spill out. "Alz think they rule the universe, but not one of them can handle real work. Let them send their own into this quagmire. My men are trained to handle traffic violations and vandalism, not open war. We're supposed to keep the terrorists off the news, but with a dozen officers dead, the media know it's more than a simple mechanical problem."

"Is there information on the location of the terrorists?" asked Mason.

The captain laughed bitterly. "Yes, they're someplace inside with six thousand hostages too dumb to walk out when given the opportunity. Other than that, we know nothing except they're monitoring our communication channels and are forewarned about raids. They are armed. Worse, they instruct the Yaz to attack us. The primitives are limited to throwing tools, machine parts, and anything else they can get their grimy hands on. When you have thousands slinging at officers who are ordered not to kill their stupid attackers, what can we do? If we stun them, they are just dragged off and replaced by others. We must kill the Yaz, perhaps all of them, to reach to terrorists. I keep telling the Alz that, but do they listen?"

"They sent us," said Alexander.

"A dozen of you against six thousand?"

"We like a challenge," said Jacob.

Captain Haleev shook his head. "Well, if you actually do succeed in reaching the terrorists, kill them, no arrests. That order comes from the High Council itself. They're afraid there might be highborn rebels involved, and they wouldn't want that news leaking out. Bad for their reputation, you know. Can't ruin the adage that all ediethean are happy with the caste of their birth."

Chapter Twenty-nine

Alexander slowly inched through the ventilation shaft, careful to avoid making noise. He crawled through semi-darkness, navigating over vertical drops in the narrow passage. Occasionally he paused to check the map downloaded to his e-band. Behind him crawled two younger brothers Lucas and Peter—his squad. Elsewhere in the vast complex, three other teams of quintessences probed towards the hub of the factory, seeking the ringleaders of the attack.

Heeding Captain Haleeve's advice, nothing of their incursion was mentioned over any communication channels, and they maintained radio silence as each group worked independently. Each squad had entered the complex from a different direction. Alexander's group had scaled a fence in a wooded back area then entered one of the outlying storage buildings. From there, they used a maintenance tunnel which ran underground, supplying water and electricity to the main building. Upon reaching the basement, they had switched to the ventilation shaft which allowed them to penetrate deeper into the complex without being seen. Occasionally he caught brief glimpses of Yaz through the grills. Each time, his squad had frozen, waiting in the semi-darkness until the Yaz moved on.

Ahead, the shaft branched. Alexander rechecked his map then turned left. The view through the grill at the next opening revealed a storage room filled with shelves of non-perishable food. No one in sight. *Might as well try it here,* thought Alexander. He carefully unfastened the grill, pushed it aside, and crawled into the room. The last one out of the shaft was Peter who placed the grill back over the opening but kept it unhooked in case a quick escape was needed. Keeping low to the floor, the squad moved along the cluttered shelves. The sound of a falling box caused the quintessences to freeze. Boots scuffed then a can rattled across the floor. Alexander moved towards the sounds and peeked around a corner.

Two Yaz poked through the food, making a mess. As the lowest of the castes, the Yaz were short and stocky, built for hard labor. The male was bald though the female had a frizz of dark curls. They wore rags over grey skin splotched and crisscrossed with healed cuts. The female studied the image of a fruit on a can. She touched the picture then rotated the can, searching for a way to open it. Finding nothing, she tossed in of the floor. The male shook a bag of chips, puzzled by the sound. Seeing its bright colors, the female tried to grab the bag from him, leading to a tug-of-war. The bag ripped open, sending its contents across the floor. Both Yaz dropped to their knees, grabbed fallen chips and stuffed them into their mouths.

"Stop that!" yelled a frustrated ediethean, walking down the aisle towards them. The newcomer, an elderly female, was taller and more slender than the Yaz. She wore a priestess choker around her neck and had a gun belted to her waist. "I let you in here to help me carry food to the cafeteria so others may eat."

"No eat now?" said the female sadly.

"No. Eat later. Now grab a box of those chips and follow me."

Hidden behind the next shelf, Alexander glanced at his brothers then pulled out his laser gun. He moved from behind the row, firing at the armed ediethean. Body armor under her clothing absolved the blast, but she was still knocked to the floor. She struggled to pull her gun free from its holster, but Alexander was faster. His second shot hit her head, causing her to go limp. Lucas and Peter fired on the two Yaz, stunning both with one hit each.

Alexander grabbed the terrorist and pulled her into a sitting position. Then he bit, searching the sentient's mind for information. Dimly he was aware of Peter warning of another culprit then shots firing. He broke off the bite and saw Peter lying of the concrete floor, a viscous burn from a laser scarring his arm. Lucas lowered his own weapon. At the far end of the aisle, another terrorist lay unconscious. Alexander reprimanded himself for being so careless in letting his guard down.

Alexander said to Lucas, "Take care of Peter. I'll see if there are more."

With gun out, Alexander dashed to the end of the aisle, looking for others. Several startled Yaz carrying boxes stared at him then glanced at each other, uncertain what to do. Alexander fired at each of them, stunning all. Seeing no more threats, he hurried back to his brothers. Peter had just finished feeding on the unconscious female Yaz, pink skin on his arm the only sign of his recent injury.

"The Yaz's mind is strange," said Peter. "So simple. Only concerned about basic needs. There was nothing about where other hostile targets are located."

"There are two dozen terrorists," said Alexander, citing the information he had found during his probing. "They have set up a command headquarters in the office area where we will head now. After we complete our orders here."

Alexander changed the setting of his gun to high then pointed it at the head of the unconscious ediethean priestess. His younger brothers watched silently as he shot, killing the helpless rebel. Then he walked down the aisle and killed the other one, an Eay youth. Alexander would have preferred cuffing the culprits for future questioning, but they could not be dragged through the ventilation system nor would he leave them for other terrorists to free. The stunned Yaz he left alone.

The quintessences pierced deeper into the complex using the ventilation shafts, reaching the sleeping quarters of the Yaz. Through glimpses in the grates, Alexander spied huge rooms filled with bunk beds stacked four high. Everywhere were Yaz. They seemed like children on a holiday. Groups were bunched together chatting or playing simple games. Some chased each other, climbing quickly up and down ladders, heedless of others trying to sleep. None took notice of movement behind the grating.

The quintessences crawled through the labyrinth of passages, no light coming from the openings they now passed. Alexander's map indicated the offices had been reached. He carefully removed a grating and stepped out into a large, dark room only illuminated by a few blinking lights warning of computers in sleep mode. Peter replaced the grating, and the quintessences moved slowly among the desks and cubicles, guns raised. Nothing stirred in the room.

Alexander headed towards the door. As he passed the final desk, he heard a faint click. Suddenly an explosion of energy burst from a hidden stun mine, overwhelming him. His body collapsed, his head slamming against the carpeted floor. He fought against grogginess, drifting in and out of consciousness. The door opened, booted feet, voices, green eyes close to him, a muzzle pressed against his head. Then nothingness.

He awoke slowly, his body stiff from lying on the floor. His vision seemed blurry until he realized he was looking through a hazy energy field. Sitting up, he saw Peter and Lucas still asleep near him. They were in a cell consisting of a few metal rods creating a frame for the energy wall. Around the huge, shadowy room were other cells, some not turned on but others held nearly a hundred captured factory employees. Alexander stood and moved closer to the humming wall to see better. Some captives slept, others talked quietly or stared at nothing. A few yelled at guards who ignored them. He was relieved to see none were his brothers.

Across the room an armed rebel and a dozen Yaz watched him. The Cuy guard left but returned shortly with a companion. The tall, elegant female walked over to Alexander's cell, stopping only inches from the sizzling shield.

She tilted her gray head, studying him with green eyes. Fiery red hair highlighted her angular face.

"Well formed. Strong, muscular. Certainly can pass as human, though the eyes are a bit off," the Alz murmured. "She chose well the design."

"You are Roobaroo," said Alexander.

Surprise flicked in her eyes. "I had not thought the authorities would be so quick in discovering our identities. We hid ourselves well."

"They still do not know, but Layla guessed you were here."

"Of course. Did she send you?"

"No, the Basanti Military at the request of your High Council."

"Ah. They must indeed be desperate to resort to outside help. Of course, they expect you to kill us and toss our bodies in the furnace, erasing all evidence of our rebellion. Cannot have news leaking out to the galaxy that insurgents exist among the most respected race of the empire."

"Layla has memories of you as happy and idealistic while in college. She greatly respected you, yet you have chosen to become an enemy to your own nation. Why?"

Intently Roobaroo stared at him. "How intelligent did she make you? How much can you understand?"

"I understand that you have become bitter since your parents' deaths."

"Murder. They were conveniently blown-up along with ten others to silence their public criticism of our government's authoritarian caste system. But their voices live on through me—and my daughter."

"Layla did not mention you had family."

"I kept it secret." She glanced at the Cuy guard standing nearby. "My husband. Our union is the ultimate blasphemy for our society, the joining of DNA from different castes. Our daughter is off world, safe. She will carry our story to future generations."

"You plan to die." Alexander needed to keep her talking, learn her motives. "How will that serve your cause? You are responsible for the deaths of many Yaz." Alexander noticed Lucas slowly awaking.

"Their deaths I do mourn, but we do this to benefit their entire race. We have gained the High Council's attention, if but a brief moment. This is the largest factory on Edieth. With its production stopped, countless other factories and businesses are also affected, each part of a huge chain. Citizens will ask questions. This time, the High Council will not be able to hide that there are deep rooted problems in our society. Never before have they dared asked for outside help."

"Is it pride or revenge which drives you along this path?"

Roobaroo studied him intently. "She indeed has designed you well. You are capable of rational thought. Until today, I imagined you only a little smarter than a Yaz but with a gun. Not a pleasant image. As for my personal motives, revenge or pride is not enough for me to betray my own caste—but the cry for justice is. You have no idea the monstrosities my caste has committed for millenniums. We hide it so well—thanks to our entire race being geniuses. Or should I say, all the identified Alz? For you see, occasionally Alz do give birth to children who are not. My older sister's was executed when she was five because her IQ was two points too low."

"You do this then to avenge your sister's death?" asked Alexander. Lucas and Peter were both standing now, silently watching the conversation.

"You have not listened carefully." Roobaroo slowly walked the outside perimeter of the cell as she talked, examining the younger quintessences. "I said the monstrosities have been ongoing for millenniums. My sister's death was the key which removed the veil from my parents' eyes. Our upper castes consider the profectus the ultimate insult, the Coalition of Human Advancement fusing our DNA with their offspring in an attempt to create beings as intelligent as us. It took thousands of years of carefully selected arranged marriages to raise our IQ's high enough to form the Alz and Byk castes. Humans had the audacity to believe they could do it in just one generation with their precious profectus." The Alz leaned close to the energy field, her green eyes piercing. "You are the end results of a philosophy my ancestors embraced nearly ten thousand years ago."

"Layla did not create us to spite your species."

"No, she is too naïve like most of the profectus. Each wrapped up in dreams of grander, blind to the overall picture. But those behind the Coalition see clearly. As did my own ancestries. Though they did not have the super intelligences of the Alz, they foresaw our creation. Mild manner middle and lower castes followed the laws that the upper castes enforced. Any who disagreed are quickly exterminated. Marriages outside one's caste is forbidden. Our evolution was controlled in two directions. Early on, leaders realized the need to have a cheap labor force to handle food and factory production. So while focus was placed on creating smarter descendants, others worked to create a simple-minded workforce. Meet their basic needs, give them some entertainment when off duty, and everyone is happy. No need to pay them. Now we reap the end results—Alz who govern not only the planet but the galaxy and Yaz, our hidden slave race. All part of our complicated twenty-two caste system, each is told what jobs they may hold, education they may have, whom they may marry—if they are permitted to marry at all. The Yaz and Xit are considered too dumb to understand the concept."

Roobaroo gestured towards the humming energy shield. "The cell you are standing is a breeding pen. Male and females Yaz are usually kept separated at the factory, but when there is a need for more, Yaz with the right traits are placed in these cells and told to breed, but they are so feeble-minded even that is difficult for them. Once the task is done, the couple never see each other again. Females nurse their young several times a day during work breaks. Once weaned, the young Yaz are separated from their mothers and given simple tasks like sorting scrap metal. Older ones clean the factory, but many die from getting too near dangerous equipment. If they survive to adulthood, they take on heavy-duty labors. By age forty, they are elders doing simple tasks again. When they become too old to work, they are euthanatized."

Alexander glanced around the shadowy room at the glowing cells. "How have the Alz maintained a slave race on their own home planet when galactic law forbids it?"

"Ironic is it not? Nearly eighteen hundred years ago when the empire was still young, it was Alz who introduced the anti-slavery bill. With the support of their many allies, the Alz easily passed the law. Of course, they made certain that the fine print was written in their favor, giving planetary governments the right to oversee prisoners and those deemed unable to care for themselves. As all Yaz are born with retarded intelligence, the Edieth government decides what is best for them."

"And now you will decide what is best for the Yaz?"

"I simply wish for my government to acknowledge its wrongs and began taking positive steps to reverse what we have done to the Yaz. We created them. They are of our own species, but we treat them as livestock, conditioning them from birth to be obedient animals who must always obey upper castes."

Roobaroo beckoned over a Yaz serving as a guard. The stocky creature came shyly, eyes downcast. At full height, the male stood two feet shorter than Roobaroo. She pulled out her gun and placed in into the Yaz's hand. The creature held it awkward, uncertain what to do with it. Roobaroo took the Yaz's hand and twisted the gun so it pointed at his head.

"Pull this button," she said to him.

Without hesitation or fear, the Yaz pulled the trigger then looked about, wondering if something had occurred.

"Thank you," said Roobaroo, taking the gun back and flipping off its safety. "You may go stand guard again." As the Yaz moved away, Roobaroo said to Alexander. "He has seen this gun kill yet understands little about death. He will obey every command I give even at the cost of his life. You have much in common with him."

"I see little we have in common," Alexander said as he noted the ventilation gratings in the room and the location of the control panel for the cells.

"Ah, but you do. You are both slaves, though the Yaz are too stupid to even realize that. I have had chats with your creator. She was angry when I accused her of creating a slave race, but she finally admitted to me she felt guilty about your fate and was relieved when you were given an opportunity to earn your freedom. Twenty-five years of hazardous service."

"We are proud to serve the empire."

Roobaroo laughed. "Another commonality with the Yaz. You have both been conditioned to obey superiors despite personal cost to yourself. Yet you have the ability to rationalize whereas the Yaz cannot. They serve their masters blindly. You do so with full knowledge of your slavery."

"Through us much good can be accomplished."

"And much evil. Who do you think decides where you go? Who tells you if someone is a traitor to be killed or a victim to be rescued? Remember, it is the Alz who hold many of the top positions in the Basanti government and military. Ultimately, it is the Alz, not the Emperor, who is your master. Just as the Yaz are terminated when they are no longer useful, so you will be. Will they really give you freedom in twenty-five years or order you into a situation which will most certainly end in your death? Make no mistake. The Galactic Senate does not care for your wellbeing. You will only be kept around as long as you are useful. Or you could save yourself by breaking your bonds. Join us. We could use good soldiers."

"I will not rebel against my creator."

"It is not your creator you must rebel against but the masters she sold you to."

Alexander thought about his forty-nine young brothers back at BGF and the many generations not yet born. "I must decline your offer."

"Why? Do you want to be a slave?"

"No. But I must think of others besides myself."

Roobaroo walked around the outside of the cell, speaking to Lucas and Peter. "How about you? Will you continue to be a slave or choose freedom?

Imagine going where you wish, marrying whom you choose. Or are you nothing more than a trained Yaz?"

Remaining silent, Peter and Lucas glanced at Alexander.

"I am their superior officer," said Alexander. "They obey me."

Roobaroo laughed. "Are you their slave master then? A slave ordering around another slave?"

"You know little about us. But I do speak for my entire race."

"I know much more than you think. I am one of your creator's closest friends, what few she does have."

"She is getting better at making friends."

Shots suddenly fired from out of the dim shadows beyond the furthest prisoner cells. One beam hit Roobaroo, knocking her down. Her husband tried to take aim at the intruders, but he was caught with a beam from behind. The dozen Yaz on guard duty dashed about looking for something to hit with the metal hammers they carried, but each was quickly stunned. Jacob and his two young squad members entered the chamber from an open side door. From behind a distant breeding cell, Gabriel's squad emerged. They had removed a ventilation grating hidden from the view of the guards by the dim light and crowded breeding pens.

"You are late," said Alexander.

"No, we were here but found the conversation interesting." Gabriel ignored the din of prisoners demanding to be let out.

"We did not want to end it prematurely." Jacob examined the control panel. He touched a button and the energy field of Alexander's cell flickered then went out. "Amiable of you to take on the role of speaking for us all."

"Did I not speak your thoughts, brother?" asked Alexander.

"Of course."

Gabriel addressed the prisoners. "We ask for you to quiet down. When we have completely secured the area, we will release you. Until then, you must be patient."

Some of the captives grumbled while others declared their rank and demanded immediate release. The quintessences ignored them. Gabriel cuffed the fallen Cuv guard. As Jacob bent to cuff Roobaroo, she stirred, slowly awaking. A protective vest she had worn under her shirt had absorbed part of the beam which hit her.

Lucas asked, "Are we not supposed to kill her?"

Gabriel answered, "Layla asked us to protect her."

Still groggy, Roobaroo looked up from the floor. "Interesting dilemma. Do you obey your creator or your master?"

Alexander glanced at his brothers then back at her. "Fortunately for you, we are rational beings."

Several hours later, twelve quintessences escorted a hundred freed prisoners and eleven cuffed terrorists through the gateway entrance of the factory. Police swarmed forward to meet them.

Captain Haleev smiled in relief, "A dozen against six thousand. Who would have believed it?"

Caleb saluted. "You will find the Yaz alive, but the factory will need repairs."

"Six thousand Yaz on a holiday can make quite a mess," said Jacob.

"The Alz can deal with that." The captain gestured to the rescued hostages. "All factory workers, to my left please. We must take your statements before you may go home." Haleev lowered his voice so only the nearby quintessences could hear him. "You did a fine job but the High Council asked for no prisoners."

Mason stepped forward. "You will find thirteen suspects dead in the factory."

"It is not the High Council we answer to," said Alexander, "but the Basanti Military. These prisoners are under the jurisdiction of the empire and must receive a trial in a galactic court."

Captain Haleev looked over the eleven bound terrorists, several from upper castes. Then he glanced at the excited news reporters behind the barricade already sending their flying cameras into the mix of freed factory workers and police officers. "The High Council won't like this. It forces them to acknowledge that highborn can be corrupted."

"They especially will not like me," shouted Roobaroo. Spotting a camera drone buzzing nearby, she stepped towards it. "I am Roobaroo Dayal, daughter of Ambassadors Baroo and Roora. I was born Alz, and I have much to tell you about the crimes of my race."

The media snapped into an animated frenzy. Every camera in the area flew towards Roobaroo as she began spewing out details. The captain yelled, "Get them out of here!"

As police officers attempted to control the excited reporters and shoo away the hovering cameras, the quintessences escorted the prisoners to several nearby vans. As the last was loaded, Captain Haleev looked at the quintessences with fear and respect. "You did that on purpose."

"Did we?" said Caleb, his expressionless face revealing nothing.

"You are indeed far more than what you seem."

The quintessences climbed in with the prisoners while ediethean officers drove them to the spaceport. Alexander sat across from Roobaroo and her husband. Some of the prisoners quietly reflecting on lost comrades while others excitedly talked about the media coverage.

Roobaroo smiled. "Thank you."

"We have arrested many," said Alexander, "but you are the first to thank us."

"You have given me the one thing I desired—media attention which the High Council cannot ignore. Being an ambassador's daughter has its advantages. My parents had powerful friends on several planets. By using those contacts, I will make the trials of my friends and I as public as possible. I expect we will get life in prison. If I am martyred in jail, it will raise many probing questions."

"Perhaps you will be let out after a few decades and see your daughter again."

"Perhaps." She leaned closer, keeping her voice low. "Heed my warning. Even if the Senate keeps its promise of citizenship after you complete your bond years, you will not really be free. Until your species has complete control over its own reproduction, the fate of your species will always be tightly controlled by the Empire."

Alexander nodded soberly, "We are a young but patient race who learns from our elders. As the Alz control by stealth, so can we."

Chapter Thirty

The hot summer breeze brought no relief though the sun had barely risen. Layla choose to walk to work, giving herself as much time as possible before she had to read her messages. Two months had passed since her quintessences had been activated by the Basanti Military, and they had yet to be sent home. The brief reports sent back claimed the Edieth mission had been successful with eleven arrests made. After that, the quintessences had been sent on a back-to-back series of high-stake missions without rest. Sometimes Layla wondered if the military was deliberately trying to kill them—or at least cause them to fail. Somehow, though, they always managed to succeed. But how long would that last?

Alexander had sent her a message informing her of Roobaroo's arrest, opening up a host of conflicts in Layla. Her friend was alive. But a terrorist. How was someone supposed to feel about that? Her best friend from college was an enemy of the empire whose actions had led to the deaths of over a hundred simple-minded Yazs and a dozen police officers. Layla could not support Roobaroo's actions, yet neither could she turn her back on her friend. Roobaroo had been allowed to send her a short letter explaining why she had chosen this path. It revealed the heavy guilt she felt for the many lives lost, and hope that due to the media onslaught edietheans would now pay attention to the Yazs' plight instead of turning a blind eye.

As Advance Department loomed into view, Layla walked slower, dreading reading her mail, battling against the fear of losing what was most important to her. The morning shift had already arrived and the caretakers were clustered in the breakroom. Tiffany proudly showed off her engagement ring while Zylar smiled sheepishly at the attention focused on him by co-workers.

"He told me we were going to his cousin's apartment to try a new video game, but when we walked in, there was nothing but a dark, empty room. Then suddenly there were stars. Everywhere hologram stars and planets zooming about. So beautiful. And romantic music playing. Then in the middle of the galaxy he drops to his knees and holds out a glowing blue ring. He told me that many have promised to give their lovers the stars but he will give me the universe." Tiffany sighed deeply along with other female listeners.

"Didn't know you could be so romantic," said Derrick, giving Zylar a friendly poke in the ribs.

"Took me nearly two months to come up with that," said the new fiancé. "My cousin helped a lot."

"When is the wedding?" asked Rosetta.

Tiffany beamed, "In six weeks, soon after my college graduation."

Layla was glad everyone was too focused on the newly engaged couple to notice her quickly leaving the room. She knew she should be happy for them, but she only felt jealousy. They did not have to hide their feelings for each other or have to wait twenty-five years to earn the privilege to marry. Nor live in the constant fear of receiving a message that their love had been killed in the line of duty. She paced about her lab, trying to force her bitter feelings into calmness. She picked up her e-tablet and scanned the many messages. The routine terrified her every time. Most related to the business of building Essence. Suddenly one sender caught her eye. Zelzer Award Committee. She stared, wondered if she still slept—but in her dreams the dreaded letter always came from the Basanti Military, not an award committee.

She tapped the title and the message opened. "We wish to congratulate you. The committee which chooses the five annual winners of the prestige Zelzer Award has selected you as the recipient for the science category for your creation of the first synthetic sentient species. All winners will attend an award banquet held at the imperial place." The message continued but Layla was too dazed to read it.

In a trance, she walked down the hall, passing a group of young quintessences on their way to class. Leana spoke to her, but Layla did not comprehend the words. When she entered the breakroom, those who still lingered to talk noticed her shocked face.

"What is it?" asked Rosetta. "Did something happen to Alexander? The others?"

Layla wordlessly handed over her e-tablet. As Rosetta read the message, her face showed astonishment. Silently she passed the e-tablet to her husband.

"The Zelzer Award!" sputtered Derrick. "But that's…that's huge. Should there not have been some warning?"

"Zelzer Award?" Zylar grabbed the e-tablet. "Doesn't that come with a million credit prize?"

"To be put back into the research," muttered Layla, sitting down. The room began to spin, and she placed her head in her hands to steady herself.

Tiffany read over her fiancé's shoulder. "I have read that the committee is supposed to investigate each contender, but we have heard nothing."

"There have been plenty of reporters," said Zylar.

"But the committee members themselves are supposed to make site visits."

Rosetta ignored the cynicism of the others. "Congratulation, Layla. You just won the most renowned award in the galaxy."

"I do not know how."

"Don't know how? Girl, you have spent over half your life working on this project to make the impossible possible. You have more than earned it."

With barely a week to the award ceremony, Layla moved through a whirl of surrealism. Palakkad and the BGF board were thrilled to hear about the award, and they quickly alerted the local media. Once again, reporters with their flying cameras probed the halls of Advance Department. Newscasters interviewed police in Austen City who worked with the quintessences, and bold reporters accompanied Steven, Tyler, and Jeff on their normal rounds, though none were allowed on dangerous SWAT raids. Tiffany and Rosetta went shopping with Layla in the city, helping her find a dress for the banquet.

A luxury spaceliner flew Layla to the vast, glittering imperial city of Diamond located on the planet Basanti. She was greeted at the spaceport by Doctor Karbiener, a renowned geneticist on the award committee.

"It is an honor to meet you," said Karbiener, giving a short bow.

"No, the honor is mine," said Layla, bowing lower than the elderly doctor. "I have studied your work for years. I used one of your theories in my design."

"I noticed that. Very insightful of you. We must discuss it more during the drive to your hotel. You will be staying at the Palace Hotel. The view is very fitting for its name. Tomorrow, if you wish, I will give you a tour of famous landmarks in our city."

"I would enjoy that very much."

As the limousine carried them to the five star hotel, Layla was awestruck being in the presence of a man whose work she had studied since childhood. As Karbiener questioned her about quintessences, she relaxed somewhat. He left her at the grand lobby and an attendant carried Layla's luggage up to the fifteenth floor. The plush suite which would be her home for the next week was more luxurious than anything Layla had experienced before, even when presidents had attempted to win her favor for Essence's site.

After the attendant left, she walked out onto the balcony. The beautiful night landscape of the city greeted her with lofty skyscrapers, city parks, and busy streets. The huge imperial palace filled the horizon. Its huge central tower rose high, topped with a gigantic diamond shaped dome lit from within by swirling light. *It is so beautiful. If only Alexander could be here to share it with me,* she thought. Loneness filled her.

Having not eaten supper, she called room service for a meal to be sent up. She had barely finished unpacking when the doorbell rang. An attendant pushed a cart into the room and left after she paid a tip. As she went to shut the door, two children dashed down the hallway chasing a runaway electronic dog. A third child waddled behind.

"Don't run in the hallway," scolded a woman, carrying several shopping bags. "Especially not here."

"Let them enjoy themselves," said a familiar man, looking tired. "At least someone still has energy."

Layla stepped into the hallway. "Richard. Alana. It is so good to see you."

"Ah, finally someone we know. We have met so many people today." Alana, dressed in designer slacks and blouse, wore her blond hair in a stylish plait.

"Are you here for the award ceremony?" asked Richard, his brown hair a bit out of place.

"Yes, I won the Zelzer in science."

"Mine's for technology."

The two profectus looked at each other then burst into laughter. Alana rolled her eyes then scolded one of her children who was trying to feed the dog a silk flower from an expense vase.

"Would you like to come in?" said Layla. "I just ordered dinner and can have some more food sent up."

For the next couple of hours the Cambridges chatted with Layla while their children played games on the large video screen. Richard had been just as astonished as Layla on discovering he had won the award.

"Came completely out of the blue. I mean, I have won other technology awards, but this is the Zelzer. Never in my lifetime did I dream it possible. The letter said it was for the software I designed relating to science."

"Ultimate Designer, that program for my quintessences?"

"Yes, though my software company has gone on to make other technical advancements in medicine and security also."

"Your DNA program is used by the majority of geneticists across the galaxy."

"And made me rich. Still that million credits we are getting will be useful in helping me design that city building program I am writing."

"Still planning to be a mayor?"

"The election is only a month off. New Hope may just consist of construction workers' trailers right now, but one day it will grow to be a good size city to house the employees of your Essence Institute. Someone needs to plan it right from the beginning. With the publicity I am getting with the Zelzer, I think I stand a good chance of winning."

His wife smiled, "You are going to win, even if there was no Zelzer. After all, you are married to a mayor's daughter."

The next day, Doctor Karbiener gave Layla and the Cambridge family a tour of the city. They saw the ancient Tree of Serenity, supposedly the site where the first Emperor of Basanti signed a treaty with his defeated enemies, uniting the planet under one government. Next they visited the Science Museum which fascinated both the adults and kids. After lunch in the museum's café, they spent the rest of the afternoon at a local zoo. That night they dined with families of the other winners at an elegant restaurant. Layla enjoyed herself most of the time, but pangs of loneness still overwhelmed her. She could not help noticing that she was the only one present without a spouse.

The banquet was scheduled to take place the next night. Layla spent a quiet, but nervous morning alone in her suite. She called friends and family. Her parents bragged about her to co-workers. Her brother and his family promised to watch the news coverage live. Rosetta and Tiffany gave her last minute make-up advice. The fifty-two quintessences on Bontinc gathered as a group to send her a video greeting. Even Roobaroo, through her lawyer, managed to send her a short text message of congratulations. The only ones she did not hear from were Alexander and his brothers traveling with him. Perhaps at this very moment they were on some deadly mission to save somebody's life. Or assassinate someone.

She lunched with the Cambridges then all the winners endured several hours of media interviews, which she dreaded. By the time Layla reached her suite, she was so mentally tired all she wanted to do was sleep. Instead, she put on a sleek, red dress and then attempted to apply make-up. Fortunately Alana came by and saved her from that disaster. Alana, already dressed in a gorgeous blue dress which highlighted her chic hairstyle, soon had Layla looking so exquisite that she could not recognize her own self in the mirror.

Limousines drove the winners and their families to the Imperial Palace. The night seemed surreal as famous scientists, entertainers, and politicians greeted Layla. She was tongue tied over and over again, relieved that Alana was always nearby, smoothing over the awkwardness of both Layla and

Richard. Finally, they were seated at tables in a huge banquet room. The food was scrumptious, but Layla ate little of it for she was terrified of the speech she must give. Millions of citizens would be watching. She reminded herself that billions of other sentients in the galaxy would not be interested enough to watch the ceremony, but the thought did not relax her.

She was the first of the winners to speak. A famous physicist gave a far too long introduction, building her up to look like a farsighted heroine destined to change the face of genetics forever. Finally, her name was called and she walked to the podium, hoping the cameras did not pick up the shakiness she felt inside. She managed to read her speech with a steady voice. The audience laughed at the right places and applauded her ending. Then it was over. Award in hand, Layla carried the heavy gold statue back to her seat. Alana smiled at her, and Richard gave a thumbs-up. Then he was called to the stage. While Richard recited his acceptance speech from memory, Layla calmed down enough to nibble at her salad.

Other speeches followed. Several prominent performers sung. After the ceremony ended, there were more greetings and conversations with famous people. It was pass midnight before Layla reached the street curve to wait for her ride. She was weary, but she tried to remember all the celebrities she had just talked with, knowing that back at BGF, her friends would quiz her.

"Your ride," said an attendant, holding the door of a limousine open.

Layla slid in before realizing that someone sat across from her. "Emperor Kalyuga!" she sputtered in shock. Had he attended the ceremony? With so many there, she was unsure.

"Enjoy the banquet?" said the monarch, relaxing in the posh seat.

"Yes, sire. I did not expect to see you here."

"It is my palace. I thought it best we meet privately out of the limelight. Congratulations on your Zelzer Award."

"It was unexpected. For me and Richard Cambridge."

"Yes, I expect it came as a surprise."

"Sire, it is a strange coincidence that both Richard and I won for research relating to quintessences."

"It is no coincidence. I asked the committee to place your names at the top of their list."

"You rigged the Zelzer Award?" Layla's mouth opened in astonishment and shock.

"Your name has been on the watch list since that first article appeared in *Galactic Times*. You were deemed too young and the research still in its infancy. Over time you would have eventually won on your own, but that could have been decades yet—and I needed the timing to be now. Your friend Richard has also been on the watch list for several years."

Disappointment filled Layla both for winning an award she had not yet earned and that the ruler she respected had resorted to fixing contests. "Sire, I would have preferred the long wait."

"Not at the cost of your Essence Institute, I presume. For that is what is at stake. I am sure you have noticed that your quintessences have been going through some grueling missions lately. That is not coincidence either, though not by my choice. There have been many political forces combating both for and against the institute, including a peculiar combination of foes working together. The quintessences are being tested so see if they can really handle what has been promised. The High Council of Edieth has been especially upset at the quintessences' continued successes, but many ediethean officers in my fleet have gained great respect for their unique abilities. Enough that even General Baarook has finally given his full approval for my original plan of producing twenty thousand quintessences a year."

"Twenty thousand!" Layla mind reeled. A hundred and forty thousand young quintessences growing up at Essence at the same time. The sheer number of workers needed boggled her mind. "Sire, Essence was not designed to handle that amount. It would require the space of a good size city."

"Fortunately, you picked a site with plenty of space. I have already contacted the architect Richton to redesign the plans. She was quite eager. Perhaps a Zelzer Award will be in her future. For my plan to succeed, I needed a bill to be passed by a proper vote of the full Senate. It did so yesterday, thanks in part to the positive publicity you and your quintessences are receiving in the media at the moment."

"You have been sending all those reporters to BGF?"

"No, they came seeking a good story. A race of clone soldiers brings out curiosity, hope, and fear in other sentients. It is curiosity and hope that must be milked at the moment. I need you to be a face that the public can identify with—a pretty, feminine face which promises a miracle race which will stabilize the internal conflicts of the Empire."

"But I am just a scientist." Who preferred keeping to her lab and not dealing with people. She had not the charm of Alana, the fashion sense of Tiffany, the friendliness of Rosette, nor the politic acuteness of Roobaroo. "I am not skilled in such matters."

"You have done well so far. If you want Essence Institute to become reality, this is the price you must pay. In public you will need to shun the media circus which your friend Roobaroo is currently enjoying. We need to avoid having your name attached to a terrorist, except that your quintessences arrested her."

"Yes, sire."

"One more thing. To pay for the expansion of Essence, the Senate raised the years of service for the quintessences to fifty years."

"Fifty years." Dizziness hit Layla and she grabbed an armrest, trying to steady herself. She would be seventy-four before Alexander was granted citizenship.

"You have written that the estimated life expectancy for quintessences is a hundred and fifty years. That is only a third of their lifetime."

"It is only an estimate. It could be less."

"Or more."

"I will not know until they begin dying from old age." *But I won't be around to see that.* "Sire, I promised the quintessences twenty-five years. Now you are forcing me to break that promise?"

"You may honor your promise for those born at BGF, but those from Essence must serve fifty years."

Layla heart rate began to slow. Just twenty-two years yet without Alexander. Years of countless interviews, meetings, supervising thousands of strangers, hiring and firing employees, bending to the whims of the Senate. A long, continuous administration nightmare when all she wished was to be contently working in her lab designing new models of quintessences—and to have Alexander by her side. *I do not know if I can make it that long.* A thought weaved in her mind, a bold plan. *But surely it will not work. It cannot be that easy.* Yet hope stirred in her.

"Sire, I will do all you require and more, but I ask for one thing in return. Just one. It will not cost anything, but it will create a positive boost in the publicity you desire."

"What is that?" asked Emperor Kalyuga.

Chapter Thirty-one

The silver hover car pulled up at Advance Department, and Layla slid out. The asphalt simmered in the midday summer heat. No one was at the nearby playground to greet her. The director headed indoors. Entering the breakroom, she found her friends in the middle of putting up decorations for a homecoming party.

"We didn't expect you until tomorrow." Rosetta held one end of a congratulations banner.

"I decided to leave a bit early."

"Does it mean the party is off?" Derrick stood on a stepladder to put up the banner.

"You can still have one. I promise to act surprised." Layla faked a shock expression.

"I was planning to bake a cake tonight," said Leana, unpacking a box of plates made from a polymer which changed colors when it came in contact with fingers or warm food.

"It will taste great tomorrow. Are the quintessences back?"

"Yes." Zylar tinkered with a machine projecting hologram images of stars and Zelzer Awards around the room. "They suddenly showed up yesterday, saying they were off active duty for a while."

"Where are they?"

"The training field," said Tiffany, wearing neon earrings morphing through bright colors.

"Good." Layla's face burst into a grin. "Very good." She walked out of the room.

Rosetta and Tiffany exchanged glances.

"She was glowing," Tiffany said.

"I noticed," said Rosette. "Something has happened. Do you think?"

"Perhaps. It would be the ultimate prize. She deserves it."

"Huh?" said Zylar. "What are you talking about?"

"Let's go see."

Tiffany and Rosetta headed outdoors. Leana, who had been listening closely to the other women, smiled and followed after. The men glanced in confusion at each other.

261

"What was that about?" asked Zylar, "Why must women always talk in code?"

"You'll get better at understanding it. Though I'm not sure what they meant this time. Come on."

Layla reached the training field. Forty-nine adolescence quintessences along with Allen and his younger sibling practiced hand-to-hand combat in the hot sunshine while their fifteen older brothers supervised. Anthony stood in the shade sipping water. The elderly man called out a greeting to Layla. She waved a hello but kept walking into the moving sea of quintessences, stopping in front of Alexander. Her friends reached the training field and watched expectantly.

"You are back," said Alexander.

"Yes." Layla's heart pounded in her chest.

"I almost did not recognize you in that dress at the ceremony."

"You watched it?"

"On video last night, after we got back. You looked…different."

"In a good way or bad?"

"Good."

For a moment the two stared at each other, unable to speak the emotions of their hearts. Around them, nearby quintessences had stopped practicing and were watching curiously. The other Fives glanced at each other warily and began walking towards the couple.

Layla was the first to break the silence. "The Emperor is pleased with the success of your missions."

"It is our privilege to serve him."

"For you, no longer."

Puzzlement flickered in Alexander's eyes. Layla pulled a citizenship ID out of her pocket and handed it to him. Alexander studied its slick surface showing his face, name, and identification number T2-A1.

"How is this possible?"

"I asked Emperor Kalyuga himself. But it comes with a price. A big one for me, at least. I am being made into a public figure who has to do tons of interviews. It is far worse than anything I have faced before. I have even been assigned a PR team. There will be a cost for you too." Layla suddenly felt doubt. "That is if you wish to travel with me. See lots of cities across the empire, being on the vids a lot. You will not have your brothers around all the time. And you will not be getting shot at—hopefully. You might find it boring."

All the quintessences now watched silently.

Alexander looked her in the eyes. "I am willing to pay this price."

Layla smiled in relief then laughed. Joy rushed through her as she bridged the space between her and Alexander. He wrapped his arms around her, kissing her full on the lips in sight of everyone. His brothers watched with stoic faces. At the edge of the field, the humans were out of hearing of Alexander and Layla's conversation.

"Didn't see that one coming," said Derrick.

"Is he allowed to do that?" asked Zylar, puzzled.

"No, it is forbidden," Anthony frowned and walked towards the couple, followed by the other humans. The younger quintessences parted out of their way. "What is the meaning of this?"

Alexander passed the ID to the retired captain. As Anthony studied it, his mouth dropped open. "Well, Alexander, congratulations on your new citizenship."

Layla glanced at the quintessences around her. "I am sorry, but you still must wait to earn your citizenship. I could only get one."

Caleb said, "Seeing our brother freed from his heavy conflict is enough for us."

Rosetta called out, "Do I see a wedding in your future?"

Layla glanced at Alexander who gave a brief nod. "Tiffany, how do you feel about a double wedding?"

"Will there be reporters?"

"Probably a lot. The Emperor wants to use the wedding as a method to boost public support for Essence."

"Everyone loves a good wedding," said Leana wistfully.

"Big budget then?" Tiffany beamed mischievously. "Sounds like fun to me."

"I guess the welcome back party has been turned into an engagement party," said Derrick.

"I'll bake the cake," grinned Leana.

"I've have to reprogram the hologram projector again," grumbled Zylar.

The month leading up to the double wedding was packed with activity. Layla cared little about wedding plans and allowed the new PR staff to handle it. The three energized blue-skinned neodites launched into full gear, planning an elaborate ceremony. Tiffany had originally planned to hold the event at a church in Taylorville, but with the guest list becoming increasing long, it was moved to BGF's training field. Tiffany was thrilled to plan the wedding of her dreams, while Zylar grew increasing apprehensive.

As he looked over the long guest list, he mumbled, "Generals, captains, top scientists, Zelzar winners, board members. You did remember to invite my mom?"

"Of course," said Tiffany. "Both our families will be there. Relax. All you have to do is show up. Our favorite band Neutron Saga will be performing."

"Neutron Saga! How in the universe did we get Neutron Saga to sing at our wedding?"

"Layla said to make good use of her PR team, so I am."

"But Neutron Saga? Layla is just a scientist, not a movie star. Even winning the Zelzer should not give her this much clout."

In the back corner of the breakroom, Layla looked up from her e-tablet. "It is the price the Emperor has asked me to pay."

"Some price. Do you think Neutron Sega will sign my tee-shirt of them?"

"If you ask politely," said Alexander sitting beside his fiancé.

Layla passed her e-tablet to Alexander and pointed to a message. "My parents are coming along with my brother and his family. They arrive in just three days."

"Good. I will have the opportunity to meet them before the wedding." Despite Layla's smile, Alexander could sense her anxiety. "What is wrong? Your visit with them went well last time."

"Of course I will enjoy having them here. We will need to shop for new clothes for you before they arrive."

"I already have a sherwani for the wedding." Alexander did not try to hide his frown as he remembered the discomfort he had felt modeling outfits in front of his fiancé, the three neodites, Rosetta, and Tiffany at an exclusive fashion store in Austen City. Zylar had quickly found a tuxedo, but Alexander had been forced to parade in a dozen traditional Indian outfits before the others came to a unified decision of the best one for him.

"You need normal clothes. Not those blacks and camos you wear every day. Do not worry. We will shop local."

"It will only be you and me this time. No PR staff."

"Of course." Layla took back her e-tablet, allowing her hand to brush along his arm. "I prefer it that way myself."

Several days later, Layla and Alexander stood in the busy lobby of Austen Spaceport, both nervous about the coming meeting, though Alexander's calm demeanor hid his tension. Layla fidgeted, running sweaty palms over her brown slacks. Without his brothers present, Alexander blended in with the crowd. Passersby barely glanced at his muscular frame covered by blue jeans and a collared shirt. *That will all change*, thought Layla, *when we become public figures. How much longer can we enjoy the privilege of anonymity?*

Alexander studied the overhead monitors. "Their shuttle just landed."

Layla held her fiancé's hand as they weaved through the crowd. "I hope they like the hotel." She wished she could have gotten them a guest apartment at BGF, but they were all taken by high-ranking individuals.

As they watched passersby exiting a security gate, Alexander said, "Relax. They dropped everything on short notice to come."

"When I saw them last year, I did not even mention that I was kind of …not seeing you. Then I suddenly spring on them that I am about to be married."

"You could not speak about me then. Now we have that freedom. They will understand."

"I hope so."

When Sargam and Kalai saw their daughter, they beamed. Behind them came Blaaze and his wife Ria, carrying luggage. Their two daughters waved excitedly.

"Namaste," greeted Alexander in Hindu, placing palms together and bowing.

Sargam studied his future son-in-law then returned the ancient gesture recognizing the divine spark of the creator in the quintessence. "Namaste."

"You have had a long trip," said Layla. "We have hotel rooms for you, but they are not fancy."

"It doesn't matter." Kalai hugged her daughter. "What matters is seeing you."

During the drive, the women chatted about the coming wedding. Zia and Sabri cut in, excitingly asking if they could meet Neutron Saga. Sargam quizzed his future son-in-law about his job while Alexander carefully kept to the speed limit as he drove the van to the only hotel in Taylorville.

The next day, Layla gave her family a tour of Advance Department. The adults asked detailed questions about the science involved, but the girls quickly grew bored and stared longingly at a group of Generation Three heading outdoors with a basketball.

Zia asked, "Can we play with them? At school I'm good at sports."

Layla glanced at Alexander who said, "Sure. They will enjoy the competition."

Outdoors, the adults gathered near the playground. Allen and his brother invited the girls to be on their team, and soon an intense human versus quintessence game was in full swing. As Zia dodged between two opponents and tossed the ball to Allen, Kalai stood aloof, misty eyed.

"Are you alright?" Layla whispered.

"Just sentimental."

Not knowing if she would have another opportunity to speak to her mother alone, Layla asked, "Are you upset that I am marrying Alexander?"

"Upset? Why would I be? You have finally found love after all these years. We have feared you would always be alone."

"But I will never bear you grandchildren."

"I have two beautiful grandchildren already."

"But no grandsons."

"Do not worry yourself. That is not your burden to carry. Your father and I knew from the moment we volunteer to become your parents that your path would be untraditional. If my old eyes are not deceiving me, do you not have dozens of sons over there playing with my granddaughters?"

Layla smiled. "Yes, I do. Quite a few."

Two days later, hundreds of guests showed up for the double wedding. Security was tight. Reporters from elite publications including *Galactic Times* had cameras swooping everywhere. Zylar nearly had a nervous breakdown, but Tiffany enjoyed the excitement. Alexander kept a calm demeanor as he and his brothers received attention from curious visitors fascinated by them. Layla focused on her family's needs, trying to block out everything but them and Alexander, but that was difficult with so many guests wanting to meet her.

The minister from First Zion Church preformed Tiffany and Zylar's ceremony. Glowing in the attention, Tiffany wore a contemporary styled white gown while her husband wore a black tuxedo, his hands fidgeting to get out of it as soon as possible. His mother beamed proudly and took dozens of photos, despite there were professional photographers present.

A Hindu priest presided over the second ceremony. Under a decorative canopy Alexander stood near a burning firepot. He was dressed in a white embroidered sherwani with a long red scarf hanging over one shoulder. Sargam led his daughter to the groom where the couple placed garland around each other's necks. Layla's red dress was heavily embellished. Her bangles clanged together whenever she moved her arms. Kalai tied the corner of her daughter's dress to the groom's scarf. Alexander took Layla hand which was decorated in intricate henna patterns. Together they circled the firepot as the priest read the seven ancient vows.

They moved in harmony until the priest cited, "Let us take the fifth step so that we are blessed with strong, virtuous, and heroic children."

Layla misstep, but Alexander squeezed her hand in reassurance. He did not care that they would never have biological children. Together they would oversee the creation of thousands of quintessence youths.

The priest continued, "Let us take the sixth step for self-restraint and longevity. Finally, let us take the seventh step and be true companions and remain lifelong partners by this wedlock."

Layla bowed her head as Alexander applied red powder to her forehead and the parting of her hair, marking her as his wife. He then placed around her neck a beaded chain from which dangled three touching circles.

The guests moved to the cafeteria for the reception. The wedding party went smoothly, despite Derrick, out of curiosity, hijacking a camera probe and half taking it apart before the angry owner caught up with him. Anthony smoothed the irate journalist with a promise of receiving the first media tour of Essence Institution when it was completed.

Palakkad thanked Layla's parents for volunteering for the profectus program so long ago. Banican silently gave Layla a brief nod, his private sign of finally accepting her as an equal. Leana, Opal, and other caregivers swapped stories about raising the groom. Members of Neutron Saga signed Zylar's tee-shirt while Zia and Sabri took selfies with them. The married couples changed outfits before the concert began. Friends and visitors danced to Neutron Saga's fast-pace music for hours.

Layla and Alexander snuck out while the concert was still ongoing. As they walked through the parking lot, they spotted Derrick leading a troop of friends in decorating Zylar's hovercar with shaving cream, streamers, and washable paints. Having been warned by Rosette, Layla had hidden her vehicle behind a maintenance shed. Soon Alexander was zipping around slower moving traffic as Layla leaned against him, blissful. Lights from a patrol cycle flashed behind them, and Alexander pulled over to the side of the road.

"Where are you going in such a hurry?" asked the officer.

"We just got married," grinned Layla.

"Congratulations," said the cop, handing Alexander a ticket. "Enjoy yourself—just at a slower pace."

As Alexander examined his ticket, his lips curled into a smile. "My first infraction."

Layla leaned close, "Welcome, my love, to the responsibilities of citizenship."

They checked into the resort hotel that Rosetta and Derrick had recommended. Their room offered a splendid view of a beach pounded by ocean surf. As Layla admired the vista, Alexander stepped behind her and brushed long strands of hair away from her neck. He bit, allowing his strong emotions to flow through her. Memories he had long wanted to share over the last few years poured into her mind. Successes, disappointments, images of sentients saved and those killed. Loneliness and longing. Hope.

Then he shifted through her memories, allowing her to choose what she wanted to share. A vast plain appeared. Mountains filled the eastern horizon while an ocean composed the western view. A herd of antelope ran across the plain and disappeared into a forest. Birds soared high in the sky on a cool breeze carrying the scent of the ocean.

"This is the location for Essence," said Layla, her long hair dancing in the breeze.

Alexander studied the layout. "It is well chosen."

"It is my gift to you and your brothers. A homeland for your race. Long after I am gone, may it be a blessing to all future generations."

It was a long time before Alexander broke the link, their souls synced. Layla turned to face him, studying the body she had designed. She touched his cheek wondering at the miracle of how data on a computer monitor had become a living being. Her husband, her lover.

Alexander stroked her dark hair then he gently lowered his lips to hers. They kissed, softly at first, but it quickly turned passionate. He drew her towards the silken bed where creator and creation consummated their love, becoming one flesh.

Chapter Thirty-two

The shuttle slowed as it descended towards the blue ocean far below. A landmass filled the horizon from which rose a vast complex of connected buildings and towers, courtyards and plazas, training grounds and hangers, a spaceport and a prison which made up Essence Institute. The architecture was sleek and polished, dangerously alluring, mocking visitors to forget that over a hundred thousand deadly warriors were currently being trained at the largest military academy in the Basanti Empire.

Alexander stood near a docking bay, waiting for the shuttle to land. He looked thirtyish but he was older—by far. Over time his shoulders had broadened, his frame becoming brawnier. His piercing eyes had caused many culprits to spill secrets while his own face revealed nothing of his thoughts. The shuttle door lowered, and Mason walked down the ramp to greet his brother.

"Was your trip successful?" asked Alexander.

"Very. The colony's rebels quickly caved in after the arrest of their leader. War avoided."

"Our infantry disappointed again."

"There was a flood on a northern continent. I sent them there to clean up and help victims. It will keep them busy for some time."

They strolled side by side, mirror twins of each other, passing a troop of four year olds practicing hand-to-hand combat in a plaza. The preteens had blond hair and blue eyes, unlike their brown-haired instructor. Layla had the research department rotate hair and eye color for each ten generations born, making it easier to identify quintessences quickly by age. During what free time she could spare, she had designed several new models, reflecting various human races. The new models had different skill sets, but the same essential personality of all quintessences.

"How is she?" asked Mason.

Alexander's step faltered for a moment. "Not well."

"She is a hundred and twenty."

"She will live to be hundred and fifty."

"She is not a quintessence, brother."

They entered the central building, the vast structure rising up fifty floors. Sentients from many species strolled through the busy forum, some heading home while others began their shifts. A two-story picture of a smiling Layla in her fifties was mounted on the wall near the arched entrance of a museum which many visitors toured on their first visit to Essence. On the other side of the entrance were pictures of the founders of the institute. Dressed formally, Rosetta and Derrick smiled from their frame. Middle-age Tiffany and Zylar looked distinguished in their portrait. A smiling gray-haired Leana was surrounded by young quintessence students. Captain Franklin appeared in full military uniform. Every human on the wall was now dead except for Layla.

Alexander paused. "She does not like that picture."

"She likes none of her pictures. Let it rest."

"She has never even been in the museum."

"Why would she? It was created by the PR Department. You are restless today. Is she that ill?"

"She is fine. I have paperwork to deal with."

He took an elevator up to his office on the fourth-fifth floor. The plaque on the door read, "Layla Rangan, director," but it had been nearly forty years since she had unofficially stepped-down from that role. She had been very active most of her life, but a serious of small strokes had slowed her down in her late seventies. She had wanted to officially pass the position of director to her husband, but when the Galactic Senate claimed they would pick her successor, she had chosen not to retire. She kept the title while Alexander and the other Fives supervised Essence for the last forty years. For decades Layla fought against the Senate, only recently earning the right to pick her own successor.

Alexander glanced at a digital frame on the wall rotating through pictures. One flashed by of Layla giving a speech in front of the Senate at the age of one hundred and two, her face wrinkled, her body frail but poised and confident. *Perhaps they had finally given in to her for fear she would never die until the amendment was passed. She can be stubborn at times.* Her semi-retirement had given her more time to design new quintessence models, but age had slowed her mind. Most of her recent work had been rejected by the research department's strict testing policy which she herself had written.

Alexander sat at the marble desk and read messages on the computer screen, but his thoughts kept wandering through a lifetime of memories shared with his wife. He stood and paced beside the glass wall looking out over Essence. Far below, young quintessences trained in courtyards. A squad of six year olds practiced bōjutsu, their metal staffs twirling quickly in the afternoon sunlight. A shuttle launched from a docking pad and rose into the sky. A monorail headed south, carrying its passengers to New Hope and Luncaster. Layla's dream had become reality.

There was a knock on the door. "Enter."

A middle-age human walked in, carrying an e-tablet. Duken Shelley had been appointed by the Senate to be their watchdog at the institute. "Did you get my message?"

"Yes, but I cannot spare so many C1 models."

"There are three thousands of them graduating this year."

"Over half of them have been committed elsewhere. I can send one thousand."

"Only one thousand? There is a war going on in Section Z4248. More infantry is needed."

"The Senate would not need so many if General Ineiz would use more wisdom in his battle tactics." It was well known that the general had bought his position, not earned it.

"You dare criticized General Ineiz?" Duken glared at him.

"I have no need to. His record speaks for itself." Normally, Alexander was more patient with the man, but today he felt on edge. "I will ask the research department to increase the number of C1 models."

"It will take seven years to see the results of that."

"That is the best I can do."

Duken frowned and left. Alexander sat back down at his desk and forced himself to work. He first sent a message to the research department, keeping his promise to Duken. Then he looked over budget estimates. As the sun began to set, he watched fighter crafts flying in a V formation over the ocean, feeling envious of his young brothers who piloted them. Though administration was needed, paperwork did not suite a quintessence's disposition.

He logged off his computer and took an elevator up to the top floor, passing a vast indoor garden and elegant suites to reach his own. He walked through the large, airy rooms to the balcony and greeted the nurse standing by the arched doorway.

"Did she eat?"

"A few bites. She fell asleep while I was reading to her."

"Thank you. Enjoy your night."

As the nurse left, Alexander stepped out onto the large balcony. The leaves of potted plants swayed in the cool night breeze carrying scents of the ocean. Alexander looked down at his wife napping in a chair, a thick blanket covering her frail body. Tassels of long gray hair danced in the breeze. For a while he just stood, watching the blanket rise and fall as she breathed. Finally, she stirred, noticing him.

Layla smiled. "How was work?"

"I managed to insult General Ineiz and offend Shelley in the same sentence."

"It was a good day then."

"Yes, it was a good day." Alexander brushed hair from her face. "It has become cool. We should go in."

"Not yet. I think I fell asleep before Mary finished reading." She gestured to the novel laying on a table. "It is just the last couple of pages."

Alexander picked up the novel *Frankenstein* and flipped to the end. He read with a steady voice, though the meaning of the text began to bother him. He paused, unable to go on.

"Please continue."

He hesitated then read, "I shall die. I shall no longer feel the agonies which now consume me, or be the prey of feelings unsatisfied, yet unquenched." He placed the book on the table.

"You have not finished."

"Nearly. Besides, you know how it ends."

"Yes, the ending I know by heart. Shall I quote it? 'But soon I shall die, and what I now feel be no longer felt.' There is more, but you look upset."

"Why must you read this book yet again?"

"For your sake. It is time to let me go, beloved."

Alexander stood and walked to the balcony's railing. Far below the lights of Essence shined in the darkness. To the south, New Hope beckoned with its gleaming homes and businesses. "I cannot."

"I signed a medical form today instructing the doctors not to resuscitate me the next time I go into cardiac arrest."

"Without discussing it with me?"

"It is my choice, Alexander. I am tired. We both know this body cannot last much longer. I am at peace with my creator. Death I do not fear."

"There are alternatives."

"You and I both will not be satisfied if I became a cyborg. I forbid you to turn me into one. Years ago you told me to let you go. Now you must do the same for me." When Alexander gave no answer, Layla said, "We have done well, have we not? We did not repeat the mistakes of the novel."

"No, you never abandoned us, and we avoided turning into raging monsters."

"I did have my doubts a few times, though," laughed Layla.

Alexander walked back over and sat beside her. "Do you regret anything?"

"No. I am honored to have been your wife for the last ninety-three years."

"Do you forget I have read your mind many times? You regret never having children."

"Why do you ask when you already know the answer?" Layla sighed. "Yes, that thought has occasionally drifted through my mind, but then I remind myself I am the mother of tens of thousands. What need do I have for biological children? I am satisfied."

"You shiver. It is time to go in." Alexander bent down and picked up his feeble wife.

She leaned against his hard chest as he carried her to the bedroom. "Still in the prime of your life, my husband, when I am nothing more than a shivered husk. Yet still you love me."

"I promised to love you always. Age does not matter to me." Alexander placed her on the bed and covered her in thick blankets.

"I have just realized one regret. I will never know the life expectancy of my quintessences. Perhaps you will see two hundred."

"Perhaps." Alexander lay down beside her, wrapping his arms around her thin body.

"Did you eat dinner?"

"I was not hungry."

"You should eat," murmured Layla as sleep claimed her.

Alexander lay awake for hours, watching her breathe, feeling the weak pulse of her heart with his hands gently touching her wrists. Many nights had passed this way. Several times in the past she had slipped to the edge of death. Each time he had quickly summoned the doctors, and they had pulled her back to him. But not next time.

Her heart skipped a beat. He knew it immediately and his body stiffened in response. A few minutes later, it skipped again. Her breathing was slow, irregular. More skipped beats. He wanted to buzz the doctor, but knew the medical staff would only stand helplessly by, honoring Layla's final wish. She gasped for breath. Knowing nothing else to do for her, he bit, entering her mind. Peace he could give her as life slipped away. Yet he could not let go, even now. He felt her mind fading as her heart slowed. He recalled a distant memory of Paton attempting to steal memories from a prisoner. Instinctively, without understanding what he did, he pulled her memories into him, pooling them together within his own mind.

Her weak heart gave one final beat then Layla died. He held her body tight and wept—for the first time in his adult life. It was not until the orange fire of dawn broke the morning sky that he arose and summoned the medical staff. He led them into the apartment, remaining stoic as they examined her body.

"She died peacefully in the night," was all he told them.

Soon several of his brothers arrived. Jacob and Caleb talked with him in the living room as her body was removed, but he understood little of what they said. For the next two days, he was aware of nothing but her absence. His creator, his wife, was gone, leaving him only with emptiness.

"The pain will pass," said Gabriel as they walked towards a huge plaza where the funeral was to take place. "It took many months for me to recover from my wife's death."

"I remember. Your grief was acute."

"It helps to stay busy, brother. Only time can heal such wounds."

The funeral took place a few days later. Thousands of quintessences stood at attention in the plaza. Squads of youth stood next to their elders. Scientists dressed in lab coats waited beside janitors and gardeners. Dignitaries and government officials watched from their reserved sections. Several of the PR staff operated camera drones to record history. As the Five walked through the sea of sentients who had been affected by the life of one scientist, Alexander studied the faces he passed. Several wives of quintessences wept openly beside their solemn husbands.

Behind the Five walked the Ten, including Stephen, Jeff, and Tyler who had joined their brothers at Essence after earning their freedom from the Austin Police Department. Next came the remainder of the Fifty, though six of their number had died in the line of duty over the years. Together the fifty-eight quintessences made up the governing center of their species, enforcing their Code and watching over the welfare of their younger brothers.

As the quintessences drew near the casket which held Layla's body, most turned aside to join the others standing in the plaza. The Five continued onward, climbing the stairs of a platform then sitting behind the casket. One by one, each gave a eulogy. Alexander was the last to speak. He looked out over the thousands of sentients watching him, his grief intense, the longing for her presence inexorable.

"What can I say that others have not? I will let her speak for herself, through a quote from her favorite book. 'A new species would bless me as its creator and source; many happy and excellent natures would owe their being to me.' Through Layla, many lives have been saved, wars ended quicker, hopes restored. Rest now, my creator, and know your work continues."

That afternoon a quiet reception was held in the indoor garden at the top of Richton Tower. The ceiling and outer wall of the huge chamber were made from glass, letting bright sunshine bathe the guests as they offered condolences to Alexander and his brothers. The Five stood together, while the Ten and Fifty moved about the bright garden, several with wives by their sides.

"She will be deeply missed," said Roobaroo. Both she and Hunter gave the Five a bow of respect. "Her friendship has meant much to me."

The ediethesan's maroon hair had begun to turn gray and a few wrinkles marred her angular face. She had been released from prison after serving thirty years, her nationality stripped from her, and the High Council had banished her forever from Edieth. To spite the Council, she and Hunter had had two more children, raising them on a planet out of the Council's jurisdiction. Her marriage had sparked a small rebellion among other editheans living in diaspora, and several had also wed across caste.

"Thank you," said Alexander politely. "She valued your friendship deeply."

Next came Allen, shuffling along with a cane, his admiral stripes showing predominately on his military uniform. The combat and tactic skills he had acquired growing up with quintessences had served him well in his military career. After his retirement, he had become an instructor at Essence. One of his kids and three grandchildren still served in the Basanti Military, while two worked as scientists at Essence. Other dignitaries gave polite inquires and moved on, but Allen remained by the Five chatting about friends and family now dead.

Duken Shelley stepped up, holding out his e-tablet. "The Senate needs you to sign this form immediately."

Allen pointed his cane at Duken. "That is Director Alexander now."

The political coordinator frowned at Allen but said, "Of course, Admiral Cashman. Director Alexander, would you please sign this form?"

"Tomorrow. I need to read over it first."

"Tomorrow, yes," said Duken politely, though his frown still remained as he walked away.

"Director Alexander Rangan." Jacob's mouth curled into a laugh. "Leader of the most powerful institution in the empire."

"Not going to let it mess with your head, are you?" Allen asked, leaning on his cane.

Alexander glanced through the wall of glass, seeing Essence spread out far below. Veins of monorails moved passengers quickly across the vast complex. Shuttles lifted into the sky, bearing quintessences heavenward to fulfill quests. Layla's dream. Her vision. He looked back at his four brothers, mirror images of himself.

"No. My brothers will keep me in line. There is still much work for us to complete."

Epilogue

Thus I died. Weep not for me. My task for which I was created is finished. My dream fulfilled. My children displaced across the galaxy, dying so other sentients may know a life of peace. It is a sacrifice my quintessences are willing to make. ·

Those who survive the fifty years of servitude return to Essence, honored as heroes. Some remain to pass on their wisdom to their brethren. Many continue their military service, though now paid for their dangerous labors. Others explore the stars, choosing their own adventures. The Five are guardians of their race. They obey—or seem to obey—the Galactic Senate, while patiently manipulating behind the scenes, a tactic they learned well from the Alz.

And I remain, dormant. As I died, my beloved broke a rule of nature, unknowingly, innocent in his grief to save me. Now I am a seed, waiting to be planted.

The Age of Quintessence began peacefully, but a raising tempest continues to build between the Coalition of Human Advancement and the Ediethean High Council, each seeking to tip the delicate balance of power.

About the Author

Books have fascinated me since I was a small child sitting beside my mother, listening to her read books I had selected from the library. Soon I was reading on my own, and I never stopped. Over the years my interests have varied wildly from stories about animals to the classics to science fiction, and much in between.

In sixth grade my English teacher assigned us to write a short story. I got a tad carried away, writing a VERY long story about the adventures of a cat. Part of the way through the writing process, I realized this is what I wanted to do the rest of my life.

So I began writing short stories and eventually novels. I also became an English teacher because I wanted to share my love of literature with others. I later branched into teaching technology, another one of my passions.

The results you hold in your hands is from years of exploring my imagination and the intensive but exciting labor of writing.

I would appreciate, if you have a moment, giving my book a rating at Amazon, Goodreads, and other sites that interest you. In the limited free time I now have, the books I choose to read are usually recommended to me by friends, so I know the power of word-of-mouth.

I hope you enjoyed reading this book as much as I enjoyed writing it.

Sincerely,

Vista Townsend

Updates for new projects can be found at:
Website: vistatownsend.net
Facebook: Vista.townsend
Twitter: Vista_Townsend

www.ingramcontent.com/pod-product-compliance
Lightning Source LLC
Chambersburg PA
CBHW070843250626
47159CB00003B/909